Dancing into trouble

 I'd forgotten how much I love this singin' and dancin' and showin' off that I completely loses myself in it all, I love it so, and then John Thomas crows out with, "You can't match this step, girl!" and I taunts back, "Can, too!" and, though a part of me thinks that maybe I shouldn't be doin' this, I lifts up my skirts to show the steps and I does the step he did and then I top it off with one of my own and then...

And then I notice that they've all stopped dancin' and singin' and foolin' around and are slinkin' back and lookin' at somethin' over my shoulder. Then I feels a heavy hand on me shoulder and I hears a squeaky male voice that says, "Come with me."

I turns around and looks up into the sweaty face of a man with round, fat, pink jowls.

"Who are you?" I ask, all fearful and stupid and not likin' this turn of events at all.

His eyes are almost buried in the folds of his cheeks and they peer down at me with a feverish glint. He wears a black hat and a coat with a high collar that bites deep into the flesh of his neck. He carries a stout stick.

"I? Who am *I*, it asks? Well, I'll have it known that *I* am Constable John Wiggins, the High Sherwiff of Boston." He smugly chuckles. "And *you*, my girl, are a dirty little twollop what's under awest for Lewd and Lacsiwious Conduct!"

Curse of the Blue Tattoo

L. A. MEYER

Curse *of the* Blue Tattoo

Being an Account of the Misadventures of Jacky Faber, Midshipman and Fine Lady

Harcourt, Inc.

Orlando   Austin   New York   San Diego   Toronto   London

www.HarcourtBooks.com

First Harcourt paperback edition 2005

The Library of Congress has cataloged the hardcover edition as follows:
Meyer, L. A. (Louis A.), 1942–
Curse of the blue tattoo: being an account of the misadventures
of Jacky Faber, midshipman and fine lady/L. A. Meyer.
p. cm.
Title: Curse of the blue tattoo.
Summary: In 1803, after being exposed as a girl and forced to leave her ship,
Jacky Faber finds herself attending school in Boston, where, instead
of learning to be a lady, she battles her snobbish classmates,
roams the city in search of adventure, and learns to ride a horse.
[1. Orphans—Fiction.   2. Sex role—Fiction.   3. Friendship—Fiction.
4. Schools—Fiction.   5. Boston (Mass.)—History—19th century—Fiction.]
I. Title: Curse of the blue tattoo.   II. Title.
PZ7.M57172Bl 2004
[Fic]—dc22   2003019032
ISBN-13: 978-0152-05115-0   ISBN-10: 0-15-205115-5
ISBN-13: 978-0152-05459-5 pb   ISBN-10: 0-15-205459-6 pb

Text set in Minion
Display set in Pabst
Designed by Cathy Riggs

E G H F D

Printed in the United States of America

*For Annetje, as always,
and for Matthew and Nathaniel*

Curse of the Blue Tattoo

PART I

Chapter 1

It was a hard comin' I had of it, that's for sure.

It was hard enough comin' up from the brig, the cell down below where they had me kept these past few weeks, squintin' into the light to see all of the dear *Dolphin*'s sailors lined up along the spars of the great masts and in other parts of the riggin', all four hundred of 'em, bless 'em, my mates for the past year and a half, all cheerin' and hallooin' and wavin' me off.

It was hard, too, walkin' across to the quarterdeck, where the officers were all pulled up in their fancy uniforms and where the midshipmen and side boys made two rows for me to walk between on my way off the ship, and there's Jaimy all straight and all beautiful in his new midshipman's uniform, and there's Davy and Tink and Willy, the boys of the Brotherhood to which I so lately belonged, and there's my dear sea-dad Liam lookin' as proud as any father. The Bo'sun's Mate puts his pipe to his lips and starts the warble to pipe me off the *Dolphin*, my sweet and only home, and I start down between their ranks, but I stop in front of Jaimy and I look at the Captain and I pleads with my teary eyes. The Captain smiles and nods and I fling my arms around

Jaimy's neck and kiss him one last time, oh yes I do, and the men cheer all the louder for it, but it was short, oh so short, for too soon my arm is taken and I have to let go of Jaimy, but before I do I feel him press something into my hand and I look down and see that it's a letter. Then I'm led away down the gangway, but I keep my eyes on Jaimy's eyes and my hand clutched around his letter as the Professor hands me up into the carriage that's waitin' at the foot of the gangway. I keeps my eyes on Jaimy as the horses are started and we clatter away, and I rutch around in my seat and stick my head out the window to keep my blurry eyes on him but it's too far away now for me to see his eyes, just him standin' there at the rail lookin' after me, and then the coach goes around a corner and that's all. He's there, and then he's not.

That was the hardest of all. I put my fingertips to my lips where his have just been and I wonder when they will again touch me in that place. If ever... *Oh, Jaimy, I worry about you so much 'cause the war's on again with Napoléon and all it takes is one angry cannonball, and oh, God, please.*

I leave off what has up to now been fairly gentle weeping and turn to full scale, chest heavin', eyes squeezed shut, open mouth bawlin'.

"Well," says Professor Tilden, sittin' across from me, "you certainly have made a spectacle of yourself today, I must say."

...don't care don't care don't care don't care...

"You should compose yourself now, Miss. The school is not a far ride from the harbor. Here," he says, handing me a handkerchief, "dry your eyes."

The Professor is taking me to the Lawson Peabody School for Young Girls, which is where they decided to dump me after that day on the beach when my grand Deception was blown out of the water for good and ever and I was found out to be a girl, which was against the rules. Being a girl, that is. *They* being the Captain and the Deacon and Tilly. *I* felt that I should have been allowed to go back to England with them. I wouldn'a caused no trouble—they could have kept me in the brig the whole time if they wanted. But, oh no, that would have been too easy, too reasonable for the Royal Navy. No, far better to kick me off thousands of miles and an ocean away from my intended husband, that being Midshipman James Emerson Fletcher, Jaimy for short. I take Jaimy's letter and put it in my seabag for readin' later, 'cause I know that if I read it now, I'll break down altogether and be a mess.

I know old Tilly, who was the schoolmaster back on the *Dolphin,* sure liked me much better as a boy. He gets all nervous and fussy around me now, now that I've become a girl. He's right, though. *Must pull yourself together now, Miss.* Can't show up at the school, where they're gonna make a lady out of me, lookin' like a poor scrub what just crawled out of a Cheapside ditch, and so I takes the bit of cloth from his hand and dabs it at my eyes. I wants to blow my runnin' nose on it but don't want to mess up Tilly's handkerchief so I just snarks it all back and swallows with a big gulp. Tilly shudders and shakes his head.

Right. I've got to put my mind on other things, like this, my first carriage ride…imagine…Jacky Faber, ragged Little Mary of Rooster Charlie's gang of beggars and thieves runnin' all wild through the streets of London, the same sorry little beggar here now, in her first carriage ride, her bottom sitting on a fine leather coach seat. That selfsame bottom is also sitting in its first pair of real drawers it's seen since That

Dark Day when my parents and my little sister died and I was tossed out into the street to either live or die. These drawers come down to just above my knees and got flounces on 'em, three on each leg. The dressmaker said that the ruffles were there to keep the dress from clinging too close to the legs. Can't have dresses clinging too close to the legs in oh-so-proper Boston, now, can we?

My dress, now, is surely a fine thing—all black as midnight and waisted high up under my chest and falling in pleats down to the tops of my feet. The bodice comes down low—much lower than I would have thought for Boston, but I've given up trying to figure out that kind of thing as there never seems no sense to it—I mean, we got drawers with ruffles to keep the legs from being too noticeable down below, yet we have the chest in danger of spilling out up top. Don't ask me to explain, 'cause I can't. Anyway, the sleeves are long and end in a bunch of black lace at the wrists. It is the school uniform and it's the finest thing I've ever had on me and I got to say I'm proud to be in it, and I know Jaimy was proud to see me decked out this way on the quarterdeck today. I could see it in his eyes when he looked in mine and the way his chest puffed up under his tight black broadcloth jacket with all the bright gold buttons gleamin' on it.

Deacon Dunne took me out the first day we were docked in Boston, to get me fitted out, as Tilly warn't up to the challenge of being alone with the female me in a female dressmaker's shop. The seamstress there was amazing fast, with her tape whipping all around me up and down and all around. Pins put here and there and chalk marks, too. She got all of my stuff to the ship today—two pairs of drawers, two pairs of black stockings, one dress, one nightshirt with nightcap, one black wool sweater, one chemise, and one black cloak with bonnet—and two hours after it arrived, I was off the ship. They couldn't get rid of me fast enough, the sods.

Everything that I ain't got on is packed away in my seabag with my other stuff that I've picked up along the way—needles, threads, awls, fishing lures, my concertina, my blue dress that I made myself and my Kingston dress, my pennywhistle, and, yes, me shiv, too, 'cause I can't figure out how to keep it in its old place next to my ribs in this dress. Not yet, anyway. And my sailor togs are in there, too—my white dress uniform that I made for myself and the boys and my drawers with the fake cod and my blue sailor cap with HMS *DOLPHIN* that I'd stitched on the band. And Rooster Charlie's shirt and pants and vest that delivered me from the slums of London and my midshipman's neckerchief and even a midshipman's coat and shirt and britches and cap that I'd got off Midshipman Elliot, who'd outgrown them. I think about that middie's uniform and how everyone on board thought it was such a great joke that I was made a midshipman before they discovered I was a girl. Everyone but me. I earned my commission, I did, and I didn't think it was a joke. Still don't.

Ain't no money in my seabag, though. After paying for my clothes, they gave the rest of my share of the money from the pirate gold to the school to pay for my education in ladyhood. Wisht they had just given me the money and let me make my own way in the world like I always done, but, no—I'm a girl and too stupid to take care of money. That's a man's job, they say. Like *I'd* be gulled out of my money, me what's as practical and careful with a penny as any miser? Not bloody likely.

Oh, look. There's a row of taverns at the end of that pier. They look like places where I might be able to play my pennywhistle and concertina and maybe make some money after I get settled and know the lay of the land...and look there—there's one called The Pig and Whistle and it's kind of seedy lookin' but it's got a sign with a fat jolly pig playing a whistle just like mine and he's dancin' about and he looks right cheerful.

Ah. There's a bookseller's. And a printer's next to it. Maybe I could pick up some work there, if I have any time off from the school. I wonder how confined I'm going to be. The school couldn't be as tight with its students as the Navy is with its sailors, though, could it? Wonder if the school has lots of books. Coo, wouldn't that be something—all you ever wanted to read right at your fingertips? It's a school. It's *got* to have a lot of books.

Now we've turned right and a big brick church is out my window to the right and a big graveyard, too, and to the left is a large open field with horses and sheep wanderin' about in the grass. Cows, too. *Pray for me, cows, as I'm feelin' in need of it and you look right sympathetic with your big brown eyes.*

"It's like havin' the country right in the middle of the city. London for sure didn't have nothin' like that," I says.

"It's called the Common," says Tilly, when he sees my interest. I think he's glad that I've stopped crying, and he goes on in his teaching voice. "It was set aside by the forefathers because Boston is essentially an island and it would be hard to get the animals off and on for purposes of grazing. I think it's wondrous restful to the eyes after the hubbub of the town. Do you not find it so?"

I nod. I know he's talkin' just to keep my spirits up, and

I appreciates it. But don't worry, Tilly, there'll be no more cryin'.

We're climbing quite high on a hill now—"Beacon Hill," says Tilly—and the horses are slowing down under the strain of it.

I look down at my feet and wiggle my toes inside my shiny new shoes. These are the fancy kind with hooks and eyes and laces that run up the ankle. I also got a pair of black pumps what slip on and off and what I think I'll like better 'cause my feet are used to being bare and my toes ain't accustomed to being all crammed together like this.

The coach lurches around to the left and... "Good Lord! What's *that*?" I say, my eyes wide as any country rube's. A huge stone building with white columns and grand entrances and a solid gold dome has come into view on my right.

Tilly peers out the window. "Oh. That is the Massachusetts State House. They hadn't finished the dome when last I was here. It is magnificent, is it not?"

It is indeed. I'm going to be going to school next to a bleedin' palace. If the gang could see me now.

We leave the State House behind us and continue along the edge of this Common for a while. The whole city is spread out below me—the buildings, the wharves and piers. It is for certain a seafarin' town. There must be at least fifty wharves stickin' out into the harbor and a hundred ships moored at them. Can't see the *Dolphin*, though, she being tucked up close to the land and hidden by the buildings. Prolly best I can't see her as it would just get the tears goin' again.

"This is Beacon Street," says Tilly. "And here is your new home."

My belly gives a queasy lurch. *Steady down now. Steady. You've been through a lot worse than this.*

We've pulled up in front of a large building. It is three stories high and has a large entrance with a lot of stone steps and two heavy wood doors dark with old varnish so that they look like they've been there forever and have closed behind many a poor, scared girl. There's a road off Beacon Street to the right of the school and there's a church there that's built in the same style as the school—stone foundation below, white wood running sideways above. There's this big tree between the church and the school, so big its lower branches touch the roofs of both, and on the roof of the church is a sharp steeple with a bell hanging in it, and on the roof of the school is a porchlike thing with a railing around it that's painted white, too.

The coachman goes over to the rack on the back of the carriage and gets my seabag and chest and brings them to the entrance and then goes back to his seat to wait for Tilly to get free of me.

Tilly lifts the knocker on the door. It is opened by a young girl in service gear—black skirt and black lace-up weskit, white blouse, white apron and cap.

"Yes, Sir?" she says, all big eyed and meek lookin'. "May I help you?"

"Yes. *Harrumph,*" says Tilly, "I am Professor Phineas Tilden and I bring Mistress Pimm her new student." The girl gives me a quick up-and-down with her eyes, then slips out of the room through a door at the far end to fetch this Mistress Pimm. I look around, jumpy as a cat.

You calm down now, you. Right now.

The room is empty of furniture and rugs—prolly 'cause

this is where people track in snow and mud in the winter. But there are things on the walls. Wondrous things. Flowers and leaves all twisted around each other—words, alphabets, apples, oranges, urns, and weeping willow trees—all made out of thread on white cloth and framed with fine wood and...

"Yes. Mistress Pimm's girls are noted for their embroidery," says Tilly, when he notices me lookin'.

Embroidery! I don't know nothing 'bout no 'broidery, Tilly, you should've told me about this. I don't know how to do this stuff. I can sew a straight line, yes, but this I can't...

The serving girl opens the door and stands aside to let Mistress Pimm stride in. The schoolmistress advances to the center of the room and brings her gaze to rest on the Professor. She is as tall as he and as thin as he is stout. Her hair is the gray of a brushed iron cannon and is pulled back hard and gathered in a bun at the back of her head, which makes her sharp features look as if chiseled from stone. She, too, is dressed in black, but her dress goes all the way from ankle to throat where it is tightly fastened by a shiny black brooch. Her sleeves end in black lace above her white hands.

"Dear Cousin Phineas," she says. She does not look at me. She does not smile at either of us. "How good to see you again." She extends her hand and touches the outstretched hand of the Professor for the briefest of moments.

"Yes. *Harrumph*," says the Professor, reddening. "Good to see you, too, Miranda. May I present Miss Jacky Faber, the girl you have so graciously taken on as a new student? Jacky, this is Mistress Pimm."

She slowly turns her head and brings her gaze to bear upon me cowering down below.

11

What am I 'posed to do? Oh Lord, Tilly, you should've thought to teach me what to do in things like this. I don't know, should I hit a brace and snap off a salute and case my eyes or should I knuckle my brow and look down all humble or should I...

The serving girl standing behind Mistress Pimm sees me in all my confusion and she takes a bit of her skirt in each hand and moves one foot behind the other and dips down, spreading out her skirt with her hands as she looks down at the floor and then rises back up and brings her eyes back to mine and nods at me and silently mouths, *Do it.*

I do it, or at least I tries, and I almost falls over sideways when I squats down but I don't, and I comes back up and puts my eyes on her brooch 'cause I don't want to meet her steely eyes and I says, "Pleased to meetcha, Mum."

Tilly sighs and says, "She's going to take a bit of work, I'm afraid. But she is a good boy...ah...girl, that is, and she is a willing worker and a quick study and she..."

Mistress looks me over. "I am sure she will prosper here," she says, finally, but she is not smiling and she don't sound like she believes it. I don't believe it, neither, not right now I don't.

She looks back at Tilly. "I believe our business is concluded, then. I bid you good day, Cousin Phineas." The serving girl goes to open the door for him.

"Right. Well, then," says Tilly to me, "you be a good girl, now."

"I will be, Sir, and I thank you for your kindness to me and the other boys. You were just the best teacher."

Tilly blinks and nods and is out the door and gone.

The door clicks shut and silence fills the room. I stand

there nervously quiverin' while Mistress Pimm looks me over.

"What is this, then?" she says sharply, reaching over and flicking her finger at my earring. I flinch back 'cause her fingernail caught my ear and it shocked me, the suddenness of it all.

"It's…it's…just me ring, Ma'am. It's like a token from me intended husband, a weddin' ring, like. We're gonna use 'em when we finally gets married and…"

"Take it off. Take it off, *now*."

"I can't take it off, Mum," I says. "It's welded shut and please, Mum, I…"

From somewhere in her dress she pulls out a thin rod, whips it back, and lays it against my leg. Even under the layers of cloth, my leg buckles under the pain. *Damn, that hurts!*

"Listen to me, girl. The Rules: You will never call me anything but Mistress, not Mum, not Ma'am, *nothing* but Mistress," she says, standing straight upright as if a steel rod was run up her back. "And you will never talk back to me or raise your voice or even *think* to contradict me. Do you understand me, Miss Faber?"

"Yes, Mistress, I do." I sobs, blinking back tears for me poor leg. "I do."

"Good," she says, straightening up and turning to the serving girl. "You. Go get Mr. Dobbs."

"Yes, Mistress," whispers the girl and darts out the door.

"And tell him to bring his snips!" Mistress calls after the girl.

While we wait for this Mr. Dobbs and his snips, Mistress continues to gaze upon me. She shakes her head and paces

13

about the room. "I have grave misgivings about this. Unseemly. *Most* unseemly."

The girl returns shortly with a dusty little man in work clothes bearing a look of put-upon impatience and carrying an evil-looking pair of sharp pliers.

"What is it, then, Mistress Pimm?" he says, with the air of one who anticipates a long, disagreeable, dirty, and thankless job.

"Take that barbaric thing out of her ear right now."

Mr. Dobbs squints at my earring and lifts his pinchy tool. He seems delighted that it is such a simple thing and soon he'll be back in the hole where I'm sure he hides himself the livelong day. "Sure thing, Mistress. We'll have that out in half a moment."

He lays his cold, vile snips against my cheek and peers at the offending ear and its ornament. I jerk back.

"Please, Mistress, it's such a small thing and I…"

The switch catches me on the leg again and I cries out, *"Oh! Please don't…"*

"What did I tell you about talking back to me?" she says to me and "Cut it out of there!" to Dobbs.

"Pardon, Mistress," says the vile Dobbs, scratching his bristly chin as he thinks about the job at hand, "but do ye wish me to cut the earring or the earlobe?" He opens his shears and puts my ear in its cruel mouth. I can feel the sharpness of the metal. "Earlobe'd be easier. Bit of a mess, though."

She seems to consider the two ways of freeing the ring from my poor quiverin' ear.

"Cut the ring," she says finally.

I'm sorry, Jaimy, I promised I'd never take your ring out of my ear but there it goes I'm sorry, Jaimy, I'm sorry.

Dobbs cuts the hoop and, none too gentle, twists the ring out of my ear and hands it to Mistress.

"Very well, Dobbs, you may take Miss Faber's things up to the dormitory. And you," she says to the serving girl, "may resume your duties." The girl bobs and leaves, and Dobbs lifts my seabag and chest and heads down the hallway.

"*You* will now follow me to my office."

We enter a hallway and proceed down its length. There's more of them 'broideries on both walls. On either side I see rooms that are prolly rooms where stuff is taught. There's a room with a lot of little tables, and there—oh, my—there's a room full of musical instruments, fiddles and harps and things. *This could be all right,* I think.

"This floor is classrooms and the dining hall. Upstairs is the living quarters. Downstairs is the kitchen and the household staff," she says, and with that she sweeps into a room and I follow.

It is a dark room with heavy curtains pulled over the windows. It has a large desk with a chair in the middle of it and cabinets along the side. Mistress Pimm goes over to a window and reaches behind the curtain and pulls a cord. The drapes part and light spills into the room and I can see the harbor lying down there below. How I wish I was down there with Jaimy, or even just sitting on a pier and playing my pennywhistle. Or gutting fish. Or doing anything but this.

Mistress comes back to the desk and sits down in her chair.

"Do you see the line drawn on the carpet?"

I look down and see that, sure enough, there is a thin white line drawn on the rug in front of her desk.

"Yes, Mistress," I say.

"Good. Now go up to it and put the points of your toes upon it."

I step over and put the shiny toes of my new shoes on the line. This puts my belly about four inches from the edge of the desk.

"Very well," she says and leans back in her chair. "Whenever you are called into this office, you will advance to that line. If you are here for punishment—and I cannot think of any other reason why you would be here—you will lay your upper body on the desk and lift up your skirts. Do you understand?"

"Yes, Mistress." I'm thinkin' fearfully that it's sort of like being bent over a cannon and having your pants pulled down and your bottom switched, which was the common punishment for ship's boys on the *Dolphin*. Never happened to me, though it was close a couple of times. Maybe this won't happen to me here, neither. I hope not. I didn't like the feel of that stick of hers.

"All right, then." She picks up some papers and holds them up. "I have read an account of your recent life aboard that ship, provided by Mr. Tilden, and I find it neither amusing nor reassuring as to your moral character," she says, crossing her arms and looking at me intently. "Are you still innocent?"

Innocent? Of what?

She notes my confusion. She narrows her eyes even more and says, "Are you yet a maiden?"

Oh. *That.*

"Yes, Mistress," I stammers. *If only just barely,* I thinks, but I don't say it out loud.

She is silent for a bit and then says, "Very well. I choose to believe you on that. I would not take you if I believed otherwise. It is reassuring that you can still blush, at least. You will, however, never speak with the other girls of your past life, as it smacks of the sordid and the unseemly. Is that clear?"

"Yes, Mistress."

Her gaze has never once left my face. "I have grave misgivings about taking you on as a student, given your origins and past life, but we shall see. Hold out your hand."

I sticks out my trembling hand half expectin' her to give it a whack with her stick for my past sins, but instead she jams my ring into it. "I never want to see that, or any kind of ornament on you again. Is that clear?"

"Yes, Mistress," I say in my misery.

"And, Miss Faber, the most important thing of all," she says, standing and raising herself to her full height, "although you may know the name of this school to be the Lawson Peabody School for Young Girls, I want you to fully understand that those are the names of the founders and trustees but that it is *my* school and *my* girls and you will *never* bring disgrace down upon me and my school by your actions and comportment. Do you understand that?"

"Yes, Mistress." I'm thinkin' that this is a lot like bein' read the Articles of War on the ship—every breakin' of a rule bein' punishable by death.

"Good. We will go up and meet my girls now." She comes around from behind the desk. "You will find that my girls have a look about them that distinguishes them from the common run of girl, and you, Miss Faber, will try to cultivate that look."

She comes up next to me. "My girls walk as if they were delicately balancing a book upon their heads. They keep their lips together and their teeth apart."

I lift my head and drop my jaw down a bit with my lips mashed together.

She sighs. "Relax the lips, Miss Faber. Make a cupid's bow of them. Now drop your eyelids down halfway. That's better. Not even close to the ideal, but better." She lifts her rod and taps my shoulders with it. "Not so rigidly straight. Remember the book on your head. You are projecting a look of languid confidence."

She steps back to look at me.

"Eventually, Miss Faber, it is further to be hoped that you will learn to control your emotions so that they do not display quite so visibly on your face as they do right now. My girls have a look about them and appearing to be about to burst into tears is *not* part of that look. Let us go."

"Yes, Mistress."

There is a broad sweep of stairs at the end of the hallway and up it we do go, Mistress first and me behind watching the swaying hem of her skirt. At the top, we turn right and enter a large room that has beds lined up on either side. There are chests of drawers and windows curtained with light white drapes on each side. There are also about thirty girls of various sizes and ages, dressed just like me. They all get to their feet upon seeing Mistress Pimm enter.

"Good day, Ladies."

"Good day, Mistress," say the girls as one.

"I've asked you to gather here before dinner to welcome a new girl, Miss Faber." She steps aside for me to come forward. "She is from England. Acquaint her with our ways and our rules."

And with that, Mistress turns on her heel and leaves the room.

Well. I breathe a bit easier with her gone. Maybe I'll find some warmth down here in the crew's quarters, but I dunno—all I see now is unsmiling faces turned toward me, lookin' all haughty and...oh, right—the *Look*, that's what it is.

Nothin' for it but to put on my most charmin' smile and beam it all around. "My name is Mary, but you can call me Jacky—everybody does," I pipes and looks around at their faces expectin'...what? Welcome, maybe. I don't see much in the way of that, though.

I hear some snickerin' and mutterin' and my smile is startin' to feel foolish on me face. Then the crowd parts and a girl, a small blond girl not much bigger than me, comes forward, her face uplifted, her eyes hooded, her back straight. *She* has the Look for certain, and she brings it all up in front of me.

She is perfect in all her parts. Her hair is perfectly piled on her head with perfectly coiled ringlets hanging down either side of her perfect face. She is a lovely cream color with touches of pink in the right places and her eyes are large and liquid and bright blue. Her nose is small and fine and her lips are full and red and shaped like a bow. Her neck is long and slender and her upper chest is soft and white without being powdered I know, and I know that her dress, which is the same color and cut as mine, is much finer in its material and drape and I feel suddenly shabby in my once-proud new dress. And in my pigtail and my tanned face and my freckles and my scarred, scrawny body.

"My name is Clarissa Worthington Howe, of the Virginia Howes," says the girl, after looking in my face for a bit. "*You* may call me Miss Howe."

By now my hopeful grin has slid completely off me face. Sweat breaks out on my brow and I know it makes me look like a scared scrub but frettin' about it only makes me sweat all the more—I can feel my armpits working up steam and sendin' the sweat tricklin' down over my ribs.

Clarissa Worthington Howe looks at me and tilts her head to the side and looks as if she is about to decide something about me. Her blue eyes roam quite boldly over my face, and then her eyes stop and I can tell she is looking at my white eyebrow and its scar from where Bliffil got me with his boot that day. The perfect lips part and she says, "So you are a Tory, then?" Sweet and soft she says it. *So you are ah Toe-ree they-un?*

I'm in total confusion. *Tory?* My mind races back for that word and I remembers it from when I was a child and riding Hugh the Grand's broad shoulders and reading the newspapers pinned to the print-shop walls for the amusement of the Fleet Street crowd. *Tory?* She's callin' me a conservative member of Parliament? I don't get it.

"Tory?" I blurts out. "I ain't no Tory. I'm just a poor girl what's lately come from sea to study here and become a lady like the rest o' yiz." *Stupid stupid stupid stupid stupid stupid.* As soon as it's out me mouth I know it's *stupid stupid stupid* and makes me sound like I just fell off the back of a Cheapside turnip wagon. *Stupid!*

"English, a Tory, and so very, very common, too. My, my," she says as she turns and floats away. "I'm afraid she won't do," she says to no one in particular, but the other girls turn away from me, too. "I'm afraid she won't do at *all.*"

Just then I hears a musical something from out in the hall and the girls, led by the perfect Miss Howe, follow the sound out of the room.

So that's the way of it, is it? Now I've got a real threatenin' glower on my face and my hands balled up in fists, but I know that ain't gonna be the way of it here in this place where Clarissa Worthington Howe rules. Goin' at her with fists a-flailin' ain't gonna do it, no. I've got to learn to fight like a lady, and so I take a deep breath and put the imagined book on my head, and with my lips together and my teeth apart, I follow them.

In the hall I discover the musical sound comes from a box what's got chimes in it that's bein' hit with a mallet by another serving girl—one who looks like the one I saw in the foyer, but not the same. Skinnier, but with the same saddle of freckles across her nose. Prolly her sister. She seems to be whackin' away at the thing with no sense or pattern but it sounds pleasant all the same, and as we all file down the stairs and into a dining room with tables set with dishes and glasses and cloths and such, it seems that it is the way the girls are called to eat.

Clarissa Howe goes over to the center of one of the tables and sits down. Others begin to do the same, so I go over to that table and pull out a chair. *Maybe this will go better*, I thinks, as eatin' together tends to make mates of people.

"I'm sorry," says a girl coming up to my side, "but this place is taken." She takes the chair and pulls it from my hand. I flush red in the face and go to another chair and pull that one out.

"I'm sorry," says another girl, doing the same thing, "but this place is taken."

I go to the other end of the table and try again there. The same thing happens. I try again. The same. Then I notice that there are more place settings here than girls and they are merely rotating around to deny me a seat at this table. I want to cry out at the cruelty and meanness of it all. I feel my eyes burning and I want to lash out and get one of 'em on the floor and pound her good, but I don't do it. Instead, I put my hands to my sides and I stand at attention and say to no one in particular, "Very well. Tell me where to sit and I will sit there."

A girl near me smirks and hooks her thumb over her shoulder. She uses her other hand to cover her mouth to stifle her giggles. I can see her eyes glance over to that Clarissa Howe to get her approval, and I see that she gets it. I follow the point and see another table, one with a single girl sitting at it. There are many empty places. I turn on my heel and march over and pull out the chair opposite the girl and plunk myself down. The girl has her head down and does not look up as I join her. She has very dark hair that is put up in a bun with side curls that hang lankly by her face. She has a pug nose and is plump—not fat plump but like she ain't lost her baby fat yet. Her hands are folded in her lap.

I put my elbows on the table and lean over and say to her

all conspiratorial like, as if we're two prisoners in a jail, "They got me for bein' English, common, and a Tory, two of which things I am guilty of. What are you in for, Mate?"

She looks up, confused. "Why, whatever do you mean?"

"Why are you sittin' here alone, away from that pack of pampered princesses, is what I means," says I. She don't reply right off.

I look at the things in front of me to see if I'll be able to handle 'em with any kind of confidence: plate, napkin, two spoons, knife, fork, an empty cup with a little dish under it, another little dish with a roll and butter on it, a glass full of water. A far cry from a mess kit and a tin cup.

"They do not like me and I do not like them," says the girl with a sniff. She looks back down at her lap.

"Well, maybe you'll like me. My name's Jacky Faber and I've just come from"—and then I remember that I promised Mistress that I wouldn't say nothin' about my past life to any of these girls so's they don't faint dead away at the unseemliness of it all or something—"from far away to study at this school and so become a fine lady. Tell me your name and why we have two spoons here."

I'm lookin' real hungrily at the bread roll sittin' there next to the butter but I notices that nobody else is diggin' in yet, so I waits.

"My name is Amy and there is to be a soup course," she says. She brings up a book and puts it on the table. So that's why she had her head down. She was reading.

"Ah," says I, deciding to watch her and just do what she does and that way avoid trouble.

I notice some older people have come into the mess hall and have seated themselves at the table by the door. *Must be the teachers,* I thinks. Then there's a rustle as Mistress strides in and everyone stands up and stops talking. She goes to her chair, which is in the center of the teacher table, and looks out across the room. When all is silent, she speaks.

"We welcome into our company our new student, Miss Jacky Faber," says Mistress, and I redden at the notice. "She will now give us the grace."

I feel like I've been hit in the belly with a cannonball. *Grace? I don't know nothin' about no bleedin' grace!*

I look at Amy in my desperation. She sees my confusion and leans forward and whispers, "A prayer in thanks for the food."

Oh.

I scours me head for some graces and I comes up with a few and thinks to myself that I can handle this *and* maybe get a counterpunch in. *Hey, is this not Jacky Faber, the saucy sailor girl who has played to lots tougher crowds than this?* I tell myself this, but I don't quite believe it.

I place my hands together in a prayerful attitude and cast my eyes to the heavens and belt out: "Oh, Lord, bless this food to our use and us to thy service." *The Regular Navy one—short and sweet and gets you to your food quick, and now,* "Bless us, oh Lord, and these thy gifts, which we are about to receive through Christ our Lord." That's the Catholic one, which I learned by listening to the Irish sailors on the ship and which now causes two of the serving girls standing by the door to quickly look at each other and make that hand cross thing they do, and now for my own special one I just made up. "I thank you, Lord, for this wonderful school, which has taken in a poor lost orphaned lamb and so warmly welcomed her into its company. Amen."

"Amen," says the congregation, and sits down, and the clatter of silverware and a gentle buzz of conversation is heard. From the corner of my eye I see Mistress looking at me, but I don't meet her eye as I sit back down.

"Well done, Miss," says Amy, an almost smile playing about her lips. She takes her cloth and puts it on her lap.

I take my piece of cloth and do the same. I want to grab that roll real bad, 'cause cryin' and bein' treated miserable always sets up a fierce appetite in me, but since Amy ain't doin' nothin' yet in the way of eatin', I holds back and waits. Soon one of the serving girls comes up and puts a bowl of yellowish soup in front of me and then one in front of Amy. She picks up a spoon and so do I.

"The other one," she says.

"The 'other one' what?" I says.

"The other spoon. You use the one in your hand for your tea."

"Oh." I switches spoons and dips the right one in and starts to shovel in the soup.

"Ohhh," I breathes, "that's prime, that is."

It is so good I want to just pick up the bowl and drink it all down that way, the way I would have done with my mess kit, but I don't. I think I'm doin' pretty good using the spoon, so I'm workin' away when I notice that this girl Amy's holding her spoon like she would a pen and she ain't makin' any noise in the eatin' of the soup, either, while I've got my spoon gripped full in my fist and am slurpin' away lustily, and so I change my grip and tries to be more dainty-like in my takin' the soup on board.

That biscuit has been tauntin' me too long, I'm thinkin'. I pick it up and give it a couple of raps on the table but no weevils fall out of it, so I rip it open and look inside and nothin' comes out but a little steam and so I rub it in the butter on the little plate and take a bite. It is wondrously soft and warm and my eyes roll back with the goodness of it.

"*Mmmmmm*. That is soooo good," I say, my eyes closed in rapture.

She looks at me a little funny. *Easy for you, Miss,* I thinks. *You ain't lately been eatin' biscuits hard enough to crack your teeth and make your gums bleed for an hour after mess call, and full of bugs, to boot.* And *that* was a helluva lot better than what I had before. But she don't know about that, and she ain't gonna find out, neither, 'cause I told Mistress I wouldn't, and I won't.

Now the girl what showed me that dip-down thing in the front hall comes up next to me, holding a platter of what I think are pork chops, and she stands there expectin' me to do somethin'. I raise my eyebrows in question to Amy.

"Use the tongs there to take what you want."

Take what I want? Why not just tip the whole tray in my plate? But I am good and take up the pinchy things that are resting on the edge of the platter and choose a fat one and manage to get it to my plate without disaster.

"Thank you," I say to the girl. "And thanks for savin' my neck this morning when I came in."

She blushes like she ain't used to being thanked and says, "'Twas nothing, Miss." And she scoots off to be replaced by her sister, who has a platter of vegetables and potatoes with tongs like before. And then a thing of gravy is put on the table.

"Good Lord!" I say. "It's a wonder that everyone here

ain't fatter than pigs if you eat like this all the time!" I regrets it instantly, as Miss Amy ain't exactly skinny.

"This is the big meal of the day," she says, appearing to take no offense. "The evening supper is much smaller. Breakfast is tea and toast or oat porridge or eggs and bacon."

A pang of guilt runs through me. I wonder what Polly and Judy and Nancy and Hughie are eatin' today, there under Blackfriars Bridge, if they're still there or even still alive. But what could I have done for them, a nothing girl like me? Nothin'. Still, sometimes I feel I shouldn'a left them. But my greed overcomes my guilt over leaving them to their fate and I eye the spread hungrily, waiting for Amy to pick up a tool and dig in.

She picks up the gravy thing and pours out a little over her potatoes and then takes her knife in her right hand and her fork in her left and cuts one piece of meat out of the chop and then puts down the knife and switches her fork to her right hand, spears the small bite of meat, and puts it in her mouth. Why not cut the whole thing up at once and why do you have to change hands? I dunno. Anyway, I do it like she does, 'cept I cuts a much bigger hunk and I pours the gravy over everything. Then I digs in, and soon I'm makin' my usual sounds of contentment that I make when I'm eatin' somethin' really good.

When I'm done, I take my last bit of bread and sops up the rest of the gravy in my plate and pops it in my mouth. I'm eyeing the pork chop bone lying in my plate and it's still got some tasty-lookin' fat glistenin' on the side, and I want to pick it up and stick it in my gob and let my teeth and tongue do the cleanup detail but I don't 'cause Amy don't do that with hers.

Our plates are picked up and I watch the remains of the chop go off, with great regret. A glass of a brownish juice is put in front of me.

"What's that?"

"It is apple cider. It is the time of year for it." She lifts her glass and tastes it. "Please don't faint from the joy of it," she says, lookin' at me all mock serious.

I laugh out loud, loud enough for Clarissa's table to hear. Good. Let them know I am not cowed. "I'm sorry, Miss," I manages to say to Amy, "but this is all so new to me, and I would purely appreciate it if you show me around a bit 'cause I don't know when anything is and where I'm supposed to go and what I'm supposed to do and…" *And* I've got that old feelin' in the bottom of my gut.

"…and I don't know where the head is."

"The *head*?" she asks, all mystified.

"I got to go powerful bad and I don't know where to do it."

"Oh," she says, and looks over to the teacher table. "Well, we cannot leave until Mistress does, but it should be soon. Ah. There she goes. Come, and I will show you." With that, she gives her lips one last pat with her cloth and rises. I pat my own mouth and follow her out of the dining room, book on head, lips together, teeth apart.

Amy leads me back upstairs and through the dormitory room to a door at the other end. "This is the privy," she says. "Do be quick. We must be in class soon."

I open the door and go in. It is a long room with six stalls on the far wall. I open one of the stall doors and peer in. There is a bench with a hole in it and I look down the hole to see a white chamber pot below. To the left is a sink with a pitcher of water next to the basin. There is also a basket with clean bits of cloth in it, and on the floor, there is a basket with a top on it and I figures that's where you put them after you use 'em. So that's how the job is done around here, then. I take a small bit of cloth.

When I plunk myself down, I notice that there's a latch on the inside of the door. Privacy, even. My, my. Sure beats the stinky old head back on the *Dolphin*.

When I am done, I put the lid on the pot, grab its handle, and head out into the dormitory and say to Amy, "So where do I dump the pot, then?"

"Oh. My. God." I hear that from a gaggle of girls who have come into the room when I was in the privy. They giggle and crow and run out of the room to tell Clarissa and the rest about my latest botch of things. I realize I have made a big mistake.

"Put it back," says Amy, wearily. "The downstairs staff takes care of things like that."

I go back and put the pot under the bench and then go sheepishly back to Amy.

"I'm sorry, Miss," I say. "As soon as I get my sea legs under me and know my way around here I won't bother you no more."

We go to class.

The first class is the dreaded Embroidery, taught by Mistress, herself, and it's true I have no skill in this regard and am discovered right off and sent to sit with a little girl who is working on her first sampler. The others snicker at my disgrace and turn their backs to me as I take my place at the foot of the class. I hear giggles and I think I hear the words *Lady Chamber Pot* whispered about.

A sampler, I find, is a bit of cloth on which a girl shows how good she is with a needle by doing the alphabet and then her name and then some gloomy verse or saying with a pretty border all around, and when she's all done, she frames it up and hangs it on the wall. I guess so possible future husbands might see it and nod in approval of her skill and maybe marry her on account of it. There's all sorts of them in frames up there on the wall, with one really big one that just has a poem on it.

> *I Pray that Risen from the Dead,*
> *I may in Glory stand—*
> *A Halo, perhaps, upon my Head,*
> *But with a Needle in my Hand.*

They sure take this stuff seriously, I'm thinkin'. Cheerful bunch, too—a lot of the verses up there go *as you read this I am now dust* and suchlike. I would sit there with a cloud of gloom over my head, 'cept the little girl next to me is even gloomier. She seems to be about twelve years old and looks to be the youngest one here. We're about the same size, 'cept I've come out a bit on top and she ain't yet.

I see from her sampler that her name is Rebecca. Rebecca Adams.

"What's the matter?" I whisper to her.

"I wish I was dead," peeps the squeaker, not looking up from her toil.

30

"*What?*" I asks back at her.

"'I Wish I Was Dead,'"she says, finally looking up at me. "That's what I'm going to put at the bottom of my sampler." She gives a few sniffs. "And then I'd be an angel up in heaven and not here."

"Here's so bad?" I say, plunging my needle in to start the ABCs on my own first sampler. The white cloth is stretched over a frame to keep it taut, and it's all clean and bright and it seems a shame for me to come along and mess it up.

"I'd rather be home playing with my dog."

I can understand that. I'd rather be on the *Dolphin* playing with Jaimy. I take advantage of the nature of this class to take a piece of the black string and put Jaimy's ring on it and hang it around my neck and drop the ring down inside the front of my dress. It is cold on my skin for a moment and then it ain't. I think of his letter upstairs burning a hole in my seabag, but I must wait till the proper time.

"Well, you'll be an angel by and by, but I wouldn't rush it if I were you. This world has many charms, you know."

"But I don't know how to do this stuff."

"Neither do I, Rebecca. But maybe we can learn to do it together. *Hmmm?*" I gives her a cocked eyebrow and a wink, and I get a weak smile out of her as we both turn to our labor.

French is next and better. Tilly had given us some French lessons on the *Dolphin*, thinkin' that since we were fightin' them we might end up captured by them and so it would be good if we could talk to our captors. Maybe on that awful day on the beach, maybe if I could have talked to the pirate LeFievre in his own language, he wouldn't have put that noose around my neck and hauled me up. I doubt it, though.

I'm behind the others, but I'll get it. The teacher is Monsieur Bissell and he gives me a book to study, and I will learn from it and catch up.

"I really appreciate it, Miss, you showin' me around like this. Sure as hell none of the rest of 'em is gonna help me." We are heading down the hall to our next class.

"I'm sorry you were treated so badly this morning," she says. "They were abominable. And I am sure Mistress was not much better."

"It warn't so bad," I says, flashin' her my best grin and showin' that I have a naturally cheerful nature. "At least they didn't strip off all my clothes, beat me up, and try to hang me, all of which *has* been done to me before." This raises her eyebrows and breaks her stride a bit. *Oops,* I thinks. *Not supposed to talk about that.*

"I wanted to smack that one so bad," I growl, glaring over at Clarissa Howe.

"It is good that you did not. You might have been asked to leave the school."

Hmmm. So that's one way out of here, I thinks. Just pop Miss Howe one on the nose. But I bet they'd toss me out and keep my money.

"Right," says I. "I reckon I'm going to have to learn to fight like a lady, then. What's next?"

"Manners and Decorum," says Amy, as we follow the others down the hallway. "Again taught by Mistress and… whatever is the matter?"

We had come to a window and by chance I looked out

over the city and down to the water and I am stunned to see the *Dolphin* standing out of the harbor. She has an offshore wind behind her and has all her lower sails set, and at the very moment I spy her, all three royals are dropped and quickly fill, just as quickly as my eyes fill with tears. There is a bank of puffy white clouds out on the horizon and soon she will be tearing along beneath them. She holds all that I hold dear and she is leaving without me.

"Nothing," I say to Amy, and wipe my eyes on my sleeve. "Just a little homesick."

And so we have Manners, Decorum, and Household Management, with Mistress, herself, teaching. Not that I get to see much of it—as soon as I walk in, I'm taken aside and put in another room with a girl named Martha to teach me how to do a proper curtsy, that dippy thing that girls do instead of bowing like the boys. She don't like it much, having to be with me instead of clustered around Clarissa, but she does it. Guess you don't say no to Mistress. She shows me how to put the feet and how you spread out the dress when you go down and how to come up all smooth and graceful. And how there's degrees of curtsies, depending on whether the person you're doing it to is higher in station than you, or lower. And how to do it in front of boys or gents, them's you like and them's you're just bein' polite to.

Right. Just you wait, Jaimy Fletcher, just you wait till Lady Jacky tries this out on you. It'll melt the cockles of your highborn heart for sure, as I know you like your ladies bein' ladies and not crude tomboys like I was. Am.

After we practice for a while and Martha is satisfied that I can handle this drill without looking totally green, we go back to class and Martha tells Mistress that I got it down sort of all right, and Mistress says, "Very well. Miss Faber, please thank Miss Hawthorne for the instruction."

I understand.

I dip down in the required way for doing it in front of someone higher than you 'cause there sure ain't nobody lower than me around here, and as I come up I say, "Thank you, Miss Hawthorne, for teaching me," and Martha dips down, but not so far as me, and says, "You are welcome, I'm sure."

Mistress watches the performance with the same narrowed eye Captain Locke used when watching his gun crews exercise the great guns. "All right," she says, apparently convinced that I will not bring total disgrace to her school in the matter of curtsies. "Now, Miss de Lise and Miss Howe. Please take Miss Faber out and teach her how to do a simple introduction." Take her out and shoot her is what everybody's thinkin', I know.

It's plain that Mistress don't think too much of my conduct upon arriving this morning. The three of us march out, books on heads, chins up, lips together, teeth apart, and eyelids at half-mast.

After we enter the room I had just left, being newly trained in the matter of curtsies, I stand there and wait, watchful as any hapless mouse in the close company of two fierce and very interested cats.

Clarissa smiles upon me and turns to the other girl and says, "My dear Miss de Lise, please permit me to introduce you to Miss Faber, of the no-account English Fabers. She's a Tory, don'cha know? Absolutely devoted to that crazy King George."

Miss de Lise does something with her mouth that I suppose is a superior smile, and she nods ever so slightly and stares over my head and says, "*Charmé.* Such a *plaisir.* I have heard so very much of ze swamp-dwelling Fay-bears."

She is French!

Clarissa turns to me and says, "*Miss* Faber, I present to you Mademoiselle Lissette Maria Theresa de Lise, daughter of the Comte de Lise, the French Consul. Rest assured, this is as close as you will *ever* get to an actual audience with one such as her. Or with me, for that matter."

French! One of Napoléon's wicked crew! Right here!

I'm startin' to burn real good now. I had heard on the ship that our King was a bit off his head, but these two ain't got the right to say so. I make a very small dip and say to Lissette de Lise, "My dear Mam'selle Lissette de Froggy, please permit me to introduce you to Miss Clarissa Howe, she of the Virginia Howes, she what's gonna have her nose busted if she don't let up on me, don'cha know?" I smiles at her. "But then you are already acquainted, *n'est pas,* being one of her chief toadies for all your airs? Toad? Frog? What's the difference?"

"Doesn't it have the most charming ways, Miss de Lise?" purrs Clarissa. "So refreshingly primitive, don't you think?"

"Ah *oui,* Miss Howe. Definitely right out of ze bog. Are we not *très* fortunate to have her here?" But our Miss de Lise is not purring—her face is dark, and if looks could kill, I'd already be sewn up in my canvas with the words said over me and my poor body dumped over the side.

Clarissa comes up to me, nose to nose, so close I can feel her breath on my face. All traces of her false smile are gone and her perfect mouth turns down at the corners and her upper lip curls up and shows a row of perfect but curiously small teeth. She says, barely above a whisper, "If you are threatening me with physical violence, you would be well advised that if you as much as lay a finger upon my person, you will be taken out and whipped and expelled from this school, a school to which, I might add, you *so* obviously do *not* belong."

It is to my shame that I can't think of nothin' to answer her back. I only watch as the two of them whirl around and walk out of the room, leaving me to follow behind. I got off a couple of shots across their bows, but I got a lot to learn about fighting like a lady.

After I spend the rest of the hour studying place settings till my eyes cross, the class finally ends and we go into yet another room that has many comfortable chairs and low tables and I flop down in a chair next to Amy. We are to be served tea and sweet tarts.

Well, this ain't so bad, I thinks, dispatching a sweet cake in two bites before I thinks to watch Amy. I brush the crumbs off my lap and look about.

The girls are in small groups and one of the ladies, whose name is Elizabeth, is pouring the tea to some and directing the serving girl Betsey to pour for the others. I ciphers it out that the girls take turns being the hostess, like she was in her own house, and Mistress over there is watching her like a hawk. Looks like you're always onstage here.

Elizabeth comes over to the group next to us and she's chattering gaily, but I can tell she's sweatin' blood. I got to be specially watchful that this Elizabeth don't dump a pot of tea on my new clothes to teach me my place, as if I don't know my place already, so when she comes up to me to pour me a cup, I got my napkin on my lap and I'm ready to spring up and out of the way if I see some unwanted liquid comin' my way. Ain't nobody gonna mess with this dress, by God.

But she don't. She's as nice as pie and we swap false smiles and then I take my tea and load it up with sugar and slide it down my throat. It's good and gives me the strength to ask of Amy, "What's next?"

"Now we have Free Study, which means we can work on what we like until supper. I plan to read. You can work on your embroidery, your French, your—"

"Letter writing?" I ask.

"Yes. That, too."

The tea being over and Mistress having left, I rush up the stairs and rip open my seabag and whip out Jaimy's letter.

James Emerson Fletcher
Number 9 Brattle Lane
London, England
August 29, 1803

Miss Jacky Faber
The Lawson Peabody School for Young Girls
Beacon Street, Boston, Massachusetts, United States

My Dearest Jacky,

By the time you read this letter you will be put ashore and I will be making preparations for getting under way, if not already at sea. It saddens my already lonely heart to think that the distance between us will grow, day by day, ever more vast. I am heartened, however, and will take great comfort in remembering the words of love you so recently and ardently expressed to me. That you should love me is the finest gift I have ever been given, or will ever yet receive.

The other midshipmen have wholeheartedly welcomed me into their company and they are all thoroughly decent fellows and I know that they all hold you in the highest esteem—Jenkins, especially, for your help in confronting the vile Bliffil—and how the midshipmen's berth exults in the bully's disgrace and absence!

Today, we all went into the town to have one last day ashore, but I could take no joy in my liberty, knowing as I did that you were cruelly confined in that miserable brig for the crime of merely being a girl. So later, as the other lads were holding forth in a tavern, I wandered off alone and walked through the town and into the meadow they call the Common.

Boston is a curiously small town for all its reputation—hardly twenty-five thousand souls, I am told. It is hard to believe that this small city could rise up and stand alone in open rebellion to Britannia in all her power and might. Not that I approve, mind you, but still you must admire the audacity of it all.

Presently, I crossed the Common and stood in front of the school you will be attending. I believe you will find it a pleasant place, Jacky, with large, well-shaped trees all about, and neat, well-tended grounds. There is a church next to the school, and it is my hope that you will find comfort and solace there in times of need.

I stood there gazing at the school for a long time. Tomorrow the Dolphin shall leave Boston, heavy laden with treasure, but depend upon it, Jacky, when the ship leaves the harbor, my eyes

*will be fixed on this house upon this hill, for I will know where
my true treasure lies.*

*Please write to me, Jacky, at the above address. I shall count
the days till I receive your first letter, having now only this lock
of your hair, bound up in a ribbon, to remind me of you.*

I remain, and will always remain

Your most obedient & devoted servant,
Jaimy

I fling myself across my bed and stuff my pillow against
my face so the others can't hear me cryin'. After I subsides a
bit, I rise and refold Jaimy's letter, and I put it back in my
bag. I know that I will read and reread this letter till the
edges fray and the ink blurs and the very letter itself falls
apart in my hands. I know that.

I go into the privy to splash some water on my face and
then I go back downstairs to find pen and paper to begin my
letter to Jaimy.

Jacky Faber
The Lawson Peabody School for Young Girls
Beacon Street, Boston, Massachusetts, United States
August 30, 1803

James Emerson Fletcher, Midshipman
9 Brattle Lane, London, England

Dear Jaimy,

*I dont know nothing about writing letters, Jaimy, this being
the first one I ever wrote and I dont know how to do it so I am*

just going to plunge ahead and hope you will forgive me when I make a mess of it which I will.

I dont know if I like it here, Jaimy, I dont know at all. Tilly and the Captain and Deacon Dunne all put out their reasons for what they were going to do with me, but I still dont get it. Why couldnt they have put me off in London? They could have kept me in the brig for the crossing, I wouldna minded. I wouldna caused no trouble just cause I was a girl. In London I woulda at least had a chance to see you or could at least known I was in the same town as you, but no...You dont know this, Jaimy, but when the Dolphin was warped out of the harbor today with you on it and me not, I could see it from a window at the school, it being up on a hill and I could see the harbor all spread out below and the ship with all its flags flying and guns saluting and looking so glorious that it fairly tore my heart out, it did.

Its my first day here and already I cant wait to get away. Oh, the bunks are clean and the grub is good, but I dont know if I like the company of girls very much. These girls here, youd think theyd be a bunch of prim pampered little princesses but, no, they aint, theyre like any bunch of thirty or so cats thrown in to a sack and shaken up good. Theyre mean in ways that boys never even thought of being. I am all at sea about this becoming a lady business, too, and I dont know if Im ever going to get any better at it. I wish with all my heart that they would just give me back my money and let me go back to you.

I know I am whining and I am sorry, but all I really want to do is bury my face in your neck and whimper and cry and have you pat my back and say everythings all right, Jacky, in your lovely deep voice, and then I would forget about everything else and be happy. I loved it when I heard you say my name. I miss it more than you could know, a simple thing like that. I loved *your letter, too, Jaimy, I did and I live only in hopes of getting another one soon.*

Please keep me in your thoughts and speak kindly of me to others if you can, especially your mum and dad. Give my regards to the Brotherhood and all the other seamen on the Dolphin. Liam especially. Tell that Davy to be good.

I regret to report that your ring is no longer in my ear as befits a proper sailor, it being forcibly removed by the school's Mistress and an evil one she is, I can tell you. The ring now is on a string around my neck and it rests against my breast, close to my heart. Know, Jaimy, that every night I go to sleep clutching it in my fist and thinking only of you. I will pray for your health and safety, and worry about you constantly, not being there to watch your back myself and keep you from charging pirates and challenging people to duels and otherwise risking your brave foolish neck, not that I was able to stop you before but at least I was there.

I know. I am a mess and I am making a fine mess of this paper with my tears running off the end of my nose and blurring the ink, but I cant help it. I will write again in a few days.

Oh, Jaimy, I just wish we were back in our lovely hammock on the dear Dolphin and I was just your secret girl again, I do.

Yours forever,
Jacky

The chimes calling us to supper ring out as I am carefully blotting my letter. I fold it and put it up my sleeve as I have neither pocket nor purse. I wipe my nose and eyes, and hoping I don't look a total mess, I go and join Amy in the dining room.

The grace is given, not by me this time, thank God, but by a bloke at the head table, sitting next to Mistress. Supper is, as Amy said, a much smaller affair than dinner, but it is still quite good. We have a pie made from some sort of bird with vegetables and gravy all in it. I'm getting better with the tools and don't have to watch Amy so closely this time. These biscuits are sinfully good.

"So where do you come from, Miss?" says I to break the silence. "Do you have a family? A mum and dad, like, brothers or sisters?"

I know she still does not quite know what to make of me. "Yes," she replies, "we have a farm in Quincy. I have a brother and his name is Randall. He attends the college across the river."

"Ah," I says, "a poor farm girl with a poor scholar for a brother. No wonder the little princesses won't have nothing to do with you. And where's this Quincy, then?"

"It is to the south. About fifteen miles."

"Ah," I say, and let the talk peter out. She is sure a gloomy one, she is.

I notice that the teachers don't come to this meal, just Mistress and that cove what said the grace and what's got on a white collar like two square wings on the throat of his black coat. All the rest of his clothes is black, too, but that ain't nothin' new around here. The other teachers prolly live close by and only take the noon dinner with us, I figures, and takes breakfast and supper with their own families.

"Who's he?" I ask, pointin' him out with my fork.

She glances over and says, "That is the Very Reverend Richard Mather. He is our Spiritual Advisor. He has the church next door. He is also a trustee and member of the

42

board of this school. We go over there for services on Sunday morning and prayer meeting on Wednesday night. He takes his suppers here. He has no wife."

I see that one of the girls is eating with them, Mistress Pimm and the Reverend sitting side by side and the girl sitting across from them, her back toward us. That selfsame back is being held rigidly straight and it does not seem to be enjoying itself, overmuch.

"That girl there?" I ask, nodding toward the head table. Amy looks over.

"That is Dolley Frazier. Each night, one of us is invited to dine with them. It is not supposed to be a pleasure. It is a test—a test of your manners, comportment, knowledge of etiquette, demeanor, and spiritual depth. And you get no warning as to when it is your turn. You will be expected to rise to the occasion."

"Ah." I look over at the unlucky girl. I know she wants desperately to be back with her mates and I note how she holds her shoulders and feet and elbows 'cause I know it'll be my turn over there someday soon.

After supper, lamps are lit in the tea room and we are left to ourselves again. Clarissa and her crew chatter and giggle, but Amy don't do nothin' but read and so I study my French book till the words begin to slide off the page and my head starts in to noddin'.

I feel myself fallin' over to one side and Amy says, "It must have been a long day for you," and I snap my head up with a jerk and weaves back and forth and says, "Right. But, I'm all right. What are you reading?"

"*The Federalist*," says Amy. "It is political matter."

"Myself, I like the novels," I says. "I just finished *Moll Flanders* and *Robinson Crusoe* and some of Captain Cook's writings about his voyages and—"

"Wherever did you get those books?" she asks, and seems to be in genuine wonder.

"Don't you have those books here?" I don't want to tell her that I sort of borrowed those books from the midshipmen's berth. "How 'bout *Poor Nell, A Girl of the Streets*? And *A General History of the Most Notorious Pyrates*?"

Her eyes widen. "No. We have no such books here."

"Well, don't worry," I says, all cheerful. "I saw a bookseller's on the way here today, so we'll get some soon and we'll curl up with 'em right here."

I close my French book and put my head back against the soft leather of the chair. I close my eyes and ask, "What do we do tomorrow?"

"Equestrian in the morning. All morning," she says. "Art, Penmanship, Arithmetic, and Music in the afternoon."

Music!

"But what's this 'questrian?" I asks.

"Horses," says Amy. "The riding and management thereof."

I shudder and turn back to my studies.

At the ringing of a handbell, we march back to the dormitory and there is a great rush for the stalls in the privy to wash up and change. Each girl takes her bedclothes from a chest of drawers next to her bed and I pull mine out of my sea chest and wait till there is a free washroom and then go in and latch the door and pour some water from the pitcher into the basin. There is a piece of soap in a little dish. I doff my clothes and wash and dry and then get into my own gown and cap. I let the water out of the basin and notice that it runs out the bottom through a pipe that goes through the wall. *Isn't this just the most amazing thing,* I thinks. Prolly goes out into the garden, or something.

I warily poke my head out of the stall, sure that Clarissa and her bunch ain't layin' for me with somethin' nasty planned, like soaking me down with water or holding me down and beating me, but they don't. They're off chattering in a circle around Clarissa and paying me no mind. Good.

I take my regular clothes back to my chest of drawers and I carefully lay my uniform dress out in a drawer of its own. There is a net bag in the bottom drawer and I do not know what it is for but I'm sure I will find out. I hang my towel on the hook at the head of my bed.

Amy comes back from the privy decked out in her own nightclothes and I look to her to see what to do next. Climbing into my bunk and going to sleep seems much too simple, and I am right. Mistress comes briskly into the room and taps her rod once on the deck and says, "Prayers."

There is the sound of knees hitting the floor as all the girls kneel next to their beds, and so I do the same. I glance around and see that everybody has their hands in prayerful attitude and is mumbling away, and I do the same. I figures "Now I lay me down to sleep" will work and then the Lord's Prayer, can't go wrong with that, and then I hear some of the nearby girls blessing their mums and dads and sisters and brothers so I sets in to blessing Jaimy and Tink and Davy and Willy and Liam and Snag and Captain Locke and Mr. Lawrence and, yes, even Mr. Haywood and the rest of the Dolphins and then puts in a word for the ones passed on like Benjy and Rooster Charlie and Grant and Spence, and then I'm mentioning Johnny No Toes and Hugh the Grand and Polly and Nancy and Judy of the Blackfriars Bridge gang when I notice Mistress standing next to me and I stops reelin' off the names. I guess I've blessed enough.

She taps her cane twice on the floor and the girls pile into their beds.

Mistress says, "Good night, girls."

"Good night, Mistress," we all say.

Mistress herself goes about and snuffs the lamps. Soon all is darkness.

A great wave of weariness sweeps over me even though I ain't done no real work today, and with the weariness comes the hopelessness of homesickness, too, that awful feelin' that things ain't never gonna get any better than they are now, and I'm startin' to wet my pillow with my tears but I got to stop it. I can't let them hear me cry, I can't. You got to look on the bright side of things now, I tells myself. The truth is no one tried to hang you today or even threatened you with it. You were not thrown naked into the street. You were beaten but not insensible. All those things *have* happened to you before, but not today. True, you've got to contend with horses tomorrow and I know you ain't lookin' forward to that, and that Clarissa is hateful and awful but at least she's not tryin' to actually kill you. Mistress is as stern as any Bo'sun or officer, but did the First Mate come to you every night on the *Dolphin* with a glass of warm milk and a kiss to tuck you in? No, he did not. So stop your complainin'.

I burrow down under the covers and curl up in a ball and clasp Jaimy's ring in my hand, and having already prayed for his health and safety, I start to fall into sleep. It is hard to believe that only this morning I woke from such sleep on the *Dolphin*. Such a long time ago, a world away it seems.

Chapter 2

Sleep is shattered the next morning by the ringing of yet another bell. I curse the ringer of the bell and throw back the covers and get out and pull my drawers and my shift from the sea chest and take my towel and stumble off to the washroom.

I'm the first one in and so have my pick of the stalls. I guess the others ain't used to bein' awakened for night watches by the Bo'sun, him what calls once and whacks second if you ain't up and on the deck right quick. I notice that the pitcher is full of water again and that the water is warm. The serving girls must have been in and I didn't even hear 'em, poor things. I wonder what time *they* had to get up.

So I whips off me cap and nightgown, takes care of the necessaries, and washes up. I runs the toothbrush what Tilly give me over the soap and then over my teeth, rinse and spit, and then I squints at myself in the mirror and decides that my hair will do for one more day, especially seein' as how I don't know how the washin' of hair is done around here and from the looks of some of 'em, it ain't been a real regular practice.

Goin' back into the main sleeping room in my shift and

drawers, my bare feet slappin' on the floor, I see that half of 'em ain't even out of bed yet, Amy included. Clarissa's up, though.

Good. I throw on my dress and stockings and shoes and quickly make my bed, and then I head out to explore. Let's see what this ship has in the way of secrets.

First, I go down the hall and down the stairs and down another hall to the foyer to see if the front door is kept locked. It is. Or, at least it's locked now, but maybe that's on account of it's early. The lock has a latch on the inside and I quietly slide it over and pull open the massive door and look at the outside of the door—there is no keyhole, which means the door can only be locked from the inside. It also means that I'll have to find some other way of gettin' in and out of this ark if I want to explore Boston like I mean to do.

I makes sure the latch is off and then I step out into the light, and there below me all Boston is laid out on this fine late August day, the Common all green with its beasts scattered about, the buildings of the town all neat and orderly, and the harbor sparkling in the distance. There is a slight breeze that blows the hair that's got out of my pigtail about my face and if I close my eyes I'm up in the rigging and we're one day out from Boston and it's, let's see, about six bells in the Four-to-Eight watch and…no, stop it.

I open my eyes and it occurs to me that this is the first time I have been free in a long, long time. I could walk down into that city and disappear forever, as far as the Lawson Peabody School for Young Girls is concerned. Sort of free, that is…free to starve to death…or to Fall into Iniquity as Deacon Dunne would have it…and all my stuff is

49

inside and how could I make my way without my whistle or me shiv or...

Click!

The door has locked behind me! Someone has... *That Clarissa!* She must have seen me leave the dormitory and followed me! *Damn!*

I go up to the door in a panic. Already I can feel the cane on the backs of my legs. I dare not pound on the door 'cause Mistress might answer it and where would I be then? Stretched across her desk with my skirt up, that's where. I've *got* to find another way in.

I run around the side of the school and see nothing on that side and then run around the back—nothing! I continue pounding around to the other side and *there*! The land slopes down and away and at the bottom there's a door to a lower level. I careens down the slope and tries the door. It's open and I go in.

I find myself in the kitchen and it is filled with the smell of frying bacon and toasting bread and there are girls chattering and laughing and scurrying around getting ready to cart it all upstairs and serve it to the ladies and in the middle of it all is a large woman in an apron standing at a huge stove and directing who's to take what.

"Betsey! The bread baskets! Get 'em up there and see if they're ready to eat yet. Annie, take up the tea!"

"Yes, Peggy, we got it we..."

That's when they notice me and the place goes quiet. There are two other girls seated at a table finishing up their own breakfasts and they stand up upon seeing me. The cook asks me, "Yes, Miss, how can we help you?"

"I'm sorry," I stammer. "But I locked myself out the front door. Could you…"

"If it pleases you, Miss, just follow Betsey there. She'll show you the way up."

The girl with the bread turns and heads out of the kitchen and I follow. I do *not* put on the Look. I do, however, take note of what's down here. After the kitchen we go through what appears to be the laundry with big washtubs and a wet floor. There's a room with brooms and mops and buckets. Also tools and a coil of rope. Then we go up a flight of stairs and the girl Betsey sticks the breadbasket on her hip and opens the latch on the door at the top and lets me through and I'm back in the classroom hallway, again.

"Thank you, Betsey," I say, and she just blushes and nods. She is the shyer of the two sisters, I see, but I make her talk by asking, "The front door. Is it always kept locked?"

"Yes, Miss."

"And if I were to go out and came back later and rapped on the knocker, you or one of the others would come and let me in?"

"Yes, Miss," she says. "Or sometimes Mistress."

Oh.

"What about the kitchen door? Downstairs."

"That's not locked, Miss. Not till after we clean up after supper and go home. Then Peg locks up."

I have gotten some useful information.

I get to the dining hall and says, "Hey, Mate," and sits down across from Amy yet again. I look around the room and it seems that this meal is a good deal less formal than the others, as the girls pile right into the tea and toast and there ain't no grace. I see some of the girls put their hands together and mumble one to themselves, but I figure I prayed enough yesterday to hold me for a long while and so grabs a roll as soon as Betsey sets 'em down. The teacher table is empty. I guess Mistress doesn't do this one. Prolly back in her room with a pipe and a cup of coffee.

I look for some sign in Clarissa that she was the one what marooned me outside, but I can't see none. She serenely holds court, the center of all attention, a goddess in her heaven. She and some of the other girls have on what I reckon are riding clothes and they look quite smart, damn them.

"What's the rule on going outside the school?" I asks of Amy.

Once again she looks confused. I find that I am good at confusing her. But then she answers.

"But of course we could never go out without an escort, so I imagine that has never been stated as an actual rule." She thinks for a bit more and then goes on. "Of course, our parents can take us out for holidays, and the local girls go home for the weekends, generally. I suppose my brother could escort me if I ever wanted to go anywhere...Not that he ever would."

"Oh yes. You said you have a brother."

"Yes, Randall. He is eighteen. The college he attends across the river, in Cambridge, is a real school. Not like this." She sniffs.

"Well, Mate, maybe someday he can come over and escort us around the town," I says. "There's some taverns down on the docks I'd like to check out."

I don't catch her reply to this 'cause a platter of eggs is brought up to me and I scoops up a couple and slides 'em on my plate and snags a brace of bacon strips to keep 'em company. I looks at the eggs in all their yellow-yolked beauty lying there on my plate.

"And what's your name, then?" I ask of the girl holdin' the platter with the eggs and bacon. She was one of the girls sitting at the table when I came in the kitchen door.

"Abby, Mum," says the girl.

"Well, thank you, Abby, and please tell Peggy I think she's some cook."

Abby smiles and says, "Yes'm."

I tears into the helpless eggs and soon am patting my belly in satisfaction. "Now, Miss Amy, I'm ready to meet those horses."

On the way down the hallway Annie comes up to me and says, "Beggin' your pardon, Miss, but Mistress wants to see you in her office. Now."

Dread crawls up my soon-to-be-beaten legs and into my belly and makes my eggs sit less easy there than they was before. Somebody must have peached on me for being outside. *Damn!*

Clarissa sweeps past with a jaunty bonnet on her head, a riding crop under her arm, and a slight smile on her face.

I grimace at Amy and leave her side as we pass Mistress's office. The door is open and she is seated at her desk. I walk inside, bob, and put my toes on the white line and wait.

"Good morning, Mistress," I manage to say. I hope my Look is all right. I case my eyes and stare over her head, expecting the worst.

"Good morning," she says. "Here." And she hands me a letter. I recognize it as my own that I wrote to Jaimy yesterday and put in the mailbox outside her door. "This letter is addressed to a man to whom you are not related. It is not seemly for you to be carrying on such a correspondence, and I will not send it on. I advise you to be more careful in your actions and comportment in the future."

"But, Mistress, we are to be married as soon as I finish school. Surely—"

"Surely you remember what I said about talking back to me," she says with a warning in her tone. "Now. Do you have a formal engagement? Anything in writing?"

"No, Mistress, but I believe his intentions are true."

"That's not enough. I direct you to put aside these girlish dreams and attend to your studies here. If you are successful in these studies, I assure you there will be a good match for you in the future. All my girls make good matches. Certainly better than casual alliances with sailors. You are dismissed, Miss Faber."

"Mistress," I says, knowin' I'm pushing my luck here, "but if I were to *get* a letter from this young man, would you—"

"I believe we are through discussing letters, Miss Faber, and we shall mention them no more," says Mistress, with menace in her voice. "Dismissed, Miss Faber."

I dip and do an about-face and head out the door, glad not to be beaten, but still steamed. She answered my question, all right—ain't no way she's ever gonna pass on any of Jaimy's letters to me. I am glad I made my explorations this morning 'cause I *will* go out and I *will* mail my letter to

Jaimy 'cause I don't want no other match but him. I just got to think about how to get that done.

Amy has waited for me, and together we go out the front door and around the corner and up the small road between the school and the church. As we leave the school building behind us, I look back and notice that the ends of the school are not the usual white clapboards but are instead completely brick, being like enormous chimneys. We leave the churchyard to our right, there is a meadow, and we come to the stables.

"Heinrich!"

"Ja, Papa."

"Fräulein Faber hast not bin on eine horse before. Give her teachings."

"Yes, Papa."

I am standing there stupidly, once again judged hopelessly behind and backward. The other girls, including Amy, are taking their mounts from the handlers like they was born to it, mounting, and forming a circle around the inside of this huge circular barn that is floored in wet sawdust and roofed in soaring wood rafters and thick wood beams. Sort of like the hull of a ship from the inside, upside down. With a snap of Herr Hoffman's whip and a *whoop!* from some of the girls, they are off at a full gallop, round and around.

Not for me, however, as I must follow Heinrich into the stables.

The boy has his light brown hair tied loosely in the back with a black ribbon and he wears a dark green jacket with gray frogging on the front and tight, *tight* white breeches

55

and knee-high shiny black boots. He has a light fuzz of hair on his upper lip and this is the first time I've been next to a boy and not under armed guard for about a month, and... no, you stop that now. Concentrate on what he's tellin' you.

He goes into one of the stalls and comes out leading a horse.

"This is Gretchen, Miss Faber," he says. "She will be your horse while you are here." He doesn't talk the way his father does. Must have been born here, or at least brought up here. "She is a very nice little mare," he goes on when he sees my look of fear.

It don't look that little to me.

It is of a light tan color with a white mane and tail. It has big brown eyes and it looks at me and I look at it. Horses to a street kid like me are big stupid lumbering things that'd crush an orphan as soon as look at 'em, but I reach out my hand and pat it on its hard slab of a forehead and it snorts in a friendly way.

Maybe we'll get along, I think, and I get the feeling she thinks the same.

The young man lets me and the beast get more acquainted while he fetches a saddle. "You might want to put on one of those dusters, Miss. To protect your dress." There is a row of light cotton cover-ups hung on pegs along the wall and I choose the smallest one and put it on. I button up the front as he flings the saddle over the horse's back and cinches it up, and then he hands me the reins. I take them, trying to keep my hand from shakin'.

"Gather them together and reach up and grab the saddle right here and put your right foot here and up you go." And I am in the saddle and looking down at the ground and thinking how much it would hurt to fall off and hit that ground.

"Heinrich," I say, trying to keep the tremble out of my voice, "wouldn't it be easier if I were to throw my leg to the other side of the horse?" Both my legs are now on one side of the horse and I'm feelin' right precarious.

"I'm sorry, Miss. It just isn't done," says he. "And please call me Henry, if you would. Now put your right limb about the pommel there." That feels a bit better, now that the pommel thing in the front of the saddle is sort of holding my thigh above the knee. Henry adjusts the stirrup for my right leg till it feels right. "Now take the reins—no, don't hold on to the saddle, and if it pleases you, Miss, sit back a bit so that your backbone is directly over hers. Please forgive my frank language, but it's the only way to say it." I believe he is flustered over calling my backbone a backbone. "Now let us go outside."

We go out into the sun and Henry takes the horse by what he calls the bridle and he walks me and the horse around a bit and I get used to the smooth roll of the horse's muscles beneath mine and that's all right, a bit nice, really. Henry shows me how to pull on the reins to make it go right and then left and then stop.

Henry ain't content to let it go at that and just let me enjoy the warmth of the morning, oh no, he says, since I'm doing so well, we must now go to trotting. He has me take the horse to a small fenced-in spot and he puts a long thin line on the horse's bridle and stands back and says, "Now, Miss Faber, firmly pull your heels up into her side and say, 'Hup!'"

I do it and the horse starts this jiggy way of going that

about jars the teeth out of my head and I grab for the pommel of the saddle.

"No, no, Miss. You must never do that. It makes you look like…an inexperienced rider."

Makes me look like a scrub, you mean, I thinks, vowing *never* again to touch the saddle.

"Get into the rhythm of her motion. Let your…back arch a little, back and forth."

I try to do it and, little by little, by getting my back and my bottom into it, I start to get it.

"Very good posting, Miss. Very good. I think you are a natural rider."

I glow under his praise and try even harder.

Henry holds the line so that the horse goes about in a circle around him, sort of a small version of the circle inside the barn, and round and round we go. "Now lean forward and chuck her again with your heels!" and I do it and she slips into this easy, loping thing that's a lot easier on my tail and I get into the rhythm of that, too, and it feels so right and easy that my heart starts poundin' in me chest from the joy of it all.

Henry has me go from the canter to the trot to walk and back again and again till it's as easy as walking a spar and swinging down to the ship's deck on a futtock shroud.

When we are done, Henry has me dismount and walk Gretchen around the field to cool her off.

"If you put her up wet, she's likely to take the colic and die, and we wouldn't want that."

No, we wouldn't, I thinks to myself, running my hand

through Gretchen's mane with growing affection, *we wouldn't want that at all.*

I take her bridle in my hand and walk her about for fifteen minutes or so, till I can reach down onto her chest between her front legs and find it is no longer steamy with sweat. I take her back to her stall and feed her an apple from the barrel that's kept in the stable for just such a purpose. Her lips take it ever so delicately from my hand.

I have taken my first equestrian lesson and Henry says I have done well. Very well, even. I know that I have tried hard, for I hate being the baby and the odd one out and I cannot wait to join that wild circle of riders pounding about that barn.

Dinner, and then Art, which I am going to like, and then Penmanship, which is all right, too, 'cept now my hand is all cramped up and is as sore from the writing as my bottom is sore from the riding. Now on to Music.

All day I've been thinking about how I'm gonna get my letters to Jaimy—and his letters to me, since sure as hell that Mistress ain't gonna pass 'em on to me. Wouldn't be *seemly.*

So what I've decided is that I'll save up everything and when a British man-of-war comes into port and is bound back to England, I'll put together a packet and then go down and ask them to take it for me, and I'm sure they will do it. At the same time I'll figure out an address he can send stuff to me. I'll ask Amy, later. She might know the way of it.

"Amy," I says, as we head for the music room, "what is this bit with Clarissa calling me a Tory? I don't know what to say when she calls me that. Where I come from, Tories are just part of a political party. That can't be what she means."

"That is not what she means. Here 'Tory' refers to an American who remained loyal to King George before and during the Revolution. Clarissa is calling you a turncoat, a traitor."

"Now, how can I be that when I'm born English and can't help it?" I exclaims all baffled.

"We were all English twenty-five years ago. Emotions still run high, especially in light of the recent troubles with Great Britain."

"Troubles like what?"

"Impressment of seamen, for one. The stopping of American ships on the high seas and the taking of seamen to fight for the crown. Mostly British sailors, but sometimes our own. And there's the British agents out west stirring up Tecumseh and his Indians to kill our settlers on the frontier."

"Oh," says I.

We enter the music room. My classmates arrange themselves in two circular lines facing a podium in the center, and at the podium is a round little man who is leafing through a stack of papers.

Amy takes me up to him and says, "Maestro, this is Miss Faber. She is new. Miss Faber, this is Maestro Fracelli."

I do the curtsy and then stand there as Amy takes her place in the second rank. I know that is an assigned place 'cause she's standing right next to Clarissa and I know she'd never stand there on her own.

Maestro Fracelli is done with his papers and turns to me and says, "Sing something, please, so that I may place you."

Place me?

I think quick and pick one that might show my range and not scandalize 'em too much, and I straighten out my shoulders and I lift my head and sings out:

> *"Oh, hard is the fortune*
> *Of all womankind.*
> *She's always controlled,*
> *She's always confined.*
> *Controlled by her parents,*
> *Until she's a wife,*
> *A slave to her husband,*
> *The rest of her life."*

There is a dead silence. Maestro clears his throat and says, "Very nice. A curious choice of material, but delivered *con brio*. I think I will place you with the altos on the left." He picks up a folder and hands it to me. "Please sing the first stanza of this."

I look at it and my heart sinks. At the top of the paper is written *"Jesu, Joy of Man's Desiring,"* and underneath that is a bunch of lines with little black bugs and squiggles on 'em and I ain't got the foggiest idea of what they mean and I shakes me head and me throat starts to tighten up and me eyes start to fill and I'm startin' to shake all over 'cause once again I'm found wantin' in *every* class and I'm so backward in *everything* here and I don't want them to see me cry, but two days of being the dummy is just too much and I'm losing control of everything and I'm about to run up and get my seabag and run off down to the docks and…me mind hears Amy say, "Pardon, Maestro, a moment, please," and she puts her arm around me and she hustles me out into the hall.

She takes me by the shoulders and says, "It's not so hard. I will teach you. You do not have to already know everything. Now, go back in there and stand where he tells you and just hum along for a while until you get it. He is a really nice man and he will help you. Now, just do it."

I'm still shakin' and cryin' and about to dissolve into a puddle on the floor. *Music! The thing I love the most and still I'm the fool and I was stupid enough to think I would stand out in this 'cause I thought I was good at it and I ain't I ain't I ain't good at nothin'...*

"Here. Dry your eyes. Put on the Look."

"Thank you, Miss, for your kindness." I gulps. "I won't forget. I promise you, I won't forget."

We go back into the music room and I walk across and Maestro points out my place and I take it and stand there with my useless folder in front of me. Incredibly, the girl next to me on my right gives me a nudge and a wink. It is the girl Dolley. I almost burst into tears again at that little kindness.

I am saved by Maestro Fracelli, who taps his stick on his podium and says, "From the beginning, one two three and *four*," and the girls burst into song and it is one of the most beautiful sounds I have ever heard. I am astounded that such beauty is coming out of the throats of these hateful girls, and I follow along the words and now that I got the tune, I sings along and adds my voice to the beautiful sound.

Amy's right. It will be all right.

I don't know if it was the tension of the past two days or just hearing some French being spoke, or maybe it was the constant rocking back and forth in the last few days between despair and joy—the despair of not knowing how to read their music and the sheer joy of hearing the beauty of the girls' chorus, the terror of my first time on a horse and the hope of someday joining the pounding ring of riders—or I don't know what, but *he* comes for me again tonight.

He comes to me as he always does when he comes to me, leering out of the darkness with the rope coiled over his arm, the noose dangling down. He reaches for me and I shrink back but my feet sink in the sand and my hands are tied behind me and I can't move and I can't get away and I keep foundering in the sand and I keep trying and the harder I try the more I'm sucked down and he reaches out and his hand goes around my arm and he draws me to him and I smell his foul breath on me and it smells of the grave and he puts the noose around my neck and it's rough and hairy and it scrapes at my neck and then it tightens and I'm standing on the keg again and it is unsteady and rocks beneath me and LeFievre looks up at me and his head becomes the head we had nailed to the bowsprit and the eye sockets are empty and black where the birds picked them out and the lips rot away and fall off and the teeth gleam in a hideous grin and then he kicks away the keg and once again I feel the rope come up hard against my neck and my own weight pulls me down against my neck and I hang there and *I can't breathe dear God help me I can't breathe I choke I choke I choke and...*

And then Amy's face comes swimmin' out of the darkness in front of me and she's got me by the shoulders and is sayin', *"Jacky, please wake up it is just a dream,"* and sense comes back to me in a rush. I must have been screamin', 'cause everybody's sittin' up in their beds and lookin' at me like I'm crazy, which I reckon I am, 'cause I got tears runnin' all down me face and I'm shiverin' even though I'm covered in sweat and I'm gulpin' down great gobs of air and I shudders and then I lets out a great sob and buries me face in the front of Amy's nightgown.

After a while I calms down and Amy gets up and goes back to her bed. I lie there quiet in the darkness, but the terror is still in me and won't go away. I try to be brave but I'm not, I'm not, I'm just so lonely and scared that finally I fling back the covers and go over to Amy and I crawl in and burrow beside her and say, "Please, Miss. I'm not good at sleepin' alone, as I ain't done it much and I just can't do it right."

If she says anything to that, I don't hear it 'cause I'm so lulled by her nearness and the gentle sound of her breathing that I slips right off the edge of the cliff into deep and peaceful sleep and *he* don't come for me again this night, neither.

Chapter 3

Amy is struggling and thrashing about as I stick her head in the basin of suds. "Get it in there, Amy. If we're gonna be sharin' an occasional pillow, you've got to wash your hair a bit more often." My own hair is already done and up in a towel.

"But, Jacky, I—"

"I know, I know, you just washed it last month. I knows the old chant, 'Onc't a year, whether it needs it or not.' Well, it needs it right now, Amy, believe me."

I scrub away, workin' my fingers in her thick, black hair, gettin' the soap down to the roots. Her hair is surprisingly long and glossy, when it's taken out of that schoolmarmish bun she's been keepin' it in. We can work with this, I'm thinkin'.

"We've got to get you shaped up, Amy. Won't be too long 'fore you're lookin' for a proper husband, and not one from back on your farm—a real gent, like."

There's a tap on the washroom door and one of the serving girls, a girl with dark eyes and dark hair and a quiet and shy demeanor, who I know is named Sylvie, comes in with a fresh pitcher of water and I take it and say, "Thanks, Sylvie," and she dips and leaves. I pour the rinse water over Amy's head and say, "All right, let's wring it out and then wrap it in this towel."

"That is nonsense, Miss," says she, her eyes squinted up against the soap. "No one will want me. I am fat and ugly and no one will ever love me and I do not care that they will not." I twist her hair into the towel, as she ain't very practiced at it. "Besides, I'm not ready for that sort of thing yet."

Does she blush just at the mere mention of a husband?

"Well, I loves ye, Amy," says I, and plants one on her cheek, "and you ain't fat, just a bit plump, and there's coves that likes 'em that way. Besides, it's just baby fat—stick with the Jackaroe and you'll be beatin' the boys to the foretop in no time, you will. And as for ugly, why, your teeth are good and I finds your pug nose downright charmin'. Better than my pointy beak."

We drop the towels and head outside to let our hair dry in the sun. It's a wondrously warm mid-September day. We go down through the kitchen and out the back—the less Mistress sees of me, the better, I figure. I wave to Peg and the girls as we pass through.

Amy and I go out into the sunlight and across the road to the field across the way, next to the church. The sun warms our damp hair and we fluff it out to dry, and it's so warm and beautiful that I twirl myself about, making both hair and skirt blossom out, and then I flop down in the grass and look up at the sky.

It's so nice to be out of the school for a bit. I've been here for about two weeks now and I'm starting to feel more easy in the place. Today is Saturday and so it's a lot quieter around the school—a lot of the girls live locally and they can go home for the weekends if they sign out and are picked up by their families. I saw Clarissa go off in a carriage with Lissette this morning, so I guess she's staying with her. There's no classes on Saturdays and we're free to do what we want. Sort of what we want. I figure I'll write a few more things to Jaimy and then take Gretchen out for a ride.

I'm getting much better at the riding—Henry's been ever so helpful and patient with me and he says I have come along in an amazing way, which pleases me no end. I had him show me how to saddle Gretchen myself so's I wouldn't bother him all the time, and even though he said it was no bother—"Not for you, Miss"—I learned how to do it. I find I like being off alone on her, looking out over the city and its harbor and buildings and marshes and fields and such, and now I can go and get her myself, without having to ask.

Tomorrow we will all troop over to the church again and have the Preacher shout at us for a couple of dreary hours. When he gets all worked up about sin and stuff, it's like he don't know how to stop, shouting and jabbing his finger at us, and me in particular, it seems. Wonder why? I don't know what he thinks we could be up to in the way of sin, living in this convent as we do. I usually let my mind wander off to think about Jaimy when the Preacher rants on and on. I wonder if impure thoughts count as sin? Prolly do, and I do think up plenty of those when I'm daydreamin' about Jaimy. Don't seem like sins to me, though. Just love, is all. Oh, well, at least we get Sunday afternoons off, too. Pretty soft, I thinks, remembering the one-in-three watch schedule we had on the *Dolphin,* night and day, day in and day out. Still rather be there, though. And then on Wednesday mornings we put our dirty drawers and shifts, all our underclothes, in those net bags that I wondered about when I first got here and we leave them at the foot of our beds for the serving girls to pick up and wash. Pretty sinfully soft, that, too. Wednesday being wash day, the beds are stripped and we will have fresh sheets that evening. Don't I feel a little guilty, though.

"Ain't it grand, Amy, so warm and nice and all."

"Best enjoy it, for the fall will be short. Indian summer will come and go and winter will come around, count on it," says Amy, ever the happy one. She already looks better, I'm thinkin', even with her hair wet and hangin' down all straight.

"So you have Red Indians here?" I say, thrilled with the thought of seein' one all decked out with tommyhawk and war paint and feathers. "Where are they?"

"Mostly out to the west now." She pauses, and then goes on. "Surely you know the British gave them guns and money to kill our poor settlers during the Revolution. They paid them by the scalp. There were the most awful massacres. On both sides, Indians and us."

Hmmm, I thinks, prolly best to skip this line of conversation. I can't believe my country would do such a thing, but then I can't believe that the child that was me was tossed out into the streets of London with no help nor mercy nor Christian kindness. I get up and stretch and say, "Let's go and look through the churchyard."

We go through a break in the low stone wall that surrounds the church and its graveyard.

"Do you think it is wise?" says Amy, all doubtful. The church looms high above us.

"Why not? We have nothing to fear from the dead, as we ain't done nothin' to harm 'em," I says. "It's the livin' you got to fear." I lean down to peer at the carving on a stone. "What do those skulls with those wings stickin' out of 'em mean?"

"Those are old stones from a hundred years ago. The carvings are called 'Death Angels' and they are supposed to depict the person that died." Amy wraps her arms about herself and shivers. "You can see that each one is different."

"And what does that 'Memento Mori' mean?" I've got some Latin, but not much.

"It means 'Remember Death.'"

"Which means?"

"It means you can have all your parties and songs and dances and you can pursue all your schemes and endeavors and ambitions and fancies and pride *but...*"—and here Amy tosses her head and looks almost defiant—"*but remember Death is coming and you'd better be ready at any time.* That is what it means. Can we go now?"

"Ah," I say, and walk on. I stoop down and read another stone. "Oh, Amy, look. How sad. It is the grave of a girl not much older than us." The inscription under the Death Angel reads:

Here lyes ye body of
Constance Howard, Beloved Daughter
Who Departed This Life on May 2nd, 1679
in her seventeenth year

Death is a Debt to Nature...

The gray and weathered stone is at a tilt and the rest of the verse is hidden by the high grass and I can't make it out, and so I kneel down and pull at the grass clumps and dirt till the words are revealed and I read them out loud:

> *Death is a Debt to Nature Due*
> *Which I have Paid*
> *And So Must You*

Well, that rocks me back on my heels. Talk about a message from the beyond!

I think for a moment and then I stand up and pull out my pennywhistle from my sleeve and I puts it to my lips and I play.

When I'm done, Amy says, "That was very nice. What is the name of it?"

"It's my own little tune, 'The Ship's Boy's Lament' I call it. I made it up as a lament for a mate of mine what died. Now it serves as a lament for a poor girl what didn't get to be no older than seventeen."

We stand there for a while and then turn to go. I look up at the windows in the church. They are curtainless and blank, like the eyeholes in the Death Angels. "That's where he lives, then."

"Who? Reverend Mather, you mean? Yes."

We leave the churchyard through another break in the stone wall and enter the open meadow. I stop. There is another grave here, outside the wall, in the meadow. It is not old and it does not have a stone.

"What do you think this is?" I asks Amy.

"A grave. But being outside the churchyard and having no stone...Maybe a criminal..." She shivers. "...or maybe a suicide."

I look up at the vestry windows and in one of them I think I see someone there, someone who ducked back upon seein' me look up.

"Our hair is dry enough. Let's go."

Why am I not shocked to hear that I am to be the one to join Mistress and Reverend Mather for supper? I am delivered of the note by Betsey, who doesn't miss my groan of despair when I open it and read it. "It will be all right, Miss," she says. I have the feeling that the downstairs staff has somehow adopted me in my feeble attempts at ladyhood.

The chimes ring out and I walk into the dining room and advance to my place at the head table and stand there at attention while all the others file in. Amy gives me a sympathetic glance as she goes by to her lonely post.

At last Mistress and the Reverend Mather walk in and I hear the rustle of the other girls rising. Mistress does the introduction and I bob and say my part as I have been coached by Amy, and the Preacher says his and nods stiffly and then pulls out the chair for Mistress and she sits down. I hear the rustle behind me again and I sit down, and then the Preacher reaches out his arms and does the grace, and it is long and *long*.

At last he sits down and the serving begins.

I have time to examine him before they start in on me.

His face is long and squared off at the jaw. His hair is black and speckled with gray and cut very short, prolly 'cause he wears a powdered wig for any big occasion like when he's preaching in his church on Sunday. His black frock coat is in need of a brushing and looks quite old and out of style, even to my eye. The skin of his face is very white and his cheek-bones poke out through the skin stretched across them. His lips are thin and purplish and held in a tight line the way a man bearing the pain of a toothache will hold his mouth. His jaw has been scraped clean of beard but is still dark from the stubble that is left in the whiteness of his face. In his temple, a blue vein pulses. Beat. Beat. Beat...

Abby appears with the meat platter and serves Mistress first, then the Preacher, then me. I don't take a lot 'cause I know I ain't gonna feel much like eating. It's Annie who brings the potatoes and greens.

"You come to us by a strange path, Miss Faber," says Reverend Mather.

"Yes, Sir," I say. I wonder how much Mistress has told him. As to that, I wonder how much she herself was told about my past.

"What possessed you to get on the ship in the first place?" He carefully places a forkful of food in his mouth and chews evenly and slowly and does not speak until he swallows, his Adam's apple working up and down in his neck. "With over four hundred rough men."

How to put this in its best light?

"I was a penniless orphan, with no relations to help me, Sir." I decide not to put on my Poor Little Orphan bit, but instead play it straight, as I think that might go down better with Mistress. "In my desperation, it seemed the best way for me to better my condition."

And I was right, I reflects to myself.

"Have you ever received any religious instruction and guidance?" Chew, chew, swallow, Adam's apple bob, beat... beat...beat of the vein in the temple.

"Deacon Dunne, the *Dolphin*'s chaplain, was very good to me and the other boys and tried to steer us onto the path of righteousness." He did try, and some of his teachings even took.

"The '*other boys*'?" he says, giving it a nasty twist. "I cannot imagine that you came through *that* experience without *some* stain upon your virtue?"

I am bringing up some food to my mouth for appearance's sake but instead put it back down. *What's he getting at?*

"I tried to be as good as I could be, Sir. I have always tried to be that," I says. I push my food around on my plate and wish I was someplace else. "And I had the good luck to have good friends who looked out for me."

"*Hmmm,*" he says, a flush rising from his collar. His eyes travel over me quite frankly. I feel a blush rising to my own cheeks and I put down my fork and stare at my hands folded in my lap. I don't like this. I don't like it at all.

"She has given me her word that her honor is intact," says Mistress. She looks sideways at the Preacher with a definite chill in her voice. "I have accepted her at her word."

Thank you, Mistress, I say to myself.

But he is not to be cowed. "Perhaps we should continue your religious education, then." He pats his thin slash of a mouth with his napkin and makes a grimace that I take to be a smile. "Individual instruction might be the best thing in this case."

That night, when Amy and I are in for the night, I say, "That preacher cove gives me the creeps, for sure."

She is silent for a bit and then says, "There are things said about that man. Be careful, Jacky."

Chapter 4

⚓ We are in Music and most of the chorus has come down from its perch and Maestro Fracelli is gathering up his music sheets when Clarissa decides to have a little fun with me. She approaches me with Lissette de Lise and a few others in tow and says, "Jacky, dear. We have heard that you can play upon some sort of fife. Will you favor us with a tune?" Fake smiles and the beat-beat of the eyelashes.

I can tell right off that they mean to make sport of me, but the whole chorus is listening in on this so I says what the hell, I've faced tougher crowds than this, and so I pull my whistle from my sleeve and place it on my lips and I starts in on "The Eddystone Light."

First I play the melody on the whistle and it's a right sprightly bouncy little jig and then I throws back my head and sings out the first verse:

> *"My father was the keeper of the Eddystone light,*
> *And he slept with a mermaid one fine night!*
> *Of this strange union there came three;*
> *Twas a porpoise*

and a tuna
and then came me!

Yo, ho, ho! The wind blows free,
Oh, for the life on the rolling sea!"

I cast my eyes about the chorus but they're all smiling
and wide-eyed and listening and not makin' mock of me so
I decides to push my luck and tootles another round on the
whistle, makin' it a bit different this time, not the straight
melody but something like it.

"Very nice, Miss Faber," says the Maestro. "I especially
like that counter melody you did on your flageolet on the
second verse."

I blush under his praise. So that's what my whistle is
called in the world of higher music. Maestro Fracelli bows
and hands his stick to me. *What?*

"Would you like to lead the chorus in this little song, yes?"

I gulp and take the baton and I step to the podium and
give the baton a few raps and say, "Everybody back in your
places. Now let's do this little song. I will sing the verses and
you will sing the chorus. And the chorus is…"

But they've already got it.

"Yo, ho, ho, the wind blows free,
Oh, for the life on the rolling sea."

So I sings the second verse.

"One night I was trimmin' of the glim
And singin' a verse from the evening hymn,

When a voice to starboard shouted 'Ahoy!'
And there was me mother a sittin' on a buoy."

And again they does the chorus and they quite naturally comes in high on the second *ho* and draws out the final *sea* like a mournful foghorn that I know they've heard out on the harbor on a stormy night. Could I make some money with this group on the right night in the right tavern when the fleet's in, or what? I sing the next verse.

"What has become of my children three?
My mother then did ask of me.
One was shown as a talking fish,
And the other was served on a chafing dish."

And again they does the chorus and I glances at Clarissa and she don't look happy at all, as this is not goin' the way she thought it would. Good. So I goes into the last verse.

"Then the phosphorus flashed in her seaweed hair,
And I looked again and me mother wasn't there.
A voice came echoing out of the night,
'To hell with the keeper of the Eddystone light!'"

With that the girls light into the last chorus and just at the end I steps out to the center and puts the whistle back to my lips and starts the dance. I plays and dances together for a bit and then I stops with the whistle and just dances, just hammers out the steps and raps the floor with my heels and they echo off the walls and the girls start clappin' in time and I'm doin' all me steps and moves and then, just at the end, I bring back the whistle and with a final flourish on the whistle and a fine rattle of my feet, I ends it and puts me hands in the air and bows low.

Silence. Then one "Bravo, Jacky!" and then another and another and wild applause all around, and I loves it so much that I just clasps me hands together on me chest and closes me eyes till things quiet down.

When I open my eyes, Clarissa is standing there with Lissette and the rest of the girls have left the choral stand and have gathered about, and Maestro is saying that yes, yes the music of the folk is the basis for all the music, and Clarissa says, "I know that kind of dancing. It's what the poor people on our estate in Virginia do. The blacks and poor whites. If it's done by the nigras, it's called buck dancing. If it's done by poor whites, it's called clogging. Sometimes they put on performances for us as we sit on the verandah in the cool of the evening. We find it mildly amusing, if somewhat simple."

Clarissa brings the power of her gaze to rest upon my poor self.

"Sounds like the poor people have all the fun where you come from," I says, gettin' all hot and comin' up nose to nose with Clarissa.

"Oh no." She smiles, all superior. "The people of your class have very little fun. They have to work for their keep, you know. As do the slaves who—"

"A slaveholder. I heard you were a slaveholder, but I couldn't believe it. Even of you." I'm lookin' her up and down and holding my hands to my mouth as if I'm about to throw up and I ain't fakin' it, no, I ain't banterin' now. "I've seen slavers at sea, Clarissa. You really ought to be ashamed."

Clarissa's smile has been replaced by a low, level stare. "I am not the least ashamed. The superior orders must keep the lower orders in their place. We take care of them and they work for us. It is the way of the world and it is as it should be."

I'm workin' up a big gob of spit and am fixin' to put it in her eye when she wheels and heads toward the door.

"Clarissa," I says, and she and Lissette stop and turn to face me. I point toward the French girl, right between her eyes. "Tell me, Princess. When you kiss the Frog, does it turn into a prince?"

There is a snicker. Then another. Then many. And, finally, all-out laughter. Lissette looks, all confused, to Clarissa—the French girl does not get it.

Clarissa, however, does get it. She shoots me a look of pure malice as the laughter swirls about her. She puffs up and comes back to face me and says, "I'll bet your mother *was* a slutty mermaid. You do smell strongly of fish; you do know that, don't you?"

A curtain of red comes down over my mind and I hear myself say in a low growl, "My mother was a lady, Clarissa, and if you *ever...*"

At this moment I am aware that Maestro has come up between us and is saying, "Ladies. Ladies, please. The sheathing of the claws, please."

Clarissa puffs up and goes to leave, but this time, *I* spins on *my* heel and *I* flounces out, leaving Clarissa in flames behind me.

I go out into the hall, flushed with the emotion of the performance and the confrontation, and I see Mistress standing there. She has heard all of it. I bob and then go on down the passageway. She does not stop me.

We leave Geography, the last class of the day, and gratefully head for the afternoon tea, and settle down in the soft leather chairs. It is Lissette's turn to serve, so I must watch out for any false moves with the teapot. Amy, sitting next to me, has something on her mind, I can tell. But I can wait.

After we are served our tea and cakes and I thank Lissette and she gives me a frosty nod, I winks at the girl Rachel who's acting as Lissette's servant and I get a small grin out of her. Amy says in a low voice that none but me can hear, "I don't know if it is my place to be telling you this, and I hope you do not think I make a practice of eavesdropping on other people's conversations, but..."—and there's a long pause.

Come on, Amy, get it out.

"But, as I was walking by Mistress Pimm's office door, I chanced to hear Reverend Mather inside asking to see the school's financial records. Mistress murmured something that I couldn't catch, but I heard a desk drawer opening and I assumed that she was handing over her ledger. He is a member of the Board of Governors of the school, after all, and has a perfect right to inspect the records. Still, and I cannot be sure, but from the tone of her voice, I felt that Mistress was not entirely pleased at this intrusion into what I am sure she feels is her own affairs."

Amy sits back and seems lost in the recollection. I have another bit of cake and wait. After a bit, she goes on.

"He was riffling the pages for only a few scant seconds when he asked outright about *you,* and how much money you had brought to the school. Mistress named a page and I heard him turning to it. He then made a sound like *'Hmmm!'* and in a moment he bid Mistress a good day and was back in the hall, putting his hat back on. He strode right on by me standing there in the hall, and I do not think he even saw me, even though I dropped a curtsy and bid him good day. He did not answer and was through the front door in a moment."

I thank her for this information and assure her it was right and proper that she should tell me this. Then I think on it for a long time.

That evening, as we ready for bed and I am in my night-dress, I take my hairbrush out into the hall and stand there brushing my hair and looking out the window at the end of the hall, the window that looks out on the church. There is a light in one of the upper windows of the Preacher's church.

What is he about? I wonders.

Chapter 5

We're returning from Equestrian, and I'm flushed with victory—Henry and Herr Hoffman had decided I was ready to join the others in the circle of riders! I rode in on my dear Gretchen, both of our heads held high, the Look firmly on my face, and with all eyes on me, I spurred us to the spot right in front of Clarissa, so that she would view my mare's behind as we circled around. Herr Hoffman cracked his whip and we were off on a fast trot, then a canter, then a full gallop, then *"Veel!"* and we turn about, and as we do I lock eyes with Clarissa and perfect understanding and perfect hatred passes between us. Then it was my turn to stare at her horse's rump, but I didn't care. Later, Gretchen and I were called to the center, and while the others sat their mounts, we showed them a bit of *dressage*—first walking in place, then turn to right, forward three paces, then back up three and turn to left and then she paces forward, one step, pause with one foreleg held up high, then another step, another pause, then step. Then stop. I get a *"Vell done, Mädchen!"* and then it's back in the circle with Gretchie and me. *Glory!*

Later, when we were walking the horses to cool them, I saw the Preacher standing off in the distance. He had climbed a small hill and was standing there, watching us. I got the uneasy feeling he was especially watching me. It put a little chill on my joy, but I shook it off.

Clarissa, of course, does not walk her own horse, but instead flips the reins to Henry for him to do it. She strides off alone back to the school, head high, whipping her riding crop at bushes and leafy branches and anything else she passes.

So the gang of us plunges back into the school. We run up the stairs and burst into the dormitory to wash up a bit and we're startled to find Clarissa standing in front of Sylvie, pointing her finger in the girl's face and yelling at the trembling chambermaid.

"I *told* you to have that dress brushed and ironed *before* I got back!" Clarissa's riding habit is thrown across her bed and she is pointing an enraged finger at her dress hanging on a hook on the wall.

"I'm sorry, Miss, I—"

Clarissa's hand lashes out and catches the girl across the face. The sharp sound of the slap startles the room into silence. Sylvie puts her hand to her face and stands there stunned. Then she begins to silently cry.

I charges across the room and shouts, "Belay that, Clarissa! She ain't here for the likes of you to slap around!"

Clarissa whirls around to face me. "You shut your dirty mouth, you low-down piece of trash!" she snarls.

That's it. A red curtain of fury comes over my mind and I launches myself at her, fists all balled up and ready to bash her, dammit, bash her so bad, and she comes at me with hands hooked into claws.

We meet in midair, both of us squealing with rage. I catch her above the eye with my knuckle, which knocks her head back some, but she gets one hand in my hair and brings the fingernails of the other down my face. I cry out and try to get her hand out of my hair, but I can't, I can't, her fingers are locked in there and she holds my head against her front so I can't see to get at her, and I can't, I can't, I can't lift my head and I know she's gettin' ready to claw me again so I pulls back me fist and puts it in her belly and I hear her grunt and so I do it again and she goes *oof!* and I go to do it again but we fall backward over the bed and then down to the floor and we roll over and over, legs entwined, and I reach up and catch her hair in my fist and pull *hard* and strain against the hand in my hair and get my head up to where we're nose to nose and eye to furious eye, breathing hard in each other's face. Then I sense her other hand comin' at my face again, but I catch her wrist in time and we lie there locked in what seems to be a draw with me on top, but then Clarissa suddenly bares her teeth and lunges her head toward me and I jerk back just in time to hear her teeth click together a scant half inch before my nose. Failing to bite me there, she turns her head aside and sinks her teeth in my wrist and I groan with the pain of it, but still I don't let go, I'd rather be bit on the arm than clawed on the face, and I'm bringin' up my knee...

...And then I ain't. A very strong hand clamps around my neck and pulls me off Clarissa. She unclamps her jaws from my arm and looks over my shoulder and I know, from the sudden silence in the room, that she is looking up at Mistress.

It is the vile Dobbs who has his hand around my neck and who untwines both our fingers from each other's hair, a smug smile on his vile face.

"Stand up. Both of you," says Mistress.

We struggle to our feet, and we stand there with our chests heaving, steam comin' off the both of us. My eyes never leave hers and hers never leave mine. I sense the other girls standing about, stunned, but I don't see them. All I see is Clarissa, who has the blood from my face smeared on the front of her camisole, the blood from my arm on her lips. She may have a bruise over her eye and I'm sure her belly's gonna be sore, but she came out the better in this battle, that's for sure, for she laid her mark upon me and I did not mark her.

"To my office. Now," says Mistress.

Neither of us turn. Clarissa is working her mouth—had I hurt her there? No, I didn't, I quickly find, for she suddenly leans in toward me and spits full in my face. As I see a thin bit of pinkish spittle hang from my eyelash, *Bloody Jack* comes unbidden to my whirling mind. Aye, I thinks, but this time it's my own dear blood.

"Crawl back in your gutter where you belong!"

When she says this, I try to go at her again, but the vile Dobbs holds my neck fast in his filthy paw.

"Mr. Dobbs, you will bring them to my office. Now!"

The vile Dobbs reaches out and, with a huge grin on his nasty face, clasps a startled Clarissa about her own neck. Mistress turns and goes to leave, but before she does she turns to the other girls and says, "You have nothing better to do than stand about and gaze at the spectacle of two of your own debasing themselves?"

The girls flee like a flock of birds. Mistress follows them out and the vile Dobbs propels us after her.

My arm is throbbing and I look down to see two neat semicircles of teeth marks, oozing redly. "I know you are diseased, Clarissa," I say, "but I can only hope you are not rabid as well."

Clarissa goes to reply, but the vile Dobbs puts a squeeze on her neck and all that comes out is a strangled gurgle. We are taken into Mistress's office and released. I advance to the desk and put my toes on the line.

"You may wait outside, Mr. Dobbs," says Mistress from behind her desk. "I will call you if I need you. Oh, and make sure none of the other girls is hanging about the door."

A plainly disappointed Dobbs says, "Yes, Mistress," and leaves, closing the door behind him. *Poor vile Dobbs, were you looking forward to a jolly good show at our expense?*

Stop it. Stop being giddy. You are in a lot of trouble here, and you must keep your mind sharp. Steady down.

Clarissa does not put her toes on the line but instead starts right in with, "Mistress, how could you let that man put his hands on me in my state of undress, how could—"

"Miss Howe, you will put your toes on the line there, next to Miss Faber." Mistress says this with a calm, cold evenness of tone. She leans back almost languidly in her throne and surveys the both of us. *Don't be fooled by her calmness, Clarissa,* I thinks, *Mistress is mad.*

Clarissa hesitates, confused. I'm sure she's never been in here under these conditions before. "But—"

"Do you recall, Miss Howe, the rule about never talking back to me? *Hmmm?*" says Mistress. "And if you want me to call Mr. Dobbs back in here to *put* you on the line, well, that can certainly be arranged."

A seething Clarissa comes up next to me and puts her toes on the line.

"Now, then," says Mistress, "let's get to the bottom of this unseemly matter. Miss Howe, you will remain silent until I ask for you to speak. Miss Faber, would you care to explain your behavior?"

I stand at attention and give her the old Royal Navy response—there is only one answer in a situation like this when a superior officer asks you a question like this and that is: "No excuse, Mistress." What's it gonna matter, anyway? She's sure to believe Clarissa's side of it.

"Come, Miss Faber. I want more out of you than that." Mistress taps her stick on the edge of her desk.

"Miss Howe was mistreating a servant, Mistress," I say, my chest still heavin' and my breath still ragged.

"How so?"

"She slapped the girl Sylvie, who is the most shy and unforward of any of your staff, Mistress. Miss Howe hit her and made her cry in front of the ladies, and I didn't think it was right." There. I have said it.

"You could have reported the incident to me."

"I am sorry, Mistress. I should have done that."

Mistress eyes me carefully for what seems a long while. Then she turns to Clarissa and says, "Now, Miss Howe. What do you have to say for yourself?"

A torrent of words pours out of Clarissa's mouth. How she was merely disciplining the girl for not doing her duty, how shocked and distressed she was to be assaulted by me and treated most cruelly—at this Mistress glances over at the nail marks on my cheek and the teeth marks on my arm—how someone like me, so lowborn, a common a gutter girl that shouldn't even be in this school, how her father will *certainly* be told of this incident and—

Here Mistress cuts her off with a sharp slap of her rod on the desktop.

"I would give more credence to your story, Miss Howe, if I did not see you spit into Miss Faber's face with my very own eyes. If I did not see, with those same eyes, the considerable damage you have inflicted upon her. And you will listen to me, Miss Howe, and you will listen carefully," says Mistress, with the iron back in her voice. "If you think for one moment that your family's stature will have any influence in this matter, you are sadly mistaken. If your father withdraws you from this school, then so be it. Adieu, Miss Howe. I will have one less student, and that will be that." Mistress leans across the desk and looks into Clarissa's now perplexed eyes. "I run a superior school here, Miss Howe, and I am happy in what I do. But I would walk out of here tomorrow rather than let my judgment in how I run my school be dictated by anything other than my own convictions!"

Mistress stands to her full height and looks down her nose at us.

"For your disgraceful behavior you will both receive no dinner or supper today. You will instead each stand in a corner of the dining hall during the dining hour, facing the wall, during which time it is hoped that you will each reflect on what it means to be a lady." Again the rod comes down on the desktop. "The Position!"

I immediately flop over the desk and pull up my skirts. *Thank God,* I thinks, *she's not gonna put me out!*

She gives me four. Four *hard* ones. So hard I cry out on each, and my knees buckle on the fourth and I have to grab the edges of the desk to keep from sliding off the desk. But I don't. It's over and I stand up and wipe away at my tears.

Mistress folds her arms and again says to Clarissa, "Did you hear me, Miss Howe? Do you want me to call in Mr. Dobbs and have him stretch you across the desk? The Position, Miss Howe."

Clarissa stands there, mouth agape, not believing that this is going to happen to her. She looks over at me. *It's gonna happen, Clarissa, believe it.* I run my sleeve under my running nose and shrug. *Better get down and get it over with,* I thinks. She shudders and bends over the desk. She don't have to lift her skirts 'cause she ain't got any on.

Mistress swings. Clarissa gasps and bolts upright on the first one, she shrieks on the second, she goes into a high howl on the third, and on the fourth, Miss Clarissa Worthington Howe, of the Virginia Howes, falls to the floor, sobbing.

And even though Clarissa's meaner than a snake, I didn't like seein' her get it. Not really.

At dinner, before the others come in, I am placed in one corner and Clarissa is placed in another. I'm sure neither one of us would care to sit down, anyway, not just yet. I try to present a military attitude—head up, back straight, arms held straight to my sides. I don't know how Clarissa's handling this, 'cause I can't see her, being crammed in the corner as I am, but I'm sure her back's as straight as mine. Clarissa's a nasty piece of work, but she is game, I gotta give her that—

who'd of thought she had that much fight in her? She whupped the hell outta me, that's for sure, and me an old Cheapside scrapper.

Hello, wall. I sigh and suspect I'm gonna be real familiar with every spot and crack in this corner.

I hear the chimes being rung for dinner and I hear them all tromping in and settling down. Then I feel a hand lightly placed on my arm.

"Miss Trevelyne," I hear Mistress say from her place at the head table. "You will please sit down, unless you, also, wish to stand in a corner in disgrace."

Amy withdraws her hand. *Thanks anyway, Amy,* I thinks, *for the kindness.*

Then there is a hush. Then a stir. *What's going on?* I duck my head and risk a look and what I see brings tears welling up in my eyes. Amy has placed herself in an unoccupied corner and stands there, presenting her back to her classmates and to her teachers. Through my filmy eyes, I resume my study of the wall and think on friendship.

During supper that evening, which was only marked by the loud rumblings in my belly, Amy again assumed her post. No one stood up for Clarissa.

Later, as we readied for bed, I took Amy aside and said, "You did not have to do that," and she said, "Yes, I did."

I was silent for a while and then I took her hand and turned it palm upward. "Spit in your hand, Amy." She is mystified, but she does it, looking at me with questioning eyes. I take my own hand and spit in it and then I lay my hand over hers, joining the spits and say, "This is the beginning of the Dread Sisterhood of the Lawson Peabody. We will now swear to always look out, each for the other, for whatever dangers might lie before us, to never betray the other in any way, and only to help the other to find happiness and joy in this life."

I clasp her hand tightly and say, "So sworn, Sister?"

"So sworn, Sister."

I had thought this day was over, but it wasn't. As we knelt for prayers that night, I noticed that my pillow was lumped up strange. I put my hand under it and found a package, neatly tied up. After all were in their beds for the night, I nudged Amy and we crept into the hallway and opened the package. It was fresh bread and butter and thin cuts of choice meat and some cheese and two little jars of pudding. On top was a slip of paper on which the simple words "Thank you" were written.

The Dread Sisterhood of the Lawson Peabody sat down in the light of the moon and had a feast, and I, for one, knew that I would never again taste one quite as fine as this.

Chapter 6

The morning after the fight, when we are all at breakfast, the girl Rachel gives me a note and I open it and it's from Reverend Mather saying I must come over to the church for counseling and guidance after classes today.

Just what I need, I think. I look over at Clarissa to see if she got a note, too, but I don't see her reading one.

"I'm to get counseled and guided by the Preacher today," I tell Amy.

"I do not envy you, Sister," says Amy.

I knock on the door of the church and then push it open and enter. It is the main door and it opens on the back of the church, such that one is looking down the central aisle to the pulpit. The Preacher is standing at the pulpit, reading his Bible. I walk down the aisle toward him. I stop and wait, my hands at my sides.

"You will kneel down right there," he says, pointing to a spot directly in front of him. There is no rug on the polished wood floor and it looks right hard, but I march over to the spot and kneel down.

"You will put your hands in a prayerful attitude and pray

silently for fifteen minutes, asking forgiveness for your disgraceful behavior yesterday."

I put up the hands and close the eyes and pray for deliverance from this place. The knees set in to aching right off, and I find that fifteen minutes can be a long, *long* time.

"Very well, you may stand," he says after an eternity of boredom and pain. I climb to my feet and put my hands behind my back and wait for what's next.

"What have you to say for yourself?"

"I got in a fight and I am sorry for it, Sir," I say.

"That's all? That you are merely *sorry* for having savagely attacked an innocent girl."

Innocent girl? Clarissa?

"Sir, there was two of us in that fight," I say. *Just look at my face, Preacher, for evidence of that! Innocent, indeed!*

"The girl you assaulted is an extremely well-bred young woman of the highest refinement. She would not have willingly entered into combat with you had you not physically engaged her."

"So you ain't gonna counsel and guide Clarissa Howe?" I asks, almost gagging with resentment.

"I gave her my condolences and conveyed my concern for what she had been through," he says. He sets his mouth in a prim line and folds his hands before him. "We prayed together for your salvation, so that you might see the error of your ways."

I roll back my eyes at the injustice of it all. *Please, God, let this be over soon.*

"You will maintain a respectful attitude, young woman!" he warns. "Remember where you are!"

"Yes, Sir," I say, dropping my hands to my sides and coming to attention, my eyes straight ahead.

"That is better," he says. He looks at me carefully for signs of disrespect, but I let none show. He looks at me for a long time and the silence hangs in the gloom of the church. Presently, he leaves the pulpit and comes down to where I'm standing in the aisle and walks slowly around me. I hold the military posture, but I don't like him behind me where I can't see him. What if he should hit me? What if . . .

I'm relieved to see him come back into my sight.

"While I would usually ascribe an incident as occurred yesterday to the hysterical vapors common to the female," he goes on in a musing way as if he'd been thinkin' on it a while, "in your case I believe it is different. I believe the sordidness of your early life has affected your judgment, your character, and perhaps even your very soul."

He goes back up to the pulpit. "We must pray together. Back on your knees."

Thump.

It went on for hours, it seemed—praying and reading from the Bible and more praying and sermons on evil and sin and me, always back to me, me and my early life, me on the ship, me and how I got here, me and the devil that's in me till I was dizzy and ready to keel over in a dead faint.

Finally, after one last long prayer delivered with his one hand on my head and the other stretched out toward Heaven, he freed me and I ran back to the safety of my school.

Chapter 7

Jacky Faber
General Delivery
U.S. Post Office
Boston, Massachusetts, USA
September, 1803

James Emerson Fletcher
Number 9 Brattle Lane
London, England

Dear Jaimy,

I'm going to be writing this letter in little bits and pieces 'cause I know I can't send it out till I see a British ship come in the harbor 'cause that's the only way I can think to get a letter to you 'cause Mistress won't mail my letters to you 'cause she don't think it's right somehow. If you're going to write letters to me, please send them to the address up there on top.

A lot of the schoolwork here is stupid and useless and I get switched a lot even though I've been nothing but good, but I do like some of the things we do. I specially like the painting class with old Mr. Peet—he's ever so sweet and nice to me. He says I have talent, but I don't know. He's showing me how to do miniature portraits on disks of ivory—it's marvelous fun slipping the colors around on the slick surface till it looks right and you can get really really fine with it because we've got brushes so tiny there's only like three hairs in them and if you make a mistake you can wipe it off. I'm doing one of you, dear boy, from my poor memory and I know I haven't done you justice but I'm still working on it. When I'm done I'll tuck it in close to my heart. Then I'll do one of me and send it to you and I hope you still want to look at it when you get it.

They have taught me how to ride, too. I never thought I'd like getting close to horses, from my time in London when it was all I could do to keep from being stomped to death by them, they being such huge beasts with mean tempers, but I find I do like the riding of them, after all. I've been assigned a sweet little mare named Gretchen and though we eyed each other most suspiciously when first we met, we are getting along right well. I often slip over to the stables and pet her and feed her bits of apple and such. Henry Hoffman saddles her up for me and gives me instruction and lets me take her out by myself into the fields behind the school, and it didn't take long at all for me to get good enough to join the rest of the girls in the circle.

Riding classes are held in this huge round arena that has a dirt and sawdust floor and we get up on our horses and go around in a circle with Herr Hoffman standing in the center snapping his whip and barking out commands. Like, for a while we'll trot, in which we have to post, which is having your bottom make a bump-paddywaddy-bump rhythm on the saddle, then Herr Hoffman shouts "Canter!" and we do that for a while and it's a kind of slow gallop, and then we gallop and that's fast and scary but exciting. When he says "Halt und veel!" we pull back on the reins and the horse stops and we wheel and go in the other direction. But then you probably already know all this because you're a nob and were born to this stuff and are laughing at me for my greenness, so go ahead and laugh.

We also go outside and get taught how to jump with the horses—there's a course laid out with low jumps and high ones. I'm just up to the lowest ones now, but that Clarissa is wondrous good at it, I got to admit. She says it comes from being brought up civilized in Virginia, not in some slum like me, and riding to the hounds and all that fox-chasing stuff. I don't know how civilized she really is though. I found out that one of the reasons that Amy won't sit with the other girls at dinner is that she won't sit at the same table as slaveholders and Clarissa's family owns slaves. I thought when I first got here that all these girls were just bits of fluff, but I'm finding that they are pretty political and this country ain't easy with itself in some things.

Clarissa sure looks good, though, in her scarlet riding habit with the black lapels and the white lace spilling out at her throat and black gloves on her hands. Her jacket has little gold epaulets on the shoulders and is tailored perfectly to her form. She has a high bonnet in the Scottish style that sits up on top of her upswept hair instead of coming down low and tying under the chin like every other bonnet I've seen around here. My own bonnet ties under my chin, and upon seeing Clarissa's, I like mine less. I know that don't say too much for me, but there it is. Clarissa looks splendid, and I hate her for it.

Clarissa ain't the only one all decked out for Equestrian— every other time, whether for class, meals, or church, the girls got to wear the black uniform dress—but here, I guess they're allowed to dress the way they want to, and given the freedom, they really do it up. Though Clarissa looks the best, there are many others who are close seconds in the way of finery, all in greens and purples and blues and every other color, and all in the finest of weaves and fabrics. I have to be content with putting on one of the dusters, which keeps my dress from getting dusty but also makes me look like a perfect washerwoman. But I am content and do not seek to rise too quickly above my station in life.

We had a bit of a tiff, this Clarissa and I, and I'm afraid she came out on top, but my wounds have healed. We stay away from each other because Mistress has warned us that we both will be expelled if we get into that sort of thing again, and neither one of us wants that. I know you're a little ashamed of me for this, Jaimy, but I'm being as good as I can be, and I hope you'll understand and forgive me.

Hark! There's the chimes for supper. More later.

Back again.

The only thing I don't understand about the riding is, why do they make us ride sidesaddle? It seems it'd be a lot more stable if we could just throw a leg over on either side, like you boys do. Amy says it's because it looks more ladylike and I says it ain't very ladylike to fall off and roll in the dirt because you can't grasp the horse between your knees and get a proper grip, like. She says it's also because they think we'll hurt our female equipment and not be fit for marriage or able to have babies and such. I think it's a bunch of nonsense—ain't I wrapped my legs around many a spar and never yet hurt myself? Amy says I should stop talking about my knees and legs and such as it ain't ladylike, neither.

Amy is my new mate. She's a bit stiff and a gloomy Puritan to the core, but I know she's got a good heart. Maybe I can loosen her up a bit and she can give me lady lessons and we'll be good for each other.

Anyway, I've been going over and taking Gretchen out during some times I can get free and we ride through the fields on Beacon Hill. Beyond the row of houses on Beacon Street it's almost all open field and meadow and it's wondrous pretty in this fall time. Henry comes along sometimes and he's good company. But don't worry, Jaimy, I'm being good.

Arithmetic is easy after all that navigation figuring we had to do on the ship, and the French teacher, Monsieur Bissell, is patient with me. I've found that not all the froggies are bad.

Penmanship and writing is good 'cause I get to write letters like this one in there and Miss Prosser, the teacher, gives us pointers like using those little apostrophe things and how to spell stuff right. That and how to write so it looks pretty.

And we have Geography with Mr. Yale who also does some history with us and it looks like good stuff for me to learn, like for when I have my little merchant ship (don't you laugh, Jaimy) and I'll need to find my way about. A funny thing—we were all up looking at a map of the world and Mr. Yale asks us to point out where we've been and Clarissa had been the most traveled because she comes from Virginia and had been to the Carolinas and was proud of that, but then I pointed out England and then the Rock of Gibraltar and the Arab lands on the north coast of Africa and then Palma and then the Caribbean Sea and Kingston and Charleston. Mr. Yale said, "A cruise, then?" and I said, "Sort of." Clarissa looked at me all narrow-eyed at that. You can tell that Clarissa and I don't get along all that well.

I've discovered that the classes are not quite so fixed as I'd thought when I first got here. Like, you might be in Embroidery but leave sometimes for an individual music lesson with Maestro Fracelli, or you might step out of Art for a private lesson in horsemanship. In other words, they don't always know where you are. Heh, heh. And you know me, Jaimy—If they ain't got Jacky Faber lashed down tight, she's apt to be up and off. And I was. I made a trial run yesterday, pretending to be going to the stables, but instead walked a bit down toward the docks. Not all the way, just enough to know I could do it, as do it I must when a ship comes in, to mail these letters. That's how I found the post office. I went out through the kitchen and came back the same way so the staff down there gets used to me going in and out.

Oops. Time to go to Music. More later.

The music classes are going well and I'm practicing as much as I can on the flute that Maestro Fracelli has lent me. You got to blow it from the side, and right off I couldn't get no sound out of it at all but now it's going better. I'm learning to read music—Amy is helping me with that as she knows how to play the harpsichord powerful good and reading music sort of goes with that. I know it's going to be handy 'cause I'll be able to write down tunes I make up and I'll be able to do other people's tunes without having to be there listening to them doing it.

So, actually, now that I've written it all out, I guess I don't hate it here at all. 'Cept for the fact that you're not here. I miss you more than you can know.

All my love always,
Jacky

Chapter 8

Dear Jaimy!

A ship! At long last a British warship! It's now the 27th of September and my month-long letter shall now go out to you! It is the Shannon and I must gather up all these papers and make a packet and I must make my plans to get out and go down to the docks!

Blot blot kiss kiss and Godspeed this letter to you!

All my love forever and ever and ever,
Jacky

I think about telling Amy about my plan to go to town today, but then I think better of it—better she should just think I am off with my dear Gretchen again, and that makes me think that maybe I should take Gretchen down 'cause it would be faster but, no, best not to attract notice. I bind up the packet of letters and the miniature of me, which I know ain't good enough but I'm sending it along, anyway, and I bind them up in oiled paper that I got from Art class to keep them safe and I get some sealing wax from Penmanship and drops a great gob of melted wax on the edge of the folder and then presses me thumb into it to hold it together and make it personal-like and then, after Penmanship, I tucks it in my bodice and shoves me whistle up one sleeve and me shiv up the other 'cause who knows what I might need it, and then I am off and out through the kitchen and out into the world. I've got a couple of hours and I am sure to be back before tea.

I cut by the side of the school so no one sees me go and cross Beacon Street and I plunge right into the Common amongst the black-faced sheep who go *baa* and I push their woolly fat rumps out of my way and I joyously run down the swale, by the cows and goats. I come out on Common Street and go up that to Tremont and then down Tremont till I hit Court Street. I don't know these streets except for their signs as I'm just heading pell-mell downhill to the docks where I see the *Shannon* sitting all pretty at the wharf.

Now I'm goin' on Court Street and I know it's that 'cause there's a courthouse there and behind it a jail and next to that, oh, Lord, there is a pillory with its head hole and hand holes. I'd seen poor blokes in these stocks in London, with their heads and hands stickin' out about to die from tiredness and shame and people throwin' stuff at 'em, and there's a stake there, too, prolly for the whippings. I hurry past all that.

Court Street turns into State Street and that leads down to Long Wharf, where the *Shannon* is moored alongside.

It is a glorious day with the sun shining and the wind whipping the *Shannon*'s flags about, and she looks in wonderful trim all polished and painted, and I trips it up the gangway and the Officer of the Watch, who is a very well-turned-out young man, comes up before me and says, "I'm sorry, Miss, but no females are allowed on board without—"

"Begging your pardon, Sir"—and here I does my best and lowest curtsy and brings the eyes up under the eyelashes—"I come not to visit but merely to ask that you carry this letter to my very dear friend Midshipman James Fletcher of 9 Brattle Lane in London," and I hand him the letter.

He bows and takes it and says, "I am acquainted with Brattle Lane and will consider it an honor to convey it to a fellow sailor who is lucky enough to be in the favor of one such as you."

I blush the blush and bat the eyelashes and say, *"Vous êtes très galant, mon capitaine,"* proudly using some of my new lady talk.

"Et tu es très belle, Mademoiselle," he says. I do not miss the familiar *tu* but I let it pass.

"Thank you, Sir," says I. "And the mail you carried with you here?"

"Already delivered to the post office, Miss. Sorry." Ah, well. It's too early for a letter from Jaimy. It's only been a month or so.

I'm looking about me at the ship with its lace and shiny brass and things so familiar to me. I look up at their foretop and my throat tightens and my eyes mist up. It is very close to the *Dolphin* in all things, and I thinks I'd better leave now before I make a fool of myself, something I find I'm very good at.

The young man notices my distress and says, "Depend upon it, Miss. Your Mr. Fletcher shall receive this letter."

"Thank you, Sir. Good-bye." And I turn and go back down the gangway and try to walk with my head up away from the ship. The old sights, the old sounds, the creaking, the...No, I will be strong.

When I am a safe distance from the ship I let myself slip over into a few tears and then I look out over the harbor. There is a wonderland of wharves down here. There are at least fifty wharves with ships at 'em just within my sight. If I was higher, I'm sure I should see at least twice as many. It is a seafaring town, no mistake about that, what with all the chandlers and shipfitters and victuallers and the taverns and the ropewalks, the huge long buildings built solely for the making and twisting of long lengths of rope.

I feel better now, knowing that my packet will get to Jaimy's house.

I don't want to leave the familiar sights and sounds of the port just yet and I figure I've got some time before High Tea and prolly wouldn't be missed, anyway, so I climbs up on a piling at the end of the pier and look about at the scene spread out before me, all flags and rope and pitch and tar and wooden ships and iron men, and I pull out my whistle and start to play.

I start out with "The Mountains of Morn," and then keepin' in the slow and sad mode, I does the "Londonderry Air," that sad, sad song of a father sending his son off to war to the sound of the calling pipes. *Oh, Danny boy...*

"Luffly, Miss. Just luffly," I hears a voice say. "But could it be that you'll play sumthin' a bit more merry for poor John Thomas and 'is mates what had had enough of sadness and woe and hard times?"

I pops open my eyes and sees a group of sailors standin'

in front of me. They look like they're just off the ship and heading for a bit of fun. A huge red-bearded brute seems to be the one what spoke, him grinnin' from ear to ear and flippin' a coin in an arc toward me.

The beggar in me reaches out and snatches the coin from the air without thinkin' and drops it down my front to free up my fingers and I hops off the piling and rips right into "New York Girls," a real rousin' tune that's sure to please this crowd.

It does. They whistle and stamp and some of 'em roar into the chorus of *"Oh, you New York girls, can't you dance the polka"* and John Thomas crosses his arms and starts in to dance, which causes his mates to cheer and shout, and so I starts into dancin', too, and that gets 'em cheerin' louder, and so I goes faster and faster and I had forgotten how much I love this singin' and dancin' and showin' off that I completely loses myself in it all, I love it so, and then John Thomas crows out with, "You can't match this step, girl!" and I taunts back, "Can, too!" and, though a part of me thinks that maybe I shouldn't be doin' this, I lifts up my skirts to show the steps and I does the step he did and then I tops it with one of my own and then...

And then I notice that they've all stopped dancin' and singin' and foolin' around and are slinkin' back and lookin' at somethin' over my shoulder. Then I feels a heavy hand on me shoulder and I hears a squeaky male voice that says, "Come with me."

I turns around and looks up into the sweaty face of a man with round, fat, pink jowls.

"Who are you?" I ask, all fearful and stupid and not likin' this turn of events at all.

His eyes are almost buried in the folds of his cheeks and they peer down at me with a feverish glint. He wears a black hat and a coat with a high collar that bites deep into the flesh of his neck. He carries a stout stick.

"I? Who am *I*, it asks? Well, I'll have it known that *I* am Constable John Wiggins, the High Sherwiff of Boston." He smugly chuckles. "And *you*, my girl, are a dirty little twollop what's under awest for Lewd and Lacsiwious Conduct!"

He's got me in the jail now next to the courthouse that I saw on my way down to mail my letter, back when I was happy and didn't know it, and he prodded and poked me with his stick the whole way here with me wailin' and beggin' for mercy but not gettin' any and once I tried to run away down an alley but he caught me and clamped his hand on me neck and I'm cryin', *"Let me go let me go let me go..."* And he says, *"Let you go? I'll let you go when your back is stwipped and stwiped!"* And I wails, *"Stripped and striped, oh no!"* and he keeps his hand on me neck the whole way back and again I see the stocks and the horrid whipping post, *oh, please...*

Now we're standin' in an open space in front of some cages and he goes over me top part and finds me shiv tucked up me sleeve and looks at it and gives a low whistle. "Well, you are a rum little tiger, ain't-cha? And with a sharp tooth, yet." And he grins and says, "We'll have to find out if you've got any more teeth on you, won't we now?"

"Oh no, Sir, please," I pleads.

He kneels down in front of me with a grunt and says for me to hold me damn tongue or he'll fetch me a whack alongside me head and so I shuts me mouth on the tears of shame that are rolling out of me eyes and down me cheeks as he sticks his hand under me dress and runs his hand up the inside of me legs and I gots to stand there and take it and take it till I thinks I'm gonna lose me mind and me chest is racked with sobs and I starts a high keening sound and my spinnin' mind thinks over and over *Dirty and shameful yes, shame on you Jacky Faber the finest of ladies, oh yes just the finest of the ladies, and oh Jaimy I'm so sorry, this is so dirty and shameful, I'm so sorry, I can't help it I can't help it I—*

"So. Up the skirts again, eh, you old dog?"

Dimly, I see through me shame and misery that a stout woman has come into the room.

The constable removes his hand from messin' with me lower parts and stands up to face the woman.

"Now, Wife, I was doing my duty checking the miscweant for contwaband," he says, all red in the face. "Just look at this wicked blade, Goody. We should stwip the female down, we should, as she might wewy well have another."

Missus Constable casts him a shrewd eye and says that we'll see about that. She pats me all around and sticks her hand in all me private places, then spins me around and does it again and says, "There's nothin' there, 'cept this toy." She holds up my pennywhistle for her husband to see and then flings it into the nearest cage, where it clatters across the stone floor. Then she puts her hand in the middle of me back and shoves me into the cage after me poor whistle.

"Get in there, you little hoor," she says. "And you can stop with yer caterwaulin', as your tears will buy you scant pity here." She takes a large key from a string around her waist and jams it in the lock to my cage and turns it home with a large clack. "This will be your new home, sweetie, at least till we take you out in the morning to Judge Thwackham's court. Then it'll be out to the whipping post with you, for sure!"

She gives me a big gap-toothed smile. "You sleep tight, now."

The constable and his wife have left the cell block and I am left alone to take stock of my surroundings and to contemplate my doom. Mistress is gonna kill me, of that there is no doubt. But will I be publicly whipped, too?

There is a narrow wooden bench along the back wall. Next to it is a slop jar. At the other end is a water bucket with a ladle in it. There is a tiny window up high and through it I can see nothing except that night has fallen. That is all. *The shame the shame, why couldn't I just have mailed the letter to Jaimy and gone back home, why can't I be good, why can't I ever be good, why can't...*

I go over and sit on the bench and I reach down and pick up the whistle and put my fingers over the familiar holes, and it gives me some comfort as I sit there and wait for whatever's gonna happen to me.

I notice that there is another cage that butts up to mine and has the same bench and same slop jar in it. Other than that, there's a pile of dirty rags in the corner.

I don't want to think about what they're going to do to me or what Mistress is going to do to me, so I lift my whistle and play, as I have done so many times before when I'm down and feelin' low, my "Ship's Boy's Lament."

I'm about halfway through it and I'm hittin' the high notes as long and as mournful as I feel and—

"That's lovely, Miss, but maybe some other time as my poor head is throbbin' somethin' awful and a high tune ain't quite the thing for it right now and poor Gully MacFarland is more in need of a drink from your bucket than for a tune from your pipe."

The pile of rags in the next cell has risen up and become a man. Sort of a man. What once was a man. A very dirty and tousled man. A man who reaches out a grimy paw through the bars toward me.

I shrink back against the wall.

"Now, now, Miss. It's just a drink from that bucket of water that you have there and I have not and that I am wantin' right now. Just a little drink of water to soothe the poor throat of Gulliver MacFarland, the Hero of Culloden Moor, who has fallen on hard times through no fault of his own, the good Lord only knows."

I look at the water bucket and its dipper and then I put my whistle back up my sleeve and go to it. The water don't look none too clean—there's a couple of dead spiders floating in the scum that sits on top of it. I pull up the dipper so that the spiders and the scum slide off the water left in it and I take the full dipper and walk across the cell. Being very careful not to have any part of me or my clothing within reach of his outstretched hand, I stretch out my arm and pass him the dipper.

He brings the ladle shakily to his lips, losing a lot of its contents on the way up. He sucks avidly at the water, some of which goes in his mouth and the rest of which runs down through the grizzled stubble on his chin, down his neck and into the filthy lace collar of his shirt. Then he stops suddenly and his ashen face turns a paler shade of white and his eyelids droop and he lets the dipper slip through his fingers and clatter to the floor. He staggers back to his bench and flops down and sticks his head in the chamber pot and throws up, long and loud with much cursing and horrible and disgusting retching sounds.

I'm looking him over, tryin' not to be sick myself. He's got on what was once a blue uniform coat and dirty brown knee breeches with loose buckles and torn stockings below, and, curiously, a tartan plaid sash across his chest.

At last he's done. He gets back to his feet and unsteadily comes back to the bars between our two cages and stands there weaving.

"Give me some more, girl."

I look down at the dipper. It is too close to his cage.

"Kick it over here and I will," I says.

He puts his leg through the bars and kicks the dipper, skittering it across the floor. I pick it up and fill it again, again without spiders, and hand it to him at arm's length. He drinks, and this time he keeps the water down. Satisfied, he flings the dipper back into my cell.

He leans his face against the cold iron bars and lets his arms dangle through. "So, what've they gotcha in for, my pretty little miss—"

I don't get to answer 'cause of loud shouting and laughter from outside the outer door through which the constable and his bride had disappeared after putting me in here, and the door bursts open and a gaggle of brightly dressed women are thrust into the room followed by Constable Wiggins with his club and his wife.

Goody Wiggins waddles over and unlocks my cell and starts shoving the women in. There has to be at least fifteen of them, and every one of them drunk and in high spirits, it seems. I retreat to my bench and sit down and try my best to look invisible.

The key once again locks the cell door and the women mill about and one of them, a large woman with a great expanse of chest and a huge mass of tightly curled bright red hair, spies the man in the next cell and bellows, "Well, if it ain't Rummy Gully MacFarland! Let's have a tune, Gully, damn your eyes! Wiggins busted up a fine party and we ain't done with our carousing yet!"

The other women shout out their agreement. Several link arms and dance about. The air is thick with the smells of perfume and ale, which have mixed with the smell of the man's sickness, and I don't think I've ever seen so much bright clothing in one room before and I'm getting dizzy with it all.

"Sorry, Hortense, my dear," says this Gully, "but that fat fiend over there has taken the Lady Lenore into his foul keeping and I am helpless to entertain you without her."

"Keep it up, Rummy, and I'll break your damned fiddle over your damned head and you'll never play the damned thing again," growls the constable as he and Goody take their leave. The man whose name is Gully don't say nothin' to that, so I guess he takes the threat with all its damnings for real.

"That one there can give you a tune, though," says Gully, pointing at me. The crowd turns as one to gaze upon me cowering on the bench, where I am trying my best to fade into the stonework of the wall.

The one named Hortense comes over and looks down upon me and grins widely, her hands perched on her ample hips. Her cheeks are rouged as red as her hair and she has a round black patch the size of a penny on one cheekbone. She is showing a *lot* of powdered chest.

"Hey, Mam'selle," she calls over her shoulder to someone in the rear of the bunch, "come see what we've got for you."

The crowd parts and a yellow apparition walks grandly through the hooting and whistling throng. She's tall and slender and is all in yellow, from yellow shoes to yellow stockings to a yellow dress trimmed in yellow lace, to a wide-brimmed yellow hat topped with a great yellow plume. She carries a folded-up yellow parasol and her hair is yellow, too, but I don't think it's natural-like. Her face is long and thin and her skin is smooth with the color of ivory and she wears an expression of wide-eyed wonderment as she brings her yellow eyes to gaze upon me.

"Oh, isn't it just the most *precious* little bit of a thing?" she breathes, and looks about as if for confirmation from the others. They all giggle and snort and nod and say that yes, I'm just about the most goddamn precious thing they've ever seen. The yellow woman's great dark yellow eyes soften and seem to mist up as they go all over me. She puts her long-fingered hands together and casts her eyes heavenward and says, "Thank you, Lord. Thank you." She says this like she really, really means it. I shrink back against the wall.

The woman in yellow comes and sits down beside me and her perfume, which smells like the tropical flowers I had sniffed in Jamaica, wraps around my head and I don't know what to do 'cept sit there like a trapped mouse. Her eyes hold mine and I can't look away, I can't speak, I can't...

"Precious. That is what I shall call you from now on, because you *are* the most precious little thing I have ever seen.

Oh, it is trembling, poor baby. Here, Precious, let me hold your hand to calm you." She reaches out and takes my hand from my lap and folds it in both of hers. Her hands are cool and soft, unlike mine, which are sweating like little piggies.

"I am Mam'selle Claudelle de Bour-bon of the New Orleans Bour-bons and *none* of that Baton Rouge Bour-bon trash, thank you, and I *am* your new best friend."

I thinks that's what she says. 'Cept she says "frey-und" for friend. Then she drops her eyes and turns her head and leans into me, and I feel her face touch the back of my neck and I hear her inhale long and deep...

"*Ahhhh*... The precious sweet smell of precious little schoolgirl neck just beneath her precious and lovely schoolgirl hair," she says, and breathes in again. "You *are* a little schoolgirl, aren't you, Precious? You are dressed as one and I, for one, find it most becomin' on you."

She pauses, then sucks in some more of whatever my neck smells like and says, "But you have been a *bad* little schoolgirl, haven't you, Precious, to be put in a place like this. Tell me, Precious, just how *bad* have you been?"

And then I feel her lips behind my ear and...

And I leaps to me feet and whips me whistle out of my sleeve and tootles a couple of simple runs, and then I puts my arms to my sides and lifts my chin and says all in one rush of breath, "Ladies and Gentleman, you have the great good fortune to be present at an appearance of the fabulous Jacky Faber, famous in legend and song, who will be singing and playing many humorous and historical songs, some happy and some sad, and telling stories for your amusement and delight!"

I goes into an easy tune and dances a few steps and gets

some delighted "oh-ho's!" and claps for it, so I winds that up with a flourish and then says, "For my first number I'll be doin' the well-known favorite, 'The Maid of Amsterdam'! Sing along with the chorus now, ladies, sing it out loud and strong!"

And they do. They are a good audience. Soon they're all singin' and linkin' arms and dancin' and bellowin' out the chorus.

> "A-roving...
> A-roving...
> Since roving's been my ru-i-in,
> I'll go no more a-roving with you...fair...maid!"

All except for Mam'selle Claudelle, who sits twinkling on the bench with the air of a proud parent watching the performance of a beloved child. "Isn't my little Precious just the most talented thing?" she asks, comin' down heavy on *thang*.

And then I gives 'em a fast jig, "The Hare in the Corn," and pounds the floor with some different steps, and then I slows it down with the sad ballad, "The Sally Gardens," and cranks it back up again with "The Flowing Bowl," and then I feels the need of a break but I know I can't stop so I tells 'em the sad story of "The Cruel Sister," wherein I tells the story and then sings the verses of the song and in between plays the melody with the whistle, and they're all sitting around like any classroom of girls and some of them are nodding off, which I don't think is a comment on my storytelling but rather on the drink, and I think it would be a good thing if they *all* fell asleep but no, Mam'selle Claudelle is beamin' at me as brightly as ever and my throat is getting sore and my voice is beginning to rasp and squeak when the door swings open and the constable comes in and says, "All right, Rummy, out with you. I won't be having you stinking up my jail anymore this night, but I catch you drunk in the street again, it will be the stocks for you and you'd better take me at my word."

The prisoner don't say nothin', no, he just shuffles to the door of his cage and waits while Constable Wiggins opens the door, and then he steps out.

"And the Lady Lenore?" says Gulliver MacFarland.

The constable goes to a cabinet along the wall and opens it and pulls out a fiddle case and, without looking, flings it in the general direction of Gully.

Gully lunges forward and catches the case just before it hits the deck. On his knees, he opens the case and pulls out the violin that rests within. He runs his hands lovingly over the curves of the fiddle's body and neck and he croons as if to a lover, "Ah, Lenore, did the beast have his filthy jailhouse hands on you, sweetness? Did the touch of his greasy fingers forever stain—"

"Get out with you, you wowthless dwunkawd," says Constable Wiggins, and he pulls back his booted foot and aims a kick at Gully's retreating rump as it disappears through the outer door, the fiddle and her case clutched tightly to his breast.

There is silence for a moment and I don't think I'll be able to get up for any more performing, and Mam'selle Claudelle is beckoning to me with her finger and patting the bench next to her and...

And then from outside the tiny window, Gully Mac-Farland puts bow to the Lady Lenore and plays "Billy in the

Low Ground" better than I have ever heard it played before, and I lifts the whistle and I play along in my poor fashion, but somehow it works together and the crowd is pleased and claps and stamps and hollers "More! More!" but then the outer door clangs open again and in steps a smallish woman dressed in sombre clothing that is nevertheless cut in the highest style and in the finest of tailoring. She is followed by Constable Wiggins and a pleasant-looking young man who wears a buff jacket and a fawn vest and white trousers in the new style. He also wears a slight smile on his round and pink face.

"Missus Bodeen!" shrieks Miss Hortense, rushing forward and wringing her hands and whipping out a handkerchief from between her breasts and dabbing at her eyes. "We warn't doin' nothin', 'cept quietly entertainin' some generous gentlemens in the Plow and Anchor when Wiggins here comes burstin' in with his badge and club and hauls us off to the slammer! It warn't fair nor sportin' of him at all!"

The women, except for Mam'selle, who continues to simper and wink at me, have forgotten all about me and have rushed to the bars and are joining in with their protestations of their innocence.

Mrs. Bodeen does not reply but instead pulls out a packet and hands it to the young man, who, in turn, bows and presents it to Constable Wiggins, who takes it and slips it into his vest.

The constable advances to the cage and unlocks the door. The women pour out the door and Mam'selle comes up next to me and whispers, "Get in the middle of us, Precious, and maybe we can get you out," and I do it and try to look small and hope arises in my chest, but it is dashed when

Wiggins's hand reaches out into the gang of women and clamps around me neck and hauls me out and tosses me back in the cage.

Resentful and without hope, I go whining and weeping and despairing back to the bench and sit down upon it. Mam'selle whispers something in the Bodeen woman's ear and she glances at me and reaches in her purse and takes out several bills and holds them out toward Wiggins and nods toward me, but he looks shocked and aggrieved and shakes his head as if to say you know it ain't done that way, and Mrs. Bodeen shrugs and puts the money away and Mam'selle pouts at the constable and then turns to me and says, "See you later, Precious. It won't be so bad, you'll see. And if they do hurt you, you come to see me and I'll make it better, I promise. I do have the most soothing and restorative salve. 'Bye now, Precious." A flutter of fingers and eyelashes and Mam'selle Claudelle de Bour-bon and the rest of them are gone and I am alone once again.

I drop exhausted down on the bench, facing out so nothin' can sneak up on me, and I turn on my side and pull up my knees. I put my hands together and put them under my cheek. My hipbone begins to ache, grinding into the hard wood of the bench. I would pray for deliverance if it warn't all my fault, which it is. *Why can't I ever be good, why can't I ever think before I do something stupid? Why?*

I want to be back sleeping between the cannons on the ship. I want to be back in the hammock with Jaimy. I want to be back in my bed at school. I want to be anywhere but here, but here is where I am.

Chapter 9

⚓ I did not think I would sleep at all last night because of the worry and the hardness of the bench, but I do sleep in spite of all and I awake in the morning with a sickening lurch when I realize where I am and what is likely going to happen to me.

I stand up stiff and aching and I think how used to sleeping in a bed I have become. My side hurts from where my hipbone spent the night grinding itself into the bench. Goody Wiggins has come in and shoved a tray under my cage and sits down in a chair by the door without a word. The breakfast seems to be a cup of weak tea and a bowl of thin gruel. I do not eat it.

A while later, the young man I had seen last night with Mrs. Bodeen comes in and looks at me and says to Goody, "What is this, then?" He has the slight smile I had noticed, even in all my confusion the night before. I have the feeling the slight smile never leaves his face, at least not in public.

Goody looks up from her breakfast, which looks a good deal better than mine, and says, "Lewd and Lascivious Conduct. Judge Thwackham's got a horse thief to deal with, then she's up."

He nods and comes over to my cage and sticks his hands in the pockets of his waistcoat and leans back and says, "Would you like to tell me who you are and what has happened that brings you to this state?"

I look up all scared and confused and say, "Are they really gonna whip me?"

"I don't know, dear," he says. "I must know the circumstances before I can help you."

Help me? Someone wants to help me?

"I am Ezra Pickering. I am a lawyer and an officer of the court. I will speak for you in court if you so wish, Miss... ah..." He lifts a questioning eyebrow.

"Fuh...fuh...Faber," I manage to say. "Jacky Faber. I go to the girls' school on the hill and I want to go home." Then I start bawling. On the word *home*, that is, which is when I start in to bawling. *I wanna go home and ride my pony that's all I wanna do... that's all I waaaaaaa...*

He listens to me cry for a while and then he tells me to start at the beginning and I do, and I tell him everything from the day I was pitched out into the streets of London till yesterday when I was taken and put here for just playin' and dancin' down by the docks, which I didn't know was wrong, I didn't. *Oh why oh why won't they let me go home? Mistress is gonna kill me, ain't that punishment enough, ain't I been punished enough for what I did, which wasn't so bad as to get me back whipped, it wasn't even...*

I tell him about the ship and the Brotherhood and the battles with the pirates and the treasure and how I almost got hanged and how I ended up here in Boston and he seems so nice and kind that I pours out all that's in me about how strict Mistress is and how mean most of the other girls are to me, a poor sailor girl what's lately come from sea, and how I just want Mistress to give me my money and let me go so's I can go back and see Jaimy and...

There is a jangle of keys and I look up and see that Constable Wiggins has come in and is unlocking my cell. "They weady now. Let's go, you."

The constable leads the way, followed by me and then Goody Wiggins and then Mr. Pickering. They take me down a hallway and I see a big room opening up ahead, and I pipes up and says that I got to go to the privy and Goody says, "Goddammit, why didn't you use the pot in the cell?" but Mr. Pickering shushes them and I am guided to a small room off to the side and get it done. I just couldn't use the pot in the cell, I ain't shy but I just couldn't, I couldn't.

When I come out, the constable takes me by the arm into the court and puts me in the middle of the room on a little stand that has a polished wood railing around it. There is a little gate in the railing behind me and he closes it as he steps back. I grip the railing and look fearfully around.

It is indeed a grand room with fine high windows all around, windows that go up at least two stories and let in a soft yellow light that falls on all within, and all within are up in high podiums and all are lookin' down at me standin' there all wide-eyed and open-mouthed and totally without hope. There's a man off to the left with a quill poised above a ledger, prolly to record my doom, and there's more men off in a balcony up to the right, all in black robes and white wigs, who look at me curiously as I am brought in and put in the dock.

They all look fearsome and dreadfully stern, but the most forbidding of all is the person directly in front of me—he is seated at the highest and most massive podium of all, one that is worked in fine dark wood and marble columns and behind him is a white statue of a woman in a blindfold holding a scale. That this has to be the awful Judge Thwackham somehow gets through the fog of fear in my mind. My legs turn to jelly and I starts an all-over shakin', which can't be good for my case, as I must look like the very picture of sinful guilt. Judge Thwackham is a big man with a big nose and a red face with great hanging jowls. He wears a powdered white wig and an expression of extreme distaste and boredom and would look like a humorous drawing of a great old hound if this were a humorous situation, which, God knows, it ain't.

The judge glowers down at my poor self cowering down here below and picks up this wooden hammer he has and gives his podium top a great whack. "What on God's green Earth is this, then?" he bellows. "More aggravation for the Court, I'll warrant!"

One of the men with quills gets up and says in a very serious tone, "The Commonwealth of Massachusetts versus the Female Jacky Faber for the crime of Lewd and Lascivious Conduct, to wit: A wanton display of female parts in the commission of a song-and-dance performance on the streets of Boston, on the twenty-seventh of September, in the year of our Lord one thousand eight hundred and three."

The words hang in the air. *Wanton display! Female parts! What? I...*

"How do you plead?" says Judge Thwackham, leaning over his bench and putting the full force of both his office and his disapproval upon me.

I open my mouth but nothin' comes out and I hear Mr.

Pickering say, "She pleads not guilty, Your Honor." I turn my head and see that he is standing at a desk to my right, with some papers in front of him.

"Ah," says the judge, sitting back in his chair. "Our own Mr. Pickering, God's gift to the oppressed, the downtrodden, and the morally suspect." This gets the judge a round of titters from the other members of the Court and this appreciation of his wit seems to please him.

"As you wish, Your Honor," says Mr. Pickering, his slight smile never wavering. "I am representing Miss Faber in this matter."

"Very well, Mr. Pickering," says the judge with an air of great weariness. "What is the State's evidence against her?"

One of the coves in black robe and white wig stands up to my left and says, "Constable Wiggins will now give an account of the arrest of the defendant."

Wiggins strides out into the open space in front of Judge Thwackham's bench and places his hand grandly over his heart and says, "I did appwehend this selfsame female yesterday at the end of Long Wharf engaged in a wild and wanton dance for the eddy-fick-cation of a group of low sailors wherein she did expose a female part, a knee, it was, to public view."

"*Hmmm*," says the judge. "What do you say to that, Counsel?"

"She is new to this country, Your Honor," says Mr. Pickering, "and unacquainted with our customs. May I ask some questions of the redoubtable Constable Wiggins?"

"You may," sighs the judge. "But be quick. My dinner is calling."

Mr. Pickering turns to face the constable and asks, "My Good Sir," he says, bowing slightly, "what sort of music was the accused playing when you apprehended her?"

"Oh, you know," says Wiggins, "that Iwish stuff. It all sounds the same to me."

Mr. Pickering clasps his hands behind his back and circles slowly around the constable.

"How big was the crowd that she was entertaining?" he asks.

"Maybe six," says Wiggins, "but I..."

"And do you think they were being whipped into a high state of carnal excitement by the performance by this girl?" He points to me and the eyes of the Court swing over to me. I make my eyes big and wide and innocent and I clasp my hands demurely before me.

"Well, no, not by the music, but by the display of flesh."

"Ah. Well. Let's get to that, shall we? How did you know that it was indeed a female knee that you did spy, and not a bit of light-colored cloth, or a petticoat or, say, a slip?"

"No, Sir," says Wiggins, reddening. "It was indeed a knee, plainly wisible wight below the dwawers and wight above the stockings!" He nods his head decisively.

"Very well, Constable, we will accept that you glimpsed her knee. Now, would you say that what she was performing was a simple country dance, one that you would see being done by simple God-fearing country folk at a country fair and not the same kind of performance one would see in a bawdy house?"

"Objection, Your Honor. That calls for speculation on the part of the witness," says the white-wigged cove who introduced the constable.

"Sustained," says Judge Thwackham. "What's your point, Counselor?"

"I am merely trying to show that this simple country girl, far from her home in England and not knowing our ways, was merely engaging in a bit of good fun and had no desire to whip men into a fever of base desire with a display of wild and licentious dancing." Mr. Pickering turns around and grandly gestures toward me. "I mean, look at her, Your Honor. Does *that* look like a temptress?"

I take my cue and put on my poor little beggar girl look from back in my London days. I work up a few tears to course down my cheeks. I drop my head and look up through my lashes at the judge.

The judge puts his chin in his hand and rubs it, and it looks like he might be thinkin' kind thoughts of me. "*Hmm.* I'm sure the knee in question is probably quite scrawny considering the rest of her..."

Mr. Pickering's gonna win this! It's gonna be all right! I'm gonna—

The white-wigged man on my left, the one that clearly don't mean me no good, clears his throat and says, "Tell me, Constable, did the accused have anything on her person when she was arrested?"

Uh-oh.

Constable Wiggins, with an air of great importance, walks over to Goody and takes something from her and then comes back to stand before the judge.

"She had this up her sleeve, Your Honor!" He holds up me shiv, the blade all shiny 'cause I'd just sharpened it and the carved cock's head with its red coxcomb lookin' all rascally on the hilt.

There is a gasp from the Court. I look over at Mr. Pickering and he's slowly shakin' his head and lookin' like he's just had his feet kicked out from under him 'cause I forgot to tell him about my shiv. All is lost, now.

Judge Thwackham picks up his hammer with a look of pure thunder and damnation on his face and rumbles out, "A poor, simple, good-hearted country girl, eh?" The hammer starts to come down, "I find you—"

All bein' lost anyway, I grabs the railing in front of me and vaults down to the floor below and there's gasps from the Court and shouts of "Hear! Hear!" but I plows ahead and goes up to the judge's bench and falls to me knees and clasps me hands in front of me face and looks up at him high above me and pleads me own case.

"Please, Sir, please don't have me whipped as I didn't know I was doin' wrong 'cause I'm a stranger here, bein' a poor orphan girl what's lately come from sea and left here with no friends by her mates who don't want her on board with them no more 'cause they found out I was a girl and they put me in the school and Mistress Pimm's gonna kill me anyway, so why do it twice, Your Majesty, why not just let her do it and—"

"What? What's that you say?" shouts out the judge, a look of amazement on his face. Suddenly, everyone in the Court has their eyes riveted on me.

I don't know what he means, so I press on. "...and I had the knife 'cause all sailors have—"

"No, no!" he bellows. "What did you say about Mistress Pimm?"

"Oh," I say, and settle back on my haunches. "I've been

apprenticed to the Lawson Peabody School for Young Girls, where they're gonna make a lady out of me..."

There is quiet...then a snicker, then a chuckle, then full-blown laughter in the Court. Even Judge Thwackham is now smiling jowl to jowl. "Oh, my joy," he says, beaming down at me. "After all these years I finally have one of Pimm's girls in my court and on a charge of Lewd and Lascivious Conduct yet! Oh, there is surely a God in Heaven and he is a just and righteous God and oh how this is going to put the old harpy's nose in a twist!"

He chortles some more and then says, "My daughter-in-law, too. Just wait till she hears! She was one of Pimm's girls and she never lets us forget it with her nose in the air and her grand and haughty ways! Joy! Pure unadulterated joy!" The judge pounds his fist on the desktop, his eyes squeezed shut in glee. "And, Brown, isn't your wife...?"

"Yes, Your Honor," replies the delighted Brown, which is the cove with the wig that's tryin' to get me convicted. "And Mr. Smith's daughters are Pimm's girls, too. We are all looking forward to great fun with this." The man with the quill smiles and nods vigorously.

"Glorious, just glorious," says the judge. "Just wait till the Governor gets wind of this. His wife *and* his daughters, all three of 'em, the poor man. One still in attendance, too."

After a few more *har-hars* the judge calms himself and turns back to one particular Pimm girl.

"So how shall we make a proper example of you, then, *hmmm*..." I swear he giggles in anticipation. As I knows that all this jollity may not extend to me, I figures I better get back in my hands-clasped, eyes-supplicatin' condition and I does it, throwin' in a little lower lip quiverin' for good measure.

Judge Thwackham lifts his hammer and brings it down and intones, "I find you, Miss Faber, *guilty* of the misdemeanor crime of Lewd and Lascivious Conduct, and I sentence you to an even dozen strokes of the cane..."

I start keening and I lean forward and put my forehead on the floor. *Oh, to have my back bared and beaten bloody for public scorn!*

"...such sentence to be suspended on the condition that I never, *ever*, see your face in my courtroom again!"

Mr. Pickering comes over and takes my arm and brings me to my feet to face the judge.

"What ... what? What does he mean?" I ask, all shaking and scared and confused.

"You are not to be beaten, Miss. I'll explain later. Thank the judge," whispers Mr. Pickering in my ear.

"Thank you, my lord," I manage to say.

"Save your thanks for the Lord above," he says, "*if* you manage to survive Mistress Pimm's wrath, which I sincerely doubt. Constable!"

Constable Wiggins looks up expectantly.

"I want you to take Miss Faber back to the school personally and I want you to walk. It is not far and it will do you both a world of good."

"Beggin' Yer Honor's pardon," says the vile Wiggins, "but I must report that the female did try to escape *twice* during her arrest and confinement."

"Very well, Constable, we must be careful, then. Therefore, I want you to take her back to Mistress Pimm..." He pauses and smiles and looks about him with a glow on his face and then says, "...*in chains.*"

Wiggins leads me out of the court and takes me to a room and wraps a length of chain around my crossed wrists and threads a strong lock through the links and snaps it shut. The chain is about six feet long and he takes the other end and heads out, leading me like a dog on a leash. He takes his stick and he puts on his hat and we are out in the sunshine.

The air is cool and it makes me feel better. Mistress is gonna whip me up one side and down the other, but that's nothin' compared to a public beating, so I am thankful and will take what comes. I resolve to be good in the future.

I am grateful, too, to see that Mr. Pickering has joined the little parade in my honor up Court Street on our way to Beacon Hill. He comes up and walks alongside me, his slight smile still in place. There are some common and low types who jeer at me as we pass and his presence makes me feel safe and gives me comfort.

"I shall go with you to the school and explain to your headmistress what has happened and maybe it will go easier for you."

I thank him and say that I don't have any money right now but I will have someday and I will pay him for his services then 'cause he did a really good job and got me out of a beating.

He nods and chuckles and asks, "Was that what you sailors would call 'The Full Waif Broadside' that you pulled back there in Court? It was quite a performance."

"'Twarn't no performance," I sniffs. "I was scared half out of my wits."

"Well, whatever it was, it worked. Judge Thwackham doesn't usually let people off with a suspended sentence."

We trudge along in silence for a bit while I thinks things over.

"Mr. Pickering," I finally say, "would it be too much to ask if you would look into how much money my mates have stashed for me at this school? In case I should want to pull up and leave, that is. Then I could pay you what I owe you."

Mr. Pickering considers this for a while and then says, "I will do that, Miss Faber, but I must advise you, as a friend, that Mistress Pimm's school enjoys a very fine reputation and you would be well advised to stay there for your full term. I suspect that you do not know that you are going to school with the future wives of judges, senators, governors, and even, it is not too far-fetched to suppose, presidents. And as your attorney, I must point out that it might be very difficult to pry that money out of Mistress Pimm's fist, you being both a minor and a girl." He pauses to gaze smilingly upon the black-wooled sheep we are passing. "Still, I will inquire into it for you."

"Thank you, Sir," I say, and then my stomach gives a lurch as I see we are approaching the school. As we draw closer, I can make out faces pressed against all the windows. *Oh, Lord.*

"Perhaps," says Mr. Pickering to Constable Wiggins, as we begin to mount the stairs, "you could release her here and I could…"

But the constable will have none of it. He fixes Mr. Pickering with a beady eye and says, "I have my orders, Sir, and I will carry them out to the letter." And he drags me up the stairs such that my arms are pulled out before me so that all can see the chains around my wrists.

Wiggins reaches the door and gives it a good pound. I don't want to look up at the faces in the windows, so I look down at the stone doorstep.

Presently, the door opens and Mistress, herself, steps out. "What is this, then?" she asks. My knees turn to jelly.

Constable Wiggins puffs up and says, "This hewe female was awested and conwicted by the High Couwt of the State of Massachusetts, Judge Hiwam Thwackham, pwesiding, of the cwime of Lewd and Lacsiwious Conduct, to wit: singin' and dancin' and distuwbin' the peace of the stweets of Boston and in the bwazen showing of a female limb, beggin' youw pawdon, Ma'am, and I am hereby wemandin' hew into youw custody if youw name be Mistwess Pimm!"

Mistress just stands there lookin' at me.

"Constable, you have done your duty most admirably," I hear Mr. Pickering say, "now if you would just release Miss Faber, I believe your job here is done."

I feel Wiggins mess with the lock and then I feel the chains fall from my wrists. Before he leaves, the constable comes up by my ear and says under his breath, "I will see thee again, giwl, and it will be tied to the stake you will be and the sentence will be cawied out in full because I knows ye for a bad 'un in spite of all this schoolgiwl talk. You can twust me on that, as I am the one what swings the wod!"

He gathers up his chain and heads on down the hill. His words chill me, but not so much as the look on Mistress's face. She drills me with her eyes.

"Disgrace…to…my…school…" is all she says, but it is enough to shake me to my bones.

"Mistress Pimm, I'm afraid there's been a bit of a misunderstanding here," says Mr. Pickering, with a helpful tone in his voice, but I know it ain't gonna wash, and after a moment he realizes it, too, and sort of trails off helplessly. "It is my hope that she is not to be beaten too harshly as she really didn't know…"

Mistress snaps her head around and looks at Mr. Pickering as if he were a particularly vile fish head that had been thrown on the steps and left to molder and stink there. "Thank you, Sir. Good day to you."

Mr. Pickering need not have worried. Mistress does not beat me. No, she does something far, far worse.

I follow Mistress into her office and put my toes on the white line and then flop over on her desk and flip up my skirts and I starts in to wailin', "Mistress, it wasn't like that at all it was like—"

"Be still, please," she says with a coldness in her voice that I don't find reassuring at all, "and stand up."

I hesitate. She's not going to beat me? What…

"Now!" she hisses, and I jerk up straight and stand there quiverin' with my hands to my sides.

Mistress comes around to face me. "Take off the dress," she says, evenly. "Now."

I am confused and scared. "What? I don't underst—"

"By your actions you have brought disgrace upon my school and all the good and worthy people in it. I do not want the symbol of this school on your back for one more second. You defile it by being in it. Take it off. Now!"

I start to pull my dress up over my head and the tears come. I blubber, "I'm sorry Mistress I'm sorry I'll never do it again I'm sorry I'm sorry—"

"Sorry is not enough, Miss Faber. It does not erase the disgrace."

I hold my dress in my hands and stand clad only in my camisole and drawers and stockings and wait for the next blow.

"You will join the downstairs staff. You shall work for your room and board. The money that was placed with me for your tuition will be put up as a dowry for you until a suitable match can be made. Now follow me."

I feel like I have been slapped hard in the face. I don't move, I can't move, I can only hang my head and let my chin fall to my chest, tears of shame and disgrace falling from my eyes and onto the front of my slip.

Mistress sees this and says, "I am sorry, child, but we both know you don't belong here. It was a mistake. Now, follow me."

We leave her office and every door has faces looking out at me walking down the hall in my undergarments with my school dress clutched to my chest, Mistress leading the way. I think I see Amy's stricken face in one doorway and Clarissa's triumphant face in another. I don't know. I am beyond knowing anything now.

She leads me down the stairs to the kitchen, where Peg is standing at the stove before a steaming cauldron. She turns as Mistress says, "This is Jacky Faber. She will be joining your staff. Get her fitted out with the appropriate clothing immediately. Acquaint her with her duties."

With that, Mistress turns and leaves.

I stand there in front of Peg and I close my eyes and start sobbing and jerking there in my misery and she says, "Come, girl, it ain't so bad down here, you'll see. We've got a right jolly bunch of girls and it'll be all right, you'll see, you'll see."

She comes to me and puts her arm around my shaking shoulders and I bury my face in her chest and she says, "Hush, now, girl, hush. Hush now, hush."

Later, I'm given clothing and Peg takes me up the stairs and past the classrooms and past the dining hall, where I hear the chatter of the ladies having supper, and then up the stairs and down the hall and past the door to the dormitory and up another flight of stairs to the attic, which is to be my room. Peg tells me that the attic room is kept for when the school has serving girls that come from the outlying farms, but all the serving girls they got now live in town and don't sleep over so it's just me in here now. I have a bed, a chest of drawers, a table, and a chair. A candle in a holder. I see that my sea chest and my seabag have been brought up. Peg leaves me to settle in.

I hang up my new serving clothes and then I kneel on the floor next to my sea chest and fold up my school dress and I place it carefully inside so that the folds lie just right. I was so proud of that dress.

After a while, I can hear the ladies down below at their

prayers, just before lights-out. Two nights ago I was there with them and now I'm not.

I warn't never meant to be a lady, I know that now. I got streaks of wildness in me that trip me up every time, and just like streaks in clothes, there's some dirt that just won't wash out.

Chapter 10

James Emerson Fletcher
Number 9 Brattle Lane
London, England
September 28, 1803

Miss Jacky Faber
The Lawson Peabody School for Young Girls
Beacon Street, Boston, Massachusetts, United States

My Dearest Jacky,

I hope this letter finds you well and that you are benefiting from your studies at your new school. Although I miss you terribly, I must say that I find comfort in knowing that you are now safely in the refined company of other girls and not that of rough seamen. I have no doubt that you are receiving excellent guidance and are growing into the refined young lady I know you will become. I am sure you have made many lasting friends among the other young ladies. I find I like thinking of you being among your new friends and gushing merrily about girlish things.

We arrived in port yesterday and I was able to take a coach to London. We had a great joyous family reunion, with all members being found healthy and well. I regaled them with tales of our adventures and I could not stop talking about you, dearest girl. I have informed my parents of our intent to wed. I have told them all (almost all) about you, and Father is most approving. Mother withholds judgment, which is not surprising considering your recent way of life, but I know you will win her over instantly with your simple charm and grace.

Please excuse the brevity of this letter, as I want to get it off as quickly as I can because—great good luck—the Reliance is leaving today bound for Boston. I have heard she is a fast frigate so you should receive this in under a month's time. Unheard-of speed!

I know that it is too soon to be hoping to get a letter from you, dear Jacky, but still I hope. I know, too, that you'll excuse my poor, stiff prose—I am not good with a pen. Forgive me and know that I send this with all my love. I am

Your most obedient & devoted servant,
Jaimy

Chapter 11

Long before the dawn comes in my window, there is a gentle knock on my door and a voice whispering loudly, "Miss. I'm sorry, but it's time for you to get up."

I mumble, "All right," and pile out of bed, the events of the days before pouring in on my mind like a huge bad dream and I…"Wait. Please wait till I get dressed 'cause I don't know what to do and someone's got to show me. Please come in." I push down the urge to cry and I splash water on my face to hide any tears that might want to come and I start to put on my clothes.

The girl Annie opens the door and comes in and sees me fumbling with my new gear. "Here. Put the blouse on first," she says, picking it up and handing it to me. I slip it over my head. "Now the skirt. The weskit straps go over your shoulders and it tucks into here and goes over the bottom part of the blouse and laces up the front. Take a breath while I cinch it up. There." She pauses in her instructions and then says, "I'm sorry, Miss, that you…"

"It's not Miss anymore, Annie, it's Jacky, and don't be sorry. It's nobody's fault but mine." I run my brush through my hair. "Do we have time to braid my pigtail?"

"We have time. Peg knew you'd need some time getting used to things so she sent me up early." She takes my hair, separates it deftly into three parts, and then braids it up with brisk efficiency. I had been wearing my hair tied up loose with ringlets hanging by my face like the other girls, but now that I'm downstairs and no longer a lady-in-training, I figure I'd better put it back in working trim. This new outfit feels trim, too. The weskit clutching my lower ribs puts me in mind of Charlie's old blue vest I used to wear on the ship to hide the fact that I was a girl. 'Cept this vest only covers up my lower ribs, leavin' my chest free to roam under the soft white shirt. Not that there's that much of me to bounce about under there, but still it's more comfortable this way, rather than being mashed down like I had to keep it when I was a boy on the ship. This skirt only comes down to mid-calf, so it'll be easier to get around in.

"This ain't a bad rig," I says, pullin' the bottom of the weskit down over the waist of the skirt.

"It isn't exactly the highest style," says Annie with a bright smile, "but if Mistress wants to dress us up as milkmaids, well, it's her school."

"What do we do first?" I ask, as I sit back on the bed to pull on my stockings.

"First we bring up the water and fill the pitchers in the ladies' privy and set the table for their breakfast, and then we ring the bell to get them up and while they're getting dressed and ready we eat our breakfast, and then one of us plays the chimes to call them to their breakfast. Some of us help Peg cook the breakfast and some serve it, and some of us come up and clean the privy and make the beds. And that's just for starters." She pauses and comes around the bed. "And speaking of beds, we should make yours. If Mistress comes up and sees it unmade you'll catch it."

"Thanks for looking out for me, Annie. You've done that since the first day I got here and I won't forget it."

Annie and I creep down the stairs and we meet the others coming up the stairs with buckets of steaming water, and I see that Betsey has one in each hand so I reach over and take one of them and we all walk silently through the hall of sleeping girls to the privy. We dump the water out of the pitchers and fill them with warm water and gather up all the used towels and washrags and clean up the basins a bit and then heads back out. When we're all out of the dormitory, Rachel, the oldest of the serving girls, rings the bell hanging outside the door and I hear groans from the ladies within.

"That's my favorite thing to do in this place—wakin' up the little darlings," whispers Rachel. The first light of dawn is beginning to show in the windows and I can see Rachel's toothy white smile shining in the gloom.

We all go down the stairs into the kitchen where the veil of silence is suddenly lifted and everyone's talking and laughing and there's a great banging of pots and pans and hissing of steam and there's Peg standing at the stove working the spatula on a griddle of eggs and bacon and Peg turns 'round and points the spatula at me and says, "This here's Jacky and she'll be joinin' our merry band! Make her welcome!"

And they do. They all plop down at a long table and Annie pats the place next to her and I sit there, and Betsey goes to the stove and gets plates of eggs and bacon and toast and puts a plate before each of us, and the girl Rachel pours the tea and I figures that they take turns in this duty so that they'll all be served like ladies some of the time.

"That's Rachel, who's going to be married in the spring," says Annie, nodding toward Rachel who is now blushing 'cause some of the other girls have got off some rude comments at the mention of her upcoming marriage. She looks to be about eighteen. "And that's my sister, Betsey, there. And that's Abby and that's Sylvie."

All the girls nod and smile at the mention of their names. I, of course, already knew their names, but still I nod and smile at the mention of each. Annie's got hair that's close to mine in color but more curly, and her sister has the same, but while Annie's got a broad nose with a saddle of freckles on it and a generous mouth and wide-set brown eyes, Betsey's nose is sharp and her mouth is small and prim and her eyes are blue. They still look like sisters, though, and it's plain they have great affection for each other.

Abby's a round-faced girl with a large chest and a mop of red hair and the devil in her eye, and then there's Sylvie, small and dark and quiet, and very shy.

We dive into breakfast and it is very good. It is a strange thing, but no calamity ever seems to be big enough to put a dent in my appetite. As I'm tucking it away, I notice them all looking at me. With my teeth in a piece of toast I raise my eyebrows in question.

"Well, that's us," says Abby, "but what about *you*?"

"Oh," I say, and leave off packing it in for a bit. I dab my mouth with my napkin. "Well, I know you all saw that I got in a bit of trouble. I saw your faces pressed to the windows when I was brought back. You can't deny it."

They all look a bit sheepish at that, as they know it's true, but I says, "I don't blame you for it 'cause my face would've been pressed up there, too, if the situation was reversed. The truth of the matter is that I got arrested for singing and dancing in the street and the showing of my bare left knee in the performance of it, and I was taken to court and convicted, and Mistress didn't take it kindly at all and said that I'd brought disgrace to her school and I didn't belong upstairs and here I am." *And,* I say to myself, *if you shun me, too, then I shall run out of this room and grab my seabag and be gone.*

But they don't. They just laugh and giggle and say that there's got to be more than *that* to the story and let's have it, Jacky, but Peg up and says, "Let's finish up, girls, it's time to feed our ladies. There's plenty of time for tellin' lies later. Let's go. Annie, Betsey, and Rachel, to the serving. Let's get those trays loaded up. Jacky, Sylvie, and Abby, to the beds and privy. All back afterwards for the scrubbin' up."

That night, while I lay curled up in a ball under the covers on my bed, I thought long and hard about what I was going to do. I had thought about running away and maybe picking up some money playing in the taverns till I got enough to get back to England and Jaimy, but I saw yesterday just how far my pennywhistle took me, which was straight to jail, and besides I wouldn't have no place to stay and winter's coming on and Amy says winters are fierce around here. Or rather Miss Trevelyne says that. I must remember my place.

No, I must stay here for now, at least till spring, where I have warm lodging and some protection. I will go see Mr. Pickering as soon as I can to tell him that I want him to try *really* hard to get me my money back. Get it back before it is claimed by some man as my dowry. I shivered at that thought—I *will* run away if that happens.

I will look around for other employment or other opportunities that might present themselves. Who knows? Something might turn up before spring.

I will stay here and I will endure my shame. They will not see me cry. I will not whine and I will not complain. I know there is much to be learned downstairs and I will learn it and I know I will profit by it. I will continue with my former studies as best I can.

I will stay here and I will be the best chambermaid that I can be.

PART II

Chapter 12

Peg was right. It ain't so bad downstairs. Oh, the first couple of days was horrible with me in an agony of humiliation and all my former classmates staring at me, some with pity, some with delight. But I got through it.

The good Peg kept me close to her for a while so's I could get used to things as they were now. I mainly made beds and cleaned the privy and hauled the chamber pots out to the cesspool in back, and that was rough till I learned to hold my breath when I was opening the cesspool hatch and pouring in the pots. The first time I did it I almost fainted with the stench, but I learned how to do it. There's a science to everything.

But there had to come a time when I had to go up and face things upstairs, and one day when Abby was out sick Peg says, "Dinner served by Betsey, Sylvie, and Jacky. Show her how to do it."

But I already know: Serve from the right, take from the left.

We stride briskly into the dining hall, pushing our carts of steaming food. I can feel their eyes on me and I put on my mask of stony indifference, which I'm sure fools no one, and I pick up a tray of sliced meat and head directly for Amy's table, where, sure enough, she is sitting alone. I come up to her right side and present the platter.

She glowers up at me. She seems thinner and more pale than last I saw her and she says, "This is not fair."

"Please, Miss. Take some. You must eat."

"No," she says, and tosses her fork in her plate. "It is not fair."

I don't know what to say to this. I straighten up and take my tray to another table where Martha and Dolley are sitting with some others, and I serve Martha and she gives me a smile and a wink and I wait on Dolley, who gives my arm a pat and tells me everything's gonna work out fine someday, and it warms me so to see them being so kind that I start to get misty, but then it's on to Clarissa's table and I ain't misty no more. Betsey tries to get to Clarissa first 'cause all the girls know how things lie between Clarissa and me, but Clarissa waves her away.

"I prefer the offerings on *that* platter," says Clarissa, looking at me in her lazy way, her enjoyment at my disgrace plain upon her face, her Look saying it all.

I keep my eyes on my platter and bring it up on her right side. Clarissa takes up the tongs and picks up a piece of meat but lets it slip before it gets to her plate such that it falls on my foot. I look down to see the meat slide to the floor and the gravy from it slip down into my shoe.

"Oh," says Clarissa, "how clumsy of you. You really must hold the tray steady. I'm sure you'll clean that up immediately, won't you?"

"Yes, Miss," I say, and I'm wantin' to dump the whole

tray over her head but I'm sure I'd be taken back to court for assaulting a real lady with a tray of meat if I did, giving Wiggins the excuse he needs to lay his rod upon my back, so I don't. What I do is take my tray back to the cart and take a napkin and go back to the table and kneel down and clean up the mess. Then I go back to the cart and take a tray of vegetables and resume serving.

It's bad, but not so bad that I can't stand it.

Later, when we're back in the kitchen, I'm put in a chair and a cup of tea is put in my hand and my shoe is taken off and cleaned and a wet cloth is put to my stocking to clean off the gravy and Rachel says, "Don't you worry, Jacky, that one's gonna get it some day, and I hope I'm there to see it!"

"From the amount of curses you all have already laid on that one's head, well, one of them's bound to take, sooner or later," says Peg, which gets a laugh from all, even me.

Peg fusses over me a bit and then says, "Go over and feed some apples to that nag you love so much. Be back in time to help with supper."

Good, good Peg, I thinks. *Bless you for giving me this bit of time. You miss very little in this world that you rule so kindly.*

Over at the stables I put an apple in the palm of my hand and Gretchen takes it oh-so-gentle and I bury my face in her silken mane and it soothes and gentles my mind. I stay there like that for a long time.

After a while I hear Henry come into the stall and I lift my head to see that he has brought in a saddle, which he throws on Gretchen's back.

"Here, Miss, take her for a ride. Just walk about the fields a bit. It will make you feel better, I know it will." He cinches her up and hands me the reins.

I take them from him and place my hand on his and say, "Thank you, Henry. But now you must call me Jacky, for I am no longer a lady." I put my foot in the stirrup and climb aboard.

"All right, Jacky. I will call you that if you want, but you will always be a lady to me, no matter what."

"But why?" I say. "I sure ain't acted like one."

"It's for how you treated a stableboy when you were one of The Ladies, is why," he says, and he leads Gretchen and me out into the light.

———

J. Faber
General Delivery
U.S. Post Office
Boston, Massachusetts, USA
October 5, 1803

James Emerson Fletcher
Number 9 Brattle Lane
London, England

Dearest Jaimy:

With my own hand I now release you from the vow of marriage which you honored me with when we were both children on HMS Dolphin, *as I have been busted down to serving girl and will never be a fine lady as you wished me to be, a lady worthy to stand by your side.*

Without going too much into the sordid details of my fall, it is enough to say that my wanton ways have got me in deep trouble again, and although I am still a good girl and am still promised to you, I am in deep disgrace.

I shall remain promised to you until such time as I receive a letter from you saying that you don't want me anymore.

Please write to me, either way. It seems like it's been a long, long time, Jaimy.

All my love,
Jacky

Chapter 13

It is on the second Sunday after my fall from grace that the word comes down from above that I must go back to the church for more of the Preacher's counseling and guidance. *Damn, and I just got out of that place,* I thinks, what with him going on and on about sin and stuff as usual and looking at me when he says it, me now standing in the back, apart from the ladies.

We were preparing the noon meal when I was summoned, and I put aside the tray of steamed greens I was making up and wipe my hands, heave a heavy sigh, and head out. The other girls give me looks of sympathy as I go, but Betsey, strangely, looks at me with real alarm in her eyes, and says *don't...* but lets it drop there and sits down and worries her hands in her lap. *Don't what?* I wonders as I cross the space between the church and the school, going past the graveyard and the unmarked grave.

I open the door and go in and again he is standing tall and severe up at his podium, his white collar tabs glowing in the half darkness of the place. He points to the aisle in front of him and I go there and kneel and put my hands up in a prayerful attitude as I did on my last visit to this place.

"We have now seen where your wanton ways have gotten you, haven't we, girl?"

"Yes, Sir, we have."

"And have you prayed for forgiveness, girl?"

"Yes, Sir, I have." *Anything to get me out of here.*

"I think it is plain to you now that the Devil is indeed in you, girl, is he not?"

"I hope he is not, Sir." *Get ready, my poor knees, for yet more pain.* "And I do not believe he is, Sir." I look up at him when I say this and hold his gaze. I am growing heartily sick of all this.

"What? You dance wildly in the streets, showing your limbs before decent people and expect us to believe that?" He takes a deep breath and pulls himself up to his full height. The light inside the church is gloomy, with dust motes floating about in the weak light that comes through the high windows. "You end up in jail and there carouse with whores and other low types the whole night long and you say the fiend is not in you, has not taken possession of you entirely?"

"It was not that way at all, Sir," I say, wearily, and settle back onto my haunches. Sounds to me like the Preacher has been talking to somebody from the jail to know so much about my night there. Prolly that Wiggins. I drop my hands from the prayerful attitude and fold them in my lap. How much more can they do to me?

"Liar!" he shouts, coming around the lectern and pointing his finger at me. "Liar! Strumpet! Minion of Satan!" He is working himself up to a fine froth and I'm starting to get scared. It is now that I notice he has a long rod in his hand. "You will put your hands back up in a proper supplicating posture and you will beg on your bended knees the good Lord's forgiveness for your transgressions against his holy teachings!"

I do not do it. I say instead, "I do not recall the good Lord saying anything about singing and dancing, 'cept maybe that thing about makin' a joyful noise unto the Lord, which is what I was doin' when I was arrested. I was makin' joyful noises unto some of his own creatures, to bring them some cheer, I was, and there was no harm in it, Sir, not a bit."

He is astounded. His mouth works up and his eyes stare at me in disbelief and I swear a line of spittle comes out the side of it and runs down his chin. I get to my feet, as I have had enough of this.

"What! No shame? No contrition? You *are* possessed! You will prostrate yourself!" he shouts, letting loose a cloud of spit droplets in the air. "Prepare to have the Devil beaten out of you!"

He raises his rod and comes toward me. I back off a few steps and says, "No, Sir. I will not be beaten by you. I have been beaten by Mistress Pimm, but I suppose that goes with being in a school, but I will not be beaten by you, not in a church." I pause for breath, for my heart is poundin' and my chest is startin' to heave. "I go to a church for solace and consolation and to be in company with my friends in the presence of God and to think about my place in His universe, not to be beaten and shamed!"

I'm in a fine froth myself by now and I don't know where I'm gettin' the cheek to speak up like this but I push on, the words just pourin' out o' me.

"I spent almost two years in the Royal Navy, and I was not flogged once, Sir, not once!" I pull myself up and throw my head back. "I ain't apprenticed to you, and I ain't a member of your household. You think that 'cause I ain't a lady no more that you can beat on me if you want, but you're wrong, Sir, as I am a freeborn English woman and I *will not* be struck by you!"

I've been walking backwards this whole time and I'm about to turn to go out the door when he rushes up to me and grabs me by the arm and lifts the rod again, shouting something about a Jezebel right into my face, but I shouts back at him, "You let go of me, Preacher! If you hit me I'll put the police on you, I will! I know where they are and how things work down at the courthouse and…and…and I got me a lawyer, too! So let *go* of me!"

With that I jerk my arm from his grasp and bolt out the door, leavin' the amazed Preacher alone in the gloom of his church.

I rush back into the warmth and safety of the kitchen and put my back to the door and stand there pantin', tryin' to calm myself down. Through the fog of my fear and anger I hear Betsey say, *"See, Peg, see! It's happening again!"* and *"Shush, you don't know, you must be quiet, hush your mouth now!"* from Peg.

I think that's what was said, but when I ask Betsey about it later, she just shakes her head and won't say a word. And neither will Peg.

Chapter 14

It ain't long till Annie and Betsey Byrnes invite me to go home with them to spend the night and Mistress says all right 'cause she really don't care what her serving girls do, even though she makes sure I'm locked up tight every night. And Sylvie comes over, too, 'cause she lives just down the street from them, and we have a fine dinner with their parents and their younger sisters and brother and one older brother whose name is Timothy who seems right pleased that I came over. Their father is a shipwright so we got a lot of things in common and we get along well, and their mother is a fussy, jolly sort, who makes sure everyone's got enough to eat, and beams proudly over her merry brood.

After dinner we play ring games and tell riddles and I pull out my pennywhistle and give 'em a few tunes and songs and raps out some steps and then we gathers about the fireplace and pops popcorn, which is the most wondrous and tasty thing and which Betsey says the early settlers learned from the Indians back when the Indians was being nice before the British started paying them to...and then she reddens and clams up, having forgot for a moment, I guess, my history and place of birth, but I laughs it off and packs in more of the salty popcorn and sings a few more songs. Timothy sits next to me by the fire and we hold hands for a while till it's time for us to go to bed. He's a sweet boy and I give him a peck on the cheek as we leave for upstairs. Then we girls get dressed for bed and have a great giggling good time in their big old feather bed, all of us, Annie and Betsey and Sylvie and even the little ones, Eileen and Gabby and Antonia, who are so thrilled to be with their older sisters on this night of merriment that we fear they shall never sleep.

But sleep they do and then we sit up cross-legged and light one candle and talk of the boys they got their eyes on, with great snickerin' and teasing back and forth. Annie and even shy Sylvie are quite frank in reeling off their list of boys who they might look favorably on, but Betsey keeps her secrets, she just smiles and shakes her head and looks off. They tell me I should marry Timothy 'cause he's taken a shine to me and he's a good boy and has got a trade and they'd love to have me for a sister-in-law, but I have to tell 'em I am promised to another.

Course they drags every detail of my recent misadventure out of me and I warms to it, being a natural show-off and storyteller, and I prolly shouldn't but I really gets into the tellin' of it, and they squeals and covers their mouths with their hands in shock and delight when I tells 'em about Mrs. Bodeen's girls and specially about Mam'selle Claudelle *day* Bour-bon. Then I puffs up like the judge and tells that part, usin' a deep voice for the judge and a high squeaky one for the constable and a sweet one for Mr. Pickering, and they says how could you be so brave to take all that, and I say I warn't brave at all as I was on the edge of wettin' my pants at any moment during the whole thing and they can take *that* as the truth, and amen to that.

Then I puts Jaimy's ring in my ear with great ceremony so that I knows that I looks like a pure buccaneer to them, and then I tell them about the Brotherhood and the *Dolphin,* as I sure don't owe Mistress no promise about not tellin' about my past to these girls. I tell them about the Brotherhood oath and I tell 'em to each spit in both of their hands, and they say, *"Yuck,"* but they all do it and so do I and we all clasp hands mixin' the spits and I say all deep and magical-like, "This being the forming of the Dread Sisterhood of the Lawson Peabody, each what pledges to the others that they will in all ways watch out for each other and never to betray another member but always help them and keep them uppermost in their hearts, and so say you one, so say you all." And we all say, "Amen," and drag the word out long and long.

And then I tell 'em all about that time in Kingston and how Jaimy and me's got an understanding about gettin' married and I get *ohs* and *ahs* and wide eyes when I tells 'em almost all about Jaimy and our hammock and our other spots on the *Dolphin,* and Sylvie up and says, "So you've bundled, then, Jacky?"

More snorts and stifled giggles from them all.

I sit up and say, "You will tell me what 'bundling' means and then I will tell you if I have done it or not." I am watchful. I don't mind bein' teased, but…

Annie clears her throat and puts on a teacher tone. "Well. There's a lot of farms around here that are so far out on the frontier that the girls don't ever get to see any boys 'cept her own brothers for maybe *years* at a time." She takes a deep breath and goes on. "Sooooo…when there's something like a barn dance or something, and a boy and girl spark a bit…weeeeellll, if that happens and it's agreeable to the parents, then later the boy is invited out to spend the night at the girl's farm…aaaaaaaand, if all goes well at dinner, then…"

"Spit it out, Annie," I says, gettin' impatient with all this hemmin' and hawin'.

She finally gets it out in a rush. "Then the boy and girl go to bed together and sometimes there's a board down the center of the bed and sometimes there's not, but usually they keep their nightclothes on and spend the night in just talking and maybe a little kissing and stuff, but no more than that, and if they find in the morning that they still agree, then they set up a date to get married and then they do and they go off to start their own farm. *We* never do it, of course, 'cause we're city girls and there's plenty of boys around here."

"You Yankees never cease to amaze me," I say, and after I have thought on this a bit and thought back on my own case, I say, "Yes. I *have* bundled and I did find it *most* pleasant."

There's hoots and I get called "Jacky Hotbottom" and there's pillows thrown and shrieks all around until, finally, down below, the father of the house takes up a poker or some such thing and gives the floor beneath us a few sharp raps and issues a muffled threat to beat us all to sleep if we don't quiet down and let a poor workingman get his rest and why was he cursed with daughters, and we do it, we blow out the candle and quiet down. We settle into the big bed with the big fat feather-tick blanket over all of us. Feeling all their bodies, both big and little, snugged in around me, their breathing growing slow and even, reminds me of the old kip 'neath the Blackfriars Bridge in London, with Polly and Judy and me and the rest, 'cept it's warm and clean here and our bellies are full, and there it warn't like that at all.

As I fall asleep with Jaimy's ring in my fist, I hope with all my heart that he and I still got an understanding. My letter is on its way to him, the one where I told him about my disgrace and told him I ain't never gonna be a lady, and he ain't gonna like that, no, he ain't gonna like that at all. Oh, I could've written lies about how good everything was going but I don't want to lie to him, not now, not ever. And if it comes out that he don't want me no more because of it all, well, I'll deal with that when I find out for sure.

Chapter 15

Tonight I resolve to check out the widow's walk, which is what the girls tell me the porch thing on top of the school is called. I had spotted the stair rig hanging up in the rafters overhead in the shadows at the other side of the long attic room the first time I was brought up here but hadn't worked out how to get it down. I had thought the ladder was fixed up there permanent to keep people from going up there, but tonight, when I bring the candle over for a closer look, I see that the whole thing is counterbalanced with weights and that a pull on the rope hanging from it brings the whole thing smoothly down to my waiting foot. I climb up toward the hatch above my head and when I reach it, I give it a shove. To my surprise, it opens and I see stars above me. I go up through and stand and look about.

Annie says porches on tops of houses like this are called "widow's walks" 'cause that's where women whose husbands are at sea pace about and worry and fret and look out across the ocean in hopes of seeing their husbands come home safe. The name, of course, hints at the fact that many of those husbands don't come back safe, or even come back at all.

I stand there and look out over the sea and hope I ain't a sort-of widow. I hope with all my heart that Jaimy is safe and has warm clothes and is in good health. I hope he's got a plate of good food in front of him and a glass of good wine in his hand. I hope all that, I do, and if you want to call that a prayer, so be it.

The town is all spread out beneath me, lights in bedroom windows twinkling and going out, one by one, and the sea glinting under the light of the full moon, which has just risen and sits low over the water. It is a lovely, warm night and a slight breeze blows my skirt about my knees as I stand there and hope my hopes and dream my dreams.

I look for faithful Polaris, which should be right—

A light in the church catches my eye. The window is right below the belfry, and in the light stands the Reverend Mather. He seems to be shouting and gesturing wildly with his arms.

I duck down so he don't see my silhouette against the bright moonlit sky and I watch him through the branches of the big tree that stands between the church and the school, touching the roofs of both.

Sometimes he's at the window and sometimes he steps back, but he keeps coming back and waving his arms and pointing, always pointing at something outside, and I can see that he's shouting and his face is contorted but I can't hear the words. Maybe he's practicing his sermon for Sunday? No, he can get real worked up in those when he's telling us what sinners we are and how we're going straight to hell, but he don't get this worked up, no he don't.

By the way he snaps his head around it looks like he's

talking to someone or arguing with 'em, but I get the creepy feeling that there ain't nobody in that room but him.

Now he's back at the window and he keeps pointing and pointing and jabbing his finger over and over again, and this time I try to follow his point and my eye goes over the churchyard and over the wall and it lands on the unmarked grave that Amy and I had seen that day by the churchyard, now a little mound of moon shadow in the gloom.

Chapter 16

We've just finished serving dinner and we're piling back into the kitchen with the dirty dishes, chatterin' and banterin', and I takes my position at the steaming tub and starts in to washing the dishes when all of a sudden there's a silence and I look sideways and I see that Amy Trevelyne has come up next to me. She does not look as if she has been sleeping well. She pokes me in my side and says, "You said you were going to be my friend. You were my friend. And now you are not."

I lower my head and say in a low voice, "We can't, Miss. I'm downstairs, now. Surely you know that things have changed?"

"That should not matter. What about all your talk of sisterhood? What about the spitting and the joining of those hands? The oath? Was that all false? Was it all a game? All a lie?"

"It was in a different time and place, Miss. I ain't complaining," I say, not looking at her. "Why should you?"

I put the scouring pad to the pan and start in to scrubbing. "Please, Miss. You're making me and the others nervous."

She sucks in her breath and I hear the rustle of her skirts as she rushes out.

We get the dishes done and are about to do some laundry when Peg up and says, "Jacky. That lawyer friend of yours was by today and said for you to drop by to see him when you get a chance, his office bein' on Union Street, right next to the Oyster House."

Hmmm, I thinks. *What's up?*

"So," says Peg, "go down and get some fish for tomorrow's chowder. About six pounds. You do know how to buy fish, don't you?"

"Peg, I was born in a market," I says, thinkin' back to the old days in Cheapside, and I pantomimes takin' a skinned fish and openin' it up where its guts used to be and stickin' my nose in and takin' a long sniff.

"All right. We have accounts with Fulton's and with Anzivino's. They're both in the Haymarket. Be back in time to serve supper."

The whole afternoon! Hooray!

"Luckeeeee," says Abby, and the rest of them hoot at me for getting out of work as I grab a basket and head out the door. It's a warm day and I won't need my cloak and I got my maid cap on as a head cover so I won't have to run upstairs and get my bonnet. I've found out since I got arrested that one of the reasons Wiggins picked up on me that day was that I wasn't wearing a hat, and around these parts that means you're advertising yourself as a bad girl. They could've told me that *before* I got nailed, jailed, and derailed in becoming a lady, but what's done is done.

This time I decide to take Gretchen 'cause that'll save me a bunch of time and it's a beautiful day and I love riding her, so that's all the reason I need. I head to the stables.

I don't get to ride with the upstairs ladies anymore, of course, but Henry lets me ride on my own 'cause I help clean up in the stables when I can sneak over to pet Gretchie. He's been ever so helpful to me since I got demoted. He's even let me put a regular saddle on Gretchen and try it that way, and I was right, it is a lot easier—boys always get everything their own way and we girls always got to do it the hard way. I know Henry was scandalized when I rode astride, with my skirt riding up to my knees, but I know he didn't look away.

He still blushes and stammers around me, but he's easier now that we're on the same level, like. I know he's glad I got sent down 'cause now we can be friends, though he don't say so. And I know that he wants to be more than friends but he don't push it, so I don't have to tell him that I am promised to another.

I spy him combing down Jupiter, which is Clarissa's horse that she owns herself. Nobody else ever rides Jupiter.

"Henry, can I take Gretchen to the market, please, say yes, please," I say, bouncing up and down and giving him the big eyes.

"I suppose, if you're careful with her, Jacky," says Henry, and he pulls a saddle off a rack and goes into Gretchen's stall and throws it on her. I could do it, but I know he likes doing it for me so I let him. She whinnies when she sees me, and I take an apple from a bin and give it to her. I love the feel of her lips in my palm as she takes it and then chews it up.

Henry weaves his fingers together and presents his hands to me for a leg up and I put my foot in his hands, but before

I jump up, I lean forward and give him a kiss on his fore-head and say, "Thanks, Henry, you're a dear," and then I take the reins and Gretchie and I head out into the light.

A sisterly peck now and then, what the harm? He seems to enjoy it so.

We cross Beacon Street and ride down through the Common and there's a good firm path there so I get Gretchie up to the gallop and go whooping and hallooing along, scattering goats and sheep that go *nay*-ing and *baaa*-ing out of our way till we get to the streets, and then we slow to a trot on Tremont Street and then to a walk on Court Street 'cause I don't want to cause no fuss here, that's for certain, but I blends right in 'cause there's lots of people in the street, both walking and riding, and Gretchen is ever so gentle in the way she picks her way through that there's never an angry eye cast our way.

As we go by the courthouse I catch a glimpse of that hated whipping post and…

…And the stocks. I realize with a start that the stocks ain't empty and the person in 'em is none other than Mr. Gulliver MacFarland, the Hero of Culloden Moor and my former jailhouse mate.

There is a hitching post at the side of the courthouse by the stocks and I dismount and tie Gretchen's reins to the rail and pet her and whisper in her ear so she'll feel safe here where she ain't been before. She flashes me a trusting eye and I walk over to the pillory.

There is a gang of boys there who have gathered up some choice pieces of dog mess and they are laughing and jeering and tossing it at Gully's helpless head held captive there in the stocks. His fists clench in rage in their holes in the stout wooden face of the stocks and his face is dirty with the dog mess that's already hit, and he curses the urchins to Hell, which only makes them laugh more and throw more mess. I stoop down and pick up some rocks and advance to a place where both Gully and the boys can see me.

"Leave off!" I say in my best command voice.

"Won't!" says the boys, and they makes as if to throw some of that stuff at me.

I picks out the worst lookin' of the young brutes and wings off a rock at him. "There's one for Cheapside!" I yells and gets off another. The second rock catches him on his broad rump and he yelps and gets off some dirty words at me, which don't bother me none, I just throws some more.

"Hard to miss *that* fat ass!" I taunts and hurls two more at his chums and connects with one. "And here's one for Blackfriars Bridge and here's another for Charlie Rooster and how 'bout one for Hugh the Grand, sure," and I've got a real rain of rocks in the air and the urchins turn tail and run and I'm glad to see I ain't lost me touch. I dust off my hands and nod to Gulliver MacFarland.

He grins up at me through his filth and says, "Good job, Miss, and I thank you. No, no, wait!"

I had turned and was heading back to Gretchen, thinkin' my job here was done. I stop and look back.

"Please. Come back. We've got to talk, me and you." He gives me what I'm sure he thinks is a winning smile but which ain't even close. I did not think that anyone could look worse than Gully MacFarland the last time I saw him, but I was wrong as he's topped himself in the way of filth. "You and me. We could be a team. You with your whistle and me with the Lady Lenore."

I know I should go on, but I wait to hear what he has to say.

"I caught your little act there that night in the tank. You were pretty good—a bit rough here and there, but then you were plainly scared...I get out of here in a little bit. Can you wait?"

"I've got to buy some fish," says I, full of doubt. I look around all careful-like, making sure that Wiggins ain't around.

"Don't worry about the constable, girl," says Gully Mac-Farland, reading my mind. "I saw him take his fat self down to the docks to collect his bribes not ten minutes ago. Besides, they got you for the showin' of your legs, not for playin' of the tunes. They haven't outlawed music in Boston, at least not yet. Do you know 'MacPherson's Farewell'?"

I pull out my whistle and play a bit of the melody, then I lift my chin and sing the chorus.

> *"Sae Rantonly, sae Wantonly,*
> *Sae Dauntingly, played he.*
> *He played a tune and danced a-roon*
> *Below the gallows tree."*

"Good," says Gully. "You've a good voice, and you ain't afraid to use it—though you'd never fool a real Scotsman with that accent. Have you got a lot of tunes by heart?"

He wrinkles up his nose as if it's got an itch. I step back—I'll be damned if I'll scratch the awful thing for him.

"Yes," I say. "Mostly sailor songs. Some murder ballads and songs of love, too."

"That's good. 'Queer Bungo Rye'? 'Patrick Street'?"

"Aye. And if 'Patrick Street' is the same as 'Barracks Street,' then yes."

"Good. Sing 'Bungo Rye.'"

I don't see any harm in it so I do it.

"Well, Jack was a sailor, and he walked up to town,
And she was a damsel who skipped up and down.
Says the damsel to Jack, as she passed him by,
Would you care for to purchase some old bungo rye,
Ruddy rye, ruddy rye, fall the diddle die,
Ruddy rye, ruddy rye."

"Good. You put a nice bounce in it. We'll do it as a duet with you takin' the girl voice and…ah, here comes Goody with the key."

I turn and see Goody Wiggins approaching holding her ring of keys and with a disagreeable look on her face. As if an agreeable one ever sat there. I turn quickly away and go back to Gretchen and untie the reins and put my foot in the stirrup and mount up. *They ain't gettin' me back in there again,* I says to myself as I prepare to head off.

Gully is released, exchanges a few curses and obscenities with the matron, and then gallops over to me, his filthy coat flapping around his scrawny, loose-limbed frame.

"Please, girl. Just give it a try. A neat bit of fluff like you what can sing and dance, and me with the Lady Lenore, why, we'll make a fortune!" he says as he comes up next to me. Gretchen is skittish and whirls about as he tries to put his hand on my leg. "When do you have to be back?"

"For supper, sir," I reply. "But I have to—"

"Fine. That's lots of time. The Lady Lenore's down at the

168

Pig and Whistle and that's on your way down to Haymarket to buy fish. Let us play together and see what happens."

His eyes are feverish. "You want to make some money, don't you? I note that you're dressed less grand than last I saw thee. I *know* you want to make some money, 'cause I know you for a minstrel no matter what you say to that. I heard you play along with me from inside the cage when I took out the Lady outside the jail after they let me go and I know you and what makes you go. So, one hour we will play together and you will decide whether you want to get an act together or not. Agreed?"

As we turn onto State Street, him lopin' alongside, I see the Haymarket down below and the taverns gathered about the docks. Squinting, I can make out the sign of the Pig and Whistle, which I had seen on my first day here and which I had wondered about 'cause the pig was playin' a penny-whistle on the sign, and I say, "One hour. No more."

"Do you have any money so we can have a bite to eat?" says Gully after we had gone into the Pig and Whistle and sat down in the gloom. The place smells of years of spilt ale and old fires but still it is a pleasant place, and, as they say of cozy pubs, it fits well around your shoulders.

I put my finger in the pocket of my vest and pull out the coin that was tossed to me by the sailor John Thomas on that day that I was taken.

"It is a dime, I think," I says.

"It will do," says Gully MacFarland, and orders. A "bite to eat" turns out to be two tankards of ale for Gully and nothing for me. I don't mind. I am well fed.

On our way here we had stopped at a washhouse where

Gully was allowed to wash up in some dirty rinse water they was about to dump in the street. He even managed to sweet-talk a bit of soap out of the washerwoman, and so, with his hair washed and his face clean, he looks almost presentable. Almost. His clothes are still dirty and they sure don't smell very good. I edge my chair as far away from him as I can manage.

Gully sticks his nose in the first tankard and takes a long, slow drink and drains it and the expression on his face turns almost holy, looking like in those pictures of cherubs that me and the gang used to see in Saint Mark's Cathedral in London on those few days we could get in to receive alms and steal what we could. He puts down the now empty tankard and sighs with relief.

"So, takin' money off little girls are you now, Gully?" says the woman behind the bar. "What's this, then? Better not be one of Bodeen's."

"No, Maudie, this here is my new partner in the performance of music and dance and joy for the populace."

"No, Ma'am. I am in service up at the girls' school," I speaks up for myself.

"Ah, well, that is a good post. Don't lose it by hangin' about the likes of Rummy MacFarland, mind."

"I ain't doin' that yet, Missus. I'm just listenin' to what he has to say," I answer.

"The Lady Lenore," says Gully, and he puts out his hands.

Maudie reaches under the counter and pulls out the fiddle case and lays it on the bar. "He left it here last night when he was hauled out by the constable, half out of his mind with drink, he was," she says to me by way of further warning.

Gully gets up to get the fiddle, but she pulls it back out of his reach and, with her eyes narrowed and her voice level and low she growls, "Listen to me, Gully MacFarland. Last night was over the top. You and me go back a long ways, but now that's done, and here's a new rule for you, Gully, and you will obey it. That rule is: None of the hard stuff for you in the Pig and Whistle, ever again. No rum, no whiskey, no brandy, no wine. Beer and ale only. Do you mark me, Gully?"

"Aw, Maudie, now..." says Gully, shuffling his feet.

"I mean it, Gully. You break the rule and I'll have my Bob take his club to your head and put you out cold, thereby savin' you the time and expense of drinkin' yourself there. And you'll never set foot in here again." She slides the fiddle case over the bar, and Gully grunts and takes it back to where I'm sittin'.

Maudie goes back to swabbin' the bar, I suppose in hopes of some customers, but there don't seem to be none comin', just me and Gully. I look over the situation and it don't take too much sense to figure out that the Pig is too far from the docks to catch the sailors as they step off their ships with their terrible thirst that has to be slaked right off in the nearest tavern, which the Pig ain't, being perched up the hill a bit.

Gully opens the case and gently pulls out the Lady Lenore.

"Look at her," he breathes. "Ain't she lovely?"

I own that she is indeed lovely, all glowing red brown in the dim light.

"Look," says Gully, pointing at a scrawl on the inside. "It says here it was made by some I-tal-ian whose name starts with an *s*. See it? And it was made in a place called Cremona."

I look and indeed it seems to be signed by someone

whose name starts with an *s* and a *t,* but it's all so old and dim and almost rubbed out.

Gully takes out the bow and tightens up the knob on the end and says, "Let's do 'Bungo Rye.'"

"All right," I says, and pulls out my pennywhistle and puts it to my lips. "But that one I usually does with my concertina."

He looks at me with joy. "Good Lord! It sings! It dances! *And* it plays the concertina! Little Miss Moneymaker, by God!"

And then he brings down the bow on the Lady Lenore.

Later, I head down to Haymarket and look at the clock on Faneuil Hall and I see I'd better be gettin' a move on. I nip into the post office just long enough to have my hopes of a letter from Jaimy crushed yet again—"*Sorry, Miss, nothing*"—and then head Gretchen down Union Street to Mr. Pickering's office, which ain't hard to find 'cause there's a sign hangin' above which says:

EZRA PICKERING, ESQUIRE
ATTORNEY AT LAW

Under the words is painted a picture of a hand holding a scale.

I dismount and tie up Gretchen and enter, the door being open. I spy Mr. Pickering sitting at a desk. He rises upon seeing me come in and says, "Ah, Miss Faber. How good of you to come."

He pulls out a chair for me to sit down in across from him. His slight smile is in place.

I thank him and he says, "I see by your costume that you have had a reversal of fortune, my dear."

"Aye. I've been busted down to chambermaid."

"I am sorry."

"Don't be. I had it coming. Besides, the life of a serving girl has its charms."

"Well. That changes things somewhat," he says, and I wonder what *that* means and he shuffles some papers on his desk till he finds the one he was looking for. "You have nine hundred and fifty-seven dollars on account at the Lawson Peabody School. Previous to learning of your demotion, I would have advised you to stay at the school. Now, I don't know."

Nine hundred and fifty-seven dollars! Enough for me to buy a small cutter! I clap my hands in delight. "So get it for me and I'll be gone!"

Mr. Pickering has his usual half smile on his pink face and he folds his pink hands. "I will try to get it for you, Miss Faber, and for—"

"Call me 'Jacky,' please. I ain't a 'Miss' no more."

"I will try to get your money, Jacky," he says. "And for my efforts I will charge you fifteen percent of whatever I recover. If I recover nothing, then there will be no charge."

I do the math. My boat just got about fifteen feet shorter, I thinks.

"Done," I says.

"There are several problems, however," he says, leaning back in his chair. "The chief of which is that you are an underage female and have, as such, essentially no rights of property."

I ain't likin' the way this is goin'.

"Oh, and speaking of property, I believe this is yours." He reaches in a drawer and takes out my shiv and places it on the desk before me. I had not hoped to see it again and I am glad to see the cocky rooster. I thank him and slip the blade in my weskit and it feels good there against my ribs once again.

He continues, "You cannot hold property in your own name if you have a father, uncle, brother, male cousin, or even a son. The instant you marry, all your property becomes that of your husband. Do you understand so far?"

"I get it, and it ain't fair," I says through me teeth. "But I don't have any of those things and so I'm entitled to my money. Right?"

"I'm afraid not. You are underage and have been placed in the custody of the school and it is acting, in the eyes of the Court, in loco parentis, or, in place of your parents."

"Finally been adopted," I snorts.

Ezra chuckles and says, "But I think I could petition the Court to break that hold on you because of the fact that the people who put you there had no real legal right to do so. They were only acting out of charity."

"They didn't know what else to do with me," I say, somewhat resentful.

"My reading of it is that they were trying to do their best by you, but never mind. The problem is that if I succeed in breaking the hold the school has on your assets, the Court would then have to appoint a guardian for you, being female and underage. Do you have any marriage prospects?"

"I do. I am promised to one James Emerson Fletcher, Midshipman, His Majesty's Royal Navy," I say primly and proudly.

"You have my congratulations. However, an engagement

will not do, especially to someone half a world away," says Ezra, leaning over the desk and lookin' at me intently. "The problem is, someone has already stepped forward and petitioned the Court to be appointed guardian of a particular female child, one Jacky Faber, late of England and now resident in Boston."

His statement hangs in the air while my mind tries to understand it.

"What!" I blurts out. "Who in the hell…"

"The Very Reverend Richard Wilson Mather, pastor of the Beacon Hill Congregational Church, is the petitioner," says Mr. Pickering, all composed and calm. "I happened to be in court yesterday on another matter when he came in to start the guardianship proceedings."

I feel a coldness come over me. "He can't! I won't—"

"I am afraid he can, Jacky. He is an ordained minister and a member of the board of the school you attend. Or attended. You are a female orphan with no relatives of any kind. You have spent time on a warship in the company of rough men. The Court knows that you have exhibited some wild behavior in the recent past and you are very probably in need of the very correction and guidance he is in a unique position to give. The Court will look very favorably on such a petition."

I jump to me feet. "That's it then. I must run away. My seabag is always packed. I'll be gone in five—"

"Please sit down, Jacky. I assumed this would be your reaction," continues Ezra, "and I took the liberty of informing the Court that I was acting as your attorney and that I would be conferring with you on this matter. I asked the Court for a stay of their judgment and they granted it. *That* put a twist in the Preacher's nose, I'm pleased to report." Ezra broadens his usual bemused smile at the thought.

"You are a very good lawyer and I am glad I have you lookin' out for me," I says, sittin' back down and tryin' to calm myself some.

"Thank you, Jacky, but it was mere luck that I was there. Otherwise, you might be sitting in his vestry right now."

I shivers at that thought. Swallowed up by that horrid old church.

"It is possible, though, that it was not my skill as a lawyer that delayed the Court's granting Reverend Mather's request but rather that other thing."

I look back all confused. *What other thing?*

Ezra makes a little tent of his pink little fingers and looks off in a considerin' way. "There was an…incident last year, in the Reverend's household: A young girl, employed by him as a housemaid, hanged herself in her room in the vestry."

I sit up in horror as it hits me. *The unmarked grave!*

"The circumstances were unusual—please forgive me here for giving you the details, but you should know—one end of one of her stockings was tied around her bedpost and the other around her neck. She was slumped against the bed. Her feet were on the floor."

"How can you hang yourself with your feet on the floor?" I asks, all dumbfounded.

"It can be done, if one really wants to do it. Condemned prisoners have done it to cheat the hangman. But to continue, she was known as a cheerful sort of girl, only sixteen, and her suicide came as a shock to all who knew her." Ezra pauses. "One other thing. It was rumored that she was with child."

I draw in my breath sharply.

"Then it had to be murder," says I. "No girl would kill herself with a baby in her belly!"

"Maybe she killed herself because of it," says Mr. Pickering, gently. "Because of the shame."

I don't say nothin' to that. I just sits and smoulders.

Mr. Pickering sighs and leans back in his chair. "Anyway, there was an inquest, but nothing could be proved. The girl's parents did not claim her body because of the nature of her death, and Reverend Mather wasted no time in getting her in the ground. There was suspicion cast on a young man of the town, but no charges were brought."

I am quiet for a while.

"What was her name?" I ask of him, breaking the silence.

"Ah. Let me think...Jane, it was. Janey Porter."

Again, there is silence. Finally, Ezra gives a little cough and says, "As for our course of action, I will file an injunction to stop, or at least delay, the granting of guardianship. We can demand a hearing, and that will give us some time. At the same time I will file a petition on your behalf to regain your money—it won't work, but it will at least show the Court that there is money involved here and that might throw some doubt on the supposed selflessness of the Preacher's petition."

I nod in agreement. *Can I pick a lawyer or what?*

I rise and say, "Thank you, Mr. Pickering, for all you have done for me. Now I must go and buy some fish. Good day to you, Sir."

"Good day, Jacky, and please call me Ezra."

I hurry through the throng in Haymarket and get the fish at Anzivino's, himself crying, "Right off the boat, Signorina!" but I sniff it all the same, and he implores heaven with his hands in the air, "The trust! Where is the trust?" It is fresh and I take five of the redfish and put them in my basket and tie it to the back of Gretchen's saddle and I head out of the market with its sounds of vendors calling out their wares in many kinds of English and its heady smells of produce and meat, both fresh and frying, and of the sea and the clam flats nearby and the horse manure to which Gretchen adds her bit but nobody seems to mind.

I head out and back up toward Beacon Hill, and as I go I think about Gully MacFarland and the idea of us getting an act together. We certainly sounded good together in our practice session. I've never heard anyone play the fiddle better than he, that's for sure. He gets some amazing sounds out of the Lady Lenore—he makes her whisper, he makes her growl, he makes her shout, he makes her plead, by turns pathetic and heroic and grand—and he knows how to slip in and out of my whistle playing and singing, doing the straight melody sometimes and sometimes countermelodies and by and large making it easy for me to sound good.

It would really be a good act, but I don't know…I'm still smartin' from my last brush with the law. Gully said that won't matter, we'd be playin' inside and Wiggins won't touch me, but I don't know. Maudie says to me that I seem like a bright girl but if I trust a drunk like Gully then I ain't bright at all, and he told her to shut her gob, but I don't know…And when Gully asked if I can get out at night to do this and I say I prolly can, he says meet me here tomorrow night and we'll have a go, but I don't know...

I do know I told him that I'd think it over and let him know soon.

I get back just in time and take Gretchen to Henry and say, "Please, Henry, could you please walk her cool, I've got to get in to serve supper. I'm sorry I'm late."

"Anything for you, Jacky. You go on." He starts to walk Gretchen around the yard, cooling her down from our final gallop across the Common.

"Thanks, Henry, I'll make it up to you," I say, and take the basket of fish from the back of the saddle and dash down toward the kitchen entrance of the school.

"It's about time, you!" says Peg. She takes the fish and smells them and then spills them out on a cutting board and picks up a cleaver and begins chopping off the heads and tails and such, all of which go into a pot for the making of stock. "Take the chimes up and call them to supper and get ready to serve it. You take the head table tonight."

I start rapping the chime thing in front of the dormitory and I turn to go back down to get ready to serve when I hear, "Wait."

I look back through the door and I see Clarissa standing straight in the center of the room. There are some of the girls around her.

"Come here, girl."

I heave a mighty sigh and go into the dormitory room. I

try to never be close to that room when the ladies are around, but this time I had no choice.

"Yes, Miss," I say, and stand there and wait for it.

Clarissa tosses her net bag of soiled underwear at my feet. Some of the others do the same.

"Wash them and dry them and iron them and have them ready tomorrow."

I put the chimes aside and stoop to pick up the bags. I save Clarissa's for last and that one I pick up twixt my thumb and forefinger and with pinky extended hold it out at full arm's length and turn my face as if the bag and its contents stink. I wrinkle my nose, turn, and head for the door.

I hear the patter of her feet behind me as she charges, and I feel her hands hit my back as she stiff-arms me to the floor.

"You *insolent* piece of baggage, you! How dare you!"

I roll over and get to my knees and look up into Clarissa's furious face and I say, "Miss Howe, do whatever you're going to do and get it over with, please."

There, on my knees in front of Clarissa, I decide that I *will* join with Gully MacFarland and I *will* make enough money to buy passage for England and I *will* go see Jaimy.

Clarissa raises her hand and I get ready for it when I hear, "No. You shall not hit her. She is not one of your slaves."

I look up and Amy is standing between Clarissa and me, and Clarissa's face is a porcelain mask of absolute fury, but she does not challenge Amy. She turns and stalks off.

I wonder why.

Amy comes to me and lifts me to my feet.

"Come," she says, gathering up the scattered net bags, "I will help you carry them down."

In serving the supper this evening I study the Reverend more closely. He gives no sign of his plans for me except to glance up as I hold the platter next to him. He smiles and it is a ghastly sight to see, a smile on the face of what I am almost sure is a murderer. My stomach churns and threatens to come up on me, and it is with relief that I turn to Mistress and Dolley, the chosen one this evening. Dolley gives me a wink as she takes her portion. She is a good one and I like her.

There are two windows in my attic, one at either end. The one on the eastern end faces toward the church and is therefore no good. The window on the other end looks out to the west over mostly open field and marsh and is on a side of the building where almost no one ever goes, and tonight, I try this window again. I had tried it before but it wouldn't open, having been sealed shut by many coats of paint carelessly applied. Some of that vile Dobbs's work, no doubt. I take out my shiv and get to work.

It takes me about an hour to free it up. I slide it open and lean out and look down. It's about three stories down to some bushes and there's a fairly large tree a ways out that will give some cover to my actions. Tomorrow I shall get some rope.

Chapter 17

⚓ "Peg?" says I, turning the ball of bread dough over and adding flour to keep it from sticking to my fingers. I resumes kneading the spongy white lump. "Did you know the girl from the church? The one what died over there? Last year?"

Peg don't say nothin' for a long time. "A sad thing, that," she finally says, screwing her face up into a grimace and shaking her head. "We don't talk much about Janey Porter. It's all so sad...what she did to herself. Not right, it wasn't."

I don't say anything to that.

"Here, girl," says Peg. "You've got to get your shoulders into it. Make your knuckles into half fists and push 'em in hard. Arms straight. Like this."

I does as she says. The dough puts up a fight but finally gives it up and becomes a smooth white ball. I put it on the rising board and I asks, "What did she look like? That girl Janey."

Peg sighs and says, "She was pretty. Bright. Always with a laugh and a joke. Like you." Peg smiles sadly at the remembering. "She was over here a lot, not that you could blame her. Who'd want to spend all their time over there? With him and all his gloom and doom."

"Don't like him much, do you, Peg?"

"All I'll say on that is that it was a sad day around here when Reverend Miller died and *he* took over the pulpit." Peg puts her dough on the board next to mine and sifts more flour into the mixing bowl. "Now, old Miller could damn us all to hellfire and brimstone for our sins with the best of 'em, but somehow it was different. Under it all you got the feeling he loved his flock and was takin' care of 'em best he could. Don't get that feelin' with this Mather."

"Amen," says I, taking the sifter and putting in it three cups of flour. Ain't seen a weevil yet, not like on the ship. The flour falls down into the bowl in dusty waves. Like white curtains blowing in a breeze.

"You said Janey Porter was cheerful…" I trail off to see if Peg will pick it up or just tell me to be quiet and get off this sad subject.

"She was, till a while before…it happened. Then she started gettin' more quiet. Like she was worried about something. No more laughin' and jokin'. I tried to get her to talk about it, but she wouldn't." Peg starts in to kneading her next loaf, and I add water and yeast starter to mine and begin mixing it with a wooden spoon. "Still, everyone was shocked when it happened. Poor thing, to die like that and be put in the ground without even a headstone to mark her time on this earth."

"Warn't nothing wrong with Janey till he done her dirty," says a voice behind me.

"Hush, Betsey. You don't know and 'cause you don't know, you should keep your mouth shut," warns Peg.

I look back and see the usually quiet Betsey sitting at the long table, shelling peas into a big wooden bowl on the floor between her feet. I finish off my last dough ball and dust my hands and go help Betsey with the peas.

I let her be silent for a while and then I pop a few raw peas into my mouth and savor their earthy flavor and say, "So?"

She looks up and I see that her eyes are full of tears. "She was a special friend of mine, Janey was, and she was good and never hurt no one in this world."

"I know she was a good girl, Betsey," I say as gentle as I can. "Can you tell me more? I'm not just being curious. It's important."

She looks up at me sharply and I think she can tell I ain't lying.

"How came she here?" I ask.

"From a farm to the west. She was so happy and excited to be here when first she came to the city. We had such a fine time. Then...well, you heard." She snuffles back tears and savages a few helpless pea pods.

"I heard about a young man who was accused—"

"Ephraim had nothing to do with it! He's a good man, the best man I know!" she says.

Ah. So that's the way of it.

"And Ephraim is...," I probes, I hope kindly.

"Ephraim Fyffe is apprenticed to a furniture maker. On Milk Street," she says, her voice all chokey. "And they didn't even..." She chokes all the way up.

"And?"

"And her parents didn't even come up to get her, after all that was done to her. She was put in the ground without friends about her, without words, without a stone. And they didn't even ring the death knell for her."

I resolve to see this Mr. Fyffe at first opportunity.

During a break in the afternoon's work, I take a look at the west wall of the school from the outside and I see right off that I don't need the rope at all 'cause there's small rungs set into the masonry of the chimney wall and they go all the way to the roof. Of course. They are there so's the chimney sweep can get to the roof and do his work without having to carry all his black and sooty brushes through the main house to the widow's walk. The rungs start about twelve feet from the bottom. To discourage burglars, I'm thinkin', but it ain't gonna discourage me.

The vile Dobbs's toolshed is not fifty feet away and I discover there are several ladders alongside it that would serve. I could go out my window, climb down the rungs, and then drop the last twelve feet. To get back in I could use one of the ladders to get to the rungs. But then I'd have to leave the ladder in place and somebody might spot it in the morning before I had a chance to go out and stash it. No, it'll have to be done with some rope, after all. I'll get about a fifteen-foot length and when I climb down I'll tie it to the third rung from the bottom, drop down to the ground, and leave it hanging there till I get back later. The bushes will hide most of it. When I come back, I'll climb up the rope, untie it when I'm still on the bottom rung, and take it inside with me and no one will be the wiser.

And that is how the job will be done.

The prayers are said, the lamps are out. All is quiet and I'm puttin' my leg out the window with me shiv and me penny-whistle in my vest and my concertina looped 'round me neck in one of the net bags we use for laundry. In there, too, is my white sailor top from back on the ship, with its navy blue flap with white piping and my HMS *Dolphin* cap. I figure I can put those on with my black skirt and stockings showing down below, and, well, I'll look right nautical and it'll make a jolly stage costume.

Down I go. In a moment, I'm off on the town.

I pick my way through the streets this time, as the usually lovely Common looks right scary in the dark. After Common Street I cuts down School Street 'cause I don't want to get close to the jail again and then down Cornhull, sticking close to the wall, just an innocent serving-girl headin' dutifully home to her lovin' parents, that's all, then on to State Street and there's the Pig and Whistle, its doorway glowin' in the growin' dark. Down the street I can see that the other taverns, the ones closest to the docks, have got big, boisterous crowds. The fleet must be in.

I peek in the Pig, all timid now that I'm actually here, and I see that there's maybe ten men sitting at tables. It don't look like they're up for much of a party, I'm thinkin'. Gulliver MacFarland is just goin' up on the little stage in back and takin' his fiddle from the case. He don't look drunk, but then he don't look cold sober, either, so I 'spect he's only had enough coin to buy some ale. I guess he's abiding by Maudie's rule, whether he likes it or not. He looks a little bit cleaner, like maybe he cleaned up his clothes some.

I open my bag and pull out my sailor top and slip it on, then put my cap on at a rakish angle, and head for the stage. Gully looks up in mild surprise as I step up and turn around to face the crowd.

"Good evening, Gentlemen! God rest ye merry and welcome to the Pig and Whistle, the finest of the public houses in dear old Boston! We are the musical team of Faber and Mac-Farland, and we will be singing and playing for you tunes that are sure to bring joy to your heart, a spring to your step, and a tear to your eye! And we will start with 'Drowsy Maggie'!"

And I rips into it with feet and whistle and Gully comes right in with the fiddle, just like we practiced it, and soon the place is rockin' with cheers and shouts and the stamping of feet. And then we heads into the jocular "Bungo Rye," which I do with my concertina and Gully sings the part of Jack the Sailor and I sing the part of the Damsel. Gully sings:

"Well, Jack was a sailor, and he walked up to town
And she was a damsel, who skipped up and down"

Then I pipes up with:

"Says the damsel to Jack as she passed him by,
Would you care for to purchase some old bungo rye,"

And then we both come in for the chorus:

"Ruddy rye, ruddy rye, fall the diddle die,
Ruddy rye, ruddy rye."

Then Gully again with:

"Says Jack to himself, 'What can this be?'
But the finest of whisky from far Ger-man-ie?
Snuggled up in a basket and sold on the sly,
And the name that it goes by is old bungo rye!"

And then both of us on the chorus, and then I come in with:

"Jack gave her a pound, 'cause he thought nothing strange.
Hold the basket, young man, while I run for your change.
Jack peeked in the basket and a child he did spy,
I'll be damned and he cried, 'This is queer bungo rye!'"

And in the middle of that verse, I hand Gully a bundle in which is a baby doll that Gully had got somewheres and he opens it up and looks properly shocked at its contents and he holds it up to the audience and they roar out with laughter. There's more verses where poor Jack goes to get the child christened and when the preacher asks what the name of the boy will be he says, "Queer Bungo Rye," and the Preacher says that's a mighty queer name and Jack says it's a queer way he came and that'll be his name, by God.

There's hoots and hollers at the end of it and my blood is up for sure and Gully whispers, "'The Liverpool Hornpipe,'" and we swing into that and I notice some coves darting out and coming back in with more coves and pointing at us and so the place is filling up.

Then Gully steps out front and says, "Now the incomparable Miss Jacky will put aside her instruments and dance," and he hits "Smash the Windows," and I steps out and I shows 'em how it's done.

We do song after song and then we take a break and I go to Maudie and say for her to give me an apron and I help serve the crowd and I learn to back up from a tableful of men without turning around, after the first time I get my tail pinched, and then I go back on the stage and we do more songs and dances and I tell a story or two and we wind up when Maudie rings the closing bell.

There are tips thrown on the stage and left on the tables and pressed in my hand. Some try to put the tips down my front after I take off my sailor shirt, but I don't let 'em.

"Look at it all!" I exclaims, wrapping my hands greedily around the pile of coins on the table. The night is over and the patrons have left and the door is locked and Maudie is cleaning up.

"Aye," says Gully. "And now we'll split it and then we'll have a bit of a drink. The Fiddler's Dram, as it were. Seventy-five–twenty-five, right?"

"In a pig's eye," I says, all indignant. "It's fifty–fifty or I walk out of here and don't come back."

"But I'm the one with the experience and the one what protects you down here," says Gully.

"And I'm the one what packed the place," says I. "It's fifty–fifty or I walk." *Don't try to scam a Cheapside scammer, Gully,* I thinks.

"All right. All right," he says, and slides a dime in front of him and a nickel in front of me. "A big one for you, and a small one for me."

"I may be a serving-girl, but I ain't stupid, Gully. Here, *I'll* divide it." And I do it and he sighs and takes his portion and drops it in his pocket and goes to the bar and says, "Let's have a bumper, Maudie."

"Just a beer for you, Rummy, you know that," says Maudie, pouring out a drink and taking his coin. She draws me a pint of ale and slides it over to me, saying, "Here, Lass, thanks for helping me out during the rush. It's the best night

I've had in a long while." I stick my nose in it and I must admit it goes down easy, my throat being dry as dust from the singing. She also slides Gully's coin over to me, but I leave it on the bar.

Gully gulps down his drink and puts the Lady Lenore under his arm and heads for the door.

"Good night, Maudie," he says, bowing low. "And good night to you, my lovely Little Miss Moneymaker. I'll see you here tomorrow night. There's more ships due in and we'll make some serious money." He starts out the door but then stops and sticks his head back in. "Oh, and work on the bridge on 'The Blackberry Blossom.' You're a bit clumsy on that."

Maudie watches him go and says, "He won't be standin' upright inside of an hour, and all his money will be gone," she says and shakes her head. Then she looks sharp at me. "It's a shame, it is, but it would be even more of a shame if he drags a nice girl like you down with him. Jacky, never, *ever*, trust a drunk."

When I get back to the school, I slide behind the bushes and find that my rope is still in place and I get up it quickly, and then, when I'm on the rungs, I untie the bowline knot and sling the rope over my shoulder and climb up to my room.

I quietly close the window and hide the rope in a corner. I put my concertina and my sailor togs back in my seabag. Back when I got busted for bringing disgrace on my school, I had put all my things that I felt were absolutely necessary for me making my way in the world into my seabag, and all my things that I could get along without into my sea chest. In case I have to bolt and run.

I spread out a handkerchief on the bed and then put my bunch of coins on it and look at it. The start of my ticket back to England and Jaimy. I tie up the four corners of the kerchief and put it in my seabag.

It was a good night and my blood still pounds in my veins. They loved us! How they clapped and hooted! I sit on my bed and I put my arms between my knees and rock back and forth in joy. They really liked me, they really did!

Chapter 18

It's Thursday and I'm on the breakfast serving crew and I slide the bowl of oatmeal in front of Amy and with it I slide a folded note. The note says:

Thanks for keeping Miss Howe from beating me. If you really want to still be my friend then you will come down to the town with me after the noon meal. Meet me at the front door.

Jacky

I've set it up with Peg to get the afternoon off 'cause I got to see Ezra again and I got some other stuff in mind. The girls will take up my slack 'cause they know I'll make it up to them, and I will.

The morning goes quickly and I'm excited about getting out in the daytime. I was out last night again and Gully and I blew 'em out of the water for sure. The word had got around about us and we had twice the crowd and made twice the money. The place was full and Maudie had a real glow to her cheeks as she dealt out the tankards and scooped in the coins. I had got the feeling she was about to lose the

Pig before and now she's got hope and it brings joy to my heart.

I had gotten back late last night and added my coins to my stash and stuck it down deep in my seabag. Then I went back up on the widow's walk to think and calm down from the rowdiness of the night.

I glanced over at the Preacher's room, but his usual haunt was dark. Maybe he slept. Maybe he was drunk. Maybe he was out visiting with sick parishioners. *Whatever he is doing,* I thought, *he ain't after me right now.* I looked back over my shoulder to make sure of that. It made me wonder how Ezra's going on my case.

I had put my hands on the railing and looked out over the city and thought: This school is my ship, I now realize, and I've got to ride her, at least for now. There is nothing from Jaimy or the others. Nothing. I am alone and cast adrift. So. The front of the school is the bow and the side with my window is the starboard beam and the blind side close to the church is port and the stern points toward the stables and the whole thing is carrying me along through this part of my life and I have just about as much control of it as I did of the *Dolphin,* but it is what I have. This widow's walk is my foretop now.

One thing that was a bit sour last night was that Gully drank too much toward the end of the evening and turned surly. Maybe he had got into some spirits at another tavern, or maybe he had a bottle stashed. He kept going on about being the Hero of Culloden Moor and how the King's soldiers had gone about after the battle and killed the vanquished Scottish wounded where they lay and how the awfulness of that day haunts him every waking hour. The drink didn't affect his playing none, 'cause he didn't really start actin' bad till late in the evening when our act was nearly done, but still... It was like he wanted to fight with the whole world. Even with me, I found, as I had to duck the back of his hand as it came toward my face. I stayed out of his way after that by helping Maudie clean up. Bob finally had to put him out.

"Don't worry so, Miss," I says to Amy. I give her a nudge to get her out the door. "We're just a lady and her maid going downtown to do some business. What's the harm in that?"

"If Mistress catches us we will be whipped in front of the other girls and I will cry and be humiliated."

"Did she say you weren't allowed out?"

"No..."

"Well, there you go."

"But we do not have an escort," she says, and I look over and see that she is trying to be brave but she quavers. "I have never been out in the city without my parents."

Oh, you are *a baby, Miss Amy.*

"Don't worry, Miss Amy, nothing's going to happen to you today."

She takes a breath and tries to compose herself. "Do not call me 'Miss Amy,'" she says. "You sound like a slave when you do that. Call me Miss. Call me Amy. But do not call me Miss Amy."

"I will call you Amy as soon as we step off the school grounds, Miss," I say. "When I am in the school I am Jacky Faber, Chambermaid, but when I step off the grounds I am Freebooter Jacky Faber, Seaman, Musician, and Wild Rover."

"There," I say as I step onto Beacon Street. "*Amy.*"

We cross Beacon Street and head across the Common. We wade through a flock of black-faced sheep, pushing their fat butts out of the way as we go. At least she is easy with animals. She did say she was a farm girl.

We come out onto Common Street and head down through the city, first on Winter Street, then Marlborough, then on to Milk Street. She looks down every alley as if expecting trouble, but she is game and we press on, and as we do I tell her some of what happened when I was taken to jail and to court and how Ezra was so kind and good to me and how he tried to help me in my darkest hour when my heart was so low and I was liable to be beaten in public, and she asks how could I survive something like that and I says you just do, is all.

Then I tell her what Ezra told me about the death of Janey Porter and she makes the connection with the unmarked grave that we had seen that day in the churchyard and my suspicions about it and about the Preacher and how he has designs on me and my money and my future and all.

And then I tell her about the Preacher's petition and how Ezra is trying to prevent it from happenin' and she is astounded. Now Amy don't seem so worried about her own self. I can tell she's thinkin' deep about all I tell her.

"So the girl Janey Porter was solely in his care when she died?" she says.

"Yes. It must have been awful for her in that place. With him." I tell her about me spying on the Preacher from the widow's walk and how strange he acted and all.

"You've been busy," says Amy, looking at me sideways.

You don't know the half of it, Miss, I say to myself, thinking about Gully and the Pig and Mrs. Bodeen and the girls and all the other stuff I ain't told her. But what I say is, "I've got to be busy as he wants me over there to take poor Janey's place."

"That is true," says Amy. "We cannot let that happen."

"It won't happen, believe me, Amy, I'll run away first. My seabag is always packed and I can be gone in a minute," I says firmly. Then I tells her about what Betsey said.

"So we go to see Ephraim Fyffe?"

"Even so, Sister."

The furniture shop to which young Ephraim Fyffe is apprenticed is not hard to find, after a few discreet inquiries. The showroom fronts on Milk Street, so named because in addition to the many shops and factories, there are a large number of cows, and, consequently, a lot of milk—milk in buckets, milk in tubs, milk being made into butter and cheese, and probably milk that will soon appear on the table of the Lawson Peabody School for Young Girls, and some of that milk will disappear down my neck as well.

The showroom has many pieces of their craft displayed within, and once again I am astounded. When I heard furniture shop from Betsey yesterday I thought rough tables and chairs like in the Pig, but, no, these are the finest examples of the craft—willowy little sticks and boards that somehow come together to form strong chairs that seem to be made of the weakest of sticks but are not and tables with legs carved to look like the legs and feet of lions, tables polished to an impossible sheen. It reminds me of a showroom I saw last week when Peg sent me out with Rachel to get several big joints of meat down at Haymarket. Rachel took me on a route that I did not know and we went by a silversmith's shop and we looked within and I, expecting clumsy little tankards and plates, was amazed to see the silver worked in such intricate ways in grand bowls and servers and ladles and such, and Rachel says that it is the work of our own Mr. Revere, Hero of the Revolution, and I ask whether he really was a hero or not and Rachel says that yes he was 'cause he warned the people of Lexington and Concord of the coming of the British Regulars. But it ain't for all that war stuff that she thinks he's a hero. It was one time, years ago, when the smallpox was sweepin' through Boston and all his children come down with it and the people from the pesthouse came and told Mr. Revere he's got to give up the children to them and he came on that porch up there and says, *"You ain't takin' my babies!"* and they don't and the kids all got better, and that's why he's a hero to her.

I thought upon that and I gave Rachel a light punch on her shoulder and said that then he's a hero to me, too.

Around the back is the working area full of sawdust and shavings, and there Amy and I find Ephraim Fyffe. He is taking his midday meal at a table with benches set up outside. He is a solid-looking young man, with a good growth of reddish brown hair on the back of his strong forearms, that same curly hair being flecked with pieces of sawdust. He has a broad forehead and a thick head of hair that is tied in back with a black ribbon. *A black ribbon like in mourning, I'm thinkin'.*

He looks at us in a guarded but not unfriendly way.

I bob and say, "Your pardon, Mr. Fyffe, but I have this note from Betsey Byrnes." I hand it over.

Suspicion is written all over his face, but he picks up the scrap of paper and reads it. One thing that amazes me about this town is that almost everybody can read and write, enough at least to get along. All the downstairs girls can. On our way down here, when we were on School Street, we passed the Chambers School where the children were out on playtime. Amy told me that it's a state law that all children shall be taught to read and write. *All* children. *Thanks, London, for nothing.*

I know the note says, *"Ephraim, you can trust her as she is trying to help about poor Janey. Yrs. Betsey."*

He looks up and says, "Would you like something to eat?" He offers to share the bread and butter of his noon meal with us but we say no, to please eat.

I tell him our names and we sit down at the table across from him. He does not rip up the note or crumple it but instead folds it up carefully and slips it into a pocket of his vest. Then he says, "What do you want to know?"

"Tell us about Jane Porter and what happened to her."

His face darkens. "She was a good girl what never did nothin' wrong." He pauses and then says in a voice full of sadness, "She...died and they came and got me and made me look upon her poor body."

At this I look at Amy and she nods and says, "It is our custom. If a person is suspect in a murder, he is brought forward and forced to look upon the deceased in all their gore, the thought being that the horror and guilt will be too much for him to bear and he will confess to the crime."

"Oh," I say, with doubt in my voice, having known some accomplished liars in my time, including myself, who might've got through such a thing without confessin'.

"Sometimes," continues Amy, "it is done right then and sometimes..." She pauses and looks down at her hands clasped in her lap. "And sometimes later. *Much* later...weeks...sometimes months...later. With the contents of the grave exhumed."

I reflect on *that* and think it'd be hard for any person, guilty or not, not to react in some way to such a sight as the dug-up contents of a grave that is no longer green.

"Did Reverend Mather help you?" I ask.

"*Help* me? He put the police on me, that's how he helped me!" says Ephraim, glowering at his now forgotten bread.

"Why would he do that?" I ask. I know the answer, but I ask it anyway 'cause I want to hear him say it.

"'Cause me and Janey had an...understanding, and he knew it. We were going to marry in the spring when I finished my apprenticing here."

"What did you do when you looked upon her?" I hate to ask but I do.

He takes a breath and I see that his eyes have welled up. "All I did was stand there and cry. Her all twisted like that. They hadn't even straightened her out and made her proper, even. Just all twisted..."

"Do you think she killed herself?" Amy gives me a bit of her elbow for my cruelty.

His eyes may be tearing, but the look behind them is pure rage. He glowers at me. "She did not do that to herself, Miss. I know that."

"How do you know it?"

"Because she was a happy girl. She was happy we were going to be married. She was happy until..."

"Until the last month or so of her life. I have heard that. Is it true?"

"What is your interest in this?" he says, looking at me

intently. "Is it for fun? For excitement? Is it a girlish lark? What?"

"I don't like seeing injustice done, for one. For two, he is after me now."

"Ah," he says, and considers this. He looks down at his strong hands knotted in fists on the tabletop. My answer seems to satisfy him, and I don't blame him for asking the question, 'cause I would ask it, too.

"Yes," he says after some thought. "Yes, her unhappiness and loss of cheer was a sudden thing and I figured it out after a few days even though she wouldn't say nothing about it and I went through hell but I told her that it didn't matter 'cause it wasn't her fault—him being a big and powerful gentleman and her being a poor helpless girl caught in his house all alone with him but she still wouldn't say nothing, just shake her head and weep."

"What about her being with child?"

Amy hisses and warns me with *Jacky* and pokes me again, but I press on. "Could she have killed herself over that?"

Ephraim rises to his full height over me and says low and even, "She didn't kill herself. She didn't kill herself over what he did to her. She didn't kill herself over a baby. She didn't kill herself over *anything*. She *didn't* kill herself, Miss Faber..." He sits back down, with the veins in his forearms still standing out over the clenched muscles in his arms.

He takes another breath, never taking his eyes off mine, and then he goes on. "I told her I would raise the child as my own."

"That was very noble of you, Mr. Fyffe. I know there are not many men who would do that," I says, puffing up my own chest and holding his gaze.

"We were going to open our own shop. We had the place picked out and all. And on that day…" His voice trails off and he looks down at the ground. The words are coming hard for him, I see.

"…and on that day, she was going to tell him she was leaving and…it is to my…my everlasting shame that I did not go with her 'cause I felt I shouldn't ask Mr. Olmstead for the time off. And now she is dead and there is nothing. Nothing."

I let the silence hang in the air for a while and then I say, "On that day. When you were brought there to look upon her. Did the Preacher look upon her, too?"

He shakes his head as if to clear it. It is plain that he is a little startled by the question.

"I don't know. When I was brought in, he was over by the window, his hands together in prayer. Looking out."

"Looking out, not at her?"

"Looking out," he says. "Looking out to the field where they buried her the next day."

I stand up and Amy stands up with me. "Ephraim Fyffe. We, also, do not believe she killed herself. But the beliefs of schoolgirls, chambermaids, and apprentices will not hold much water against the power of the Reverend Richard Mather and his position as a gentleman and a man of God. We must go slowly. But we *will* go forward, I promise you that, Ephraim Fyffe. I promise you that Preacher Mather will look upon Janey Porter again, and if he is guilty we will bring him down. We will bring him down from the pulpit he does not deserve to be in, and we will bring him down and we will make him answer for his crime."

When we stood to part from him, I laid my hands on his arms and said, "If we need you, will you come?"

He looked at me steadily. "Depend upon it, Miss. You know where I work and Betsey knows where I live. It is on Olive Street, right near to your school. You have only to send word and I will be there."

And there we left it.

"That was certainly fraught with emotion," says Amy, as we head down to the docks for me to mail yet another letter before going to see Ezra.

"Yes. Well. I had to know," says I. Ephraim Fyffe was all I hoped he would be: strong, good, and mad as hell. "Look, Amy! There's the *Intrepid*! Isn't she glorious?"

Amy tucks her bonnet down a little lower on her face and says, "It looks like a dirty killing machine to me, no matter how prettied up with flags it is, and I do not like it."

I forgive her words 'cause she doesn't know my past. As I look down at the *Intrepid*'s gun ports and know well the hulking cannons that lie quiet behind, I have to agree with her, having seen guns like these at their murderous work. *Intrepid* is a killing machine, but I also know she is not dirty, and that within her, there will be some instances of uprightness and honor.

We get closer and Amy gets more frightened the closer we get.

"God. Isn't she lovely?" I sighs. She's an eighty-eight-gun First Rate Ship of the Line of Battle and has two levels of gun ports instead of just one like the *Dolphin* had. "Come on!" I says to Amy and skips up to the *Intrepid*'s side. "Well, come on!" I have to about drag her up the gangway.

"But surely we are not allowed…"

"'*Allowed*'?" I counters. "We're *allowed* to do anything in this world until someone says we *ain't* allowed and that someone can back it up."

We get to the top and step on the ship.

"Permission to come aboard, Sir!" I pipes, hand to brow in a snappy salute. The quarterdeck is all fancied up with shiny brass and bright white rope lace going from post to post to mark off the holy area. There is also a young midshipman on the quarterdeck as Officer of the Watch and he is handsome and bright, too, and he looks properly astounded at the sight o' me.

"No...No girls allowed on the *Intrepid*, I'm sorry, Miss," he finally manages to say, blushin' very prettily.

"I just want to send this letter by you to my very good friend Mr. James Fletcher of the *Dolphin*. He is a brother midshipman and I hope you will do it." I bob and flutter my eyelashes and give him the letter. There is a Bo'sun's Mate of the watch there, too, but he ain't blushin'—he's all smirks and leers as he looks at Amy and me and thinkin' he knows somethin' about us.

Well, he don't.

The midshipman gives the letter to the Messenger of the Watch, which used to be one of my jobs on the *Dolphin*, and I stand there and point out to Amy all the things of interest on the ship—the foretop, the mainmast, the shrouds, the spars, and all, and then the middie comes back with the news that the letter will indeed be sent along. I give him my very best curtsy and heartfelt thanks and I give the Bo'sun's Mate my very best damn-your-eyes look and we turn and leave.

I'm twisting around and looking at all the familiar sights of rope and line and tackle and, of course, the foretop, which looks exactly like the foretop on the *Dolphin*, and

Amy has to tug at my sleeve to get me down the gangway and onto the pier.

We're heading up State Street over to Ezra Pickering's office on Union Street, and I'm looking around at all the shops and signs and such when I notice something. Not something that's there—something that *isn't* there.

"Amy," I asks, "how come there ain't any orphan beggars around this town? In London we'd be knee-deep in 'em by now."

Amy keeps peering down every alleyway as if she expects a parcel of rogues to leap out at us at any second. Satisfied, for the moment, that none are poised for such an attack, she says, "Well, it is because anyone who is orphaned and has no other relations or means is generally given to a farm family in the outlying towns. Many times on the frontier, beyond the Alleghenies. The farmers put them to work in exchange for their keep."

"That's good for the orphans, then?"

"Sometimes. Sometimes they are taken in and treated as a member of the family. Adopted, even, or they marry into the family when they are old enough," says Amy, scooting across a dark alleyway. "Sometimes, though, they are just worked like indentured servants."

I reflect that if I was an up-and-coming young orphan instead of the grizzled and battle-hardened veteran orphan that I am, I'd still choose to take my chances here in the city rather than out there in the woods.

"And there is the New England Home for Little Wanderers, and for those boys big enough to lift a shovel, they are filling in the Mill Pond in the northern part of town.

They're scraping off part of Beacon Hill to do it and anyone who can lift a wheelbarrow can—"

"Hey! Ahoy! It's the little nightingale from the Pig!"

"By God, 'tis!"

Uh-oh.

There's three men standing in front of us, grinning and lifting their caps and it looks like they are seamen and they look a little familiar, like maybe they were in last night's crowd, and by the way they are weaving, it looks like they've had a few.

"Oi believes ye be right, Seth Hawkins," says the man in the middle. "The one what could sing and dance so pretty it fair broke me poor heart, it did!"

"Aye, you were right blubbering in yer beer, ye were, Amos, ye sorry sod!" says his mate, slapping him on the back.

"Don't care," says the one named Amos. "She put me in such mind of my own dear daughter back home who I may never see again that I could not hold back the tears…"

"She may have put ye in mind of your daughter, but that didn't stop you from tryin' to steal a kiss!" roars the other man.

I do remember this crew, I thinks, and I did have to be right nimble to stay out of their reach when I was helpin' Maudie durin' our break, but I did feel there was no harm in them for all their bawdy behavior. I sneak a look at Amy— she looks like her most terrible fears have come true. Ah, well.

"Gentlemen," I says, all bright and brave, "I am very pleased that you enjoyed our show, but now I must bid you all a good day, 'cause me and my sister must be gettin' back to school, and if we're late we're sure to get a whuppin'.'" I hear Amy let out a whimper behind me.

"Ah, Miss," says Seth Hawkins, "if ye could give us just one tune, for we right now are going back to the ship and we sail on the tide and may never see land nor ale nor pretty young things ever again." He takes off his cap and gives me the mournful eye.

"Very well," says I, and I draw out my pennywhistle. "Just one now, mind." And I tears into "The Queen of Argyle."

Seth and Amos link arms and whirl about in some demented dance while the other hoots and hollers and Amy tries to sink into the masonry of the nearest building.

We're rippin' along pretty good and I adds a few steps of my own and I'm headin' for the end of—

"*TWEEEEEEET!* You! Stop there!"

Oh, Lord.

"Cheese it, boys, it's the constable!" shouts my trio of admirers, and they fly off down the street. They could've saved themselves the trouble 'cause it's me that Wiggins is after, not them.

"Run, Amy! If he catches me I'll be tied to the stake and whipped for real! This way!"

I grab her arm and we pounds down the alley and out into some yards that I sort of recognize and I heads through some rose arbors and out another alley and onto Union Street. I spies Ezra's office and haul Amy through the door and into Ezra's office sayin', "Save us, Ezra," and out the back door and through the backyard and through some gardens and then on to Water and then up High, but the constable keeps after us, movin' real well for such a big bloke, I gotta say. I sees somethin' up ahead, maybe a way out of this.

"That stairway, Amy! Head for that!" I shouts, and we makes it to it and storms up the stairs and through the door. I slams it after us and throws the lock, me back to the door. Amy's breath is comin' in huge gaspin' rasps and her eyes are wild in her head.

There is a woman there, sitting at a small desk. She looks up slowly, unruffled by our sudden disturbance.

Soon there is a loud poundin' and a tryin' o' the lock.

"Hide us, Mrs. Bodeen, *please!*"

Mrs. Bodeen calmly gets up and goes to the window and pulls the curtain aside, ever so slightly, and looks out.

"All right. I'll take care of it. Get in that room there." She points to a room at the end of the hall.

I grabs Amy's arm and we runs down and dives into the room. I puts me back to the door again and closes me eyes and takes a couple of deep breaths and then I opens me eyes. Everything is *yellow.*

The walls are yellow and there's a yellow dresser with a yellow pitcher of water and a yellow basin, a yellow chair, and...

I hear a rustle of cloth and a wave of a very familiar perfume rolls across the room and breaks across my nose.

"Why, if it isn't my Little Miss Precious, come to visit her dear aunt Mam'selle Claudelle day Bour-bon. And she's brought a little fray-und with her. How nice."

Lord.

I turn and look, and there is Mam'selle herself reclining on her bed, wearing a yellow day dress and snuggled up against big, fluffy yellow satin pillows, which I'm guessin' is

207

silk 'cause it's all kind of shiny. She is holding a little lapdog, which being white has somehow escaped the yellow brush. It does, however, wear a yellow ribbon around its neck.

Well, I sighs, *let's tough this out as a lady, shall we?*

"Good day to you, Mademoiselle," I says, and dips a bit and turns to the astounded Amy. "May I present my very good friend, Miss Amy Trevelyne? Amy, this is Mademoiselle Claudelle de Bour-bon of the New Orleans Bour-bons. She was kind to me when I was in prison."

Amy recovers enough from her astonishment to dip and shakily say, "*Enchanté,* Mademoiselle de Bourbon."

"Charmed, I am sho-ah," says Mam'selle, moving her head to make her golden earrings jangle. "What a lovely little friend you have, Precious, and she even speaks Frey-unch." She pets her little dog and looks up through her impossibly long eyelashes. "Shall I call you Little Miss Dumpling, then, Little Precious's special fray-und? Yes, I believe I shall."

Mam'selle pats the bed next to her. "Now, come over he-ah, both of you, and let me relieve you of some of your garments...It's rather warm in here, don't you think? Would you like some refreshment? *Hmmm?*"

"It's a lovely room you have here, Mam'selle," says I, moving out to the center of the room and looking about.

"Why, thank you, Precious," simpers our hostess. She looks at Amy cowering by the door. "Does my apartment not make it plain that I am for the discriminatin' gentleman, the one who desires somethin' rare and refined and exotic in the way of female companionship?"

"It does, indeed, Mam'selle," says I, tryin' to think of somethin' else to say.

Mam'selle puts her finger to the side of her nose and

looks at me all tender. "I can see by your clothing that you have had a fall in your station in life. Poor, poor little Miss Precious, it is such a hard life, isn't it? Why don't you come over he-ah and put your dear little head in Mam'selle's lap and I will pet you and caress you and make it a little bit better. Now doesn't that sound good, Precious baby?"

Actually, with her singsong purring voice and my tiredness from the events of the day, it *does* sound kind of good, but there's a light knock on the door and I shakes my head to clear it of Mam'selle's soft and insinuating voice.

"You can come out now, girls," we hear Mrs. Bodeen say from the other side.

Amy has the door open in a flash and is outside in an instant. I pause to thank Mam'selle for her kindness and to apologize for Amy's rudeness in not saying good-bye 'cause she is scared and don't know her way around yet.

Mam'selle smiles and says, "That's all right, Precious, I understand. Just you be careful now, because I am quite fond of you and I know you to be one of those that *aren't* scared when maybe sometimes they should be scared, *hmmm*?"

We go back out into the foyer. Mrs. Bodeen looks at us and shakes her head.

"Girls, don't you know you've got to pay off the police?"

"Please, Missus," I says, "we warn't doin' nothin', just singin' and playin' in the street, we warn't…"

"Still got to give John Law his bit, Miss. Anyway, he's been taken care of." Mrs. Bodeen casts her shrewd eye over the both of us standin' there. "If you're ever looking for full-time work, girls, you know where to come. I run a clean house."

I don't have to look over at Amy to know that she is

brick red in the face and ready to fall through the floor. "Everyone knows you run a clean and honest house, Missus," says I, my face hot, too. "And we thank you for the invite, but we're still in school and..." I trails off, not wantin' to offend her who has just saved us.

Mrs. Bodeen lets a knowing smile come to her lips as she looks me over.

"I recall you from the jail," she says, dryly. "You do get around for a schoolgirl, don't you? Ah. Here's our Mr. Pickering, come to collect you."

I had not expected to arrive in Ezra's office in quite such an inelegant fashion. If he could have brought me in by the scruff of my neck, I'm sure he would have.

Amy weeps quietly in her chair, her hands coverin' her face, and I'm sittin' here all straight with my hands folded in my lap and my best Jacky-takes-her-punishment look on my face. We are both a bit mussed from our run. I stick out my lower lip and blow away a lock of hair that has found its way into my eyes.

Ezra, sitting at his desk, is looking at me most severely. I have finally managed to erase his little smile.

"It is possible that you are insane," he says. "Perhaps I can have you committed to the female asylum. That might keep you out of the Preacher's hands."

"I was told that music wasn't against the law in Boston," I says in my defense.

"No, but creating a public disturbance *is* against the law."

"We warn't doin' nothing but—"

"If you had been caught, you would have been taken to

court and charged. You would then have been thrown back in jail, a place I recall you did not enjoy overmuch the last time you were there, and I do not have the slightest doubt that the Court would have declared you a wayward child. The Preacher's petition of guardianship would then have been immediately granted and you would have been taken directly to his house. *After* you were taken out and caned, that is. Remember, you *were* convicted of lewd and lascivious behavior, and although the sentence was suspended, it would be carried out if you were arrested again. Does any of this make sense to you?"

Amy whimpers all the more on hearin' this. I swears there's a steam of shame risin' off her like a fog. She may be in a state of fatal mortification. She was barely able to produce a decent curtsy when I introduced her to Ezra.

All right, Ezra, all right. I get it.

"I am sorry, Ezra…," I say, and put on my best I'll-be-good look.

"Sorry. *Hmmm.*" He picks up his quill and points it at my nose. "Shall I describe the rod? It is about three-eighths of an inch in thickness, and although it is called a cane, it is actually quite whiplike. You would be put on your knees and your back bared and your hands tied to the post. You would have to use your elbows to prevent your shirt from slipping forward and baring your breast to the crowd. Not that you'll care about *that* after the first stroke of the cane. Constable Wiggins swings the rod, and he makes it no secret that this is the part of his job that he finds most pleasing. *Especially* if the victim is a young and pretty girl. As the welts begin to form, succeeding blows would cause them to bleed and, eventually, scar. Is that a sight you want to present to your future husband? Your Mr. Fletcher?"

"No, Ezra, I don't," I whispers and hangs my head, and this time I takes it to heart.

"All right," he says, and sits back in his chair. He allows the half smile to return to his lips.

"The Preacher was back in court today to press his case. Once again, I was able to keep things up in the air, pending an inquiry by the Court. Of course, if he gets wind of your actions today, I'm sure he will press even harder, you exhibiting delinquent and immoral behavior and all."

He pauses, and then he goes on. "If he came over to take you without a court order, would Mistress Pimm hand you over to him?"

"In a minute," I says. "To her I am nothing but a serving girl."

"*Hmmm*," says he. "Then maybe it would be better if you could leave the school for a short period of time. For the weekend. Till we see how the wind blows, as it were. I'd rather be working to prevent you from being taken than working to try to get you back. He can't do anything more today, and neither can we, the court being closed and not being open again until tomorrow, Friday at nine. You would not have to leave till morning. Is there anyplace you can go? I regret that propriety prevents me from offering you shelter here, me being a bachelor and all." He looks at Amy when he says this.

I says, "I can stay at the Pig and Whistle and…"

"*That* would *not* be appropriate," says Ezra in a warning tone.

I'm wonderin' what's wrong with the Pig when Amy

comes up with, "We will go to our farm. In Quincy. She will be safe there."

Ezra smiles and brings Amy to her feet and escorts her to the door. "That will be perfect, Miss Trevelyne. Please visit with me upon your return."

I nod and go to the door.

"Please be good, Jacky," he says in parting.

"I will, Ezra, I promise," I say. *At least, I'll try.*

"Coo, Amy, this will be such fun. We shall slop hogs and sleep in the barn and...you do have hogs, don't you?"

"Yes, we have hogs," says Amy, her voice weary with the events of the day, "but we also have a problem. There is no coach to Quincy tomorrow. How shall we get to the farm?"

"Why, we'll just take Gretchen and Brunhilde," I says. "Henry Hoffman trusts me. I've been helpin' him with the stables, the brushin' of the horses and stuff. It's only an easy day's ride, you said, so what's the problem?"

"Two girls can't go riding off alone in the country, not without a male escort." She sighs, weary, also, of my lack of knowledge of New England ways.

I think for a minute, and then I says, "I know someone who'll escort us. So put it out of your mind. We've got to stop in here for a moment."

We've come up next to the Pig and Whistle as I planned, takin' a route back that would bring us here.

Amy gasps. "No more, please, Jacky, I can't take any more." She's close to tears, I can tell.

"Now, don't worry. I've just got to get a message to someone. Come on."

We go in and there's Maudie at the bar and I says, "Good

day, Maudie, could you tell Gully I ain't gonna be able to play this weekend as I got to leave town right quick?"

"Don't worry about it none, Jacky. He's back in the slammer again, and he'll be in for a few days, at least. He took a swing at the constable," says Maudie, sadly. I know she's thinkin' of the lost business.

"I'd be glad to do a solo act, Maudie, but I really..."

"That's good of you to say, Jacky, but you go on. We'll see you when you get back."

And we're back outside. "I won't even ask what *that* was about," says Amy, as we trudge back up the now familiar path through the Common to the school.

As we are about to duck back in through the kitchen, I have a thought and say, "You know what, Amy?"

"What?"

"I think our Mr. Pickering likes you," and I give her a nudge with my elbow.

"Oh, Jacky, *please*," she says, as she heads upstairs.

At lights-out I imagine them all down there kneeling by their bedsides saying their prayers, their white nightgowns ghostly in the moonlight, and I know Amy is thanking God for her deliverance, relatively intact, from a day with the wild and wanton Jacky Faber. I kneel down beside my bed, myself, though it is not my way to do so, and I call down the blessings of heaven on my long list of names, starting with Jaimy and Davy and Tink and Willy and Benjy and Liam and Mum and Dad and Penny and ending up with Snag and Burnt Tom and Johnny No Toes. This night, I adds another.

"And please bless and keep by your side Janey Porter, a

young girl cut down in her prime, who you know never did no wrong. Amen."

Amen.

Mistress taps her cane twice on the floor and they climb into their beds and are quickly snugged up and very soon asleep. Me, too.

Chapter 19

"Now, you just be outside the back door in half an hour and I'll go get our escort," says I to Amy, all excited to be off to visit Amy's place. She don't look too happy just yet and I knows it's 'cause she's ashamed of the dirty little farm where she comes from but she don't know the places *I've* been so it will be all right. "Tonight we shall sleep in your barn all covered with hay!"

Amy nods. "All right. And I'll leave a note for Mistress saying I'm feeling poorly and we are off to home for a few days. She won't care if we go, but she'd care very much if we didn't tell her we are going."

"Tell her we're off to Timbuktu for all I care," I says. "Out back. Half an hour." I pick up my seabag and sling it over my back and rattle down the back stairs.

"You have a good time, Jacky, but you be careful of those handsome plowboys!" sings out Annie as I tear through the kitchen. It's my weekend off, and they're gonna cover for me today and on Monday till I get back. They know I'll make it up to them.

A wave to all and a promise to be good and a quick peck

on dear Peg's cheek for havin' bagged up some sandwiches for us and I'm out.

"Henry! Dear Henry, quickly! Amy Trevelyne and I are going to her farm for the weekend and we need Gretchen and Brunhilde saddled up! Please, Henry." Bat, bat of the eyelashes, hopeful smile on the lips.

"Mistress said it was all right," I pleads. It's sort of the truth—she *will* know that we are gone, she just won't know how we went.

Henry looks doubtful. "Maybe I should check with Mistress."

I look all hurt and abashed and I stick my lower lip out like I'm going to cry and he gives it up. "Oh, all right. For you, Jacky."

I clap my hands for joy. "Bless you, Henry," I say. "And Henry, if you would, please put a regular saddle on Gretchen."

He protests, of course, but I say I know what I'm doing and I'll be right back, please please please.

I take my seabag and duck into an unused stall. I open the bag and reach in and take out the midshipman's uniform I had got from Midshipman Elliot during my last days on the *Dolphin*. I had put it at the top of my bag so it would be easy to get at today.

I take off everything I got on—weskit, blouse, chemise, stockings, slip skirt, and then the drawers—'cause nothin' I had on would fit under this uniform, not even the drawers, 'cause the uniform is so formfitting, and with the flounces on the drawers, it just wouldn't work.

Standing naked in a stable is a new one, even for me, and I hope that Henry don't get done too quick and come lookin' for me. I hurries into my new rig.

First I put on the white shirt with the white lace at the neck and wrists, then the white stockings, and then the tight white breeches that buckle under the knee and over the stockings. I dust the hay off my feet and slip on the shiny black pumps. Now the black jacket with its shiny brass buttons that button all the way to the neck, letting the lace show above and at the wrists. The jacket comes down to my waist and is of heavy broadcloth and is tight and feels good on me.

I fold up my girl clothes and stuff them in the bag. Then I put on my cap, which is black like the jacket and has a shiny black leather brim, stuff my hair up underneath, pick up my bag, and stride out. Henry is just bringing up the horses, all saddled and ready. Gretchen whinnies out a greeting as soon as she sees me. Henry's mouth drops open as he takes me in, but not a sound comes out.

I turn my back to him and tie my seabag to the straps on the back of Gretchen's saddle and then turn back to Henry, who is now a bright shade of scarlet. Well, maybe these britches *are* a bit tight.

I take the reins from his hand and put my foot in the stirrup and swing my leg up and over and settle into the saddle. Then I lean way over and whisper into Henry's ear, "You won't peach on me now, Henry, will you?"

I let my lips brush his cheek as I come away and straighten up. I give him a wink as I give Gretchen a little cluck and we head out, leading Hildy, into the light of day.

———

Amy is dutifully waiting at the appointed spot, now looking back anxiously to see if Mistress has come out to snatch her back, now looking around for me.

I pull up in front of her and dismount and bow. "Miss Trevelyne?" I say, making my voice low and trying to keep a straight face.

"Y-yes," she says, all confused. "But who are you and where is..."

Then I give her my best grin and salute.

"Oh, Jacky, *no*..."

"Do you like it?" I say, spinning around. "Ain't it a good fit?"

"Jacky, we cannot!" she wails. "After the events of yesterday, I thought you would be somewhat chastened, but oh no...This is scandalous! You will be arrested and you will be taken and...and someone will *see* you! Those are your... your *limbs* there."

"Oh, fiddle-dee-dee," says I, taking her bag and fastening it to the back of Hildy's saddle. "All they'll see is a lovin' brother and sister, ridin' home for the weekend to see our lovin' mum and dad. We'll ride straight through, not stoppin' at no inn for refreshment, and no one will be the wiser. Who'll know?"

Her bag being secured, I say, "Up with you, now," and I take her hand and lead her to her mount and help her up, just like any decent gent. She sits there, shaking.

I return to dear Gretchie and I mount, swinging my leg over seabag and horse's rump. Amy shudders and looks away.

"Believe me, Sister," says I, to make her easy, "folks sees what they expects to see."

And with a *whoop!* from Midshipman Jacky Faber, newly back in naval harness, we clatter off down the street.

We head south in the city, first a wild gallop across the Common, scattering livestock out of our way, and then by the ropewalk and a burying ground and onto Pleasant Street at a brisk trot, down to Orange and across the causeway and out of the city of Boston. The town thins out very quickly and soon buildings give way to rolling fields and farmhouses. We go at a quick walk for a while to give the horses some rest.

"Ain't this just prime?" I exults as we leave the cobblestone streets of the city and head off into the country.

"This will be just prime if we do not get caught," says Amy, ever the optimist. "Oh no, someone is coming!"

I see a gent up ahead, approachin' in a small open buggy pulled by one horse. "Our first test!" I says, all gleeful, and wipes the smile off me face and puts on a serious but pleasant face.

"Good day to you both!" says the man cheerfully as we come abreast. "And a beautiful day it is!"

I drops me voice down a notch and says, "And a very good day to you, Suh!" And I raise my riding crop to my brim by way of salute. Amy drops her eyes and nods demurely.

"Played like a pro, Amy, my dear," says I, when the man and his rig have passed. "You were the perfect sister, and you see that we have nothing to fear."

"I suppose," sighs Amy.

I take a deep breath and feel the jacket tighten around my chest—it is of heavy material and cut so close and snug that I did not even have to strap myself down. Not that there's all that much of me to strap down, but still…I smile to think back to my old Deception.

It is so good to be out and free and back in sailor gear again that I just can't keep down the joy bubblin' inside my chest.

"Free!" I have to shout out. "Free of the school, free of Mistress, and free of that awful Preacher. Free! Free of switches and constables and rods and—"

"Hush, Sister…or rather Brother," scolds Amy. "We do not want to attract attention."

"Right," says I, and I stands up on the saddle, which is something I wanted to do ever since I got a little bit good at riding but which I could never do in front of Herr Hoffman or even Henry.

"Ta-da! Miss Jacky Faber, Queen of the Circus, for your delight and amazement!" I announces, the reins in my left hand, and my right hand in a grand sweepin' gesture as my feet step up on Gretchie's dear broad rump.

"Jacky, you are going to fall!" pleads Amy. "Get down, now!"

I drops back down and my bottom makes a soft *whump* as it hits the saddle.

"You are going to hurt yourself, you are," she says, sounding like she's fed up with me and my ways.

"Ah, no little babies for little Jacky, now, eh?" I tease.

"Hummph," says Amy, but I think I almost get a smile out of her.

"Let's have a song, then."

And so the day wears on. We pass many people on the road, but no one suspects us of being anything other than what we appear, a brother and sister riding along talking and singing amidst the glorious colors of the fall.

We trot for a time, and then canter awhile. Then walk, then gallop, then dismount and walk the horses to let them rest and cool down. There are ripe apples hanging from branches overhead and we feed them to Gretchen and Hildy and we eat some ourselves.

We stop for lunch next to a brook where the horses can water themselves, and we sit on the grass beneath a tree and eat the sandwiches that Peg had made for us. Earlier we had come upon an old man selling cider by the wayside and I pulled out a coin from my jacket pocket, one of several I had put there last night, and bought a jug of it.

"I am sorry I do not have any money," says Amy, looking a little ashamed. "I have never been given any."

"Ah, who expects a poor farm girl to have any coin o' the realm, and, besides, I say it's a pretty poor sod what can't stand her mate to a bit of a treat."

We pass the jug back and forth. The sandwiches are made from slabs of meatloaf tucked in thick pieces of bread on which Peg has put some sort of gravy and they are wondrous good. *Thanks, Peg.*

"You Yankees have fine soft land here," says I. I tips back the jug again and takes a long swig, then sprawls back on the grass, knees in the air.

"Let us hear you say that in a few months when we are in the dead of winter, dear," says Amy. "And you had better be careful of that cider. It is quite hard."

"'Hard'?"

"It has fermented and has some alcohol in it."

"Ha. Don't worry about that. I know to be wary of old

Mr. Booze. Ain't I seen his handiwork lyin' outside many a tavern? No, Jacky Faber ain't gonna be one of his victims, I can tell you that."

I think of Gully then and how he's wasting his great gift on the drink and how I don't understand that at all.

"You know, Amy," I says after a while of looking up at the sky with its fluffy white clouds and birds scudding by. "We sound awfully good singing together. We might think about getting up an act. To play in the taverns, like."

I hear a choking sound from Amy and figure she's taken a bit too big a bite of her sandwich.

"We could do songs, of course, and dancing, but we also could do recitations of your poetry and dramatic readings and such. We could be the Fabulous Valentine Sisters. 'Valentine' sounds all exotic and romantic, don't you think?" I says. I suck a bit of meat out of my back teeth and go on. "Trouble is, that harpsichord of yours ain't too portable."

"Come," says Amy, getting up, "we have several more hours to go."

"I shall think on the problem as we ride," says I.

We're gettin' pretty close to the end of our journey, accordin' to Amy, who has, for some reason, gotten more jumpy with the nerves the nearer we get. I figures she thinks I'm gonna be disappointed with her little farm, but she's wrong. She don't know yet just how humble my beginnings really were, so if we get there and it's just a lean-to and a pigsty, it'll look like home to me. In truth, I'd be glad to be gettin' just about anywhere, as my bum is gettin' sore from sittin' in the saddle all the day long.

I'm babblin' along, talkin' about this and that and how

maybe we could mount the harpsichord on wheels, when Amy says, "Turn here."

She pulls Hildy's head to the left and starts down a smaller road that goes between two great stone pillars. On one of the pillars is fixed a brass plate with "Dovecote" writ on it.

"Wot's this?" I says. "The name of the village your farm is in?"

"No," says Amy, real low, "it is the name of our farm."

"Your farm's got a name? I never heard of such a thing," says I, givin' Gretchie me heels and pullin' up next to Amy as she goes over a small rise and the woods end and the prospect opens up. "But, then, that's sort of sweet it is, to name your little...Oh, my God..."

"I'm sorry, Jacky," cries Amy, lookin' at me all trembly and worried. "I thought if you knew you wouldn't come!"

I look down over the prospect. There is the great house with its three stories and its huge chimney at either end and its grand entrance, gleamin' all white in the afternoon sun. There is not one, but one two three four *five* barns. A stable. A racetrack with white fencing all about. There are horses in paddocks and cows in fields. There is a small river running down on the left and, on the right, neat fields, newly harvested. There are men and women and boys and girls, all out on their many tasks, and beyond all is the sea, all sparkly and bright.

"What is done now, my Lady? You'll have to help me 'cause I don't know what to do," says I, hanging my head all humble. "Do I get off and lead your horse down? Where are the servant quarters? Should I go there direct? Should I—"

"You stop with that now," hisses Amy, reaching out to

clutch my arm. "Are we not still the Dread Sisterhood? Are we not still the Fabulous Valentine Sisters?"

I laugh and lean over and give her a nudge and say, "Of course we are, Sister, and I'm glad you're rich and I wish you the joy of it! But I shall pay my way when I am here, I shall gladly curry the horses, and if any hog needs slopping, well, I'll slop the hell out of him!"

We ride down toward the main house when I spy there a young man dressed in a fine uniform and talking to one of the stable hands.

"He's a pretty one, he is," I says.

Amy starts up in her saddle. "It is Randall. My brother. He is not supposed to be here." Her brow furrows, and she does not seem pleased.

"Your *brother*?" exclaims I, delighted. "Why are you not glad to see him?"

"You will see," says Amy, and she will say no more.

"Well, then," says I, the evil fizzing up in me again. I feel it comin' but I can't stop, I can't be good I can't I can't. "Let's have some fun! Play along! Follow my lead! Let's go!"

And with that I give poor Hildy a swat on her rump with my crop and give poor Gretchie a dig with my heels and together we gallop down to meet Brother Randall in a fine cloud of dust.

When we gets there, I wheels Gretchen about and dismounts as I does it, which looks rash and dashing. I bounds over to the astounded young man and pulls myself to attention and salutes and roars, "Midshipman Jack Faber. At your service, Suh!"

He manages to nod, astonished.

"Your sister Amy has honored me beyond measure by

inviting me here for the weekend, to sample the charms of your beautiful estate and her own sweet company! I am blessed beyond measure!"

I bow to Randall and go to Amy's side and help her down. I take her bag off of Hildy and get my seabag from Gretchen and hand the reins to the astounded stable hand. Bowing again to her brother, I take Amy by the hand and lead her toward the big house. I turn and salute again.

"You must excuse us, Suh, but my time here is not long, and 'gather ye rosebuds while ye may,' and all that! Off to your chambers then, Milady! Adieu!" Puttin' my arm around Amy's waist, we run, laughing, to the house, over the porch, and inside the door. "Do you have a room?" I ask, startin' to unbutton my jacket.

"Yes! Up here!" Amy is grinning widely and is fully in the spirit of the thing.

We storm up the stairs and into her room. I throw my seabag on the bed and rip it open. I pull out my serving-girl gear and tear off my jacket and shirt and put on the blouse and step into the skirt and on with the weskit and lace myself up tight. I'll get out of the white britches and stockings later.

Done!

I go to the window and look out and see Randall standin' there not knowin' what to do. I open the window a crack and put my mouth to it.

"Oh, Amy," I cries out and lets it go at that.

It is enough. I look out the window and see that he has reached a decision and has drawn his sword and is headin' this way.

"Quick!" I squeaks to Amy. "Stand over here. How's my hair?"

I hears him thunderin' up the stairs and then he's beatin' against the door and then the door bursts open and there stands Randall Trevelyne, sword in hand and blood in his eye. And looking quite handsome, I might add. I've always liked a man in uniform.

"May I present my friend Jacky Faber, from my school," says Amy, all cool and aloof. "Jacky, this is my brother Randall."

I bounce up and down on my toes, about to burst with excitement for the trick played upon this Randall, but I drop my eyes and bob my best curtsy. "My lord," I say.

He looks me over quite frankly. He does not bow. "So you would play tricks on me with your serving wench, would you now, Sister?"

"She is not my servant. She is my friend, although she constantly gives me reason to think otherwise."

Randall Trevelyne puts the point of his sword on the lip of its scabbard and rams it home. It is plain that he does not like being made sport of.

"What brings you home, Brother?" asks Amy, all puffed up like a pigeon. "I would have expected you would be at your studies...or at Mrs. Bodeen's for the weekend."

That gives him a start. It occurs to me that being with me has given Sister Amy another arrow in her quiver in her war with her brother, for war it quite plainly is.

"The Sheik is being brought down early tomorrow," he replies coldly. "Father thought it best I see him settled in myself."

"Ah," says Amy. "The last nail in the family coffin."

Randall whirls on me and says, "Get out."

I bob and duck out of the room.

When I am outside the door I hear them going at it for real. I can't hear it all, but I hear snatches.

"Damned impertinence! Our family's business is not to be spoken of in front of the help!"

"Help? I'll thank you not to order my friends about, Randall!"

"Your 'friend'? A cheap trollop going about dressed as a man is your friend? Then you have fallen in bad company, Sister! You bring something like that here to mock me, to mock our family, to…"

"Our family! Oh, our sacred family! Oh, the holy name Trevelyne, which is going straight to ruin in a…"

I figure I have heard enough, enough to realize that all is not well here at Dovecote. I feel uncomfortable and I head out to find the stables and make sure that Gretchen and Hildy are taken care of proper, walked and brushed down, like.

Then I go to find the kitchen and that is where Amy finds me, helping Mrs. Grubbs, the cook, with the evening meal, and that is where we take our dinner.

Chapter 20

I'm awakened in the morning by the sun streamin' in the window and roosters crowin', and I roll over and stretch and give Amy a poke. I look all around and say, "A room of your own, Amy. Such a thing." She grunts and does not stir.

I don't think I've ever been in a prettier place, all bright and cheerful with new white and blue paint, filmy white curtains on the window, and thick rugs on the floor. There are framed paintings on the wall, mostly of fields and mountains and trees, but there's one of a fluffy white cat and there's one of three oranges in a plate. And, besides the bed, there's a chest of drawers with a mirror over it, a small desk and chair, and a dry sink with a basin and pitcher on top of it. The pitcher has little red roses painted on it, and so does the chamber pot on the floor.

I get up and pull off my nightdress and toss it over a chair and give the pot a visit. There is soap and washcloths and towels laid out on the sink and so I pour some water from the pitcher into the basin and lather up and wash my face to get the sleep out of my eyes. Then I give my armpits and some other parts a bit of a scrub down as well. Behind me, I hear Amy stir and then let out a loud *tsk!* and sigh.

"I swear, Jacky, you have all the personal modesty of a monkey," she says, her voice still thick with sleep.

"A clean mind in a clean body," I chirps all cheerful and bright, and proceeds to towel off. When I am done I dives into my seabag and pulls out my sailor togs from back on the *Dolphin* and I puts 'em on. It's the uniform I made to wear when we had Inspection and other fine days like port visits. My white duck pants with a drawstring waist and my white duck shirt with a flap on the back with blue piping. My black midshipman's neckerchief goes under the flap and ties in front. I digs deeper in my bag and comes up with my dear old *Dolphin* cap and slaps it on.

"Ta-da!" I sings and poses, hands on hips. "What do you think? Can I wear it today, here on your little farm?"

Amy opens her eyes and she looks at me and her eyes roll back in her head. "Might as well," she sighs. "You are not going to listen to me, anyway, and I am sure everyone here already knows you for a hopeless eccentric."

I give a delighted squeak, so glad to be back in my old gear, and go over to the mirror and admire myself in it. Not bad for a girl what was a dirty and near-naked urchin not two years ago, but seein' the uniform reminds me of Jaimy and the lads and that takes a bit of the shine off my pride. I miss them all so and I hope they are all right.

I take off my hat and let out my braid and sit on the edge of the bed and commence to combing my hair, facing away so Amy can get up and go do her necessaries. My hair is quite long now—not so long as Amy's, as she could sit on hers if she wanted—and I decides to wear it looser today, maybe just gathered in back by a ribbon. A blue one. To match Lord Randall's jacket, I thinks, with a touch of evil in my thought.

"What service is Randall in?" I asks, all innocent.

"He is a lieutenant in the local militia," says Amy from the sink. "That sounds grander than it actually is—mainly, they just drill and parade around shouting things."

"Still," says I, "how dashing he looked with his sword drawn, ready to storm in and pin me to the wall to save his sister's honor!"

"He was not there to save *my* honor," snorts Amy. "He was ready to save the *family* honor, so that it would not reflect badly on him. He cares nothing for me and I care nothing for him."

"Surely that can't be true. That's just brother and sister talk."

"Would you love someone who was a constant torment to you as a child? Would you love someone who gets to go to Harvard College while you are thrown into the pit misnamed the Lawson Peabody *School* for Young Girls? *And* someone who is squandering that education in favor of drink and sloth and lechery? And finally, would you love someone who planned to marry the darling Miss Clarissa Worthington Howe? Now, would you?"

Now *that* hits me like a stone on the side of my head.

I mulls this over a bit. So that's why Clarissa didn't destroy Amy that time when I was on my knees before her amid the bags of underwear and Amy stopped her from hitting me. Why rock the matrimonial boat over some harmless fun shaming a mere serving girl?

"So he's really gonna marry the Queen, hey?" I probes.

"Oh yes. It will be the social event of the season. Clarissa's family is quite rich, you know. My father is very pleased with the match. My mother, too. It will put her up a notch on the social scene."

"Where are your mum and dad? I sort of expected them to be here. That's why I was on my best behavior."

Amy snorts and then gradually collapses into helpless laughter, and it occurs to me that this is the first time I have heard her really laugh hard, and it is a most pleasant sound, even if it is at my expense. "On. Your. Best. Behavior," she manages to say and then returns to outright laughter. I didn't think it was all *that* funny.

Eventually, she calms down enough to say, "They are in New York, for the winter social season. They will be back for Christmas and then will go back to New York and not return until spring. That is why I am in the school: They do not want me here alone; and they do not want me with them in Society."

Amy comes into my view wearing a riding outfit, all wine colored with touches of dark green and very finely tailored.

"Well, look at you, now. Ain't we the grand one, Milady," says I, popping up and going to her and smoothin' back her lapels and the fabric over her shoulders. "Looks like hangin' with the Jack has been good for you. Runnin' from the police and such." I pull out the sides of her jacket. "You'll have to have this taken in a bit."

Amy looks pleased. She blushes and says, "Let us get some breakfast."

Out we go to the kitchen, where Mrs. Grubbs whips us up some fine bacon and eggs and tea and toast, and it's all so rich and fine with the fat sausages and hams hangin' down from the ceiling and the big wheels of cheese all stacked up. There's jars of things put up for the winter and pickle urns and foamy pitchers of milk and loaves of lovely fresh bread, but in my contrary way I thinks about Polly and Judy and Nancy and the rest back on the streets of London and how it ain't fair, it just ain't fair that some have so much and some so little.

And it's strange, I thinks, how quickly I get used to all this, like I takes it for granted that I have always lived this way and will always live this way. Even when I know it ain't gonna be true.

We go outside in the warm autumn air and look upon chickens and cows and a new litter of piglets, which I feed a bit of grain, and their squishy little noses pressin' at the palm of my hand makes me wish bacon didn't taste so good. In the henhouse, we take baskets and gather eggs still warm from the chickens. The eggs lie in the cozy little nests and it is like a fine game to collect them.

I meet the people of the farm—the plowboys, the milk-maids, field hands, herders, and all. Dovecote is like a little village, sufficient unto itself—there's a miller and a weaver and even a blacksmith, with little cottages all around for the people to live in. They all seem to really like Amy, and they greet her most warmly. Maybe she warn't always so solemn and gloomy.

There's children, too. Lots of them, and they stare all openmouthed at me, strangers bein' rare here, especially ones decked out in sailor togs, but that's all right, I just whip out my whistle and give 'em a tune and dance a few steps and that delights 'em and makes 'em laugh and dance about. We have a little parade for a bit.

There's some raised eyebrows about my dress, but they get over it.

We're walkin' over to the stables to saddle up Gretchie and Hildy for a ride around the place when a black-and-white thing appears from nowhere and capers all about me. I goes rigid and stands there scared.

"What is it?" I wails. "What does it want?"

"It's just Millie," laughs Amy, grabbing the beast by its ears and—*yuck*—kissing it. "She's our collie sheepdog and is just the dearest thing."

"Make it go away," I begs. To me, dogs was vicious beings that we fought with over scraps of food on the streets of London. The dog comes back to me and pokes at me with its pointy nose.

"What's it doin'?" I wails. "Make it stop!"

Amy is lookin' at me with a small smile on her face. "The redoubtable Jacky Faber, scared at last." She calls the dog back to her and says, "She was herding you. She wanted you over here by me, and that is how she goes about it."

"I think she was bein' mighty familiar, if you ask me," I fumes.

"Poor Millie, a sheepdog who has lost her sheep," says Amy in a musing way. "And does not know where to find them." The dog rolls its eyes and actually seems to smile under her petting.

Amy's smile is gone now and she continues in a clipped tone, "But it was not poor Millie who lost our sheep. It was Father. With one cut of the cards. Five hundred sheep. *And* the pasture on which they used to graze. That field over there, beyond the river. That one. Gone. Let us see to the horses." Amy strides briskly toward the stables. I hold my tongue and follow.

We get to the stables and I meet the grooms and stable hands. One of them is the boy that Randall was talking to when we rode up yesterday. His name is Edward and I remember him lookin' real daggers at me when I was prancin' around in my male finery and seemin' to be all tight with Amy. *You are not as unloved as you think, Sister.*

With Gretchie and Hildy saddled up, we gallop off across the land.

"This is the Neponset River," says Amy, when we pulls up after a while. "It is the border of our land to the north."

"It's lovely," I say, lookin' out over the sparklin' waters movin' down to the sea. "Too bad it's a bit chilly. We could swim...and look, that huge tree hangin' out over that pool is just beggin' to have a rope hung on it for swingin' out over the water. Do you know how to swim? I could teach you if you don't."

"I do not know. I have never tried. I have never been in the river. It was always assumed that I would catch cold." Amy looks out over the land, back toward the buildings— the houses, the stables, the barns, all laid out neat and tidy.

The dog Millie has followed us out here and is happily dancin' about, chasin' the small birds that burst out of the high grasses. Prolly tryin' to herd them, too.

"You know, Jacky," says Amy after a while, "one of the reasons I did not tell you of the extent of Dovecote is that it is all, in a very real way, an illusion."

I don't say anything. I don't have to. She will get to it.

"My father, Colonel John Trevelyne, a hero of the Revolution, who was at Valley Forge and Yorktown and who was decorated by General Washington himself, has an affliction. He is a gambler, and he is going to gamble away every bit of this. He has been doing it, little by little, but now he is going to bet it all." She pauses. "*All*. On the Sheik, that horse that is arriving today."

"But, why?" I asks, all mystified. "Why would anyone risk all this on a bet?"

"I do not know why, but it has been getting worse and worse. I think he misses the excitement of the war, or, oh, excitement of any kind. Gambling brings the element of risk back into his life."

"So you're gonna be poor, just like me, someday," I says, and I ain't sayin' it to be mean, just to lend some comfort. "But don't worry, we'll get along. Remember, we're the Fabulous Musical Singing Valentine Sisters, and we will make our way in the world!" I says to jolly her up a bit. "Ta-da!" I sings, but it's weak and I knows it's weak and it don't wash. She seems so sad and downhearted. It's easy to see why she's been so gloomy all along. It's a shame, all this lost for a bit of a tingle.

Amy sits up straight. "Look. He comes. The Sheik of Araby, the Pride of Dovecote," she says with no small bitterness. "And the likely agent of its downfall."

I turn and look and see a group of horsemen coming along the same road we came down yesterday when first I came to Dovecote. There are four men, two on either side of the huge black horse between them. The black horse does not have a rider, only a blanket. They pull up in the stable yard and dismount.

"Father bought him for a huge amount of money in the spring. Then the stallion was brought to Boston by ship, which cost even more money, money that my father has raised by mortgaging our land," says Amy. "The Sheik is a British Thoroughbred with Arabian blood, and he is supposed to be as fast as the wind. There will be a race and bets will be made and my father will cover those bets and if the horse loses, the farm is gone."

The horse his ownself is kickin' up quite a fuss down there—it's takin' two men hangin' on the reins to hold him. He rears up, dragging them forward so that they are in danger of his flailing hooves. He tosses his head back and forth and whinnies. Screams, really. He is some horse.

"When will this all happen?" I asks.

"In the early summer. During racing season, if Father has not already lost everything at the cards and dice before then," says Amy. "Come, Sister, let us go see this Sheik of Araby."

We turn our horses' heads and ride down to the stable, with Millie joyously leading a rather silent pair of sisters.

When we come into the yard, there is a crowd standin' about admirin' the beast. He's got a big body and a long neck and a small, finely shaped head—no common hammerhead he, even I can tell that. As he moves, I can see the big muscles bunching and sliding around under his glistening hide. The stallion is all black except for a white blaze of a star on his forehead, between the black eyes that roll about all wild, showing their whites and making him look hot and fierce and not to be taken lightly.

It's not hard to see the difference between this creature and my poor little Gretchie, who don't like him at all and who ducks her head and shies away, not wanting to get close. *Don't you mind him, Gretchie, let's have your little walk.* I slides off her back and walks her about a bit so she can cool, and when I can stick my hand in her chest and not find it all sweaty, I leads her back to her stall and sets her up with some oats and combs her down a bit. Then I goes back out to look at the Sheik more close.

They're taking him to his stall now, or at least they're trying, him still puttin' up a fuss and resistin' their efforts to calm him down, him all snortin' and blowin' and generally bein' difficult.

But they finally succeed and there he is, all tucked in, with his head poked out of a little window into the stable yard. There's a cry and a curse as a man behind him in the stall gets a kick, but then things quiet down and the horse seems to calm.

From a barrel of apples tucked beneath an overhang, I takes one and goes over to his Sheikship. There's a stool by where his head sticks out and I gets up on it next to him and puts my hand on his neck. I feel the hard muscles move under my hand as he swings his great head around to fix me with his eye. He don't look pleased.

"Nice horsie," I says, givin' him my best smile. "Here, have an apple."

"Jacky, be careful," I hears Amy warn from behind me. *Careful of what?*

I holds out the apple and he pulls back his lips over his huge teeth and he bites me.

"Damn you!" I cries, clasping my bitten hand to my breast. "You bit me!" And without thinkin' I takes that same hand and swats him across the nose with it.

"Miss! Please! You can't treat him so!" pleads the head hostler. "He's too—"

"You miserable piece of…" I growls, and then launches into a string of sailor's curses that cause the stable hands to wince and cover the ears of the younger onlookers. I don't remember much of what I said 'cause of my shock and pain in bein' bit, but I'm afraid I took the Lord's name in vain a few times in wishing the damned nag to the lowest levels of Hell, and I think I might have said a few bad things about his mother.

The Sheik looks confused and abashed—it's plain he ain't used to bein' treated this way. He ain't near so fierce lookin' now.

I jump to the ground and pick up the spurned apple and hop back up to confront the horse again. "Now, horse," I says, "let's try it again. Have an apple, and if you bite me again, I will smack you again. And, remember, this is Cheapside Jacky talking to you, horse." I offer the apple on my open palm.

The horse looks at the apple and then looks nervously up at my other hand raised and ready to strike him on the nose should he be so bold as to try another assault on my poor hand. He looks back down at the apple and then, very gently, the Sheik of Araby takes the apple.

"That's better," I say, reaching back and combing his mane through my fingers. "We will get along."

Chapter 21

"Amy."

"Yes, Jacky."

I put my face down on the hay and look over at her. It is raining on this Sunday, our third day at Dovecote, and, after having gone to church, we are lying above in the stable hayloft where it is warm and dry and redolent with the smell of the horses. Faithful Millie lies down below at the foot of the ladder, whimpering because she can't come up.

There is a small piece of board missing on the side of the barn and we lie side by side looking out across the autumnal fields. The fields set up quite a pleasing pattern as they roll down to the sea, and the rain has brought a blush of green back to the earth. The rain has also kept us here another day, which is all right with me.

I'm thinking back on Jaimy and what he wants me to be and on Mistress and on my demotion and I asks, "Am I crude, Amy? Others have said I am, which is why I'm asking."

She waits a little too long in replying.

"I *knew* it," I says, and flips over on my back. "I *am* crude and common and awful and I'll never be a lady. I shall go down and slop the hogs as that is my station in life and I should be glad of it and not try to get above myself."

Amy looks at me for a while, thinking. "It is not so much that you are crude, as it is that you are…impulsive…simple…straightforward…and maybe a bit too direct and plainspoken for our society. In a charming way, of course," she adds quickly and puts her hand on my arm to show I ain't to take offense. "An unpolished gem, as it were."

"Oh?" I gets up on one elbow to face her direct. "And what do I do wrong that makes me all those things?"

She considers the question, and, at length, she plunges forward. "When you hurt, Jacky, you cry. When you are unhappy, you whine. When you are mad, you curse, and when you are threatened, you resort to violence. You talk with your mouth full and lean over your plate. You dash madly about when an impulse takes you, and you never walk when you can run. You say the first thing that comes to your mind, and the profanity, like with the Sheik yesterday, oh, Jacky, you have just *got* to stop that."

As if recognizing his name spoken, the stallion wickers and snorts down below. "You hush up, horse," I orders, "or I'll see you salted down in a barrel and served up to poor sailors who'll curse you for your toughness and lack of flavor, I will." I have already cajoled my way onto the back of the Sheik—the stable hands are finding me hard to deny, 'cause of my persistence.

She pauses to take a breath and then goes on. "And that way you have of grinning with your mouth open, looking like a vixen that has just killed a poor goose and is reveling in the blood that drips from her jaws, well…There, you're doing it right now. Stop it. Please."

"Shall I make that prissy little Clarissa smile?" I screw my lips up into a prune shape and cross my eyes.

I can see she is warming to her task in spite of my clowning. "And your references to your personal things: It is *not* your petticoats, *not* your shifts, *definitely* not your underpants, it is your *linen.* As in, 'I must have my *linen* cleaned,' not, as you would have it, 'Oi've got to scrub out me drawers!'"

For this I give the sad-eyed, abashed look and say, "You must be very ashamed of me, Sister."

"Not at all," she says. "I love you as my life. But you did ask…"

"All right, all right. Go on." I sprawls on my back again. "Lay on, Amy, and get it all out."

"Well. Then there's that right there. You should never lie or sit with your limbs apart like that."

I snaps my legs together.

"And they are your *limbs,* Jacky, and that is how you should refer to them, not as your legs or arms or anything else."

"Even when it's just us girls?"

"Even so." Amy's mouth is set in the same thin line as Mistress Pimm's.

"Farewell, legs. Hello, limbs," I says. "What is this, then?" I point.

"Your *knee.* Part of your limb. And, yes, your *thigh,* too, is part of your *limb,* and never discussed."

"And me rump?" I asks, pointing to my bottom.

"Your *derriere.* The less said, the better."

"And these?"

"*Décolletage* would be best. Or *breast,* but singular, never plural."

242

"And this?"

"That is your *abdomen,* dear, not your *belly* nor your *stomach.* Discussed only with your doctor." She knows that she is being played with, but she goes on. "And no more picking of the nose, should you get around to pointing to that part. And as to that, a lady does not point, either."

I take a deep breath and let out a long sigh. "Farewell, nose, friend of my idle hours. Farewell, too, my belly. Maybe as Miss Ab Domen you will not trouble me so much with your wants."

I grin what I now know is my foxy grin and lift my hand and am about to point to the really good stuff when she drops her head and says, "Now you are going to shock me and it is not fair, for I am such an easy target."

She looks down at her hands wringing in her lap and doesn't say anything more. I see from her expression that I was about to go too far with her.

"I'm sorry, Amy." I rustle about and straighten myself out on the straw and say, "I don't want to be a lady like Clarissa, but I do want to be a lady like you, and I will listen to you and learn."

In spite of all my foolery, she seems touched by what I say.

I lift my hand to my brow and make a salute. "I, Jacky Faber, Maiden First Class, await your further instructions, Ma'am!"

I thinks then about Jaimy and our hammock and then adds, "Better make that Maiden *Second* Class," and I wrap my arms about myself and rock back and forth, giggling.

"I do not believe you are one at all," she blurts out. "There. I have said it." Her face is blushing furiously.

"Are one what?" I asks, wondering what she's gettin' at.

"A...a maiden," she whispers in mortification.

I drop the smile and give a low whistle. "What you must think of me, Miss," I say.

"No, no...I am sorry. Forgive me. It is just that...that I worry about you, Jacky. Things you have said, things you have done...I'm sorry," she says, and covers her face in shame. "Let us talk about something else, please, Sister. I am sorry."

I gaze upon her and remember Mistress telling me to keep my mouth shut about my past, but that was before I was kicked out of the ranks of the ladies.

I consider that and then I says, "Would you like to hear my little story, then?"

"I would, yes, I suppose I would," she says in relief and in, I think, some dread.

"Even the rough parts?"

She gulps and then nods.

"All right, then," I says, lying back. "And if afterward you want to put me out, I'm all right with that and won't hold it against you. I know I'm free and easy in my ways, and I know that might not sit right with someone like you who was brought up proper. My seabag is always packed and I can be gone in five minutes. Agreed?"

"I would never put you out. Never."

"Never say never, Amy. It has a way of coming back on you."

I put my hands behind my head and look off into the high rafters of the barn, and back through the Caribbean and the Mediterranean and the *Dolphin* and Jaimy and the

244

Brotherhood and Cheapside and Charley and the gang and back to that day, That Dark Day.

At last I close my eyes and begins to speak.

"My name is Jacky Faber and in London I was born, but, no, I wasn't born with that name. Well, the Faber part, yes, the Jacky part, no, but they call me Jacky now and it's fine with me. They also call me Jack-o and Jock and the Jackeroe, too, and, aye, it's true I've been called Bloody Jack a few times, but that wasn't all my fault. Mostly, though, they just call me Jacky.

"That wasn't my name, though, back on That Dark Day when my poor dad died of the pestilence and the men dragged him out of our rooms and down the stairs, his poor head hanging between his shoulders and his poor feet bouncin' on the stairs, and me all sobbin' and blubberin' and Mum no help, she bein' sick, too, and my little sister, as well.

"Back then my name was Mary."

It was much harder to tell than I thought it would be and much, much later when I am finished and I lie shuddering and sobbing in her arms, Amy says, "How silly we must all seem to you."

And then, as I quiet down and subside, she says, "Never, *ever* again think that you are less than any lady."

Chapter 22

J. Faber
General Delivery
U.S. Post Office
Boston, Massachusetts, USA
October 18, 1803

Dear Jaimy,

We're back at the school, Amy and me, and I'm mooning out the window, watching the clouds roll by like great big puffy sailing ships and putting together in my mind the stuff I'm gonna tell you about in this letter. All about Amy's farm, Dovecote, and how beautiful it is and what a great time I had there. And about how on Sunday, after church—can you believe it, Jaimy, the place is so big it has its own little chapel—after church, they put a saddle on the Sheik, he's this big Thoroughbred, and were walking him around the paddock just to give him a little exercise, and after a little begging, they let me get up on him and you wouldn't believe how big he is and how strong. He'd a little jockey-type saddle on him, the kind where the stirrups are real high so that your knees are right up by your chin when you're sitting, but you don't sit, you stand in the stirrups and put your bottom in the air and your face over the horse's neck. Or rather, your limbs and derriere and visage. I'm trying, Jaimy, I am trying to become a lady, even though I ain't in the lady school anymore.

Anyway, we're walking around and around and I'm thinking of kicking him up to a trot, what could it hurt after all, when a breeze comes up and the paddock gate swings open because it wasn't latched proper. Now, I swear it wasn't me that took the horse out that gate, that it was the horse his own willful self, but nobody believes me, but one thing for sure, we are out and gone. The Sheik gathered himself and leaped straight into a full gallop and we were off across the yard and down the road, my face bein' whipped by his flyin' mane, my lower limbs clutchin' his back, and we fly. How we did fly!

We were pounding down the road and I saw the main racecourse up ahead and I managed to steer him toward it 'cause I thought it'd be better to run him there 'cause I didn't want him stepping in a hedgehog hole out in the fields and breaking one of his precious legs, and we got on the track and I knew this is a place he knew real well 'cause he got right up against the rail and he flew, Jaimy, he flew! The white fence posts flickered by in the corner of my eye as he roared along, hooves pounding and throwing up great clots of turf and the foam from his mouth and the snot from his nose blowing in my face but I didn't care for wasn't I having the ride of my very life!

Once around, twice, and still he showed no signs of wanting to stop but I thought it might be best that he don't burst his noble heart just now and I started pulling back on the reins and at first he resisted, but then he gave in and started to slow and I saw the stable hands running toward us with ropes and I pulls him back harder and he reared up on his hind legs and I yelled in his ear, "Scream, Sheiky, Scream!" And he did. He screamed out all his defiance and his rage and his joy and everything that's wild and wonderful in him. Glory!

Then I slid off his back and took the reins and led him over to George, who gave me a murderous look and took the reins and led the Sheik back to his stall, but not before the Sheik of Araby looked back at me as if to say, "See, little human? See?"

So now you can put Horse Stealer next to my name along with liar, murderer, mutineer, beggar, thief, and, I suppose, lewd and lascivious dancer, but I swear I didn't take the horse out. But then, I don't want to swear on anything too sacred, either.

I met Amy's brother Randall, too, when I was at Dovecote. He's quite a dashing young man, a lieutenant in the Yankee militia and about the same age as you, dear, but not nearly as handsome. Actually, if you two ever were to meet, I think you'd be at sword's point in no time, as he is a bit of an arrogant rotter. But not without some charm, I think. On the second day I was there he was a bit more civil to me and even called me by my name, even though I am merely a serving girl now. I told him how I got demoted and he seemed to feel for me in my distress over the incident. He even showed me around a bit.

Amy and I left Dovecote to go back to school on Monday and we did it the same way we came down—with me in full fig as Midshipman Jack Faber—and all went well on our return ride.

When we got back to the Lawson Peabody, Amy wanted to sneak in quietly but I would have none of it. A delicious situation like this and we should waste it? "Oh no, my Sister, we must launch you into legend and song," I said, and I led us clattering into the street behind the school, where the dormitory windows look down but Mistress's windows do not, and I wheeled us about in grand fashion, with the horses' whinnies *and their hooves making a great loud show of it, till I spotted a few faces in the windows and then I bounded down and gave up my hand and helped Amy off of Hildy. I escorted her to the top of the back stairs and bent over in an elegant bow and kissed her hand, saying, "Your reputation is made, my dear, just keep up your end of it—if anyone asks about that young man, just smile all mysterious and shake your head, as if you could not possibly tell."*

Waving farewell, I leaped back on Gretchie and galloped off, hallooing like any love-struck lad. You should have seen it, Jaimy. It was grand.

Here I put up my pen for a bit to recall how, after I'd dropped Amy off, I went back to the stables to drop the horses off, but then I figured I had to talk to Ezra about how things stood so why not ride Gretchie down into town and save me the walk? Besides, I didn't want to go back into the school till I knew how things stood with the Preacher— didn't want to just walk on in and find I was already delivered into his hands.

So I rode down into town and, of course, as soon as I turned off State Street, whom did I encounter but Constable Wiggins, swingin' his stick and peerin' up at me. He nodded and brought his stick to his brow by way of salute, but I put on my best young aristocrat damn-your-eyes, couldn't-be-less-interested-in-a-lowly-constable look and ignored him. As I passed on, I knew that he was standing back there scratching his head and wondering just where he'd seen me before.

I pulled up to Ezra's door and tied the good Gretchen's reins to the hitching post and got inside quick.

"So, Mr. Pickering," I said when I spotted him at his desk, behind a pile of papers, peering over his spectacles at me, "it looks like you increase and prosper. Perhaps I have brought you luck." I flopped down in a chair and crossed my limbs. "What news have you for me, then?"

Ezra gazed at me for a long while. Then he said, "You no longer amaze me, Jacky, as you beggar the imagination. You are completely incorrigible and I suppose I must accept that fact in my dealings with you. I will do so. Starting as of now, I will no longer give you advice as regards to your personal conduct. I will only give you legal advice. Agreed?"

"Yes, Ezra," I said, all meek, 'cause that's the way he seems to want it.

He harrumphed a few times and then said, "The Court on Friday accepted Reverend Mather's petition for review. I entered a counterproposal stating that if you had to be assigned guardianship, you preferred it be the Boston Asylum for Women. It is a refuge for females in distress and also takes in orphans. It has a fine reputation, and if you had to go there, I believe you would agree with my assessment. At any rate, this move delays action on his petition by many weeks."

"Good. You worry the Preacher from your end and I'll work on him from mine," I said.

"What's that supposed to mean?"

It means I got a plan, Ezra, that's what it means, I thought to myself, but I didn't say nothin', I just shook my head and looked off.

Ezra looked hard at me and told me not to do anything stupid, and I said that I won't and I put on my innocent look and that seemed to satisfy him.

He shuffled some papers and held one up. "I took the

liberty of drawing up incorporation papers so that, should we reclaim your money, you would have a place to put it where it could not be easily taken from you because of your minority and femaleness. Essentially, your corporation is a separate legal entity in which you would own all the shares. It is a layer of protection." Ezra looked at me to see if I understood. I did.

"Ain't you some smart, Ezra," said I, beaming in appreciation. "I could not have a better lawyer or a better friend."

"What do you want to name this corporation?"

"Faber Shipping, Worldwide."

"No sense aiming low, is there?" said Ezra, taking up his quill and dipping it in his inkwell and scratching away. "There. Faber Shipping, Worldwide. One hundred shares, all held by J. Faber, President. So recorded by E. R. Pickering, Esquire, Clerk of the Corporation. I shall file this copy with the Court Registry, and you shall have this other copy. If you ever make changes, such as sell shares or appoint officers, you must tell me. Do you understand?"

"I do, Ezra, and I thank you." I stood and took the paper and slid it inside my jacket and prepared to leave.

"Your friend Amy. Is she well?"

"Yes. She is back at the school. Resting, I suppose. Knowing me has proved a bit of a trial to her, I think."

"I can well imagine," he said, his small smile back in place. He got up and escorted me outside. I gathered Gretchen's reins and stuck my left foot in the stirrup. Ezra sighed and averted his eyes as I swung my right leg across. I looked down on him as Gretchie started to caper a bit. I knew she wanted to get home to her little stall. Knowing me is rough on her, too.

"I know you don't approve of me or my ways, Ezra, but I got to make my way in this world the best I can. I got to work with what talents I got 'cause ain't nobody gonna look out for me but me. I *will* play my music, I *will* sing my songs, I *will* dance my dances. And sometimes, as I have found in my life, it's easier being a boy. That's the way of it. Till later, Ezra."

I turned Gretchen's head and off we trotted. She wasted no time getting back to her stable, her stall, and her oats.

I shake those thoughts from my head and go back to my letter.

You know, Jaimy, you might hear things about me from sailors crossing back and forth across the great ocean—about me singing and dancing and playing music in taverns and sometimes getting in trouble with the law and such, but I've been a good girl for you, Jaimy, I really have, so don't put no stock in it at all. I've been learning lots of things from Peg, the head housekeeper, and the downstairs girls are sweet and I've been keeping up with my higher studies, and all the teachers ('cept Mistress) have been ever so kind in helping me on the sly and so I've been keeping up. Amy helps me, too, and I love her for that and for being my friend.

I believe I see HMS Excalibur *being brought to the dock. I must hurry and get this all down on paper and get it ready to send.*

Please write to me. I'm afraid you have forgotten me, Jaimy. I'm afraid of that, I am.

Yours,
Jacky

Chapter 23

It being Wednesday, we're deep into the washing, the water hot and sudsy and steaming and all of us sweating with our paddles going, swirling the sheets and pillowcases and net bags of small clothes around about in the big tubs. Later, the bedclothing will be wrung out by hand and hung to dry outside. The ladies' *linen* will be taken out of the bags and scrubbed out against the washboard and done singly so as not to mix them up. I try not to notice whose linen I'm doing when I do that job.

Betsey is working next to me and I tell her about Amy and me meeting with Ephraim and she listens with keen interest, nodding sharply at each recollection of his words and his suspicions.

"Betsey, tell me what Janey looked like," I says. I run my forearm across my forehead to take off the sweat. "Her hair and how big she was and all."

"Here, take the other end," she says, and I reach in and grab the other end of the sheet she is beginning to twist, and I haul it out and start twisting my end in the opposite way so as to wring the water out. Then she says, "She was small, not much bigger than you, and she was tight like you, too, wiry and strong and not afraid of work. In fact, you remind me a lot of her, in her cheerfulness and happy nature and all…" She pauses and I know this is hard for her. She takes a breath and then goes on. "'Cept for the hair, though…Her hair was almost white blond and she wore it in the Dutch fashion, you know, the bangs cut straight across over the eyes and the rest hanging straight."

"Did she dress as we do?"

"Yes. The same."

We fall silent, and then there is a jangle as Mistress's bell rings over our heads. It is a bell on a cord that goes through a hole in the ceiling, up through the floor, and into Mistress's office where it runs through a pulley system and ends in a black (of course) tassel hanging by her desk. The rule is, one of us has to answer the call before she takes her hand off the cord, or watch out.

"Betsey. You," says Peg, and Betsey dries off her hands and squares away her apron and cap and runs upstairs.

In a moment she is back with a note that she hands to Peg, who opens it, reads it, and sighs, and says, "Mistress has invited a bunch of the boys from the college over for the afternoon tea. Miss Howe is to be the hostess and she has picked Sylvie and Jacky to serve. We are to finish up with the laundry, serve dinner, and then you all are to help the ladies prepare." Peg claps her hands. "Let's go, girls. Mistress has done it again!"

Sylvie and I look at each other. Of course. The one Clarissa slapped and the one who fought her, right there under her control. Shows us who's boss, now, don't it?

As I rush about doing my duty, I'm thinking that Mistress prolly sprung this as a surprise so that the ladies would just spend one day getting ready, instead of a whole week. *And* keep them on their toes and get them used to preparing on the spur of the moment—never can tell when the President's gonna drop by, don'cha know. And I figures Mistress set this whole thing up so's the ladies could show off their refinement and good manners and social skills in mixed company. And maybe to scout out some future marriage prospects, *hmmm*? Mistress did say that all her girls made good matches.

The place is in a dither of excitement all day as the ladies rush about furiously powdering and perfuming and combing and primping. There's not much done in the way of school-work after the noon meal, that's for sure. All us girls are pressed into service, combing and putting up hair, brushing out and ironing dresses, and suchlike, but finally, all is done and the boys arrive and are met at the door by Abby and Annie all starched and primped and in their best uniforms. Swords and scabbards are unhooked from sword belts and are placed in the cloakroom next to the entrance foyer, and then Mistress appears and she takes the young men up to the tea room, where the ladies anxiously await their coming.

There are introductions and bows and curtsies and dimples and giggles, blushes, and female eyes peeking out over the tops of fans and males strutting about, and oh, but there will be a lot of posing and posturing this day, depend on it, and all, *all* under the very watchful eye of Mistress, for woe be to any boy who would venture to as much as touch any of the ladies, and even more woe to any lady who would allow such a thing to happen.

Except that Mr. Randall Trevelyne is allowed to take Miss Clarissa Worthington Howe's hand to bring her up from her curtsy, 'cause they're engaged to be married, so it's all right. And even those lovely hands are in snow-white cotton gloves, white gloves that she had me wash and dry before the fire earlier today. At least I didn't have to comb and set her hair—she didn't trust me to be so close to her face with the hot curling iron, and well she shouldn't.

There are clusters of easy chairs grouped around low tea tables on which the cups and saucers and spoons and napkins are set, and Clarissa leads Randall to the one she has selected for herself—the grandest one, the one with the largest bouquet of flowers on it and, as the central one, visible to the entire room. Randall pulls out her chair, she places her lovely bottom in it, and all are seated. They do look splendid together, I got to admit—Clarissa in a dress of white with touches of pink here and there, low cut in the latest French style, her shining blond hair piled high with cunning little ringlets to the side, and Randall is the very picture of male beauty in a velvet coat of the deepest crimson with white lapels and white lace at the throat and cuffs, snow-white breeches, and black boots to the knees. A lot of the boys are wearing crimson, I notice. Prolly the school's color.

Also seated there is her pet Lissette and a few other carefully selected toadies and some young men of various sizes and shapes, one of whom seems especially taken with the Frenchy, with her exotic manners and haughty ways. He is trying to speak to her in stumbling French and is making a fearful botch of it, I'm afraid. His name seems to be Chadwick and she is not being very nice to him at all. I get the feeling that she'd much rather be next to Randall, and for that, I would not blame her. Amy's at this setting, too, in a state of cold fury, she being family and all and required to be there.

Clarissa beckons to me and I take teapot and tray and over I go.

I pour Clarissa's tea first, then the rest of the ladies, and then Randall. He looks up at me as I fill his cup. "It is good to see you again, Jacky," he says.

This surprises me a bit, but I recover and dip and say, "It is kind of you to say so, Lieutenant Trevelyne. I trust you are well." I notice the male chest swell a bit at my use of his military rank. I meet his gaze and then drop my eyes and go to fill the rest of the cups.

I am not the only one surprised by this—I heard a sharp intake of breath from Clarissa's direction at this exchange of pleasantries and I steal a glance at her. The Queen is *not* pleased, that's for sure. Her eyes are narrowed as she stares at me with undisguised loathing.

"You," she says to me, "take care of the next table. And try to do it right."

I wait a moment before I say, "Yes, Miss." Not a pause long enough to make me guilty of outright insolence, but long enough for her to get the point. I go off to another table, but on my way I look back at Randall and find that he is looking back at me, and I lower my eyelids and let the slightest of smiles come to my lips as I turn away. Clarissa misses none of this, I can tell—the pink of her cheeks has gone to a much less becoming shade of red.

Sylvie handles Clarissa's table for the rest of the party.

All in all, I reflect later when it's all over, a *most* satisfactory tea.

That night, after all the giggling over the events of the day subsides and prayers are said and Mistress retires, Amy sneaks out of her bed into the darkness and goes out into the hall and up the stairs to my door, where she opens the latch and slips into my room, where I am waiting for her. We sit on my bed in our nightdresses and talk real low till we are sure that all below are asleep.

Amy looks around at my room, what she can see of it in the light of the lamp. I had gotten tired of the guttering candles that Mistress issued to me and bought this whale oil lamp yesterday when I had snuck down to the Pig to see when Gully was gettin' sprung. It didn't cost much and works really fine—good, even light and not much smoke, so I get to read and study my French and Music and work on my miniatures far into the night. I don't seem to need a lot of sleep, prolly 'cause of all those watches I stood on the ship.

Amy notices my miniature I did of Jaimy that I hung on my bedpost so it is the last thing I see at night before I snuff the lamp and the first thing I see when I wake.

"That is your young man?" she asks, and I say yes, but it's not a good likeness 'cause he's much more handsome than that and my poor skill does not do him justice at all.

"He is a lucky young man," says Amy, and she turns to looking at my books. She picks up one and reads the title, "*Barnabas Bickford, a History of Wantonness and Dissolution.*" And then another, "*The Rake's Progress.*"

She considers these for a moment and then asks, wonderingly, "Where ever did you get these? Surely not from the school library?"

"No. I got them from dear old Mr. Yale, who has the

bookseller's shop on School Street. He lent me the books in return for me sweeping up a bit when I can," I says.

"No moss ever grows on you, does it, Sister?"

"Well, I was down there the other day, and I figured, why not give it a try?"

"You were abroad in the town again and you were not arrested?"

"I am not always arrested, Sister, as I know my way around."

"Why did you go, other than pure contrariness?"

"I had to find out when Gully was getting out of the slammer so as to know when we're gonna put on our act again."

"And when is that?"

"Friday night. Then Saturday afternoon and Saturday night. Three full sets."

"I wish you would not do it, Jacky, I really do wish that. You are going to get in trouble. Again." She wrings her hands, and I know that she is genuinely distressed.

"I must do it, Amy. I must get some money together so I can leave if I have to. Have I told you that Mistress means to marry me off as soon as a 'suitable match' is found?"

"That is horrid and wrong," she says. "I cannot believe it. Not even Mistress would do that."

I snort out a quick bark of a laugh. "When you fall in Mistress's eyes, you fall hard and far, that's for sure. A 'suitable match' indeed! Prolly to some no-account scoundrel who'll take my money and work me to the bone and then turn me out when I'm broke down and useless. Well, believe me, Sister, it's not gonna be that way. I'll run away first, I will, and if I have to cut and run because of it, well, I'd rather have some money in my pocket than to go out in the world all penniless again."

"Where would you run to?" asks Amy.

I consider this and say, "If I didn't have enough money to book passage back to England, I would go to New York, I think. I hear they might be more tolerant of my ways than Boston seems to be. I would work the taverns there till I had enough money to cross the pond."

I lean over and turn the wick on the lamp down as low as I can without it going out, as I don't want to have to creep down to the fireplace in the dormitory to light it again. "So you see that I must do what I must do. Come, let us go up on the widow's walk."

I rise and go over and pull down my stairway to the stars.

And stars there are. It is a brilliant night and the moon is just rising and the stars are as jewels in the heavens and I name them and point them out to Amy. I especially point out my old friend Orion and Polaris, the North Star, which always tells the poor sailor where north is and what latitude he is on.

We both lean on the railing and look out over the town, struck by the beauty of the tiny lights that twinkle in the city and the moonlight gleaming on the harbor beyond.

We are silent for a while and then Amy asks, "What do you want out of life, Jacky?"

I don't have to think hard on that, as it's what I always wanted since first I stepped on the *Dolphin*. "I'd like to have a small ship, one that could take cargo here and there around the world. So I could get my Bombay Rat and Cathay Cat, and see the Kangaroo."

"And what does that mean?

"It's just a line from a song I heard sailors singing back in London when I was on the streets. It sorta summed up for me the yearning I felt to better my condition and see the world and all its wonders. That yearning I feel yet, strong as ever."

"And if your Mr. Fletcher wants you to stay at home and keep house?"

I smile at that. "Ah, Jaimy knows me better than that, he does. He knows I got a streak of the wild rover in me and would soon get restless and unhappy in a calm and settled life." *My Mr. Fletcher,* I think, the smile slipping from my face, *is he really?* It's been almost two months and still no letters. *What's wrong, Jaimy?*

"And what do you want out of your life, Sister?" I ask Amy in return. I suck in the cool night air, looking out over the water to where Britain lies. She is quiet for a time.

"I want to write poetry and prose and I want to publish it, and I want to lecture about my writing and the writing of others before halls of educated people and I want..." She stops. "It does not matter what I want, because it is not going to happen. Women do not publish, as it is *unseemly.* It is just not done—their sensitive natures, you know, and the disgrace to their families, well, it is just not done, not in New England, anyway, and I do not want to talk about it anymore."

"Seems to me you could publish what you want to publish, if you've got the money to pay the printer. I know there's women in England who write novels and sell them," says I, a little mystified as to what one can and cannot do in this world. Seems to me that money drives what you can and cannot do. "Mr. Yale has a print shop next to the bookstore, should you need it."

Amy cuts her eyes to mine. "As a matter of fact, I *do* have a project in mind—"

"Hush! Amy, get down! He's there!" and I pull her by her sleeve down to the deck of the widow's walk and we lie there and peer out through the railing posts at the Preacher's lighted window.

First he opens the window and leans out and peers intently at Janey's grave and then he pulls back and the arm and the finger start pointing and he starts into talking and he starts saying words like *demon* and *devil* and *Satan* and *Babylon,* and Amy and me, whose faces are right close together, look at each other in amazement.

Then the Preacher goes into his thing of talking to someone not in the room and we hear snatches like *"Grandfather, I know!"* and then *"Something will be done, I swear!…"* and then he steps back into the room and we can hear only muffled sounds. After a pause, he lunges back to the window and says, *"I know she is one, too, and she will pay, oh I swear it, Grandfather, I swear it!"* and I get the feelin' that he ain't talking about poor Janey now, and I wonder what I'm guilty of. Besides the usual, that is.

I look over toward Janey's grave and I shudder, 'cause I know for certain that if he gets me over there I will soon lie beside her.

I look at the overarching oak tree and resolve that I will hear the Reverend Mather a lot more closely tomorrow night.

After the Preacher subsides and turns out his lamp, Amy and I get up and go back down to my room.

"Please, Sister," I say as we come back into the small circle of my lamp, "stay with me tonight, as I feel the nightmare coming on."

Soon we are abed and I snuff out the lamp and I burrow into her side and the nightmare does not come.

Chapter 24

I take the packet of black powder and open it and pour the contents into the steaming pail of water I have prepared and then I take a stick and stir. This done, I take the britches that I got off poor Charlie the night he died and plunge them into the dye and poke them down with the stick and swirl them around. I'll leave the whole thing sit for an hour or two and then I'll pour off the dye and rinse out the britches and hang them to dry. It won't be a great dye job, but it will do for my purposes.

I had been keeping the pants in my seabag 'cause, though they are tight, I can still get them on. There's a New England homily that I heard Peg say one day that goes "Use it up, wear it out, make it do, or do without," and I holds to that motto, as it appeals to my practical nature.

I got the dye this morning at the chemist's at the end of Sprague's Wharf when Abby and I were sent down to the market to get some fresh-killed chickens. We don't usually kill our own hens, as long as they keep on laying eggs, but we do kill the roosters when we get too many of them or when we have a pressing need. A while back I was taken out and shown the ax and the chopping block with its two nails stuck in it about an inch apart, which is where you put the chicken's head and then stretch out his neck out and then…I couldn't look, and one day when Peg said, "Jacky, go kill two chickens. I need 'em for the broth," I took the ax, but I dragged Annie outside and begged and pleaded for her to do it and she did. In spite of the nickname I picked up on the ship, Bloody Jack don't like killin' and she ain't particularly partial to blood.

I also bought a watch cap, one of those black knit woolen things that sailors wear rolled up on top of their heads when it gets a bit chilly and pull down over their ears when the weather turns harsh. I've already got one, of course, but I'm going to need another. Abby looks at me funny when I pays a penny for that, but I just say that winter is coming.

"It ain't exactly the fashion," says Abby, with a laugh. It's always a joy to come to town with the plump and jolly Abby, she of the red curls stuffed up in her cap, she with her wandering eye for the lads—won't be long before she's married and dandling a fat baby on her knee, I'll wager.

"Don't matter," says I.

This morning, too, I gather up some sooty ashes from the edge of the fire and put them in an old cracked jar, and, let's see, I'm going to need an extra bucket of water in my room and some old ragged towels that no one will miss, an old mop.

I get all these things and I sneak them up to my room and stash them in the shadows where the roof rafters meet the floor.

Then I go down and attend to my duties.

———

I am easy in my duties now. I know how to make bread and am skilled in washing and ironing, and under Peg's sweet guidance, I am learning to cook. I keep up with my studies on the sly and steadily improve in my painting and my music—I can read the little musical notes now and Maestro Fracelli is showing me some things on the fiddle as I have shown interest 'cause of listening to Gully. I'm even doing some embroidery. Mistress would be proud, if she knew, but if she knew she'd prolly beat me for neglecting my duties, so it's better she don't know.

In turn I've been helping Rebecca with her reading and writing and math, she being the little girl I talked to my first day here as we sat all miserable doing our samplers. Poor thing, she's really too young to be here and seems so lost. So, anyway, I'm paying back in instruction for the instruction I've been getting, and that seems fair to me.

Clarissa doesn't bother much with me anymore, now that I have been, in her eyes, completely destroyed, and am no longer worthy of her steel—though she does keep a wary eye on me since that little thing with Randall at the Grand High Tea. The serving of the meals is no longer the humiliation that it was at first. I am used to it now, and so is everyone else. It is merely a job to be done and, it is to be hoped, done well.

We do the noon dinner and then clean up, and later I help Dolley, Miss Frazier, that is, serve the afternoon tea, as it is her turn. She is gracious and charming and she orders me about with a brisk but kind manner that I hope I will be able to show someday if I ever have servants, which ain't likely. Dolley is going to be a fine lady, I can tell. She already is one.

When I help serve the evening meal, I notice how the Preacher's eyes seek me out every few minutes for a split second and then dart away. Not plain enough for anyone else to notice, of course, he is much too careful about that. But I do, and if I had any doubts as to which girl he was talking about last night, I don't have them now.

What I can't figure, though, is how he can appear almost sane now, in the daytime, and then turn into a raving lunatic at night.

Maybe he's a werewolf.

This night I sit and talk with Amy and I give her *The Rake's Progress* to read and I say for her to take it with her downstairs but she says no, Mistress will take it if she sees her reading it—*unseemly*, you know—and so she will read it only when she is upstairs here with me.

And so we each curl up with our books and we read till we hear the call for prayers downstairs and I tell Amy not to come back up 'cause I'm going to be all right with the nightmares tonight and she shouldn't risk getting caught hanging about with the servants—*unseemly*, you know—and she agrees and goes below.

I read for a bit and then when things go completely quiet in the school, I get out of bed and take off my nightdress and pull on Charlie's pants that are black now and quite tight from the dye bath, but that's good 'cause I don't need any extra fabric flappin' around me tonight. I put on my black sweater and over that my black vest. I think about shoes, but I know I can climb better without 'em, so I stick to my bare feet, which have always served me well in the past, no matter what the rigging.

I cram my faithful old black watch cap down over my hair and low on my brow. Then I go to my jar of soot and take some and rub it over my face to take the white shine off of it and I do the same to my feet.

Then I go and pull down the stairway and go up to the widow's walk.

He is not yet at his window, but somehow I feel he will be tonight, because of the glances he sent my way at supper this evening, so I put my foot on a stout branch of the overarching oak tree and begin to climb.

The moon is rising and that makes it easier for me to make my way through the branches, but it also makes it easier for me to be spotted in spite of my burglar's gear and so I am careful to move slowly.

Soon I am over the trunk of the tree, midway between the two buildings, and I pick out the branch that will lead me to the church. I begin to climb out on it and it sinks under my weight until it touches the roof and makes it easy for me to step onto the tiles of the church roof. When I get off, the branch lifts a bit, so I will have to leap up for it on my return.

I quickly pad over the roof to the gable above the window from which he holds forth, and I nestle down into the shadows of the gutter to await his arrival.

It occurs to me while I sit there and wait that most girls might find this a strange and scary thing to do, but to me it ain't much different from being on watch at three in the morning and sitting astride the main royal yardarm and taking in a line to trim a sail that don't want to be trimmed 'cause of shifting winds.

Then, too, I reflect on how me and the gang in Cheapside would climb to the tops of high buildings—first up on a low shed, then up to a low roof and then to a higher one, then higher and higher as the buildings were all close together and we could jump from one to the other till we got to the top of the highest one. We did this sometimes for safety, like when some of the bigger gangs was at war and we needed to stay out of the way, or when the police was keen on nabbing us, 'cause of what we'd been up to, but mostly we did it 'cause when we was up there we could spy out any profitable mischief down below—a pie cooling on a windowsill, or some clothing hung out to dry that we could pinch and sell to the ragman. And we did it 'cause it was fun.

I don't have to wait long. I hear a shuffling down below and then a lamp is lit and light pours out the window. I crawl to the end of the gable, straddling it with my legs to either side like I am riding a horse.

I sit and listen. I hear the window opening.

The arm and the hand at the end of it come thrusting out of the window so suddenly that I start back. I could lean over and touch the hand with the pointing finger, I am that close.

"There that one lies and well it should and the other one shall lie beside her and so shall all the evil witches in this hellish world by the living God I will make it so…what? Grandfather, what did you say?"

It chills me to hear these words, but I make not a sound. The hand is withdrawn and I hear a clink like…like what? Ah…like the clink of a bottle on a glass. Ah yes.

"Yes, Grandfather, in your day she would already be hanged…or burned…or drowned…but in these unholy times I must have proof or they will take me and end my ministry. Satan's minions control the courts. That damned popinjay of a lawyer she has enthralled, he thwarts my every move...that *damned little man, he mocks me to my face!*"

Good work, Ezra, I thinks, high up above on my perch.

Again I hear the clink of bottleneck on rim. I think I can even hear the gurgle of the spirits sloshing into the glass. I'm thinking that this explains a lot—it is the drink that pushes him over the edge into lunacy at night.

It is a pity. I much preferred him as a werewolf.

"I have been gathering evidence, Grandfather, I have learned that she carries the very mark of the Devil—a pitchfork!—on her belly, she does, and I am gathering other evidence, oh, do not mistake me..."

Now, how the hell did he find out about my tattoo? *Which, by the way, you demented lunatic, is an anchor,* not *a pitchfork. And it's on my hipbone,* not *on my abdomen.* I think on this...it had to be that louse Dobbs, who surprised me one day when I was taking a bath. Peg warned me to hurry up and get out 'cause Dobbs was comin' soon with wood for the fires, but me in my contrary way said don't worry I'll get out in a minute and I sank back into the lovely suds but he did come burstin' in just as I was gettin' out and I thought I got the towel up in time, but I guess I didn't. So the vile Dobbs is in the Preacher's pocket...Good to know.

"Yes, Grandfather, there will be the judgment. First the discipline, then the judgment. Just like the other one."

So there we have it. From his own mouth.

I have heard enough and make ready to make my return

when I have a idea. When he starts in to ranting again, I lean over and say real low in a wee, sad voice, *"Please, Sir, don't..."* just as I imagine Janey Porter did when first he came at her, she in all her innocence and he with worms crawling in his brain. Then I leap back over the roof beam of the church, the pads of my feet silent on the roof slates.

For sure that stopped his ravings real quick, and though I can't see him, I know he's craning his head around tryin' to see where the sound come from, but I also know he can't see nothin' but blackness.

I hadn't planned on doin' that tonight, it just come to me, but I figure it was a good opening shot across his bow. *Sleep well, Preacher.*

When I am back in my room, I sit on the edge of my bed and breathe deeply and think for a while. I had stayed up there on the church roof until the Preacher turned off the lamp and even a little longer after that to make sure he wasn't sitting there waiting to hear something like me getting back into the tree, which I can't do totally silent, and, sure enough, a little later I hear the window slide shut. Only then do I creep back into my tree.

I get up and take off my black clothes and scrub my face and ankles and feet with the water from the bucket and towel off with the ragged towels and hide them. Tomorrow I shall wash them on the sly.

Then I wash teeth, armpits, and parts in my usual way and get my nightclothes on.

But instead of turning to sleep, I turn up my lamp a bit and take out my new watch cap and my needle and thread.

Then I take the old mop and, with my shiv, cut strands of it off, some long, some quite short, and I begin sewing on the whitish strands. The long ones on the sides and back, the short ones on the front.

Like bangs.

Chapter 25

⚓ "Jacky, please don't go," implores Amy. We're up in my room, after supper, and I'm getting ready to go out.

"I got to go. Gully expects me," I says. "We've been making some serious money. After this weekend I may have enough to buy a cheap passage to London and Jaimy. The fleet's in and we play tonight and then twice tomorrow, and it should be good."

I've made a small bag built like a sling and it goes over my shoulder easy, and into it I'm stuffing my concertina and some stuff we use in the act, like my sailor shirt, the doll, and my *Dolphin* cap.

"But I worry about you so, out there all alone in the night," she says, low and whispery.

"So, come with me, then. It'll be fun."

Amy sits back down on the bed.

"But I'm scared," she says.

"Me, too. But if you're going to be poor like me, soon you'll have to go out in the world, scared or not."

"I suppose."

I lace up my weskit and slide in my pennywhistle and my shiv.

"What will you do if you're put out in the world, Sister?" I ask.

"I suppose I'll be made a governess to someone else's children...unless a match can be made for me."

"Not much fun, that. More fun to make your way on your own. It can be done. Even as a girl, alone. Come, we can rig you out with bits and pieces of clothing from downstairs and you'll look just like me. The wild and contrary Valentine Sisters, out on the prowl!"

"But I'll be missed at prayers tonight."

"Hmm...all right. You can't go out tonight, that's certain. But we'll do it tomorrow afternoon, for we do a Saturday afternoon show, as well as the nighttime one."

Ready now, I turn and go to the window.

"Please be careful, Jacky."

"I will, Sister. Turn off the lamp when you leave."

She says that she will, and I hook my leg through the open window and fit my foot on the first rung.

Much later when I return, smelling I'm sure of spilt ale and tobacco smoke and with much jingle in my purse, Amy is there in her nightclothes, sprawled across my bed with a book on her chest and the lamp long since gone out.

I open my seabag and add my handful of coins to my hoard and then get into my night togs. I rouse Amy enough to get her under the covers and on her side. She murmurs, "Thank goodness," and then falls back into sleep.

Dear Amy, I thinks, crawling in beside her and pulling the blanket up over both of us, *you need not have worried.*

The crowds were cheerful and well behaved and generous with their applause and their money.

We've added a closing number to our act and it went over wonderfully. It's called "The Parting Glass," and it's a slow song, almost a lament. Gully plays the straight melody and sings over it.

> *"Oh, all the money that ever I had*
> *I spent it in good company.*
> *And all the harm I've ever done,*
> *Alas, it was to none but me."*

I play a breathy countermelody over it all on my whistle to add a wistful touch, and after we do the final verse...

> *"And all I've done for want of wit*
> *To memory now I can't recall.*
> *So fill for me the parting glass,*
> *Good night and joy be with you all."*

Gully bows low and I do a deep curtsy and we are off. A perfect way to end the set and the evening.

"Always leave 'em wanting more, Moneymaker," says Gully, putting the Lady Lenore gently back in her velvet-lined bed. He had even cleaned up a bit and stayed almost sober the whole night and insisted on walking me home after our set. I said he didn't have to and was even a little suspicious and made sure my shiv was handy, but he was a gentleman and it was good walking and talking with him and not having to stay in the shadows.

He left me at the foot of my ladder, chuckling at my

arrangement. "Och, you're a rare 'un, you are, Money-maker," he whispered, and disappeared in the dark.

I put my hands behind my head and look off into the dark, too keyed up to sleep just yet, and I think back on another funny thing that happened tonight. These two gents come up to me after I was steppin' off the stage at the end of a set and they bow all polite and I'm watchin' 'em real careful for any false moves but they don't invite me upstairs or anything like that. Instead they hand me a small white card that says

Fennel & Bean
Thespians
Theatricals & Revues

I looked at the card and then blankly up at them.

"Actors, Miss. I am Mr. Fennel and this is Mr. Bean"—a sweeping bow. "We are always looking for talented young actresses. Are we not, Mr. Bean?"

"Yes, we are, Mr. Fennel," says Mr. Bean.

"But I'm not…"

"Oh, yes, you are. And we notice that you are not at all shy in performance," says Mr. Fennel.

"And you are also not shy about donning costume," says Mr. Bean.

"Please keep our card, Miss Faber. We will be staying the season at the Bull and Garter, giving performances at various fine halls about town. Please feel free to call on us at any time. Shall we go, Mr. Bean?"

"Yes, we shall, Mr. Fennel," says Mr. Bean.

I think on all that for a while, and then I turn over and go to sleep.

Chapter 26

Amy and me rolls into the Pig at about two the next afternoon and there's already a crowd gathering. My reputation grows. I know 'cause I get looks and even a small round of applause just by walking in. I hate to say it, but it warms me. I lower the eyes and dip a bit in answer to the claps and then take Amy up to Maudie at the bar.

"This here's Amy, Maudie. She'll help out during the rush. For tips. All right?" Me and the other girls had cobbled together a version of our uniform for Amy, so she don't stand out.

"For sure, Amy, any friend of Jacky is a friend of mine," says Maudie. She's lining up freshly washed glasses along the bar. "There's aprons hanging there. Put one on and get some change for your pouch, dear, for it looks like it's gonna be a good night." Maudie is fair beaming at the thought. I hear her man Bob rolling in another keg, and he looks right cheerful, too.

I give Amy a slight shove and I can feel her shoulder shaking under my hand, but she goes over and picks an apron and puts it on. *Do it, Amy. It's a skill like anything else and it never hurts to pick up another skill.*

"A nickel a pint and no one runs a tab," says Maudie. "Just dish it out and don't stand for no foolishness."

I can see that some of the glasses on several of the tables are getting low so I take an apron myself and says, "Here. I'll show you." I put the apron on over my head and tie the strings behind me and take a tray and go to the nearest table and say, "Gentlemen?"

"Aye. Three more, lass. And then come sit on my lap, like a good girl," says the biggest rogue of the lot, patting his leg. His friends guffaw and say, "Well said, Mike."

"I'll not try your lap, Sir," says I, "but I will get your pints."

I turn to Amy beside me and say so that they can hear, "You reach way in to get the glasses, that way they can't get too close to you, and always back up from the table so they can't grab your…can't pinch you. And if they do grab you, call for Bob and he'll come runnin' with his shillelagh and bash a few of 'em till they behave."

The men snort and say that they ain't afraid o' no Bob with no club, but I notice they don't give Amy no trouble when she goes back with the full glasses and collects the money.

"I have gotten a tip," she says, when she comes back to the bar. "The first money I have ever earned in my life."

"May it not be the last, dear," says I, as Amy heads back out to another table. I believe she will enjoy this. I know I do.

"So where's Gully?" I ask Maudie.

"Don't worry, he's about. He's being careful about the British warships in the harbor. He thinks he'll be pressed if they catch him, him being a seaman and Scottish and all."

"That and being the Hero of Culloden Moor," I says. "If

they take him, they'll surely hang him," says I. "He's got to be careful."

Maudie don't say nothing, but I get the feeling she ain't too worried about him being hanged for that. Two more tables come in and sit down.

"I guess I'll go up and do some solo," says I. "Get 'em warmed up, like."

"That would be good, Jacky," says Maudie.

I pull off my apron and take out my concertina and mount the little stage that Bob had built at the end of the room and begin to play. I don't give my usual show-opening patter but instead just play, 'cause I don't want them to get real worked up yet.

I do "The Blue-Eyed Sailor" and then step down from the stage and walk among the tables playing "Rosin the Beau," just playing, no singing or dancing, just something to get them in the mood. I brush by Amy and we exchange glances. She seems to be doing just fine.

The place is filling up and I see that some of the men have brought their wives with them—the word must be getting around that we run a clean act in a respectable public house. I had told Gully I didn't like singing the really bawdy songs like "The Cuckoo's Nest" and "Captain Black's Courtship" 'cause I didn't like the way the men looked at me when we did them—all smirks and knowin' winks and such—and Gully says that some men would look at me that way if I was up there in a white gown with wings and halo singin' the bloody *Messiah*, so leave off. But I say I don't mind being looked at—I am a performer, after all, and I like bein' the center of attention, but I don't like bein' snickered at or laughed at. So I get my way.

I know that Maudie eyes the women and makes sure they *are* wives, and not something else, before they are welcomed and seated. There are some taverns where Mrs. Bodeen's girls and their like are allowed, and some where they ain't, and the Pig is one where they ain't. "I run a good, clean public house and I don't need them here," she told me early on. "I don't need the men fightin' over 'em, and I don't need angry wives burstin' in with muskets loaded to blow the heads off wayward husbands. If I can't run a respectable house, then I won't run one at all."

I go back to my bag and pull out an old lace shawl that I got down at the rag shop and I put it on my head and whips one end around my neck and I step back on the stage. I note that there's a lot of Irish in the crowd and more coming in, so I decide to do "The Galway Shawl," which is about a young man on the road who meets a maid wearing a Galway shawl, like the one I'm wearing. This song is usually done with just the voice, but since I ain't done it before in front of an audience, I take out my pennywhistle and plays the melody, with a few embellishments, and then drops it and lifts my chin and sings:

> "In Erinmore in the County Galway,
>   One fine evening in the month of May,
>   I spied a Colleen she was tall and handsome,
>   And she nearly stole my heart away.
>
>   She wore no jewels or no costly diamonds,
>   And as for silken stockings she had none at all,
>   She wore a bonnet with a ribbon on it,
>   And o'er her shoulders hung a Galway shawl."

The maiden in the shawl takes the young man back to meet her father, her father who was six-foot tall, and the boy charms him by singing "Brown-Eyed Sailor" and "Foggy Dew" and the girl sits with the lad by the fire and they hold hands through the night. I warbles the last two verses.

"Early next morning I was on the High Road,
On the High Road out and bound for Donegal,
And as I wandered thoughts strayed wildly from me,
Dwelling with the maiden in her Galway shawl.

So all young men from me take warning,
Don't you love no maiden be she short or tall,
She'll wander with you in the mists of morning,
She'll steal your heart in her Galway shawl."

Just as I'm ending and bowing my head, Gully strides in with the Lady under his arm and the applause breaks out and Gully takes it for his and bows grandly and bounds to the stage and says, "Good one, Moneymaker, we'll add it to the act," and I flush with pleasure, and as Gully pulls out the fiddle and rips into "Bonny Kate," I nip off the stage and grab my bag and pull out my sailor top and sailor cap and pull them on. As Gully finishes up, I bound back on the stage to cheers and starts on the whistle and we swings into our act.

We're flying along and the crowd is in a state of near delirium with the music and the drink and we're coming up on our break and I ends with a fine rattle of me hooves and we bow and there are cheers and whistles and the lovely clatter of coins being thrown into the Lady Lenore's open case when there's the sound of horses pulling up outside and in a moment six young men swagger in. They're finely dressed, with swords clanking by their sides, and they look like they're just itching for trouble, and at their front is Randall Trevelyne and he has his best arrogant, sneering, damn-your-eyes look on his face.

Oh, Lord...

He walks up to the stage as if he had expected to find me here in this place. I can feel the ill will of the crowd toward these unwelcome puppies and I hope I can cut the fuse of this situation and calm things down. Randall hooks his thumbs in his sword belt and says, "Your reputation has extended across the river, Jacky, even unto the ivy-covered halls of academe. When I heard rumors of a girl in a sailor suit who sang and danced and played a tin whistle in one of the sailor bars, I knew it could be none other than yourself." It's plain that his friends find him a rare man-about-town in speaking to me as if he knows me well. *Well, he don't.*

"You are welcome here, Lieutenant Trevelyne," I say, and again I see the chest swell a few inches when I say it. "Please be seated and we will attend to your needs."

I turn to Gully and say under my breath, "College boys. Half drunk. Trouble. Do you know any college tunes?"

Randall strolls back to his table to the admiring looks of his chums and the black looks of the usual Pig patrons while Gully thinks and says, "I know some...mostly obscene, though...Ah, I know. *'Glorious!'* A real rouser! All will enjoy. Concertina, key of G. Chord along. Introduce it, Jacky, and tell 'em to sing along with the chorus."

I pick up my squeeze box and take a breath and announce to the crowd, "We have with us some fine lads from the college across the river and to give them a proper Pig and Whistle welcome, Mr. MacFarland and I will do 'Glorious' and we invite all to join in the chorus in the spirit of brotherhood and good fellowship!"

With that, Gully puts fiddle and bow to his sides and booms out the chorus.

> *"Glorious! Glorious!*
> *One keg of beer for the four of us!*
> *Glory be to God that there ain't no more of us,*
> *The four of us can drink it all alone!"*

I start droning out the chords on the concertina, but it's Gully's deep voice that's carrying the tune.

> *"The first thing we drank to*
> *We drank to the Queen*
> *Glorious, glorious, glorious Queen!*
> *If she have one son, may she also have ten!*
> *Have a whole bleedin' army cry the sophomores,*
> *Amen!"*

Gully does the chorus again, and the crowd, getting the form of it now, joins in with gusto, and then Gully sings the next verse, which is about the Prince and his horses, 'cept the crowd don't sing *"sophomores"* and other college words, they put in *sailors* or *soldiers* or whatnot, dependin' on their trade. The ladies in attendance pretend to blush like they ain't never heard words like these before. Then it's the chorus again and on to the last verse.

> *"The next thing we drank to*
> *We drank to the King*
> *Glorious, glorious, glorious King!*
> *If he have one mistress, may he also have ten!*
> *Have a whole bloomin' brothel cry the seniors,*
> *Amen!"*

I guess I should have seen that coming, but what's the harm in it, I thinks, the place is jumping and they all roar into the last chorus thumping the tables, stamping their feet, and making the rafters ring with their roaring, and they are as brothers.

More coins are tossed to us as we leave the stage, and just then Amy comes up to the table where the college boys are seated and says, "Gentlemen, another?"

"By God, yes!" says one of the boys, and Amy leans in to pick up the empty glasses. I see out of the corner of my eye that Randall is still looking at me, leaning back in his chair, his legs in their white breeches crossed, his knee-high black boots gleaming in the lamplight. He has lit a cheroot and draws on it and sends a puff of smoke in my direction.

"Watch your hands, Sir," warns Amy, and Randall, distracted from his examination of me, looks languidly over in the direction of her voice. That's the last languid thing he does this day.

He shoots to his feet. "Get your hands off her, Chadwick!"

"Wot? Trevelyne has dibs on all the dollies? It ain't fair!" protests the baffled Chadwick, as Randall grabs Amy's arm and hustles her off to the alcove at the end of the bar, where they will not be seen by his cohorts, and he puts her up against the wall.

"Just what in hell do you think you are doing?" he says, furious.

John Thomas notices all this, however, and makes a move toward them, but I put my hand on his chest and hold him back with "Don't, John. It's a family matter." John Thomas has become the self-appointed guardian-at-the-Pig of me, during his time ashore, and now of Amy, too, 'cause he feels responsible for getting me thrown in jail that time, and I can't say I'm sorry to have his rough protection.

I go to the bar to get a tray to take up Amy's slack and I catch a bit of what is said between the warring Trevelynes.

Amy squinches up her nose and comes back at him with, "I am learning a trade, Randall. What do you think *you* will be doing when Father loses everything? Join a grand regiment? Somehow I do not think that the finer units are hiring very junior officers from country militias just now!"

"You watch your mouth, Sister!"

"You let go of me, Randall! I am not afraid of you anymore."

"Here, here!" says Bob, coming up with his club.

"Get away, barkeep," Randall snarls. "Back to your slops."

"*Tsk, tsk,* you must think I'm one of those barkeeps what don't like pounding the nobs of spoiled little rich boys," says Bob with a grin. "You are sadly mistaken in that notion, lad." He hauls back his club and starts his swing at Randall's head.

"She is my sister!" says Randall, hunching up his shoulder to take the threatened blow. "Now leave off!" he says with what little dignity he has left.

Bob looks dubious but Amy nods and Bob lowers his club and says, "Well, hurry it up. She's needed out front."

I go by them to the bar and I see that both sets of Trevelyne teeth are bared.

"'Tis by keeping company with that low-life vagabond that has made you this way," he hisses.

"She is giving me instructions in how to make my way in the world while poor and destitute, Brother," Amy hisses right back at him. "And I assure you, she is an excellent teacher!"

Low-life vagabond? Well, I've been called much worse since first I set foot in Yankeeland, and actually, it sums me up pretty well, so I shan't take offense.

I don't hear more, as I take the tray of glasses meant for the college boys and go to their table. One grins and goes to grab my bottom and I scoots sideways. *Boys! I swear, why can't they be good?*

"You must behave yourselves in here, young gentlemen," I says. "There are some in here who would cheerfully rough you up and throw you out all bloody into the street."

The lad follows my glance over to John Thomas who has resumed his place by the wall and is glowering at the young man with very little love in his eye. "And here, in these close quarters, your fine swords would be of very little use, for this is the world of the bludgeon, the fist, and the sting of the hidden and wicked knife." The young man withdraws his hand and puts it on his glass.

"Thank you, gentlemen," says I, as I gather in the coins. "Please enjoy yourselves." I smile on all and say, "All are welcome at the Pig and Whistle."

Presently, Amy comes back into the room with her tray and goes to serve a table of British seamen in the corner.

Randall stalks back to his table and says, "Come on, we're going."

"Wot?" says his comrades. "We just got here!" but they down their glasses and stand.

I'm stepping back up onto the stage and I feel his eyes on me. I turn and meet his angry gaze.

"Come," he says to his friends, "there's better music down the street."

I hold his gaze and put the whistle to my lips and play a bit of "Yankee Doodle" and then I sing out the fragment, *"And with the girls be handy..."* and I let the final note hang in the air and then go flat and sour.

With that as a farewell, Lieutenant Randall Trevelyne turns on his spurred heel and retreats from the Pig and Whistle.

"He won't peach on you," I promises Amy, as we wind our way through the night-darkened alleys and backstreets on our way back to the school. I've worked out a route that takes me back and forth to the Pig with the least danger. I know what yards don't have barking dogs and are safe to cross. I don't cross the Common at night anymore, 'cause I've tripped over too many drunks sleeping it off in the grass and too many amorous couples who ain't exactly happy to hear my "'scuse me's," neither.

"Why not?" While she ain't really happy to be out in the city in the dark, she ain't as jumpy as she used to be.

"For one thing, what has he to gain? He just has the quick pleasure of seeing you in trouble and then what? Nothing. Except that *you* could then peach on *him* for being in a low dive. Do your parents know that he goes to places like the Pig? Or know who Mrs. Bodeen is? Nay, I'll wager Randall's been telling your mum and dad he's been taking tea with his divinity teacher Reverend Bluenose of a Saturday evening or somesuch. Smoking? Does he smoke at Dovecote? Aha. I thought not. Ah, here we are, back home."

We get the ladder the vile Dobbs keeps by his shed and lean it up against the wall such that Amy can climb up it and get on the rungs and so into my room—Amy is coming along, but I know she is not quite ready yet to climb the rope.

I put the ladder back, go up the rope, pull it in, and soon we are in bed and asleep, as it has been a long day.

Chapter 27

Preacher Mather ain't quite up to his usual fire and brimstone this Sunday morning. He don't look like he's been sleeping well. I can't look at him much, though, knowin' what he done. But he gets through it and damns us all to hell for being base sinners and then it's over and I'm thinking I'll be changing churches, me being Church of England and all, who's to keep me here, me not being a lady no more? I can't even sit with Amy, no, I got to sit in the back. Lookin' at the boys ain't no fun anymore, neither, since the Preacher's eyes are on me all the time. Who could object? Mistress would hit the roof if I went to church with Annie and Betsey and Sylvie, them being Catholic and all. I think Abby and Rachel go to another church nearby. I'll have to check it out. It would be fun to go with them.

I help Abby and Rachel serve the midday meal to the few ladies who are at school today, and then go get Gretchen and I'm off on the town. Maybe I'll go see Annie and Betsey. It being Sunday in Boston, ain't nothin' open, so I can't possibly get in trouble. Just a leisurely ride on a really warm fall afternoon, just going out to enjoy the weather, just going out to visit dear friends.

Amy stays back, needing the rest, she says, after yesterday's work at the Pig. She plans to spend the afternoon scribbling in her book. She seems all excited about it, but I don't see why—it seems it's all about my own poor adventures, and who could be interested in that? She's always asking me questions about what I told her back in the hayloft at Dovecote that day—things like, "Jacky, how did you and the others survive the really cold days in winter? You couldn't have lived through *that* wrapped in rags and shivering under a bridge. It's not possible," and I'd think back and say, "Well, you know Cheapside was the market part of London, just like Haymarket is here in Boston, and so there was a lot of horses and 'cause of that, there was a lot of blacksmiths, and on deadly cold nights the smiths would let us curl up next to their forges for the night and the waning warmth of the forges was enough to keep us alive till the next day. We were always careful not to take anything or throw any more coal on the banked fires, though, 'cause then they wouldn't let us do it anymore. I watched the smithies fire up their forges in the morning and learned how to do it myself so that after a while they let me do it for them and so me and the gang would be allowed to stick around the heat for a little bit longer before we were put back in the streets. So, you see, not everybody was mean to us."

She nods and writes.

"And so you also see how no skill, no matter how lowly, is ever learned in vain. I was very proud of the way you handled the serving yesterday in the Pig."

She blushes and continues to write.

It is very warm for this time of year—everyone's been saying it's been an uncommon fall—and townspeople are
standing outside their doors to take in the last real heat of
the year. I look at the *Excalibur* lying down in the harbor. I
had gone aboard her several days ago to post yet another letter to Jaimy, but there was nothing from him. I don't know
what's happening with that. I just don't know.

Gretchen and I walk lazily downtown and I hold my face
up to the warmth of the sun and let my mind wander. I figure I'll visit Sylvie over in the North End and then maybe I'll
go see Annie and Bet—

There's a commotion down on the pier where the *Excalibur* lies. I give Gretchie a bit of a kick and we head down to
see what is the matter. It don't take long for me to find out.

Oh no! They've got Gully!

It's a press-gang and they've got him good and they're
hauling him aboard. He's puttin' up a mighty struggle, but I
can see it ain't gonna be any use. They've got him for sure,
and when they finds out he was the Hero of Culloden Moor
they'll hang him for sure. Gully MacFarland ain't much, but
I'd sure hate to see him hang.

And there goes our act, for certain. *Damn! And it was
going so well! Damn!*

They've pulled him up the gangway, his gangly arms and
legs flailing uselessly about, 'cause he ain't strong, he's all
just skin and bones, and they've got him on the quarterdeck
and rope is being brought to bind him up.

I leaps off Gretchen's back and I runs up the gangway
and goes to my knees in front of the Captain and cries, "Oh,
Captain, please, if you take our poor Papa all us girls will

starve for sure, Mama being sick and all, and poor Baby Agnes, oh, Sir, what will become of poor, poor Baby Agnes?"

I got real tears runnin' down me face, half believing this drivel myself, and I drives on. "Oh, what will become of her when poor Papa is gone across the sea and can no longer bring home the few pennies he does now? She's poorly, Sir, and we fears the worst, and the other poor tykes ain't got no milk, neither, Sir, and we won't be able to buy milk or medicine for poor Baby Agnes, she's such a dear little thing what don't ask for much…"

The Captain is starting to look a little doubtful and is scratching his chin when a voice calls out from above, "Rummy Gully MacFarland ain't got no kin, Captain… 'cept maybe the bottle." There are low, throaty chuckles all around and the sod goes on, "'Cept maybe the bottle, what he cradles to his breast like any Poor Baby Agnes, I'll own."

Damn!

There is outright laughter now and I know this battle is lost.

All right. Plan two. I jump to my feet and whip off my cap and pull off my shoes with my toes and pull down my skirt and roll everything up in a ball and throw it all to the dock and then I hook my toes in the mainmast ratlines and, quick as a flash or any ship's boy, I am up to the maintop and I lean out over the edge and look down at the astounded Captain and crew below. "Ain't no sailor alive what can catch Jacky Faber in the riggin'!"

And with that taunt, I heads higher. If it were not for the fact that Gully's fate hangs in the balance, my chest would be poundin' for pure joy in being aloft again. Still, it does pound as I climb the ratlines that run from the maintop to the main topsail yard—yards bein' those things that go crossways from the mast and what hold up the square sails—and I turns to look down.

"Bring her down!" thunders the Captain, and two fit and fast-looking seamen head aloft after me. I know I must look foolish climbing in drawers with flounces on 'em, but up I go, anyway, up and up past the main topgallant yard, on up to the main royal yard, and there I wraps my legs around the mast and pulls out me shiv and puts it on a line that is thick as my forearm and hard and stiff as iron from the stress that is put on it, keepin' the mainmast from bein' taken over by wind and weather.

I calls down: "Captain! Stop your men. Call them back down. I have my shiv on the main topgallant stay. I can cut through it in a flash. In front of me are the fore royal braces and aft of me are the main royal braces and the main top-gallant braces. I can reach them all and cut through them before your men reach me, and you will be a week fixing the damage and I know you're supposed to leave today. What will the Admiralty say when you come in a week late? Is it worth one pressed seaman?"

The two men stop about fifteen feet below me and look back down at the Captain, who's lookin' up at me with pure hatred writ all over his crimson face. I move the knife to another line and say, "But let's watch the main royal sail fall to the deck first, shall we?" and I pretend to saw away.

"Stop!" roars the Captain, and I stop.

"Look at the pilings on the pier, Captain, and you'll see the tide is ebbing. The same tide you're supposed to be sailing on, Sir," says I. "You must hurry or you will miss it. What will the First Lord say?"

"All right. Let him go," says the Captain, not taking his furious eyes off me.

They take their hands off Gully and he jumps to his feet and runs all gangly down the gangway and across the pier and disappears around a building. Gully is saved. Our act is saved. But now, who will save poor Jacky?

"Tell your men to go back down," I says. I've still got my knife poised on the stay. The Captain nods and the feet of the two men quickly thump on the deck. Why bother chasing me, they're figurin'—I got to come down sometime. I put my shiv securely back in my vest and tighten down the vest's laces, and I start down.

They make a circle about the deck in the place where I must come down so that I won't be able to make a dash for it. The men are hugely enjoying this, of course—what a story it will make, and who cares about one more seaman on board, more or less? Ah, but the Captain, he is not so amused. He mutters something to a sailor next to him and the sailor leaves and comes back with the Cat. He slaps the Cat's nine tails against his palm and grins up at me. The Bo'sun, for certain.

When I get down to the topsail yard, I wails, "Surely that Cat's not meant for me, Sir!" They don't say nothin'. They just waits.

I put my foot in the ratlines that lead down to the maintop, the ratlines on the pier side, to throw them off. I climbs down to the maintop platform, blubberin' and cryin' like I'm afraid I'm about to be whipped, but when my foot touches the main yard, I yelps, "Ha, ha!" and runs the length of it toward the seaward side of the *Excalibur*, and now they're startin' to shout in alarm, but *it's too late, Mates, you can't catch me now.*

I'm at the end of the yard, hangin' out over the water. I turns and grins and dives off.

I tries to make the dive as graceful as possible, havin' an audience and all, and I hits the water right neatly, just like I practiced back in my lagoon down in the Caribbean. Just like the Caribbean. Except for the *cold.*

The day's warmth had charmed me into thinkin' that the water would be as warm as the air. It ain't. The water grabs my chest like an iron fist of cold that means to squeeze all the air out of me forever. I fights the panic that wells up in me and opens me eyes and looks about. It ain't near as clear as the water in my lagoon, but I can make out the looming hull of the *Excalibur* in the murk and I makes myself swim toward her, underwater.

I comes up gasping next to the rudder and I moves next to the pintle where I know they won't be able to see me and hangs there, tryin' to make my chest stop shudderin' and shakin'. While I collects myself, I listens to them shoutin' up above.

"Stupid girl! Drowned for sure!"

And...

"'Twarn't our fault. God knows, it 'twarn't our fault!"

And...

"Oh, the poor thing! She'll haunt us for sure!"

And...

"We've got the wind and the tide! Let's get the hell out of here! We can't hang about for a Goddamed inquest! Damn that girl!"

That from the Captain.

"All hands aloft to make sail! Cast off lines One, Two, and Four!"

I take a breath and go back under and swim over under the pier. My feet touch the muddy bottom and I stand and wrap my arms about myself. Teeth chattering, I hear the swoosh of the sails dropping and filling and the bow of the ship begins to swing out from the dock.

"Cast off Three and Five! Take a strain on Six!"

The Captain *is* in a hurry, taking his ship out without using small boats full of rowers to carefully warp her out of the harbor.

"Take in Six! Shift Colors!"

The *Excalibur* is under way, free of the land. I swim over to where the water comes up under the dock. I had hoped to find one of those ladders that go down in the water for the loading of small boats, but no such luck and I have to slog through the muck to the shore. There's over a hundred years of harbor filth in that mud, but I got to crawl through it. I am lucky that there ain't no sharp stuff buried there and so I don't get cut. I stay away from the barnacles on the pilings themselves, 'cause I know they'll cut me deep if I so much as brush up against them.

I'm about to gain the shore when I slip and go down, up to my elbows in the slop and my hair flops down in it and I have to kneel in the glop to free my hands but I do, and I figure it's all better than a whipping.

I get to the head of the dock and see that the *Excalibur* is about twenty-five yards from the pier, too far out in the channel to come back to get me, so I strolls out to the end of the dock. I can't let them think that I'm dead, as it would ruin their voyage. I'm sure the most superstitious of the sailors have already seen my ghost, and great portents of bad luck and disaster have already been cast 'cause of the death of poor me. I can't let them sail out under the shadow of something like that.

I put my fists on my hips and bellows out, "Good sailing, Mates!" I waves and they are not so far out that I can't see the heads snap around and the smiles of relief on their faces when they see me standing here filthy but alive and waving and grinning from ear to ear. I hear whistles and cheers and I see some thumbs held up.

I can see the Captain, too, as he rushes to the rail to glare at me, mouth open in curses I can barely hear. The legend of this day will not go easy on him and I think he knows it. He snaps his jaw shut and gives me a gesture with his finger that I take to mean something nasty. I resists the temptation to turn about and drop my drawers and give him a good look at my bare and muddy backside, but I quells the urge. After all, I am a lady. Sort of.

I have to put my skirt back on over my muddy drawers 'cause I'll be arrested if I don't, so I do it. Then I go and fetch the faithful Gretchen, who is waiting for me at the end of the dock and whose nostrils quiver as she gets a whiff of me, but she is good and forgives me and lets me lead her to the Pig, where I find Gully stuffing a bag with his things and I ask him what he's doing.

"Och. I'm leavin' this town, Moneymaker. Too hot for old Gully, the Hero o' Culloden Moor. There's more o' King George's ships due in and one of 'em 'll get me, soon enough!"

"Leaving!" I says, standin' there stinkin' and drippin' on the floor and not believin' any of this. "But what about our act? We was doin' so well! You can't break up the act!"

"I got to go, Missy. Don't ask me to take you with me 'cause I can't—got to travel light to keep ahead of the King's minions."

"But I wouldn't have saved you if I'd knowed you was gonna cut and run!"

"Saved me?" he snorts. "Ah, nay, I was just about to bust loose from them blaggards when you come up. All you did was prevent me from hurtin' some o' them."

Gully slings the Lady Lenore around his shoulder and heads for the door. "I'd kiss ye good-bye, Moneymaker, but ye stinks too bad."

And he is gone.

I get up on Gretchen and ride slowly back to the school. I'm lucky there ain't many people about to wonder at my condition and I get into the Common where it don't matter, so I pokes along, thinkin' about things.

I know I've been fooling myself about a lot of things. I'd made enough money by last week to buy a cheap passage back to England and Jaimy. So why didn't I go? Is it 'cause I'd lose my money that Mistress is holding? No, I don't care about that. Is it 'cause I'm afraid that Jaimy's found another girl, one better and finer than me? No, that ain't it. That would hurt me deep, but that ain't it.

I know it's because I got all these other things pullin' at me. Amy losing Dovecote. Randall marrying that awful Clarissa. And most of all, poor Janey Porter lying unquiet in her grave because of the terrible evil done to her. Ephraim

Fyffe walks the earth without joy and he and Betsey can never come together in happiness till that pall is lifted from them. That pall on which is stitched the name Reverend Richard Mather.

I'd left friends once before, that night back in London, when I put on Charlie's clothes and lit out, and I ain't been easy with myself about that ever since. Oh, I know, what could I have done for 'em, me bein' a mere girl and all, but the thing was, I was clever and cunning and they were not. That's the thing that gets me up some nights and robs me of sleep.

I bring Gretchen to a stop and look out across the town and down to the sea.

That's it, then. I will stay till things are resolved, one way or the other, for good or ill.

Peg has her hand around the back of my neck and she pushes my head back under the sudsy water and she keeps me down there longer than I think she really has to.

"Why can't you ever be good?" she scolds when she brings me back up. I had hoped to sneak in and clean up on my own, but Peg caught me and stripped off my clothes and threw me in a laundry tub and poured in the hot water, all the while yelling at me.

Rachel and Abby are over at the side basins trying to save my clothes. My secret tattoo is now common knowledge to all.

"But Peggy, I had to—" But then my head is plunged underwater again and Peg gets her scrub brush workin' the harbor grit out of the roots of my hair.

"'Had to,' nothin'," says Peg, "Had to get in trouble,

that's you all over. Why a nice girl like you has to carry a knife like that...and *tattooed*?"

"You're the fastest girl we know, Jacky, and we're proud to know you, ain't we, Abby?" chortles Rachel. Abby nods in delighted agreement.

"But a sailor *always* has a kni—"

Back down under. "But you *ain't* a sailor. You're *supposed* to be a good girl is what you're *supposed* to be, and you ain't even close."

Then the door opens and Amy comes in to join the throng pointing out my faults and is quickly brought up to date on my latest crimes against ladyhood. "Why don't you *ever* think before you act?" is her addition to the conversation. That, and a worried look and a hopeless shaking of the head.

Once again my head is pushed down between my knees. It occurs to me that bein' the only naked one in a room when all about you are clothed and yellin' at you ain't the most comfortable of situations. The warm water does feel good, though, after the chill of the harbor.

This time when I come up, however, I hear neither scolding nor banter.

I open my eyes and see, through the blear of the water and the strands of my hair hanging down, the disapproving face of Mistress Pimm. I put my arms across my chest and I am glad that my tattoo is underwater. My mouth drops open but I don't know what to say, and I rummage frantically about in my head for a saving lie.

"The foolish thing was sent down to the market to buy fish and fell off the pier," lies dear Peg for me.

Mistress says nothing to this. Instead she says, "Dobbs has discovered a ladder leaning against the outside wall under your window. We have investigated and discovered that your room has been ransacked. I trust you had nothing of value in there. You will be well advised to keep your window latched from now on."

Mistress turns and leaves.

The first thing I check for is the money and, of course, it's gone, every penny, the poor little bag lying flat on the floor. The rest of my things are scattered about, where he emptied my seabag and overturned my chest in his search for other things that might be worth selling. Did I even tell him that I kept my money in my seabag when he expressed concern that I might lose it and must be careful? I might have. Did I really think it was a kindness when he walked me back home the other night, when all he really wanted to do was case the job?

How could I be so stupid?

I look over the mess and then flop down on my bed, facedown.

Chapter 28

James Emerson Fletcher
9 Brattle Lane
London
October 24, 1803

Miss Jacky Faber
The Lawson Peabody School for Young Girls
Beacon Street
Boston, Massachusetts, USA

Dearest Jacky,

I hope this letter finds you safe, well, and happy and that you are continuing to profit from your schooling and that you are enjoying the companionship of your new friends. I am sure that you are most popular with the others, considering your wealth of charm and your infectious high spirits.

I am sorry to tell you that the crew of the Dolphin has been broken up. Upon our arrival in Britain, an inspection of the repairs needed to get her back shipshape showed that they were much more extensive than we had previously thought, and she would have to go into dry dock for a long time. The Brother-

hood is scattered, I'm afraid—Davy to the Raleigh, Tink *to the* Endeavor, *and Willy to* Temeraire. *I am posted to the frigate* Essex, *along with George Elliot, whom you will remember as being a fellow midshipman on the* Dolphin. *He is a very decent sort and we have become quite good friends. It is a very good posting, the* Essex, *and we have Captain Locke to thank for it, for it was his recommendation that secured it for us. We will soon set sail to join Lord Nelson's fleet, which has bottled up the French fleet at Toulon. It is important work, for Napoleon intended to use his fleet to invade our country, and he has been thwarted in that attempt. May Britannia always rule the seas!*

It is rumored that we might even meet the great man himself, can you believe it?

Perhaps it is well that I have left the dear Dolphin *because in my time on her after your departure, when on watch or in the performance of my regular duties, I would see you in all our old nooks and crannies and it would both delight me and sorely oppress my mind. The day before we left her, I climbed to the foretop and carved our initials there—JF + JF—I wonder what future generations of ship's boys will make of that? At least in leaving the* Dolphin, *I will no longer be subjected to the looks of envy directed toward the scoundrel who wormed his unworthy self into the affections of the redoubtable Jacky Faber, Girl Sailor, Midshipman, and the Scourge of the Seven Seas.*

Well might they be envious, for I am a very lucky man to have been loved by such as you. I hope that I continue to be lucky by remaining uppermost in your heart, but I fear that I may be mistaken and unlucky after all—I have received no letters from you, Jacky, and the Shannon *has returned from Boston, as well as the* Sprite *and the* Plymouth. *I check with my mother each time I am home, but she informs me, to my infinite* sorrow, that there is nothing from you. I am cruelly disappointed and I am beginning to be worried.

My mother further implores me to seek out alliances of those "within our own set," but I will not allow her to continue in this vein. I inform her that there is none for me but my brown-eyed sailor.

We leave on the tide tomorrow. There are many rumors flying about, but it seems certain we are about to blockade the French fleet at Toulon, and will be on station for many months. I shall continue writing, but I fear the delivery of my letters will be chancy, at best.

Please be careful. I worry about you, given your propensity for plunging into trouble. And please write to me.

Your most devoted servant,
Jaimy

Chapter 29

I mope around for a bit, but then, like always, I get over it.

In a few days I take tea with Maudie and we both grumble over our losses.

"Never trust a drunk," says Maudie, again.

"Older and wiser now," says I. "How much did he get you for?"

"Some lodging, some board," sighs she, who warned me in the first place but who I guess didn't take her own advice. "But what I hate most is losin' the business his fiddle and you brought in."

What I hate most is being taken for a fool. I just found out that the Battle of Culloden Moor was fifty some years ago and Gully couldn't possibly have been there. Jacky Faber, Cheapside scammer, was scammed again, scammed royally. And all my money gone. I had noticed that my concertina was gone. I find out later that Gully had sold it at the pawnshop and it's gonna cost me two dollars to get it back.

"Aye," I says. I could do a solo act, but we both know that without Gully's fiddle and without his wild craziness, it wouldn't work. Just some afternoon shows with me makin' a few sailors cry in their beers with my sad songs—not the thing that fills the coffers. I mean, I'll do it, 'cause I *really* need the money now, but it ain't gonna be the same.

I bid Maudie good day and go out and climb aboard Gretchie, her saddlebags bulging with the stuff from the greengrocer's that I was sent to buy. I bring her up to a brisk trot 'cause I want to get back quick to show Mr. Peet my latest poor attempts at miniature portrait painting and to get his kind advice, and I got a math problem I can't figure out that I want to see Mr. Sackett about.

And then, after I'm done with the work of the day, I must make my preparations for tonight.

I put the last strand of the mop to the top of my watch cap and sew it in tightly. Then I patiently unravel the mop strand as I have done to all the other strands I have sewn on to the cap.

I have long since sent Amy down to her own bed, complaining of sickness that I do not want to pass on to her.

I am going out to visit the Preacher, but this time I do not put on my black gear but instead keep on my serving-girl outfit. And this time, instead of blackening my face, I take flour and spread it over my face, rubbing it in so it won't dust off. Then I rub it on my hands. I have already worked it into the strands of my watch-cap wig.

Now I take a little dish and put some soot and a little water in it and mix it around with my finger till it's a black paste, and with my biggest watercolor brush, I fill my eye sockets with black and then paint six up-and-down lines of black from my upper lip down to my chin, to look like the teeth in a grinning skull. Then I put on the white, Dutch-boy wig.

I wrap my black cloak around me like a shawl to keep me from being spotted in my white blouse, and I open my window and go down the rungs, tying the rope to the third rung from the bottom, and drop down to the ground.

I stick to the shadows and work my way around to the graveyard, looking up to see that the Reverend has yet not come to the window of his study. He may never come to the window this night, but I must be patient—if not this night, then the next. If not then, then the one after that.

Patience.

I dart across the road and fling myself down next to the stone wall that lies between Janey's grave and the church. I worm my way along on elbows and knees till I am lying next to the grave, and there I lie and wait, hidden from the church by the wall and hidden from the road by a row of bushes. The side of the school that faces this way is the opposite side from my rung ladder and, like my side, is made up mostly of massive chimney. It is the blind side of the school, without even one window.

The moon is rising and casting a fine light on the graveyard. I wait, my eye on the window.

What to do while I wait? Maybe I'll compose another letter to Jaimy: "Dear Jaimy, I hope you are well and passing your time in joyous pursuits. I myself am lying next to a grave in the middle of the night waiting for a demented witch-hunter to—" Hush! There he is!

I hear him before I see him. *"Sorceress! Witch!"* comes clearly across the churchyard from the window. Then,

"Demon!" I put my eye to a cleft between the stones and I can see him, but he cannot see me. He is gesturing and posturing like before, but this time I can see his crazed face straight on and it is not a sight to make one sleep easy at night. While he seems to be shouting and pointing directly at *me,* of course he is not. He is pointing at poor Janey in her grave.

I know the way he moves through this performance of his, having watched it twice already, and I wait for one of those times when he steps away from the window to rant and rave inside and pour another drink and gather fury for another bout of arm-waving, pointing, and hissing.

There he goes! Now!

I get up and stand on top of the grave. I step carefully so as to leave no footprints. The earth is hard, but still . . .

I just stand there with my arms to my side, in my white hair and bangs, my white face with empty eye sockets and painted teeth. No grimacing, no saying *boo,* no waving of arms—just standing there, stock-still in the moonlight.

He comes back to the window and launches into his routine with the accusing finger pointed directly at me and then he says, *"Corruption,"* and then, *"Wicked,"* and then he opens his eyes and he jerks back and don't say nothin' at all, he just stands there with his mouth wide open and his tremblin' finger still pointing. His eyes are wildly staring. I keep my own eyes as slits so he don't see the whites, but still I can see him plain.

Then he says, *"Nooooooo,"* and it sounds as if it's coming from the very bottom of his twisted soul, and he stumbles back and there's the sound of a chair being overturned and a crash of maybe a bottle and he disappears from my view.

I take that opportunity to nip down behind the wall and begin my creep back. Don't want to overdo things. That will do for tonight. I have a branch from one of the bushes, and I sweep it behind me to cover any traces of my being there.

When he gets up the nerve to look back out, all he will see is the grave lyin' there all still in the moonlight.

Still, but not quiet.

I pause by my rope and dust the leaves and twigs off my clothes as best I can, then up I go to the rungs, untie the rope, sling it over my shoulder, and climb up to my window, congratulating myself on a job well done.

As I've just got head and shoulders through the window, I stiffen as I hear someone in the room. The lamp is turned up and there is Amy Trevelyne, staring at me as if at a very demon from hell itself, which, if you look at it from her point of view, she has. Then she says, *"Ooohhhh,"* and her eyes roll back in her head and she faints onto the bed. On the bedside table is a bowl of chicken soup, now quite cold, that she had brought up for me. *How sweet of you, Sister.*

I have taken off the wig and rubbed off some of the flour and soot from my face. I am patting Amy's hand and slowly bringing her back into this world. She comes unwillingly, but as she nears full consciousness, I put my arms about her and whisper, "Sister, please! It's just me, Jacky! Come on, now. Wake up!"

Her eyelids flutter and she looks at me and says, "Oh, Jacky, no…" as she has so many times before.

Chapter 30

After that first time I appeared to Reverend Mather as Janey, I let things lie for a couple of days. I watched him on the next day, though, and, sure enough, he came out to the gravesite and looked about for signs of something real and not ghostly there, but he found none. His movements were jerky and his face was sunken. *That's it, Preacher, stew in your guilt for a while yet. Then we'll up the ante.*

Each night after that, Amy and I would creep up to the widow's walk and watch the Preacher to see the changes in his actions. For certain he don't rant and rave and point no more. Rather, he peeks out timidly every few minutes to see if the specter has come back. It would be comical to see, if it weren't for the real tragedy of Janey Porter.

But after several days, I figured he needed another shot, so last night I got back in costume and headed out on another moonlit night, leaving Amy wringing her hands back in the room.

Again, I snuck up next to the wall and waited for him to turn back into the room. Then I stood, and when he came back and looked out, there I am as Janey on the grave. His eyes went big as saucers and he put his hands to his mouth to stifle a moan of horror, but he didn't jerk back into the room this time, this time he just stood there lookin'.

Well, I couldn't stand there all night and I certainly couldn't just walk off as if to say *Good night, Preacher, we're done with tonight's haunting and I'll be going now. Haunt you next time.* So there we stood as the minutes ticked by, and then I had a thought.

Slowly, slowly, I brought up my right hand and pointed an accusing finger at him, my other fingers on that hand hooked into a claw. His eyes grew even larger and then, suddenly, he buried his face in his hands and I took the opportunity to drop like a stone behind the wall.

I watched through the cleft in the stones to see what he did then. He looked out again, rubbed his eyes, and I could see profound despair was writ on his face. He appeared to be mumbling something. Prolly asking his grandfather to get him out of this. I shall have to go back up on his roof soon to hear what the two are talking about these days.

I got back to my room without incident. Amy breathed a sigh of relief at seeing me come through the window.

Word had come this Saturday morning that Ezra wanted to talk to me again, but Peg was having none of it. "You'll come back all tarred and feathered or else will run off with the circus. No, you ain't goin' nowhere, Miss Nothing-But-Trouble," but I got down on my knees and clasped my hands together and pleaded, "I'll be good I promise and you can send Betsey with me 'cause she's so sensible and Amy Trevelyne'll come, too, and she's a lady as cautious as any dormouse and…"

"All right! All right!" said Peg, giving it up. "But if you come back in disgrace one more time…"

She didn't go into what she'd do if I came back in such disgrace again, but I was promised it would not be pretty. I yelped and went upstairs and got Amy and then I grabbed Betsey by the arm and the three of us were out the door.

I had wanted to have Betsey along 'cause I planned to visit with Ephraim again to bring him up to date with what was happening with the Preacher, and Amy 'cause I wanted to put her next to Ezra again, to see what happens.

We're goin' across the Common and I can see that Betsey's a little shy to be with Amy and so I stop them and join hands with both and say that when we're in the school we're girl, girl, and lady, but when we are out on the town we are all just members of the same Dread Sisterhood. Agreed? They agree, and we walk down the path as Sisters.

We go first to see Ephraim and his eyes light up upon seeing Betsey, and hers light up upon seeing him, and that gladdens my heart, and then we take him in tow and head down toward Ezra's office, and as we go, we fill him in on all that's been going on with the Preacher. His mouth is set into a firm line of satisfaction that something is being done, and he demands that he be allowed to do his part, and I say for him not to worry as his time will come.

"I've been haunting the Preacher, Ezra. It's as simple as that. He would not look upon Janey on that day. He will look upon her now," I say with firmness. Ezra is at his desk and we are seated facing him. Introductions have been made.

Ezra looks upon me with wonder. "And what good do you think this will do?"

I fluffs up and says, "His guilt will overcome him and he will confess."

"And then we will take him out and hang him, I suppose," says Ezra.

"I had thought more in the way of the lunatic asylum. As long as the name of Janey Porter is cleared of shame."

Ezra looks at me long and hard. Then he turns to Amy. "You knew of this, Miss Trevelyne?"

"On the widow's walk we heard the Reverend admit his guilt," says Amy, steadily. *Good on you, Amy,* I thinks. She gives him a short account of the Preacher's words and actions.

"Why didn't you report that to me? Perhaps we could have charged him with his crime?"

"On the word of Jacky Faber, convicted of lewd and lascivious conduct? Jacky Faber, what sings and dances in taverns, and what plunges into Boston Harbor at the slightest provocation?" snorts I. "I am well aware of my reputation in this town."

"Besides," says Amy, "what he said, though plain to us, was vague enough that any good attorney could successfully defend him. One such as yourself, Mr. Pickering."

"That is very perceptive of you, Miss Trevelyne," says Mr. Pickering, fairly beaming at her. "And you are right. I have no doubt I could get him off.

"And you, Mr. Fyffe. You approved of this?" Ezra asks of Ephraim, who sits stolidly in his chair, his hands in fists which rest on his knees.

"I didn't know of it, but I approve. Jacky is a brave girl. Janey was a brave girl, too, what didn't deserve what happened to her," says Ephraim. Betsey puts her hand gently on his shoulder.

"And you, Miss?" Ezra asks of Betsey.

"She was friend to me," is all she will say, but it is enough.

There is a small silence and I throw a question into it. "Who was the Preacher's grandfather?"

Ezra considers this for a while and then says, "He is probably referring to Cotton Mather, a towering figure in the early colonies, both in religion and law." Ezra pauses and looks at me and then goes on. "Cotton Mather was instrumental in the Salem witch trials, wherein forty-nine people were executed for witchcraft—largely on the evidence of several hysterical girls."

I shiver and resolve to be more careful.

Ezra goes on. "He was directly involved in the trial of a young girl here in Boston in 1682. It concerned the death of her baby. She said she had rolled over the infant in her sleep, causing its death by accident. The Court, urged on by Cotton Mather, convicted her of murder. On the day of her execution, she had to sit there and listen to a two-hour sermon on the sins of youth, delivered by Reverend Mather, before she was taken up and dropped." Ezra puts on a thoughtful attitude. "Poor thing. Had I been her, I would have offered to go first."

I'm sittin' there tryin' to keep my gorge down when Ezra brings his eyes again to lock with mine. "It is reported that Reverend Mather marched immediately around the corner to have his sermon printed up for distribution, even as the girl still hung on the gallows. So you see, Jacky, the Mathers are *very* serious people."

I take his warnings even more to heart.

Ezra Pickering looks about at the assembled gang of conspirators and says, "There have been some developments. Our Reverend Mather has redoubled his efforts at getting his petition of guardianship granted. He has hired an attorney, a Mr. George Blish, a man I personally cannot abide but who is nonetheless extremely competent. Blish has entered into the Court record a deposition describing your recent physical fight with another girl at the school and your propensity for singing and dancing in public houses. Reverend Mather seems to have excellent sources of information, and you, of course, do everything possible to further their case." Ezra looks at me sternly.

The vile Dobbs, I thinks, *and prolly Wiggins,* but what I sighs and says is, "There'll be no more singing and dancing. I shall try to be good."

"And I shall try to block this petition at every turn, but it is getting increasingly difficult. And I shall continue looking into the matter of reclaiming your money, but somehow I do not think this case is entirely about the money."

"It isn't, Mr. Pickering," I says. "I believe he has convinced himself that I am a witch. The same thing he convinced himself about Janey Porter, and we all know what happened there."

Ezra is silent for a while on that, and then he says, looking steadily at me, "We must *all* be very careful then, mustn't we?"

After we leave Ezra's office and return up the hill, I see a strange thing in a side yard of a stable. It seems to be a wooden figure of a man with a cone-shaped hat on his head sitting in a chair that's on a narrow platform, and right behind him is another wooden figure, a devil with pitchfork and horns and tail, painted red.

I say, "What's that?" and Ephraim says that it's a Pope's Day wagon that will be paraded down the street on the night of November fifth, and the gangs from the North End will try to knock over and destroy the Popes of the South End gangs, and all will have torches and the fights will go long into the night.

"And there's supposed to be at least three British ships in, which should add some spice to the mix," he says. He gives his arm to Betsey and she takes it. They smile at each other and I think it's the first time each has really smiled in a while.

I'm thinking it's a lot like Guy Fawkes Day back in old London town when me and the gang would get wholeheartedly into some serious mischief. "Sounds like fun," I says, ever up for some excitement. "Can we come, too?"

Chapter 31

"Come on, Henry," I'm sayin', dragging on his arm. "You can be my gallant escort, come *on*!"

"But the horses—"

"Sven can watch the horses, can't he, Herr Hoffman?" Herr Hoffman has appeared as I am trying to haul his son out of the stable and into the riot of the night. Halloween's come and gone and now it's Pope's Day!

Herr Hoffman puts his hand on his son's head and ruffles his brown hair. "Ach, ja, Heinrich, go with the young people. Have fun, boy. The responsibilities of age vill come soon enough."

With that, Henry grabs my arm and we are off joyously into the night.

The others are right down the street. There's Sylvie and Abby and Rachel and her young man, Paul Barkley, whom she will marry in the spring, and they plan to go west to claim a homestead and farm. He brings along his brother, who is pleasant and soon accepted by all and who quickly falls into step with Abby, who don't seem to mind. Amy has climbed down the ladder route and is dressed in her common gear to fit right in with us milkmaids, and we're to pick up Annie and Betsey on our way down. We walk the road between the school and the church, and I look up and sure enough, there he is at his window. *I'll leave you alone tonight, Preacher. May you not enjoy the rest.*

"The others are waiting down the road, and Maudie has said we can go up on the roof of the Pig and watch the whole thing from there! Won't it be grand?" I crows.

Henry allows that it will be and thanks me for taking him with our merry group, and I say, "Thanks nothing, you are a finely turned out fellow and I'm proud to walk by your side." I am a little surprised to learn that Henry does not know all the girls of the Sisterhood, what with him working so close to them and all. I guess their paths just don't cross is all. Like, he had never really met Sylvie before. Now, upon their first meeting, she gives him a shy bat of her dark lashes, and he can barely stammer out his own name.

Darkness has long since fallen and already we can see groups of torches gathering in the streets down below. I assume there are others over there in the North End as well. There is the sound of sporadic firecrackers. I'm sayin' that I hope it's not gunfire, but Amy says Pope's Day isn't as big as it once was, before their Revolution, when the gangs of Protestants from the North End would clash with the gangs of Catholics from the South End and injuries, and even death, would occur. It sort of ended when General Washington told everybody to knock it off because he had both Catholics and Protestants in his army, everybody fightin' for liberty and such, and he didn't need them at each other's throats. Sylvie says that's true, but some of the old customs hang on, 'cause they're too much fun to give up right off.

It is good to hear Amy talk so easy and unfearful with everyone. I have put her through a bit since coming into her life, but I think she is the better for it.

Annie and Betsey come out of the darkness to join us and Ephraim appears at the corner of State and Cornhull. He don't approve of all this but comes along to lend his protection. *Boys*, I clucks to myself, *so careless of their own conduct, so careful of ours.*

"So, how did you get out?" he asks Betsey, who is already on his arm and looking up into his face. "I'm sure your father knows nothing of this."

"We told him we were going to spend the night with Sylvie," says Annie.

"And I told *my* father that *I* was staying with *you*," laughs Sylvie.

It turns out that everybody is staying with someone else.

"Some are sure to get in trouble," warns Ephraim, with a dark look.

"Not if we get back before our fathers get back! They are out there, too!" says Annie. "Ours is fighting for Ward Number Ten!"

"And mine for Ward Number Four!" cries Abby. "They'll all be kept busy, and I'll wager they'll all be too tired to beat us when they get back!" Wards, I am told, are voting districts and go from Ward 1 in Boston's North End down to Ward 12 in the South End.

Actually, it turns out that all of them plan to go to the school in the wee hours and so avoid capture by any father, which seems like a good plan to me.

A gang of young boys comes up to us and they beat sticks upon their crude Pope and Devil figures. Some wear masks and some are fully costumed as devils, and they sing out to us.

> *"Don't ye hear my little bell*
> *Go chink, chink, chink!*
> *Please give me a little money,*
> *To buy my Pope a drink!"*

"Not very respectful of the Holy Father," says Annie, giving each of the boys a treat. "But I suppose they don't really take the sense of it at all."

Each of us girls has a basket that is filled with small balls of dough that were fried in lard until brown and then rolled in sugar. Peg made 'em for us sayin' that we wouldn't get far without givin' out some treats. They are very good, if you don't eat too many. Here's another bunch of boys with a wooden figure that looks like it's supposed to be King George and they have another chant.

> *"Pray Madames, Sirs,*
> *If you will something give,*
> *We'll burn the dog,*
> *And not let him live!"*

"Not very respectful of His Majesty," says I, also dropping treats into the outstretched hands of the boys. "And where are your sisters, boys?" I asks.

"Why, home where they belong, Miss," says one boy, eyes wide with the stupidness of my question.

"Right," I say, and let it go.

We give out the pastries to each group of small boys who

come up and demand a treat, and they are appreciative, but the boys are getting bigger and bigger and their demands are not for sweetmeats but for other kinds of sweets, and I am glad when we reach the Pig and get the ladder from Bob and climb on the roof and pull it up after us.

What a great perch! We can see the various groups as they make their way up the narrow streets, slowed down by their very numbers and slowed down even further by meeting the resistance of rival gangs.

Young men down below whistle and tell us to come down and they'll show us a treat, and we go to the edge and say that we know what kind of treat they plan for us and though they are all very pretty they can all go and sod off. This gets us hoots and hollers, but all seems in good fun.

Maudie and Bob have got the good sense not to open up the inside of the Pig but instead are dealing the ale and rum out the front door with the lower half of the door shut. The tankards have small lengths of light chain attached to their handles so they can't be carried off by the revelers.

There is a mob in the street below, waiting for one of the Popes to try to get through and so I go over to the edge of the roof over the doorway and pull out my pennywhistle and toots out a high and shrill bit that'll carry over the noise of the throng and I gets some cheers and so I goes on and gives 'em a few more, but then there's a real roar, "*Here they come!*" and a Pope cart appears at the end of the street, surrounded by very determined-looking defenders. I'm told that the object is to get your cart to Cobb's Hill against all odds and there to burn it on the bonfire that is already raging in the distance. That is, you throw it on the fire there before your opponents can destroy it and burn it in the street.

The cart gets closer and we can hear the chant of the South End stalwarts what are pushing it along.

> *"It's up the long ladder and down the short rope!*
> *The hell with King George and up with the Pope!*
> *If that doesn't do, we'll tear him in two,*
> *And send him to hell with his red, white, and blue!"*

The chant incites the attackers to great violence, and from the crush of fists and clubs comes the chant of the North Enders who have now come out of the night... *"Here comes another,"* is the shout, and they have their own Pope and Devil up on their shoulders. Their Pope has a barrel for a body and there is someone inside, prolly a small boy, who turns the grotesque head about and about, and it glares at all who gaze upon it. They have a chant, too, but I can't make it out over the roar of the crowd, but it don't matter, anyway. I jumps up and down and cheers and shouts and the blood is up in me for sure and me heart is beatin' in me chest hard enough to burst out and I know I shouldn't like this wildness so, but I do, I do. I take my whistle and I just blasts on it to add my bit to the mayhem and the chaos of the night. Amy reaches up and pulls me down to sit next to her and she says, "Be good!"

The two groups come together with ruinous intent and there's the bellowing of threats and curses as the Pope and Devil figures rock back and forth in the press of the combatants and then there's great shouts and the South End cart goes down in the sea of bodies and there's crackings and splinterings and a huge cheer and the North Enders have won—this battle at least.

The crowd surges back and forth and it's hard to tell who's who in the way of the teams and there's blood on some faces and some are on their knees recovering from blows, and the crowd eventually surges up the street in the direction of Cobb's Hill, and the defeated ones pick up the pieces of their vanquished Pope and Devil and follow, in as good a cheer as can be expected.

This leaves the street almost empty for a bit, except for...

There's a bunch of men and boys over there and they got someone pinned up against a building and that person is... *Mam'selle?*

The bunch of scum is pokin' at her with sticks and she is tryin' to keep her dignity under their attack, her head up, but that ain't gonna happen as they keep pullin' at her yellow dress and have already torn off her yellow hat with the yellow plumes and trampled it in the dust, and she has cradled her little lapdog to her breast to keep it from bein' hurt, but they're pokin' at it, too, and I can see her eyes all scared and she knows that soon she will be down in the dirt, too, and they will kick her and stomp her and they will step on her little lapdog and kill it but there is nothin' she can do. Some bastard must have lured her out o' Mrs. Bodeen's with a promise of a fine parade or somesuch and this is what she gets....

"To me!" I shouts. "We got to save her!" and I'm already shoving the ladder over the side, and Ephraim and Henry and the other boys follow me down and someone cries, "But why?" and I says, "'Cause she tried to save me twice is why and she's different, which is why they're at her," and I'm down and racin' up the street and I yells to John

Thomas, *"Help me, John Thomas!"* and he leaves his post at the door of the Pig and follows me without question.

I charges into the pack of slime and says, "Leave off, you curs!" and their shocked faces turn on me and some say, "We'll not! We was only havin' some fun with this...thing," and I goes to pull out me shiv, which I only oncet before pulled with serious intent and that when me very life was in danger, but I don't have to get it all the way out 'fore John Thomas's balled fist smashes into the mouth of the cove what was talkin' his trash talk to me and blood squirts out of the cove's nose and he goes down and Ephraim has the heads of two of the dogs under his strong arms and is proceedin' to squeeze the life out of 'em and brave Henry puts his fists up in the face of yet another knave, but the knave retreats and the others retreat and so leave the field of battle to us.

I bend down and pick up Mam'selle's battered hat and hands it to her.

"Why, if it isn't my little Precious come to save her dear auntie Claudelle from harm," she says, dusting off the hat as if it was just an unfortunate accident of the wind at the races in New Orleans. "Thank you so very much for your intervention. I cannot believe the ungentlemanly nature of some of the citizens of this city. I do fear the ruffians would have made sport of me for a tedious long time. Will you and your brave consort not accompany me back to my lodgings?"

"We will, Mademoiselle," I say. Mam'selle murmurs to her puppy and she puts her yellow parasol out before her and we proceed in as grand a style as we can manage back to Mrs. Bodeen's.

On the way, Mam'selle says, "You know, Precious, I know this will break your dear little heart, but your auntie Mam'selle Claudelle has decided to go back to New Orleans—no, no, dear, please do not protest, it is for the best, for this clime does not agree with me and neither does the quality of the folk hereabouts. I shall take ship within the week."

When we reach the stairway up to Mrs. Bodeen's, Mam'selle turns to me and says, "I will give you a token, Precious, to remember me by." She reaches behind her neck and undoes a clasp on a gold chain. "Lift your hair, Precious," she orders.

I reach back and lift my pigtail from off my neck and she leans over to me and puts the chain around my neck and fastens it. There is something dangling off the chain and it hangs on the bodice of my dress. It is a little beaded bag, about one inch by one inch, and has strange designs worked into it.

"It is an asafoetida bag," says Mam'selle, and she pulls my bodice out and drops the little bag down there. It rests there where Jaimy's ring usually sets, 'cept now it's in my ear for the night. "It is powerful magic, Precious, and don't forget it. It was made especially for me by Mama Boudreau, herself, a famous conjure woman, and it is full of magic and power. Did it not bring me you, Precious, when I needed you most?"

"What's in it?" I asks stupidly.

"Ah, Precious, no one ever knows what's in each bag—could be a piece of bat wing, rare and poisonous herbs, strands from a hangman's noose—who knows? Only the conjure woman knows, she what made it and put the magic on it and she what knows the *hoodoo,* the *voodoo,* and the *gris-gris,* and it's not best to mess with it, dear little one. You got to let the magic be, and let it work for you, that's all."

She puts her foot on the stair and says, "Good-bye, Precious. If you ever come to New Orleans, please come visit your dear auntie Claudelle." With that, she goes up the stairs and Mrs. Bodeen opens the door and Mam'selle goes in and I see yellow no more.

Mrs. Bodeen gives me a nod. Of recognition? Of thanks? I don't know. Other girls come out on the landing and say, "John Thomas, come up, come up, John Thomas," but he says that nay, he's workin' and can't let their considerable charms keep him from his duty, and we all head back in the direction of the Pig.

So we're rollin' back up the street, my bully boys and me, and I still got my shiv half out of my vest, for show, really, since I don't plan on pullin' it out, most of this fightin' bein' in fun and not in deadly earnest, when there's a line of striped shirts in front of us and we know they are British sailors and it don't look like they mean to let us pass without a fight, and Ephraim squares his shoulders, as do the Barkley brothers, and Henry raises his puny but brave fists and John Thomas prepares to do damage to the line of battle when I hear a familiar voice say, "You know, Jacky, when I thought of you back here in the States, I really thought you'd be sittin' in a rocking chair with a shawl about your little shoulders, some needlework in your lap, and a prayer on your lips. I *really* did."

I squint into the night and there's a sailor in the center of the line who's grinnin' at me and then all the noise and revels drop away from me. *It's Davy! Oh, good God, it's Davy!*

I leap forward and wrap my arms around his neck and my legs around his waist I'm so glad to see him, and I start blubbering and crying and...

The rogue kisses me full on the lips and shouts out, "Didn't I tell you, Mates, one in every port!" Cheers from his mates. I blush and reflect that I seem forever to be making boys' reputations at the expense of my own.

I unwraps my legs on that one. Davy ain't changed, not in that way. He has gotten taller and under my hands the muscles on his arms have become harder and more well defined, but I'm hardly noticin' 'cause all that I can think about is... "Jaimy! Where's Jaimy? Oh, Lord I didn't know the *Dolphin* was comin' in. Where's..." I'm pounding on his chest with me fists and lookin' wildly about as I'm sayin' this.

"The *Dolphin* ain't in, Jacky, and you should calm down. The *Dolphin*'s crew was broke up as soon as we got to England. Too much hidden damage—she had to be put in dry dock and they scattered us out to the nearest ships around. I'm on the *Raleigh*, Tink's on the *Endeavor*, and Willy to the *Temeraire*."

As my stunned mind is soakin' this in, Davy's pals wave off and head down the street to one of the open taverns, thinkin' the only dolly-mop in sight is already taken up by their mate Davy, and my crew looks Davy over and figures things out pretty much and we all start movin' again toward the Pig.

"And Jaimy," I say, full of dread. He could be killed, or dead of some fever, or...

"He's on the *Essex*, on station off Toulon, last I heard," says Davy, putting his arm around my shakin' shoulders. "Now, you just forget about Jaimy, 'cause he's sure forgot about you, the snob. Now let's me and you go get married and have a fine toss in the hay and then we'll talk about other things." Davy looks out across the crowd. "Let's us lovers find a preacher." He points at a tall man in a black coat. "Sir! You there! Are you a preacher? Well, who cares, you'll do, now just say the words, now..."

Then I starts blubberin' and put my face in my hands. *For one moment I really thought I was gonna see Jaimy again and now no...no...* and Davy sees my cryin' face and says, "Ah, now, I was just foolin' wi' ye. The last time I saw Jaimy, all he could talk about was you—it fair made me sick, it did...disgustin', I can tell you."

"He did?" says I, through my tears, "Really? I ain't got no letters..."

"Really, Jacky. Now let's have some fun. I'm back to sea in three days and if you think I'm gonna spend any of my liberty in talkin' about your Jaimy Fletcher, then you don't remember your old pal Davy very well. I means to rack up some memories to hold me when the wind blows cold. Who's all this, then?" and I introduce him to Ephraim, who don't look like he's got a whole lot of use for him, and Henry, who don't know much about the world and is glad to meet anyone who's seen some of it, and John Thomas, who sees Davy as one of his seagoin' brethren and claps him on the back, and we all surge up the street and put the ladder back up at the Pig and the girls' faces are lookin' down at us in relief that we got back without damage and we climb up and I do more introductions and then Davy's lookin' at Annie and Annie's lookin' at him and I come back to my senses and say, "No. No, Davy. She's a nice girl. You stay away from her."

I get between them. "Annie, don't…"

But it is too late.

Well, at least I can keep them to hand-holding tonight. But there's so much I want to ask him! I guess it will have to wait till later, after they're done with the sparkin'.

Amy comes over and stands next to me and puts her hand on my arm to bring some sense back to me, I guess, and then I hear a call from down below and there's Ezra, and Amy looks at me with narrowed eyes and I just shrug and feign ignorance, but of course I did send word to him that we would be up here tonight. I direct him to the ladder and he comes up and bows to Amy and she dips in return. Ladies and gents, even on the sloping roof of a tavern in the middle of a night of devilment, I swear.

Then I turn around and notice that I have lost my own escort. Henry and Sylvie are over on the roof beam, sitting together, holding hands, and looking into each other's eyes. Ah well.

The street revels are winding down and the Popes and Devils alike are being thrown onto the bonfire on Cobb's Hill and it's safe enough for Maudie to send up a trayful of ales and we gratefully quaff them, our throats dry from shouting and singing. And then Ezra buys another round and we sing and dance and…

Lord, what a night!

On the way back, I look at the couples in the moonlight and it strikes me that unlike on the *Dolphin* when I was the only girl with a boy, here I'm the only girl without one.

We turn up the road twixt the school and the church and we're startled to see a man with a dog on a leash, patrolling the graveyard. The Preacher has hired a watchman! All who are in on the plot exchange glances: Changes will have to be made in our plans. I shiver a bit—I could have been so easily caught. I was lucky to have seen him this night.

When we go round the school and arrive at the kitchen entrance, most get into amorous embraces till Amy coughs, "Ahem," and the lovers part. Paul and his brother go off down the hill and I go and get between Davy and Annie, which ain't easy. With a final squeeze of his hand, she turns and gives him a wave and then she joins the other girls, who all go in the kitchen door, opened by Peg in her nightgown, clucking over her girls like any mother hen. Sylvie, I'm sure, would go into the hayloft right off with Henry but good sense prevails, and after a long good-night kiss, she, too, disappears through the kitchen door, and Peg's strong arm reaches out and pulls the door shut. There is the sound of a latch being thrown.

Henry, in a daze, wanders back to his bed after what has to be the finest night of his young life. Ezra and Davy escort us around to our rung ladder and look at our rope trick and Davy says something like, "Can't keep that one down, for sure." Ezra takes Amy's hand and bows over it and kisses it. Amy lets him do it and then turns and goes to the rope. When Amy goes up, shinnying up like I taught her, Ezra looks away like a gentleman. Davy don't, and I 'spect he won't look away when I go up, neither. I can't wait to get that little weasel alone for a while, but it ain't gonna happen now, I know.

"I gotta talk to you, Davy," I whispers.

"I know, Jacky, I know," says he, "but I got the duty tomorrow and they won't let you on the ship, not to talk to the likes o' me, they won't. But it will all keep. I'll see you on Monday. I'll come here."

I bet you will, thinks I. I've got to get that Annie aside and tell her some of the facts of life. And of sailors.

I go up the ladder, and Ezra and Davy walk back downtown together, seaman and lawyer, brothers at least for this night.

Chapter 32

"But I like him," says Annie.

I had gotten up close to her on Monday morning, when we're in the kitchen scrubbing up the breakfast pots.

"You don't know the little weasel like I do. You'll catch something from him. Or he'll give you a baby and run away to sea."

"I can't believe that," she softly says.

"What's he promised?"

"That he'd think of nothing but me when he's out on the sea."

"That's prolly true," I admits, "but that don't mean much. Will you give him any token?"

"A lock of my hair, braided and tied up in one of my ribbons."

"Aye, and it's lovely I'm sure, Annie, and he'll show that to all his mates so they'll think he's a mighty lover what's broken many a young girl's heart, yours included, you can be sure of that, too."

"But what's the harm in that? I know that I'll probably never see him again after tomorrow, but it's nice to dream on things, sometimes."

"Harrumph," I grumps. It occurs to me that I'm prolly acting a lot like Mistress right now.

"He said he'd swing in his hammock at night with the lock clutched in his hand and next to his heart and all fear banished from his mind, knowing I was safe and warm back on land, no matter what cruel fate awaited his poor self."

"Oh, *please,* that's what they all say. Davy does have a gift of gab, I'll own, if nothing else," I say, thinkin' back to when he talked himself aboard the *Dolphin* when there was plenty more boys bigger and stronger than him. Then again, I done the same thing. But he's prolly not lyin' about lying there in the dark with the token to his breast, for it does get cold and lonely out there. "All right. Just you be careful is all. The Davy I remember don't think with his head, that's for sure. What's the rascal got planned for today?"

"Just a walk in the Common. Then a bite to eat, and then I got to go home at my usual time, you know that, or else my father would kill me."

"Well, you mind the tall grass in the Common, Annie."

"I know how to be careful, Jacky. You're the one what needs to be more careful, from what I've heard."

I ain't got nothin' to say to that.

Davy comes up the hill at about eleven in the morning and I'm layin' for him. I've been about jumpin' out of my skin all yesterday and today, I'm so keen to talk to him.

I head him off at the kitchen door. "Come with me," I say, and we go around to the side and then we're up in my room.

"Keep your voice down and if anyone tries that door, you dive out the window, you hear?" I had put a small wooden wedge under the door to keep us from being surprised.

"Pretty nice kip," says Davy. "How come you're separate from the others?"

"I got busted down from lady to serving girl," I say, makin' myself not hang my head.

"Sounds like something you'd do." He tests the bed. "Why don't you call down for Annie to pop up here for a bit?"

"She's a good girl and a nice girl and a good friend to me and I don't want the likes of you to hurt her—"

"Ah, Jacky Faber, the Mother Superior, lookin' out for her little flock, ain't that sweet..."

"I mean it, Davy..."

"Still the bossy one, ain't you, Jacky? *Now boys, dress up in these pretty little uniforms I made for ye! Now boys, stand up all straight in a line here! Now boys, wear the cute little caps! Now boys...*" He looks at me all serious. "Look, Jacky, she's the first real girl I've met since I got on the *Dolphin*—you don't meet many of 'em in my line of work, you might recall—and, hell, I've only been ashore about a week and a half total since I signed on to this jolly seafarin' life."

"Still..."

He sneers and pokes me on the breastbone with a stiff finger. "No real girls, 'cept for you, of course, but you never did me much good in that way, savin' it all for Jaimy like you was...and is, I reckon. Aww...is that your Jaimy up there on your wall now?"

Davy and I are back in our old stance—nose to nose, eyes narrowed, lower lips jutting out, fingers pointing, each at the other, and snarling.

"You don't know what it's like to be me, Davy, then or now."

"Maybe I don't care what it's like to be a bossy, pig-headed little Cockney chambermaid what thought she was gonna be a lady."

That hurts me and I jerk like I've been hit. I got nothin' to say to that. He knows he hit home 'cause he looks a little ashamed and he don't follow it up with any more jibes.

I make an effort to settle down. Fighting with Davy over female virtue ain't exactly what I had planned for this morning. "I'm sorry. I just don't want you to hurt her is all."

"I'm not going to hurt her, Jacky." He says this gently and I half believe him.

"All right," I say, calm now. I sit down in my chair and fold my hands in my lap. "Please, now tell me what's up with Jaimy."

Davy goes over and flops down on my bed. He *has* gotten longer and leaner, for sure. He is turning into a fine-looking man and it is easy to see why Annie is taken with him. "All right, Jack, I'll tell you." He picks up my pillow and sniffs it and then crams it back under his head. I'm glad to see there is no tar in his hair.

"On the way back to England, he was Mr. Midshipman and Tink and me and Willy was Ordinary Seamen, so our paths didn't cross much anymore, but I will say that Jaimy never lorded it over us but always found a way, like if he had to give us an order, to do it in a way that didn't make us feel like dirt. And, sometimes, if we was some of us on watch in the middle of the night, we'd sit and talk and joke like in the old days. Then we rounded Margate and were taken into the docks on the Thames and little men with notebooks swarmed over the *Dolphin* and declared she was not fit for sea, her knees having been weakened by the blast

of the pirate's fireship that day," says Davy. "You got something to drink here?"

I had sat on the edge of the bed to listen and I got up and
got him a glass of cider from the jug I had put up here for
just such a purpose. It is a little bit hard, and I figure,
shamelessly, that it might loosen his tongue a bit.

"Ummm," he says. "Good."

He puts the glass down on my bedside table and taps it
with his finger. I fill it up again. "I like you as a servin' girl,
Jacky," he says. I give him a low growl. He goes on.

"Anyway, we're back and the *Dolphin*'s crew is bein'
broke up and Tink and Willy and me volunteer to go on the
Raleigh, and bein' seasoned man-o-war's men we are taken
on, and we're happy that at least some of the Brotherhood is
still together, but then some brass hat from the *Endeavor*
comes aboard and he outranks our Captain and he takes a
bunch of men, includin' Tink, to his ship, and then two
days later *another* bleedin' Captain comes up and takes
Willy and some others for the *Temeraire*. Pissed us off, it did,
but what could we do?

"But anyway, the *Raleigh* is layin' next to the *Essex*,
which Jaimy is posted to, and he comes over and says to
come to his house and where's Tink and Willy, but I says
they're gone to sea, it's just him and me now, so we go off
together, brothers again as soon as we're out of sight of the
Royal Navy and we gets in a coach and I'm feelin' like a
proper nob, I am, and we're laughin' and rememberin' old
times, but then we get to his house, which is a pretty fine
place, I can tell you, and we go in and I meet his mother, and
that dragon takes one look at me and I'm off to the servants'
quarters for a meager bite with cold tea and then I'm out the

back door by myself. I ain't seen Jaimy since then as the *Raleigh* made sail the next day and I was gone."

"He didn't try to find you after his mother sent you off downstairs?"

"He was going upstairs to change clothes and I'll wager when he come back down his dear mother had some sort of story for him. Like I ran off after a scullery maid, or got sick or something." Davy draws a long breath. "It was like she didn't want Jaimy to have anything to do with his past life or anybody who was in it. Which is funny considerin' the money that put her family back on its feet come from the likes of us."

I thinks on this and says, "Life ain't fair sometimes, Davy."

"For sure, Jacky."

"What about Liam?" I ask, avoiding the big question for a bit.

"His plan was to take his prize money and light out for his farm in Ireland where his wife and kids were. Whether or not he made it past the press-gangs, I don't know. Saw Snag in a tavern a little later and he seems to think that Liam made it."

Good for you, Liam. I wish you the joy of your farm and your family.

"Jaimy. Did he say anything about me?" I prepare myself for the blow.

"He talked about nothin' but you and I know he checked with every ship that come in from the States to see if you had sent him a letter, but he never got one. There was the *Plymouth* and the *Juno* and the *Shannon*..."

"The *Shannon*?" I cries, and jumps up. "I sent a letter on the *Shannon* and the midshipman who took it from me

337

knew where Jaimy lived and swore that he would deliver it to the house and I believed him!"

"And I'll bet he was as good as his word, Jacky," says Davy quietly and shuts up, letting me figure it out on my own. Which I do.

I sit back down on the edge of the bed. "His mum prolly wants him to marry a fine lady. Which I ain't. And which is why she ain't lettin' my letters get through to him. And now he ain't got no letters from me and prolly thinks I've gone off with someone else."

"That's the way I'd cipher it out, Jacko," says Davy. "And the story of you running around in the riggin' of the *Excalibur* and takin' a dip in your drawers didn't help none, neither."

"You heard of that?"

"*Everybody's* heard of *that*," he says, and then mimics my voice. "'*Ain't no sailor alive what can catch Jacky Faber in the riggin'!*' Oh, you're famous, you are! Famous in legend and song, just like you always wanted!" He rocks back and forth with glee.

"Hush now, you!" I hisses at him. "Someone will hear!"

"Captain Morgan of the *Excalibur* has let it be known that he will run his sword through you at next meeting, and if he has to hang for it, so be it!" he crows. "And I hope to God I'm there as witness!"

"All right. Enough," I says. "I will have a letter for you on the day after tomorrow, when next you have liberty, to deliver to Jaimy. Be good to Annie or I'll find a sword to run through *you*. Now get out. We've got to get ready to serve dinner."

Davy gets up and says, "Gladly, as I got someone to meet." With a wink, he is out the window.

Chapter 33

Jacky Faber
In care of Miss Amy Trevelyne
Dovecote Farm
Quincy, Massachusetts, United States
November 8, 1803

Mr. James Fletcher, Midshipman
On Board the Essex, on Station

Dear Jaimy,

If you are reading this letter, you will know that I met Davy in Boston when his ship made port here. It was a great joy to see him and it was an even greater joy to hear from him that you were well the last time he saw you.

It was with great sorrow, though, that I learned that you have not gotten even one of the many letters that I have sent to you by way of the ships of the Royal Navy that have come to this harbor. It fair broke my heart, it did, to know that you have not been assured of my love for you and have probably gone off into the arms of another by now. Alas, I have not gotten any letters from you, either, and that has been the hardest part of my life here, not knowing how you fare and if you think of my poor self, if at all.

I must now write of something that may distress you: In talking to Davy, he said that you said that you didn't get a letter when the Shannon docked there. Jaimy, I sent a letter on that very ship by way of a very kind and honorable officer who knew your address and promised me that you would get the letter. I know he was as good as his word. There's only one thing we can cipher from this: Someone in your house has not been passing my letters on to you. I will not insult you by telling you who I think it is, but I think you will be able to figure it out. From now on I will send my letters to you on your ship direct.

Whoever has been reading my letters knows that I continue in my love for you in spite of your long silence. If you should want to write to me, please do it to the above address, as I don't know where I will be from one day to the next and I am sure that Mistress Pimm here at the school would not give me any of your letters, as she doesn't approve of sailors and she ain't given me any yet.

All that I have written of my life here has been lost and into it all again I cannot go, at least not now. Let it be enough to say that I am happy and have many new and dear friends, but I have been demoted to serving girl because I got in a bit of trouble. After I got busted down I sent you a letter saying if you didn't want me anymore because of that or anything else, then I was releasing you from your vow of marriage to me, which I here repeat again.

I am enclosing a miniature painting I did of myself in hopes that you might like to look at it sometimes. I have done one of you such as my poor memory and even poorer talent serve, and it hangs over my bed. Your ring rests close to my heart.

It filled my heart with hope to hear from Davy that you did talk fondly of me the last time he saw you. I am still your girl, if you still want me to be that.

With all my love,
Jacky

Chapter 34

⚓ I'm putting the finishing touches on my miniature painting of Annie—one more little dab of blue right...there. Good.

We set her up on a stool in the kitchen 'cause the light's better down there and she's sittin' there all blushin' in my blue dress that I made on the *Dolphin*, the one with the low front 'cause I copied it from the one Mrs. Roundtree was wearin' that day she set me straight on the facts of life— Mrs. Roundtree bein' one of the ladies on Palma, where we made our first liberty call, and copying my dress from hers, considerin' her particular profession, was prolly a mistake—well, what did I know, at the time?

I really think I got Annie pretty good: honey brown ringlets hanging by her cheeks, a ribbon in her hair matching the dress, her upturned nose all jaunty, and a saddle of light freckles over the blush of her cheeks. I'm right proud of this one and it is with a fiendish delight that I lean over my work and paint the bodice of the dress even lower than it actually is 'cause I know it'll drive that imp Davy stark raving mad with lust when he's far away at sea. And with

Annie havin' a lot more on top than me, I say let's make those parts extra plump and peachy, what's the harm?

"There," I says. I put the oval watch glass over the ivory disk and snap the frame down. Then I put Annie's braided lock of hair around the whole thing and bind it up with the blue ribbon. *You really don't deserve this, Davy.* Then I show it to Annie and the Sisterhood.

Squeals all around.

"Oh, do you think I should?" says Annie, crossing her arms over her chest, her face a comely shade of pink tending to the red.

"Oh yes," says Rachel, our oldest and wisest. "Oh yes, you will give it to him!"

"Better not let Father see that," warns Betsey.

"Believe me, he shan't," says Annie, looking at the thing in wonder.

"It's amazing," says Sylvie. "It looks just like her. I can't believe it." She hesitates and then asks, "Jacky, could you…"

"Of course, Sylvie," I say. "Let's drive Henry mad, too. Let's drive them *all* mad!" Shrieks and cheers from my Sisters.

Course this means I got to do all of them, but it's good practice for me and it delights them, so it is all for the good.

But if Annie hoped to spend time with Davy again this day, she is to be disappointed. As we're clearing the dishes at the noon dinner, I lift my head and cock my ear and I hear, far off, the sound of ships' bells and foghorns and trumpets, even, all coming from the harbor. *Uh-oh…* I take my tray of dirty dishes and put it on the cart in the hall and dash to the front door and peek out. I don't like what I hear and see.

"Something's up down at the docks," I say, as I rush back into the dining hall and take the wide-eyed Annie by the arm. "Come, up to the top."

We rush up to my room and I pull down the ladder to the widow's walk and up we go. I grab my spyglass on the way and while she's viewing the scene with *ohh*s and *aah*s, I put the glass to my eye and train it on the three ships down below. Sure enough, there's men running about in a hurry, doin' things that I know is done when ships is about to get under way. The *Guerriere* is flying the commodore's flag and a line of flags is hauled up the masthead. Red square, then white square with blue *X*, then the numeral pennants: one, three, zero, zero. The other ships answer with the same flags racing to their own mastheads: All ships get under way at 1300 hours. For some reason known only to the Royal Navy, all shore leave is canceled and I can hear the seamen's complaint now: *Goddamn Captain prolly had a goddamn fight wi' his goddamn mistress ashore and now I'm missin' me goddamn liberty, I am!*

Davy will not set foot on the United States for quite a while yet, if ever.

Damn! And I ain't talked everything out of him yet!

I take the glass from my eye. "The fleet's leaving early. They'll be at sea by mid-afternoon."

She takes the news calmly. She drops her head and says, "Ah, well."

"Ah, well, nothing!" says I. "I *will* send my letter by him! Do you have your miniature?"

"Yes, it's here in my vest. I was going to give it to him today."

"Maybe you shall yet do it. Let's go!" and I lead the way

344

back down, snatching up my packet from my bedstead on our way through my room. Down the stairs to the first floor and then down into the kitchen. "Cover for us!" I yell as we go out the back door.

We run up to the stables and I take a bridle from the rack on the wall and I go into Gretchen's stall and put the bit in her mouth and slap the harness over her head and back her out of her stall.

"Surely a saddle, Jacky!" says Henry, coming upon us in our haste.

"No time, Henry! Open the barn doors!" I leap onto Gretchen's back and move her over to the hay crib, which has a side like a ladder. "Climb up here, Annie, and get on behind me! She can carry us both. Arms around me now and hold on!"

When I feel she's on, I give a "Hyah!" and dig my heels into Gretchen's sides and out we bolt from the stable and down the road we go. I've been riding long enough that my legs are strong enough to grasp the horse's sides without the need of stirrups, and I've tried it a couple times bareback so I know I can do it.

We get to a full-out gallop down through the Common and Annie's hangin' on so tight I can hardly breathe, but she's game and don't cry out and when we get to the street we hardly slow down at all and some people look up in alarm and some shake their fists at us for riding so fast through the town but I don't care, *we've got to get there in time!*

We're down School Street, and the boys and girls at the schoolyard there gaze in wonderment as two crazy girls on horseback thunder past them, and then it's on to Water Street and then a hard left on Kilby and then a right on State and then the cobblestones of the street give way to the planks of the pier and we're on Long Wharf, where the ships are tied alongside.

There's last-minute provisions being taken on all three of the ships, but the one on the end of the pier and closest to sea, the *Java,* was already pullin' in her gangway and startin' to throw off lines. The next one in line is Davy's ship, the *Raleigh,* and the final one, flying the commodore's flag, is the *Guerriere.* It will be the last to go.

I push Gretchen into the melee around the *Raleigh*'s gangway and earn myself a few curses for my cheek. I'm lookin' around for Davy and I scan the riggin' but somehow don't think he's aboard yet, and I'm lookin' over the heads of the crowd on the pier and—

"Jacky! Annie!"

I wheel Gretchen about and see Davy bounding toward us. As I suspected, he was ashore when the call to return to ship went out and he waited till the last possible moment to go back aboard.

I throw my right leg over Gretchie's head and slide off and then I help Annie off and she slips down with a fine flash of petticoats.

I got to get my business done first 'cause Davy sure ain't got eyes for me. I hand him my packet and say, "Put your hand on your tattoo."

"Which one?" he says with a grin.

"Your Brotherhood tattoo, you ninny. I've no wish to see whatever else you've had stitched on your nasty butt," I huffs. He shrugs and puts his hand on the proper place.

"Now, swear, Davy, that you will try to deliver this to Jaimy and you will place it in no one's hand but his."

"All right, Jacky, I swear on my tattoo. I will do my best to get it to him."

"Thank you, Davy, and be careful of it. There is a miniature painting in there that's on ivory what can break, and make sure it don't get wet, neither, as they are watercolors and can run."

"All right, Jacky," he says, and turns to Annie.

They embrace and I turn around to give them what little privacy they can find on a crowded pier. I hear some *whoops* from the ship, and I know that Davy's reputation is being made. I wait, patting poor Gretchie, who's standing there snorting, her chest heaving like a bellows. *Ain't you the best girl, then? Poor Gretchen, you had a lot easier life before I got here, didn't you?* She nuzzles my cheek and forgives me.

"Here, Davy, is a token to remember me by," I hear Annie say with a slight quiver in her voice. "I think Jacky made me too pretty."

The show-off in me wants to turn around and see what he thinks of my work, but I don't have to, as I hear him draw in his breath sharply.

"No, no... not too pretty at all. Not by half, dear Annie. Trust me, this will warm many a lonely night."

"Good-bye, Davy. God be with you. Be safe."

"Good-bye, Annie. I will write to you. I will be back."

I turn around and he has his hands on her shoulders and she has her arms around his waist.

Davy plants a final one on her forehead and they part and he lopes back to his ship. I did not think it would happen, but my chest tightens upon seeing Davy bound up the gangway, him lookin' again all gangly and boyish 'mid all that cruel machinery of war. He leaps up into the top to his station on the main royal yard, he raises his fist and shouts down, "Good-bye again, dear Annie, and good-bye to you, too, Jack! Bless the Navy and up with the Brotherhood forever!" I raise my fist in return.

The Sisterhood, too, I thinks, as I gathers up Annie and we ride at a much slower pace back to the school. We take a different route so we don't have to say, "Sorry" to anyone we might have run over on the way down.

We get back. We are not caught. I cover for Annie as she goes back up on the widow's walk to watch the ships leave the harbor and put to sea.

Chapter 35

Davy's gone and the fleet's gone and my letter's off and I guess things will settle back to normal, or as normal as things get around me. Sylvie and Henry are forever sneakin' off and moonin' and spoonin', and Annie heaves great sighs heavenward to the gods and goddesses of love.

I'm keeping busy doing miniatures of all the girls to make up for all the times I've said *"Cover for me!"* on my way out to some mischief. And I'll do a Henry for Sylvie and a Davy for Annie. *And* an Amy for Ezra. But I won't tell her who it's for, 'cause, as she always says, "I'm not ready for that sort of thing yet."

I take all my miniature paintings to Mr. Peet for his comments and he shows me where I've done right and where I've gone wrong and he gives me hints on how to do better. I keep up with my arithmetic and pass my homework sheet in to Mr. Sackett, who corrects it and hands it back, and I study French with Monsieur Bissell when he and I can find a moment.

It is such a moment when, having finished the morning chores, I find time to talk to Monsieur Bissell about some problems I've been having with the French language and we are both leaning over a desk and he's explainin' to me why the verb "to be" goes through so many twisted versions. "It's just like English, Jacky. In English we say, 'I am, you are, we have been, we are, he is, they are, we will have been, they...'"

There is a rustle of black silk and a coldness in the air, and I turn my head fearfully about. It is Mistress standing there.

"Is this part of your duties?" she demands, knowing very well the answer.

I stand and say, "No, Mistress."

"She is a good and willing student, Mistress," says Monsieur Bissell, gallantly.

"Thank you, Monsieur Bissell," says Mistress. "Faber, go to my office."

Oh Lord, I'm gonna get it now.

I follow her to her office and advance to the white line and put my toes on it and then flop down on the desk and pull up my skirts, feeling very sorry for myself. A tear works its way out of my eye and it goes across the bridge of my nose and falls to the blotter on Mistress's desktop. I breaks the rule about talkin' to her without bein' told to but I don't care, I'm just gonna get beat anyway. "I don't know why you want to hurt me so, Mistress, I really don't. I'm middlin' good. I do my work, I do, you won't find me shirkin' any of it." I sniffs. "I was just trying to learn."

I wait for the sting, but it does not come.

"Oh, do be quiet and stand up, girl," says Mistress. She sits down as I straighten up in confused relief. *What?*

She looks at me standin' there quiverin' for a while, and

finally she says, "You thought, did you not, that I did not know what you were up to?"

What did she find out? The Pig? The singing, the dancing? Oh no...

"I d-don't know what you mean, Mistress," I quavers.

"You see, I know everything about my school. Everything," says Mistress. She has a pen in her hand and is tapping it on the edge of her desk. "For instance, I know that you have continued your studies, when, as a serving girl, you were not expected to do so." *Tap...tap...tap.*

"Yes, Mistress," I admits, hanging my head and looking contrite.

"And, furthermore, I know that you have been tutoring young Rebecca Adams." *Tap...tap.*

"Yes, Mistress."

She lets me stand there some more, wonderin' what she's gonna do with me. *Tap...tap.*

"Actually, I find all that quite commendable," she says at last, and relief floods through me. "You will continue to help Miss Adams. Set aside an hour each day, as she needs it. She is too young to be here, I knew from the start, but it is hard to say no to Mr. Adams. I would send her back home, but her family is overseas on diplomatic duty. Do you think she can catch up on her studies?"

"Oh yes, Mistress," I say. "She is a bright girl. She is coming along nicely. She just needs some help and some kind words."

"Which you shall provide. I cannot have the other teachers give her individual instruction as it is not a profitable use of their time." Still she taps. *Tap...tap...tap.*

"Yes, Mistress, I will be pleased to do it."

Mistress continues to regard me. "So you see, do you not, that I know *everything* concerning my school?"

I think she is saying this with some satisfaction, almost smiling, in fact. And still…*tap*…*tap*.

I think, as I stand there waiting to be dismissed, on what she does *not* know about her school, or about me. I think back on what Ezra told me that last time in his office, about the Preacher closing in on me, and I decide to press my luck.

"Then you know, Mistress, that Preacher Mather has petitioned the Court to gain custody of me and my assets."

The tapping stops.

Although I am staring over the top of her head, eyes cased, as is my usual posture when standin' on the Line, I can see well enough that she did *not* know that. I go on.

"Please don't let him take me, Mistress. I don't want to go over there. I want to stay here. Please, Mistress."

Saying that, I feel my eyes get all hot and I think I'm going to cry 'cause I really meant what I said.

"Look at me, girl," says Mistress, and I drop my eyes to hers and I see the fury in them. I sense that she is outraged to the very marrow of her bones. "Tell me. Have you learned humility?"

"Yes, Mistress," I manage to say.

"And have you learned that your conduct reflects not only on your own reputation but on that of the school and all in it as well?"

"Yes, Mistress."

"Do you now have a clear notion of what it means to be one of my girls?"

"Yes, Mistress, I do."

She continues her steady gaze into my eyes. I want to look away, but I can't. At last she speaks.

"Very well then, Miss Faber, you may come back upstairs and resume your studies."

It hits me like a club and I am staggered.

"And, Miss Faber, please do your best to make the transition smooth. Without your usual histrionics."

"Yuh—yes, Mistress," I manages to stammer.

"Very good. You are dismissed."

Mistress turns in her chair and faces away from me, and I turn on my heel and go out into the hall, my mind all awhirl. I place my back against the wall and try to collect myself.

My thoughts are spinning wildly about my head, but one thing stands out: *She is trying to help me.* I don't know if she intended to reinstate me before I told her about the Preacher or not. I don't know if she's thinkin' about my money. I don't know if she just hates the idea of *anyone* messin' with her school. I don't know nothin'. I just know she is trying to help me and she has bought me some time, and I thank her for it.

I take three deep breaths and then I stand up straight. I put on the Look. I turn and go to my room. I take my school dress from my sea chest and carefully unfold it and lay it upon my bed. I take off my serving gear and put it neatly away. I put on my school dress once again.

I go back down the stairs, and hearing the chimes, I go in to dinner.

PART III

Chapter 36

The day of my reinstatement as a possible lady, I walked into the dining hall, the Look in place, and I headed for my old spot next to Amy, who looked up in complete surprise and then delight. The ladies and the serving girls looked and wondered at seeing me once again in my apprentice-lady rig, and as I got to my chair, Dolley Frazier rose from hers and started clapping and then Martha Hawthorne did the same and then little Rebecca and then others till the place resounded with their applause. Clarissa, of course, sat in stunned silence, a sour expression on her face. Annie and Betsey and Sylvie were serving and beamed their pleasure at my joy with their broad smiles.

Mistress came in and marched to her place and called on me for the grace and I gave it, thanking the good Lord for the food and for all those, both upstairs and down, who have bestowed on my poor self the precious gift of their caring love and friendship.

That evening, the Preacher was not at the supper table, nor would he ever again reappear there this winter. Two girls are called each night to dine with Mistress, instead of just the one.

The next morning, I got up early, washed, dressed, and went down to the kitchen, where I knew the staff would be having their breakfast. They looked up in surprise as I took a tray of eggs and went around serving them to show that Sisterhood is more powerful than any notions of class or standing, and Rachel says, "Now that you're a teacher as well as a fine lady, shouldn't you be sittin' at the head table, then, Miss Faber?" and I say, "You'll call me Jacky when I'm down here or I'll tip this platter of eggs over your head, and won't you make a fine bride for your Mr. Barkley, then, Miss Rachel?" and the other girls hoot and laugh and all is easy between us.

And so we passed the winter, the Dread Sisterhood of the Lawson Peabody and I. We attended to our studies or did our duties, depending on whether we were lady or girl. We read. We painted. We stitched. We had oceans and oceans of time, and we filled our hours with music and song and talk, endless talk. And I waited for a letter that did not come.

The snows came at last, and I do not have to fear them as I did when I was on the streets of London. We are quite cozy here, with all four fireplaces blazing away, and it is pleasant to study and stitch in front of the glowing fires and maybe roast a potato on the edge of the coals for a hot treat.

Course, with the snow on the ground I can't haunt the Preacher no more, not the way I was, 'cause the snow would show my footprints on Janey Porter's grave and then the game would be up, as ghosts don't leave tracks. No, I must content myself with putting on my black burglar's outfit and, on those dark nights when the moon is down and the snow has slid off the church roof, crawling over and scratching at the tiles over his head and giving out a piteous moan or two. The Preacher still has the night watchman making rounds now and then, but he can't see me up on the roof.

I see the Preacher every Sunday, of course, and he seems to be coming apart, piece by piece—he is a shadow of his former self, with sunken cheeks and black circles under his eyes. His hands shake as he turns the pages of the Bible up on the pulpit. I would pity him if I could, but I know what he's done, and I can't.

There's now some empty pews on Sunday and people are beginning to talk. Amy tells me that Puritans are now called Congregationalists 'cause they ain't got a central authority, like us Church of England types got the Archbishop of Canterbury and the Catholics got the Pope. Each Congregational church is unto itself alone, and there ain't no higher authority to complain to if you got a problem with your preacher, which is why, I guess, that the Preacher has lasted here. He's a Mather, says Amy, and he's got powerful supporters in the congregation. We'll see.

I went with Amy to spend Christmas at Dovecote, with her and her family. I met her mum and dad, bows and curtsies all around, and I think I acquitted myself well in that regard—can hardly tell me from a real lady now. Amy's mother is sweet and says how nice that Amy finally has a little friend, which causes great mortification in Amy. Mrs. Trevelyne is the exact opposite of Amy—happy, gay, and fluffy—and she is fun to be with. Amy's father, Colonel

Trevelyne, is a strapping, thick, tree trunk of a man, given to wearing sporting clothes and smoking big cigars.

A tree, a very sweet-smelling spruce, was brought in as is the new custom, borrowed from the Germans, and we had great fun decorating it with popcorn strings and small candles and bits of crystal. Mrs. Trevelyne had brought back from New York boxes of colored glass balls, and these were hung on the tree, where they gathered and reflected the light from the candles most wondrously. Even the high-and-mighty Randall joined in the spirit of the thing and helped decorate the tree.

On Christmas Eve we had songs and carols and happy conversation, and the household staff and the field people were all brought in and I got up and sang "The Cherry Tree Carol," which everyone said was top-notch, and all received from the Colonel their gifts of money and geese and turkeys to share with their own families on Christmas Day. The Colonel, for all his faults about money and gambling, is not an ungenerous man.

Afterward, when only family and me was left, we exchanged gifts. I gave the elder Trevelynes a miniature portrait of their daughter, the only thing I have to give, really, and they proclaimed themselves delighted. I gave Amy the portrait of Ezra, him sittin' there in profile lookin' all right and proper with his little smile on his lips, and she blushes and all tease her, but I think she likes it even though again she said she's not yet ready for that sort of thing.

Amy, for her part, gave me a large package bound in bright ribbon, and I opened it, and in it was a fine riding habit, all maroon with turned-back lapels of warm light gray and skirt of deepest green. When I say it is too much, I can't possibly accept it, she waves me off with, "It is too small for me now, and I have no younger sister to give it to." Once again I have to blink back tears. I will no longer have to wear the duster in Equestrian class.

Randall Trevelyne has forgiven me, I guess, for having dragged his sister down into the haunts of the poor, for he gave me a fine Spanish mantilla, made of black lace, which he offhandedly said he had picked up in a secondhand shop in Cambridge for almost nothing, but I don't believe him. In return, I gave him a portrait, not of Clarissa, which I *would* not do, nor one of himself, which he would surely give to that selfsame Clarissa, but rather one of the many I have done of myself for practice. It is shameless, I know, but still I do it and say, with my eyes so low cast down, "Just to remember me by."

It was a wonderful, wonderful time, that holiday at Dovecote. And, of course, I never missed a chance to get up on the Sheik when I was there.

During this winter, too, I went and looked up Mr. Fennel and Mr. Bean, the actors who had given me their card back in the Pig that day. I got put in some small parts like Puck in *A Midsummer Night's Dream,* and other such elf parts. Being that I can play the pennywhistle sort of fits right into that, and I've got a real smart outfit, all green stockings and a little short kilt and a top that looks like it's made out of green leaves and a pointed green cap. I'm billed as "Jack Tar" so as not to be discovered as a girl 'cause that would be a scandal. 'Cause of the costume and all.

I only do these parts on weekends when I know I won't be caught, as I don't want to be busted again. I do love to take the bows and hear the applause, though. And, it makes me a little money, money that I keep in a little money belt that I have made for myself, which fits flat around my waist. When I get enough copper and silver coins from the acting jobs and from doing my solo act at the Pig on some Saturday afternoons, I change them into the tiny ten-dollar gold pieces, which fit more compact on my belly. I have several now. I take the belt off only to wash.

I do not completely escape the sting of the lash this winter, though. We were all in Household Management class one dreary gray day and I was bored beyond all sense and began making faces and crossing my eyes to make Rebecca Adams, sitting next to me, laugh and giggle, which, of course, she did. But then Mistress rose up and said, "Miss Adams, would you like to stand up and tell us just what you find so humorous about providing a clear and complete accounting of household expenses to your husband? What mirth is to be found therein that we dullards have overlooked?"

Little Rebecca went white as a sheet and got to her feet with great difficulty, as if rising to mount the scaffold and face Eternity itself. She was unable to speak, but only stood there, shaking in mortal terror.

"Come up here," said Mistress, picking up her rod and tapping it on her desk. The poor child looked like she would go off in a dead faint, and didn't move.

I rose to my feet 'cause it was my own stupid fault that this happened, and I pushed Rebecca back down in her seat and said, "Begging your pardon, Mistress, but it was not her fault as I was playing the fool with her." Not waiting for an invite, I marched up the aisle, went around Mistress's desk, and flopped down upon it, my skirts up and my face looking out to the class. It occurs to me that this is what the crowd must look like to those poor sods strapped to the guillotine.

Mistress raised her rod and gave me four and then I returned to my seat. Strange thing, though—Mistress did not hit me hard. It was as if she pulled back on each blow just before it landed. Although it made me wince and I had to snuffle back tears of humiliation as I went back to my seat, the beating did not hurt at all. Strange, that.

Rebecca looked at me with absolute worship in her eyes, and at supper that evening she left her table and came and sat with Amy and me. Then we were joined by Dolley and Martha, who gave my shoulder a squeeze as she sat down.

The winter does wane and the Sisterhood does increase.

I've even been doing some decent needlework. I've worked for some days on the edges of a silk pillow slip, embroidering it with intertwined roses and briars, and a few blue anchors thrown in for good measure. I wonder, as I do the stitching, whether Jaimy's head will ever lie next to mine upon this pillowcase.

Nothing, *nothing* from Jaimy.

Chapter 37

James Emerson Fletcher, Midshipman
On Board HMS Essex
January 25, 1804

Jacky Faber
The Lawson Peabody School for Young Girls
Beacon Street, Boston, Massachusetts, USA

Dear Jacky,

At least I know that you are not dead, and that is some comfort to me. There was a new group of sailors brought on board the Essex yesterday and one of them was lately come from the Excalibur. I later overheard him regaling his fellows on the fo'c'sle with an account of a girl in Boston racing seasoned seamen through the Excalibur's top rigging. I knew it could be none other than you, my wild and foolish girl. I have chosen not to believe their tale of the girl taking off her dress and diving into the water, and attribute that to the sailors' love of tall tales.

That is the only news of you that I have gotten since we parted. I exchange letters quite often with my mother and she informs me with each letter that I have received nothing from you and I am cast down into darkness each time she so informs me.

Why, if you were on the Excalibur for your sport, why did you not send me a letter by her? I know you to be many things, Jacky, but cruel and hard-hearted and indifferent are not among them. You must tell me why you are treating me so.

I throw myself into my studies to try and get you out of my mind, but I am never completely successful. I shall be testing for lieutenant within the year, but it will be a hollow honor if I succeed.

We keep the French fleet bottled up here, with endless patrols back and forth, back and forth across the mouth of the bay, but they've got to come out eventually, and when they do, well, maybe a cannonball will cure my black despair.

Please write, Jacky, if only to tell me I am no longer in your heart. I am desolate.

Your most humble,
Jaimy

Chapter 38

⚓ *Spring!*

By God it's finally spring! Spring, when a poor girl can poke her head out of her cloak without fear of it bein' frozen off at the neck! Spring so long in comin', oh, cruel winter would just not let go, oh no, he wouldn't! Then suddenly one day the clouds of winter broke and the heat was on the land and the snow patches melted and shrunk and slunk away and then were gone and incredibly there's a green blush on the grass and by God, it's spring! Hooray!

I dance up the path to the stables and say to Henry, "My horse, Henry, my horse! For it is spring and it is Saturday and no one is lookin' and I have my fine riding habit on and I will ride wild and free and I will go downtown and I will—"

"Please calm down, Miss Faber," says Henry. He goes and gets Gretchen and puts the sidesaddle on her and will not hear of any other. "You're a lady again and you will ride sidesaddle or you will not ride at all."

I think I catch a glimpse of Sylvie's skirt disappearing around a corner of the stable. Ah, 'tis spring and everyone's thoughts turn to those of love.

"And I shan't ride till you call me Jacky again, Henry, I won't."

"All right, Jacky. Up you go."

And I'm up and off!

Gretchen and I thunder across the Common and I can feel her beneath me and I know that she is just as glad to get out as me and she fairly kicks up her heels and we go crazily rollicking across the land, hallooing as we go and making general fools of ourselves until we pull up at the dear old Pig and I slide off.

"What's the good word, Maudie?" says I, as I enter and pull back my cloak. I revel in the feel and the look of the maroon riding jacket and I know I am committing the sin of pride, but right now I don't care. It is spring and I think I can be forgiven.

"Death and taxes, dear," says Maudie, full of cheer as usual. I survey the half-empty house and reflect that it ain't as good for Maudie and Bob as when Gully and I played the house, but it ain't as bad as it was before. They'll get by.

"It is our own dear Puck, Mr. Fennel, and looking especially fine!"

"She is indeed, Mr. Bean! A glass of wine with you, dear Puck!"

I spy the two rogues sitting at a table by the fire. Though 'tis spring, there's still a nip in the air. I go over to them and Mr. Fennel pulls out a chair and I sit down.

"A cup of tea will be fine, Maudie, thanks," says I. "What's the news?" It's plain that they are quite pleased with themselves about something.

"We have rented a bigger and better hall, the very Fenwick, itself, for the season, have we not, Mr. Fennel?"

"We have, indeed, Mr. Bean, and therein our gallant troupe shall reach even greater heights of theatrical glory. We plan to do the complete *Lear*, not just the ending! How fine will that be! We shall be the toast of Boston!"

"Yes, and come summer, we shall take the whole thing on the road and then become the toast of the entire coast, from Boston to Richmond, shall we not, Mr. Fennel?"

"Yes, Mr. Bean, we shall. Now, dear, once again we beg you to take the role of Cordelia. What say? You would be perfect for the role. *Hmm?*"

I shake my head. They had wanted me to do Cordelia in the bit of *Lear* they have been doing, but I just couldn't do it. The part where Cordelia is hanged at the end, well, I can't even *watch* it, let alone play her. As written, that part of the play takes place offstage, but Fennel and Bean have staged it in full view of the audience for the shock value. And shock value it has, for sure—they have devised a dress, a black one, that has a bunch of straps inside it that go around various parts of the actress and then up her back to a loop, and the noose hooks on to that, not to her neck. But it sure looks real. When the Executioner kicks the chair from beneath her feet and Cordelia falls, the shriek from the audience can be heard clear out on the street, which is where I'm at during this part, covering my ears with my hands and trying to keep old memories from wellin' up.

I did see it done once, when they first rigged up the actress, and when they did it, I had to run outside and throw up. I hear they have several faintings at each show. "No, Sirs,

I cannot do that," I say firmly. "Best let me keep doing the small parts as I have been doing with great joy, for who knows where I'll be come summer." Maudie brings me my tea, and I thank her and sip at it.

I joke with the merry pair for a while, but the pull of the new spring sun is too much and I bid them and Maudie a good day and I'm out the door. I take Gretchen's reins from the hitching rail and walk dreamily along beside her, my face held up to the sun.

We walk past the alley next to the Pig and a clawlike hand reaches out of the shadows and hauls me in. Gretchen whinnies and shies away and I drop the reins and try to get at me shiv, but...A familiar smell hits my nose like a hammer.

"Gully?" I say. "Gully, what?..."

If it's possible, Gully MacFarland is even dirtier than last I saw him. There's a wild, crazy gleam in his eye, and I waste no time in stickin' my finger in that eye and snarlin', "Gully, you miserable son of a bitch, where's my money? I'll have it right now or I'll call the constable and have you hanged for a common thief!"

He bats my hand away from his face and something like a grin splits his grimy face as he says in a cracked and ravished voice, "We got us a job, Moneymaker." He has even less teeth than before, and what teeth are left are green and rotten. His rancid breath would put our cesspool to shame.

"I ain't playin' anywhere with the likes of you, Gully, not now, not ever. You stole my money, you lyin' bastard!"

"Back up on the top of the world again, ain't-cha, Moneymaker? A fine lady again, you are, I can tell by how ye're dressed—and fine dress it is, Little Miss Tidymouse."

He is unsteady on his legs, but still he reaches inside his coat and pulls out a bottle with a vile-lookin' greenish milky juice in it, and he puts it to his lips and swallows long. It is disgustin' to see his gristly Adam's apple bob up and down.

"How long you think you'll be in that fine gear when I tells your schoolmistress what you been doin'…playin' in low taverns, showin' of your legs, spendin' nights at Bodeen's…entertaining gentlemen…"

"That ain't true and you know it! I'm gonna tell Maudie and Bob you're back, and they'll fix you good."

"You tell them that and I'll go straight to your school-marm."

"How could you be so mean, Gully?" I says. My mind spins around but all it comes up with is *I'm trapped.*

He shrugs and says, "I'll meet you here on Thursday night, Moneymaker. There's some ships in. We'll make some money."

"Right, which you'll steal, you drunken sot…"

He puts the vile bottle to his lips again. That stuff is a new one on me—it ain't rum nor whiskey, that's for sure—and it don't seem to be doing Gully much good. I ain't never seen him *this* bad, and I've seen him pretty bad.

"So, meet me in front of the Plow and Anchor at ten Thursday night and just bring your whistle—it's mainly the dancin' you'll be doin', anyway. We'll be playin at Skivareen's."

"*Skivareen's!*" I shouts. "Gully, that's the lowest dive in town. Even Mrs. Bodeen won't allow her girls in there!"

"Ten o'clock. Here. Don't be late. We go on at half past ten. Remember, Moneymaker, you show up or I'm on the steps to your school first thing in the morning with many a fine tale to tell."

He lurches off down the street, clutching his bottle. The Lady Lenore is strapped to his back and it looks all forlorn hanging there amid his rags.

Damn! And everything was goin' so good!

Chapter 39

I've got my serving gear on, 'cause I can hide my shiv in my weskit, and my whistle in there, too, and 'cause I certainly don't want to be in Skivareen's in my school dress, as I sure don't want to be before Judge Thwackham on my knees in that dress again. This evening, after supper, I went up to my old room and took out my serving clothes and laid them out on the bed. Then, after prayers and lights-out, at nine, I lay there in the dormitory for a while, and when all the breathing about me is slow and regular, I pull back the covers and creeps out of the room and up the stairs.

I'm pullin' my nightdress over my head when I hears a footfall. As I pokes up my face, I sees that it's Amy standin' there, wringin' her hands.

"Please, Jacky, tell me you're not going out," she whispers. "Please tell me that."

"I got to, Sister. Gully MacFarland is back in town and he wants me to play with him."

"But you can't! You're upstairs again!"

"He has threatened to go to Mistress and tell lies on me. Damned lies, to be sure, but lies he can make stick. All he has to do is accuse me and I'm expelled. He is a changed man, Amy. A very sick one, too."

"Oh," she wails. "This is going to turn out badly, I just know it."

"Hush, you'll wake the others." I've finished dressing, and after I put in my shiv and my whistle, I pull up my skirts around my waist and say, "Wrap those lengths of rope around my waist and hips now. Tight, so they don't slip down. Now, don't ask, just do it."

Whimpering, she does it and I fix the ends so they won't fall out.

I put my regular escape rope around my shoulder and go to the window.

"I will wait here for you, Jacky. Please be careful."

"This will be the last time with Gully, I swear. I'm gonna take care of that," I says, and then I am gone.

Gully is sitting at the appointed spot, his back against a wall, mouth hangin' open and legs sprawled out on the cobblestones. I nudge him with my foot and says, "This is it, Gully. I ain't doin' this no more."

"Yeah, yeah," he says without listenin' to me. "Le's go." He struggles to his feet and we head down to the lowest part of town.

The fleet is definitely in, 'cause I can see their mastheads and rigging hangin' out there in the gloom on Long Wharf. Looks to be four of them, one a First Rater with two decks of gun ports, one over the other. Eighty-eight guns, what a thing. Plenty of sailors, too, on the wharf and thronging the streets. Maudie should do good tonight. I don't bother asking Gully why we ain't playing in no decent tavern—it's plain none of them would let him anywhere near their places, the condition he's in now. If Maudie found out he was back, she'd have her Bob beat him half to death for running out on his room and board.

I see a lit doorway at the end of Market Street by Sprague's Wharf, where some dirty little tubs are tied up. Skivareen's don't even got a sign. Gully goes in first and then I go in, and already I don't like this crowd. There's a cheer upon seein' me, but I look around and don't see none of my regulars. I see some men smirk and point at me and some wink at Gully and he winks back. *What's going on here?*

Gully takes his fiddle out and tunes up. He steps to the low platform that serves as a stage in this hell. The place stinks of piss and sweat and some other things I don't wanna know about. I step up also and pull out my whistle—the sooner we get this over with, the better.

Gully says "Saddle the Pony" and we tears into it and then we do "The Pet o' the Pipers" and things seem to be going all right, and though my heart ain't in it, I does my best, 'cause I hates to give a bad performance, no matter what. But then Gully turns from the fiddle tunes and the funny ones like "New York Girls" and calls for a whole string of the dirty songs, which he know I don't like to play. Things like "The Cuckoo's Nest," and all the men are lookin' at me funny, like they're expectin' somethin'.

I'm glarin' at Gully after the last number and he says, "Put away the whistle. Just dance from now on."

Then he plays a long, long jig and I'm bouncin' up and down and clatterin' me feet as fast as I can. Then he brings that one to an end and plays *another* jig and I look at him all curious.

Then it happens and all comes clear.

There's a disagreeable-lookin' cove, who looks like he ain't washed in a month, at the table next to the stage and he gets up and comes over to me and holds a fiver up in front of my nose.

"Ain't you just the prettiest little thing, bouncin' around up there so gay." Before I can do anything, he stuffs the bill down my shirtfront. "Now let's see how you bounces without yer shirt!" The rest of the house roars its approval.

I turn to Gully with my mouth open and say, *"What?"* and he just shrugs and says, "Why not?"

I look back at the crowd and another bloke has pulled out another crumpled bill. He throws it at my feet. It's a twenty, and we ain't never been tipped a twenty before.

Really scared now, I looks to Gully for help, but he just looks at me real hard and says, "Do it."

I look hard back at him "So now you're a pimp, as well." I pull the bill out of my bodice and throw it on the floor and ram my whistle back in my vest and heads for the...*by God, they're tryin' to close the door! I'll be trapped in here!* I whip out me shiv and hold it out in front of me and the bloke who's closin' the door thinks better of it and moves back and I'm out the door and into the cool night air.

I put me shiv back in its usual spot in me vest and stand there, my chest heavin' with the anger that's ragin' through me. Then the door is jerked open and Gully lunges out and I rushes at him and sticks my finger in his face and shouts, "What the hell were you thinkin' of in there? What kind of girl—"

The back of his hand hits my face and I go to my knees. He pulls my face up to his and says, "Listen, bitch. You're gonna go back in there and do exactly what they say. Understand? *Exactly* what they—"

Through the fog of my shattered mind, I realize the men are pouring out the door, calling out to Gully.

That's it, teach her a lesson!

Show 'er 'er place!

Damn bum show. Waste of time, it was...

Gully yells after 'em, "Wait! Wait! Come back. She'll do it...Damn, they're leaving! Goddammit! Twenty-five dollars and that was just to start! Now, nothing! You..." And he rounds on me kneeling there helpless, and he balls his fist and brings it crashin' down on my eye. My head explodes in pain and shock, and he lets go of me neck and I fall in a heap of weepin' misery to the cobblestones. He gives me another curse and goes back inside.

I lie there for a while and then I get up and stagger over to an alleyway. I get in there and I lie back down 'cause I'm so dizzy with the force of his blow that I can't stand right. I put my hand to my eye and feel that it is already beginning to swell. In a while I get up and go to the Pig.

When I get there, I don't go inside but instead go around the back to Bob's work shed and take his wheelbarrow from where it leans against a wall. I set off rattlin' back down to Skivareen's, and when I gets there, I puts the wheelbarrow back in the shadows of the alleyway. I can hear Gully rantin' and ravin' inside, and I sits down to wait.

He's thrown out into the street at about two o'clock in the morning, barely conscious. The Lady Lenore comes flying out soon after, but I manage to break her fall.

I bring the wheelbarrow up next to him and I say,

"Come on, Gully, we've got to get you home. Up now." I put my hands under his arms and help him to his feet.

"Moneymaker?" he says, his voice all thick and stupid. "Where you been?" He tries to focus on me, but he can't. "Lenore?"

"I've got her, she's safe. Over here now, Gully." I get him between the handles of the barrow and eases him back. I need him far enough forward with his weight over the wheel so that I'll be able to lift him. *There. That's good.* "Lie back, Gully. Lie back and sleep."

He does. Soon he snores.

I lift my skirts and untie the lengths of rope that I had tied there. I tie each of his ankles to the wheelbarrow handles then I tie one end of a piece of rope around one wrist and pull that arm over the side of the box and I take the rope underneath and wrap it around the wheel housing a few times and then bring it up on the other side to his other wrist. I tuck in the ends so they will not drag.

Then I take the small ball of rags that I had put in my pocket and I pinch Gully's nostrils shut and when he gasps and opens his mouth, I crams the gag in.

There. Time to go. I sling the Lady Lenore over my shoulder and I grab the handles and lift. Not too bad. I've got about two hundred yards to the water. I can make it.

I rattle off down the street and the jarring motion of the hard wooden wheel over the cobblestones wakes Gully and he looks about in confusion. He notices that his hands and feet are tied and he starts struggling.

"I knows how to tie the knots, Gully, as I've been to sea. The more you struggle, the tighter they'll get." He struggles anyway, mumbling into his gag.

My eye is almost completely swollen shut, and now I can't see out of it at all.

"You hit me, Gully, you did. You was my partner and was supposed to look out for me, but you didn't. What you did was take me to that place where I didn't want to go and try to make me do something I didn't want to do, just so's you could buy more of that green stuff."

Gully's shaking his head back and forth.

"You prolly don't even remember doin' this to me, Gully, right? I see you shakin' your head, but you did it, Gully, you put your mark on me, and you'll do it again the next time you get drunk and I can't let that happen, I can't. I got to get rid of you, Gully. I'm sorry, but I do."

At this, his eyes grow wide and he cranes his head about to look where we're goin' and he sees that we're goin' toward the water. The look in his eyes changes from one of confusion to fear. He makes a loud sound into the gag and redoubles his thrashing about. It don't do him no good.

'Cause of my tiredness and my throbbin' eye, I'm startin' to ramble and sometimes I make sense and sometimes I don't.

"What's it gonna be like if I lose me eye, Gully? If my Jaimy comes again for me, will I lift my face to him and show him a gaping empty eyehole? Or an eye that's all filmed over, disgustin' milky white, staring out all blind at nothin'?

"You don't know this about me, Gully, but in some quarters I'm known as Bloody Jack 'cause I killed two men by my own hand. Yes, it's true. It's also true that they had it comin' just like you got it comin', Gully, but it still weighs heavy on my soul."

The fear in his eyes has been replaced by pure terror. He cranes his head and twists his neck around again and sees that we're about halfway to the water. He makes mewling sounds.

"You know, Gully, it's such a shame. We had a really good act. People really liked us. Good people, not like those scum back there. And, yes, I know you're sorry and you'll make it right and I know you'll say that we'll get the act back together again and it'll be like it was, but we won't, Gully, 'cause you'll just get drunk again and mess it up."

I stop and put the barrow down for a second to rest. "Surprised I can do this, Gully? Well, I'm little, but I'm strong, I am." Then I lift him up again and we press on.

His eyes get bigger and bigger and he looks frantically about for some passerby to save him, but there ain't nobody out this late, and if we do run across someone, well, I got a story already cooked up: *Poor Dad, when he's like this, it's the only way we can get him home. What a trial he is to poor Mum, Sir, you can well imagine...*

"Yes, Gully, it's a shame. You were a great fiddler, you just weren't much of a man."

Gully groans in despair as we roll up onto the planks of the wharf. We go on for a while and then I pulls up next to the eighty-eight-gun HMS *Redoubt*, looming up there above us in the gloom of the early morning. I put down Gully and the barrow.

"Ahoy, the quarterdeck!" I shouts up.

An officer steps out on the gangway and says, "What do you want?"

"Beggin' your pardon, Sir, but this here gentleman has expressed a desire to return to sea."

The Officer of the Deck barks out a short laugh. "He has, has he? He looks like he's right tied up in knots about it."

"Aye, Sir. He is Gulliver MacFarland, a prime seaman *and* a British citizen—Scottish, he is—so you won't anger the locals by takin' him. He was foretopman on the *Solstice*—that much is true—the rest he tells you will be lies."

Other men are called and they start down the gangway. Gully, his fear of death gone, looks at me with cold hatred.

"They're finally getting the Hero of Culloden Moor, ain't they, Gully," says I. "I found out about that, too. You warn't the Hero of Culloden Moor, you warn't the hero of nothin'. You only found glory at the bottom of a bottle. What a fool I was."

The sailors come and stand around Gully. "You are sure he is a Scotsman?" says the officer.

"Yes, Sir," says I, and reaches down and pulls out the gag and a torrent of curses pours out of his mouth, thick with a Scots accent. "See?" says I, and I jams the gag back in. Gully's curses turn to gurgles.

"He is Scots, for sure, but what do you expect to get out of this?"

"Nothing, Sir, just a good English girl doin' her duty for King and Crown. And for the good of the Service, like."

"Wait. Did he do that to you?" The good officer puffs up in outrage.

Ah, the eye. It must be a sight. "Yes, Sir, but he was out of his mind when he did, so don't hold it against him. I would, however, warn you that he is more slippery than any eel. Perhaps if you held him in the brig till you sail?"

"We'll hold him," he says grimly and turns to his men. "Take him."

"Wait, Sir. One more thing." I go over to Gully and open his coat and take out his bottle of the greenish liquid. I lean over and look down at Gully's eyes as I say, "He has a problem with the drink, Sir. I would deny him his rum ration, at least for a while." I can imagine what Gully is calling me right now, but nothin' gets by the gag 'cept a gargling sound.

The Bo'sun takes the bottle from my hand and uncorks it and sniffs at the neck. He makes a face. "Wormwood. Rotten Frenchy wormwood. Rots the brain. Might as well drink lye!" He throws the bottle over the edge of the wharf and we hear it shatter on a crossbeam down below.

The men untie Gully and pull him upright, one good strong sailor on either arm. They leave the gag in.

I take the fiddle case from my shoulder and am about to hand it over when the officer says, "Ah no, Miss. No fiddles. The Captain can't abide them and won't let any aboard."

I sling the case back over my shoulder and look at Gully, and this time his eyes show only a deep, deep sadness.

"Sorry, Gully, I really am. But I'll take good care of the Lady Lenore for you, and if we ever meet again, I'll give her back to you."

With that I pick up the wheelbarrow and I turn and take it back to Bob's shed.

The sun is coming up when I see Amy runnin' toward me when I turn up Beacon Street. Annie is with her and their relief at seein' me back is gone the instant they see my eye. Amy's mouth opens but nothin' comes out.

"Sweet Jesus," says Annie. "We got to get her to Peg right off!"

There is a kind of thick juice comin' out from between the slit of my eyelids. *Please God, don't take my eye.*

I'm led into the kitchen. "Oh, my poor little girl," moans Peg. She puts her hand on my forehead and looks at the eye.

Her hand feels wondrous cool and soothing. "Sylvie! Go down to the apothecary shop and get three...no, five leeches! Quickly! Abby, to the icehouse! Run!"

Peg wets a towel and takes me to her room in back. "Get in here. We can't let Mistress see you like that. Stretch out on the bed." I take off the Lady and I lie down, gratefully.

"Who did that to you?" she demands. "I swear I'll have the man that did that..."

"He's gone away, Peg, and he won't be back for a long, long time," I says, and falls into a deep, deep sleep.

Much later, when I swim back into something close to wakefulness I feel a cold ice pack held to my eye. I open the other eye and see that it is Amy who is holding the compress. I fumble around and find her other hand and hold it to me. "Dear Amy," I whisper, "thank you."

Then I hear Peg say, "All right. Let's take a look." With my good eye I see her squinting at my other eye. "The swellin's down. Let's get 'em on her."

With great joy I find I can see a little out of my hurt eye—just a little slit of light, but it's something. Peg brings something black and shiny and wiggling over into my sight and puts it down, cold and clammy, on the top of my cheekbone, close to my lower eyelid.

"One there, and one over here...and two up top..."

I see that Amy's look of tender concern has been replaced by one of stern disapproval. "I told you something like this would happen," she scolds. "What do you have to say for yourself?"

I considers this for a bit. "You know," I says, as I feel the leeches' rasping mouths workin' their blood-suckin' way through my skin, "I'm thinkin' of giving up show business."

Chapter 40

Amy thinks it might be a good idea to get me out of the school for a few days, what with my eye and all, and I think it is a *great idea,* so we go to Dovecote for a few days this weekend. I spent all Friday in bed, claiming to be sick, and when Mistress came in to check on me, I flipped over on my side and pressed my bad eye to the pillow so she wouldn't see. Amy makes our excuses to Mistress and this time there *is* a coach and we take it. The coach is anything but comfortable and we get bounced around something awful—I'd much rather have ridden Gretchen—but we chatter and laugh and soon the journey is done and we are dropped at the big house at Dovecote.

We drop our bags in Amy's room and I go over to the mirror and squint at myself in it. Not too bad—the leeches did their job in getting the purple bruises out. Now it's just a few smudges of yellowish tinge.

Amy sees me looking in the mirror and says, "Come. We will go to Mother's dressing room. She will have some powder there."

"Coo, Amy, look at all this," says I. The dresser top is full of little jars and bottles and things with stoppers. "I thought you Yankees was all Puritans and didn't hold with this stuff."

"We have a saying here in New England: 'Pray in Church, Sin at Home.' Here, hold your face to the light." She picks up a squat jar and opens it and takes a soft brush and dips into it and applies it to my bruises.

It's easy to imagine Amy's mother sitting here at this dressing table. As different from Amy as the night from the day, Clementine Trevelyne is as pink and flighty as Amy is dark and serious. It is certain that Mrs. Trevelyne has never read a book and her talk centers totally on things of a social nature—the parties, the dinners, the glittering balls, and who was there and who was not. She does not seem to care a whit about the danger her husband's gambling poses to her present way of life, but goes about being gay and frivolous and charming. Or maybe she doesn't know. Whatever, she was kind to me when we met at Christmas, clucking over me and saying how nice it was that our Amy has a little friend. She was kind and I liked her.

Amy steps back and surveys her work. "There. That's better."

I look in the mirror and sure enough, I can hardly see the bruise. "Good work," I say. I pick up a bottle with blue juice in it. "What's the rest of this, then?"

"That is perfume. From France. Try some if you wish."

I pull out the stopper and put my nose to the tiny bottle. "Ooohhh, that's so lovely!" I want to stuff the whole thing up my nose.

"Put some on if you like...No, no, not like that." She sees that I was about to shake the open bottle over my head.

384

"Like this." She takes the bottle and puts her finger over the open end and tips it and then takes her finger and puts it behind my ear. "Like that. Behind each ear. Maybe a touch at the throat."

I do it and as I am doing it, Amy's attention is captured by something outside and she goes to the window.

"It's Randall," she says, not sounding entirely pleased, "home for the weekend. *Again.* I've never seen him home so much. It's strange."

By the time she turns around, I have put another big dab of the perfume down on my breastbone, loosened my hair from its usual pigtail, and dragged a lock of it over my damaged eye.

She narrows her eyes upon seeing me do all this, but I just smile all innocent and get up and go down to our room to brush my hair and tie it back with a ribbon.

"Ah, you rogue, you! What have you been up to since last we met? Oh yes? Well, I've heard you've been havin' quite a jolly time with the girls, you rascal you! Several babies already on the way? I'm not surprised. Now, don't you blush like that!" Saying that, I wrap my arms around his head and plant a great kiss on his forehead.

The Sheik seems to be glad to see me, too. I had heard him whinny when we approached the stable—I guess he caught a whiff of me, though how he could through all this perfume, I don't know. Maybe he recognized my voice, talking to Amy and Randall as I was. Whatever, his eyes roll and he fairly screams at the sight of me.

I give him pieces of dried apple, which he takes off my palm with great gentleness, and I say to George Swindow, who's the head hostler, "Please, George, tell me you'll allow me to ride him later." Amy don't even bother anymore tryin' to tell me not to do it, and Randall puts on his air of not carin' what I do.

"*Exercise* him, Miss. You may *exercise* him *inside* the track," says George. It's plain he's thinkin' back to those wild rides I've already had upon the Sheik.

"Thank you, George. I'll be back as soon as I change!" And I lift the front of my skirts and run back to our room and put on my sailor pants and shirt and I get back as they are saddling him up. The people here are used to seeing me in this rig—they have shrugged it off and they let me be the tomboy I guess I am.

I go up next to the Sheik and he lowers his great head, nuzzles me, and then shakes his mane and snorts and stamps, which means he's ready to run and asking why are we just standing here?

Randall appears to hand me up and I settles myself on the saddle. He is dressed today in a red velvet jacket with white front lapels and a high stiff collar that goes up above his ears and his dark hair curls over both collar and ears. Above his black boots stretch spotless white britches. He looks up with hooded eyes and then reaches up and pats me on the leg and says, "Be careful now, Jacky." I smile and nod. The Sheik shies away and I turn him and we are off.

The first time around the track I take him around slow—slow for the Sheik, that is—my hair is flying out straight behind me and the great muscles of his shoulders flex and stretch and roll under my legs and the white fence posts fly by. When we get to the last turn, we go by a small pasture that has some mares placidly grazing and I've been told that three of them are with foal by him and we shall have some fine colts and fillies by summer. I know the Sheik notices them, 'cause he speeds up a bit as we pass, as if to say, "Ain't I some fine horse?"

As we pound by the grandstand I notice that Amy and Randall are standing at the rail, watching, and I stick my bottom up a little higher in the air—to gain better balance, of course. Ain't I some fine rider?

And this time around we really let go.

After the last lap, I pull up the Sheik, all hot and frothing but still ready for more, but no, that's it for now—George had waved the flag and I knew I had to bring him in or else not be allowed to get up on him again.

Sheik's capering around, wheeling and whinnying, and he rears up on his hind legs, but I soon get him calmed down by whispering in his ear and patting his sweaty neck. As he's standing there blowing, I slide off and hand the reins to...*what?*...

It is a tiny little man, no bigger than me, wearing the silken colors of Dovecote Farm—green and white striped top, tight white knee pants, white silk stockings, and a green cap. He wears also a little man's cocky grin and says, "Ain't it a wonder, a female jock," and since I don't hear an accent, he must be another Cockney.

"Hullo, Jock," says I. As we stand, I look directly level into his eyes, something I ain't used to doin'. "London? Cheapside?"

"Couldn't be more right, Missy. Peter Jarvis, called Pete.

Sometimes Petey. Whelped and weaned in Ludgate. You, too?"

"Takes one to know one," says I, patting the Sheik on his flank. We lead him, all blowin' and snortin', on a coolin'-off walk. "Jacky Faber, Blackfriars Bridge."

"You lived near the bridge?" He looks quizzical.

"Under it," says I.

"Ah," he says, and he don't press it. "You ride real fine, Miss. The nag seems to like you."

"That's some horse. Is he the best you've ever seen?" I ask, wanting the real expert's opinion.

"He's right up there, Jacky," he says, looking up with admiration at the Sheik. "But, then, any horse can be beat, given the wrong day, the wrong rider, the wrong luck."

When we're done walking the big horse, we go back to the stable and I see Randall waiting by the racetrack gate. Not that he gives any indication that he's waiting for *me*, exactly, just sort of lounging about and surveying the scene and talking with some others.

I follow Petey into the stable and we put the Sheik into his stall and I get his oats and put some in his trough and he eats.

"I wonder why you get on so well with the horse, Jacky," says Pete. "He'll do things easy for you that he won't do for me."

I thinks for a bit and then says, "You know, it may sound stupid, but I think it's 'cause he knows I'm a girl."

Pete raises an eyebrow.

"Aye, and don't think this rogue don't know it. Aside

from runnin', gettin' with the mares is his main occupation. So he knows."

"Ah, what's the big difference?" asks Pete, the track-hardened jockey. His age, after you get over his boyish size, is about thirty, thirty-five.

"The difference is, with male jockeys, he sees competition, like...and so he acts that way. He runs good for you 'cause he wants you to see just how good he is, so you'll go away in shame. With me, he sees someone he wants to... well, *impress*. He wants me to admire him...and like him." I blush a little at this speech, but I think it's true.

"Pretty deep there, Jack-o," says he, laughing.

I laugh, too, and think how long it's been since I've been called by that Cockney name.

I spend a good deal of the rest of the afternoon with Pete, learnin' the tricks of the trade, listenin' to his stories— *and that time at Ascot when I was on a big dumb hammer-headed black, and four o' the bleedin' bastards had me boxed in against the wall and I...*

He's a good sort and we become fast friends. When I leave the stable, night is falling and Randall is no longer at the gate.

I go into Amy's room and she is sitting there scratching her quill in her manuscript, as she calls it. She rises and we dress for dinner.

We take our evening dinner with Randall at the great long table in the grand dining room. Amy wanted to take our dinner in the kitchen, all jolly and easy like we usually do, but Randall insisted, so here we are. I like being here, and look about like any simple country girl. Candles are lit in a crystal chandelier above the table where we sit, and the lights from it reflect warmly on the polished top of the huge table. It reflects, also, on the fine china and silverware laid out before me. At least I know what to do with it now, and don't have to cringe in fear.

There are about twenty, twenty-five chairs ringing the table, and we three sit in the middle, Amy and I together, and Randall across from us. There are windows at the end of the room and they are covered with thick red drapes, gathered with gold cords. Behind me is a big double door that opens on the hall and through which we came in, and on the other side is another set of wide doors that open on what seems to be a big, dark ballroom. *What a thing*, I thinks, *to go to a real ball in there.*

"So how go your studies, dear Brother?" asks Amy. A soup is brought and placed in front of each of us, and I lay into mine thinkin' I just might keep my mouth shut just now and let these two go at it. "I'm sure you are finding Homer and Virgil most exciting."

"Boring," says Randall. "How goes the girly school? I'm sure you're finding your courses in the changing of the baby's nappies quite entertaining?"

A man in livery—a footman? Randall's valet? the butler? I don't know—comes to serve the wine.

"And you?" he asks, raising an eyebrow to me.

"I like my French and I love Art and Music. Could do without Embroidery, though, and as for Household Management, which is where the changing of a diaper might someday come up, well, Amy and me don't like it much, but all knowledge is useful, is what I hold. And as for Equestrian, well, you know I like that. I've gotten so I can do medium jumps now." I figure a little girlishness wouldn't hurt just now, and I flutter my eyelashes and clasp my hands all helpless and flighty. "It's dreadful scary, but I can just do it."

"Indeed?" says Randall, puffing up till I swear his waistcoat buttons will pop. "Well, perhaps we shall ride to the hounds in the summer." He raises his glass and looks at me over the rim.

"Only if you spare the fox, Sir." I raise my glass in return and look back at him over my own rim. "Or the vixen. Whichever one is being chased."

"That would depend on how fast the vixen runs." Randall smiles lazily.

"Or how clever she is in evading capture," says I.

He nods his head in a kind of bow.

Two girls with trays come in and serve the meat, potatoes, and greens. I take some and thank them. They dip and go.

Randall notices this and I know he wants to say that I'm too familiar with the servants but he don't.

"Another glass of wine with you, Jacky?" Randall is feeling good, I can tell.

"Just half, please." The man fills my glass halfway. "Thank you." I take my water glass and top off the wine, turning it from deep red to pink.

"A travesty," snorts Randall, leaning back in his chair. "Leave it," he says to his man and the man places the bottle on the table and leaves the room.

He turns to his plate and shovels some in and while he's chewing and tossing back the wine, I think how different he is from his father, as different as Amy is from her mother.

Well, maybe it's only in appearance that they are different, Randall being tall and slim and the Colonel being medium-sized and built like a door. But I got to admit they got the same arrogant kiss-my-royal-bum look in their eyes. The Colonel was civil to me over Christmas, but it was plain that he had very little use for such as me.

Randall pushes his plate away and wipes his mouth and fills his glass again and lobs the mortar: "The Sheik will race all comers on Saturday, April the nineteenth."

Amy drops her fork to her plate.

"Yes, and Clarissa will arrive here at Dovecote, the day before. You know Clarissa Howe, do you not, Jacky?" He smirks, obviously recalling the grand tea party at the school.

I own that I have had the pleasure of her acquaintance. I look over at Amy. She is not happy.

"You will excuse us, Brother," says Amy. She throws her napkin down and rises.

He takes out a long thin cigar and curls back his lips and places it between his teeth. "Perhaps we'll retire to the piano room?" He looks at me with his sly look.

"Perhaps not," says Amy, and brother and sister glare at each other as I get up, a bit more regretfully. Pity. I was having fun.

So. We will return in a month to see a fine horse race, where the Sheik will certainly conquer all who dare to challenge him...

...Or we will witness the fall of the House of Trevelyne.

That evening, after we're dressed for bed and I'm brushing out Amy's long, black, shiny hair, I ask, "What's a piano, and why does it have a room?" She has already brushed out my hair and I have put on my mobcap, which now has an anchor worked in blue thread on top of it—might as well use that embroidery, I figure. Although I still ain't near as good as the other girls, I got to admit it looks right smart. I think Faber Shipping, Worldwide shall use that as its flag. The Blue Anchor Line, from Cathay to Bengal, from the rocky shores of New England to the sandy beaches of Mexico, from the—

"Come. I'll show you." She gets up and puts on her own cap and takes up the lamp and goes to the door.

We creep down the broad staircase and down a hall and into a darkened room. Amy goes forward and puts the lamp down on a big...what? It's got four thick legs and is flat on top and is all rich and smooth and glossy and warm and...

"It's called a piano," she says, sitting down at a bench in front of the thing and lifting a wooden cover that slides back to reveal a row of gleaming black and white keys. "Or, actually, a pianoforte, which is Italian for 'soft-loud,' which is appropriate because, unlike my harpsichord, it can make a note loud or soft depending on how hard you hit the key. Like this." And she strikes a white key hard and lets the sound die out, and then does it again, only this time lightly and the note is much quieter.

"That's wonderful," I say, and can barely keep my fingers off the keyboard. "Can you play something?"

"Well, Father has only recently brought it here, but I have started a few things," she says, shyly. "Like this pretty little tune. It's by Ben Jonson, from back in Shakespeare's time, and is called 'Drink to Me Only with Thine Eyes.'" She arches her fingers above the keyboard and brings them down and plays and fills the room with rich and sweet sound. After she plays the melody, she sings a verse:

> *"Drink to me only with thine eyes,*
> *And I will pledge with mine.*
> *Or leave a kiss but in the cup,*
> *And I'll not look for wine."*

I am sitting all wrapped up in the music and don't notice when the door opens and Randall comes quietly in, but Amy does and she stops playing.

"I was about to ride up to the tavern in Braintree," says Randall, "to find more convivial company than was available around here, when I heard the noise."

"Please leave, Randall. We are not dressed," orders Amy.

"No, wait," says I, rising and facing him. "It is just Randall, and if I am your sister, Amy, is he not then my brother, and all is right and proper? Isn't that right?"

A bow of agreement from Randall, a snort from Amy, but she don't press it.

"Shall we have a song, then? Have you a good voice, Randall?" I asks.

"I have a passable baritone," says he. "What would you like to sing? 'The Riddle Song'? 'Captain Marshall's Courtship,' 'The Maid Who Lost Her Cow'...?"

"Ah no, Sir, none of those songs where the maid sets forth these riddles to try to protect her virtue from the advances of the man and the man is not supposed to be able answer them but he does, the rascal, and the girl *always* loses and we both know what she has to do then." I plant my finger in the center of Randall's chest and push him back. "No, Sir, we shall not sing those. Perhaps we will dance, instead.

"Amy," I say, "that pretty song you were playing, the one about 'drink to me only'…Could you play that again, please? For me?"

Amy turns back to the keyboard and, with a reluctant sniff, begins to play. I turn to Randall. "Shall I teach you a simple country dance, then, Lieutenant Trevelyne?" He seems willing.

"Very well, put your right hand here on my waist. No, here on the small of my back—a little higher, please… that's it. And put your other hand in mine and then we move together, like this. Your feet make a pattern like this— watch me, I'll lead, and then when you get it, you'll lead. Good. Shuffle, shuffle, and turn. Smooth and light. See, by pushing and pulling me with your right hand, I know what direction you're gonna go in, and I can follow, and we glide about together like this. Isn't this nice?"

I think he finds it nice. I'm liking it, too. When we started the dance, there was some space between us—there ain't no such space now. When the music comes around to the beginning again, I start to sing the verse into his ear: *"Drink to me only with thine eyes…"*

He brings his face to mine and I pull back, but he comes on further and I lift my fingers and place them on his lips and lightly push him back. He retreats and we dance like that until Amy finishes.

She makes it plain that she is done by pulling down the keyboard cover. "Good night, Randall," she says firmly.

Randall bows and I curtsy.

"Good night, Jacky."

"Good night, Mr. Trevelyne. You be careful tonight."

"I shall. Thank you for your concern. I look forward to showing you about tomorrow." He bows and leaves.

I sit down on the bench next to Amy again and put my head back and smile in the darkness and let out a sigh and... *"What?"* I say to Amy, who seems right steamed about something.

Chapter 41

The next morning, after chapel, I say I'm gonna go give the Sheik a pet and Amy goes off to our room and when she's well off and gone, Randall appears. He had sat between us during the service. It seems he never passes up a chance to make Amy angry.

"May I show you around Dovecote now, Jacky?"

"I think dear Amy has shown me most of it, Mr. Trevelyne," I say, all demure in my lovely riding habit that Amy gave me, my soul newly scrubbed free of sin, but I have no intention of letting him get away. I had spent most of the service checking out the fit of his clothes from the corner of my eye. It's none of my business, but aside from the flaws in his character—arrogance, a tendency to swagger, false bravado and all—he is really a most beautiful boy, and, deep down, I think a very sweet one, too.

The young groom Edward brings out Randall's horse, a big bay gelding with a good head and fine white boots all around that Randall has named Comrade. Randall puts his foot in the stirrup and smoothly mounts.

"She cannot show you the place like I can. I know of places she does not know. Come"—and he extends his hand. There is no mention of rigging up a buggy, I notice, like I know he would for Clarissa. Well, we must know our place.

"Wait. I'll go get…"

"No need," says Randall. "Climb up here behind me. Comrade can carry us both."

I consider this for a moment and then I hand my hymnal to the groom and say, "You'll keep this for me, won't you, Edward?" He nods, but he don't look happy. He sends a glare in Randall's direction and I lean over and whisper, "Oh, don't worry, Eddie, I can take care of myself."

"All right, Mr. Trevelyne, go over by that feed box, if you would," I say, and he does.

I put my foot on the box and then leap up behind Randall onto Comrade. I get settled with a leg to each side and wrap my arms around Randall's middle and says, "So, show me."

Randall touches Comrade with his spurs and we are off.

It is a glorious spring day with all the world rejoicing in it. There is a steam rising from the ground and the birds rise with it and whirl and sing and we ride down along the river till it meets the ocean, and the sea is as blue as any sky I have ever seen. There is a long beach made flat and smooth by the tides and we gallop along it, tossing up sand, and Comrade even goes into the water and I squeal at the spray thrown up by his hooves and I pound on Randall's back and tell him to stop it, my clothes are going to be ruined, and we go back up along the riverbank and Randall points out a boathouse that he says has several small boats in it, and I say maybe I'll teach him to sail if I come back here in the summer and he says I must.

We go farther along the river, leaving the main houses of Dovecote to our right and then far behind.

"Where are we going now, Mr. Trevelyne?" I ask from behind him. I twist my head around. There don't seem to be any buildings or anything else around here.

"Please call me Randall, Jacky. I think we know each other well enough now to do that."

"Very well, Randall," I say. "Where are we going now?"

"I thought I might show you a spot that was quite dear to me in my youth. A place where I used to come to read and think and be by myself with my thoughts and dreams."

Aw, ain't that sweet, I thinks, *the young lord off by himself dreaming like any silly boy or girl.* I look up at the back of his head with its black curls looping over his collar. Without thinking, I hugs him a little tighter.

We come to a bend in the river, the bank of which is covered with bushes that are already putting out their leaves. Randall pulls up and, throwing his leg over his mount's head, he slides off and then reaches up for me. Before I can lift my own leg and slide off in my usual manner, he reaches up and grasps me by the waist and lifts me up and off and puts my feet on the ground.

I look about and there's an opening in the thick bushes, leading to a dark glen within.

Uh-oh...

"Randall, I don't know..." Suddenly I ain't quite so brave anymore.

"But Jacky, this is the place I want to share with you."

"Mr. Trevelyne, I've got to tell you that I am promised to another," says I, all prim. "And I think you've been promised to Clarissa Howe."

"Of course, my dear," he says, his hand still reaching for me. "This is only a little visit between friends—think of us as brother and sister sitting on the banks of the river to rest from the ride and to have a nice talk. You did say last night that if Amy was your sister, then I am your brother?"

"I guess," I say.

"We have to be friends, Jacky. You're not like other girls—prissy and afraid of their own shadows—no, you're different, you are, and I knew the minute I saw you the first time, dressed as a midshipman and so pleased with yourself that I thought you might just explode with joy... and when you were onstage at that tavern, so confident, so unafraid..."

While he's sayin' this his mouth is getting closer and closer to mine and I'm pullin' back but he goes on. "That's why we're so much alike, Jacky, and why we have to become very good friends, Jacky, we have to become such *very*, very good friends, a friendship that goes beyond who we are promised to, Jacky, beyond who we will marry, beyond the very bonds of convention itself."

His breath is on my face, and I say, "But..."

"But nothing. You know it's true. Now I will kiss you, Jacky. Close your eyes, Jacky, just a brotherly kiss, now, Jacky...Jacky..."

His words are making me dizzy, sleepy even...

...And then we hear hoofbeats and Amy storms up on her horse, furious.

"Just what the hell do you think you are doing, you philandering cur!" Amy pulls up and takes a swing at Randall's head with her riding crop.

"Minding my own business, Sister!" he roars, ducking his head such that the crop swishes over it.

I figures it's time for Jacky to disappear and leave them to it, and I cuts and heads back to the house. And they do go at it for real.

Millie comes up and bounds by my side as I'm trudging along and then I hear hoofbeats. *Oh no, Randall, you'll not again...* But, no, it's Amy on Daisy and she comes up behind me, her face the very mask of doom and damnation.

"Amy, I..."

"Just keep walking, you," she says, not looking at me. "Millie. Mind her."

Millie takes that as an order to keep me moving and on the path. She pokes at me with her nose and seems just out of her mind with joy.

"Nothing happened," I throw back over my shoulder.

"I know," she says. "I was in time. Just. Millie! Mind her!"

Millie comes after me as I try to veer off the path to escape Amy and her wrath. She brings me back.

"I thought you was my friend," I hisses to Millie, but she just shrugs a doggy shrug as if to say, "A job's a job," and keeps me to the straight and narrow. I look back, but Amy still won't look at me, so I keep walking.

"You'll not give me a ride, Sister?" I say, a little miffed. It's a long way to the house, in disgrace or not.

"Ladies ride. Tramps walk," is all she says, and with that, she wheels Daisy about and gallops back to the main compound, leaving me there in the dust.

Fine, I says to myself, *my seabag is always packed.*

Later, anyone standing outside our window, by Millie's whining side, would have heard us go at it.

"My seabag is packed. I always said you could put me out at any time, and I don't hold it against you."

"It is only because I love you and don't want to see you hurt, and I would never put you out no matter what stupid thing you have done."

"I know how to take care of myself, thank you, I've done it all me life and I means to keep on doin' it."

"You think you are so smart and cunning in the ways of the world, but all I've seen of your cunning is you getting beaten and ill-used..."

"I've made it this far from a pretty low start—"

"You may think you know how to manage low ruffians—"

"My mates ain't low ruffians, my mates are them what loves me and have, mind you, been loyal and kind to me and stood beside me, unlike present company!"

"You may think you know how to manage low ruffians, but you have no defenses against smooth-talking gentlemen who have nothing on their mind but to have sport with you! Randall is good at what he does, and you wouldn't be the first link in his chain of broken hearts, Jacky, I can tell you that. Father has had to get him out of several scrapes of that nature so far. There are at least two local girls who are older and far, far wiser now."

"Don't care don't care don't care..."

"Put down that bag. Stop that. You are not going anywhere. It will be dark soon."

"Yes, I am. Jacky Faber don't stay where she ain't wanted. Don't worry, I can make my way—"

"Oh yes, I had forgotten: the redoubtable Jacky Faber and her magic whistle! How could I have forgotten that wonderful life-sustaining talent! Tell me, Sister, how will it be when it is the *old* Jacky Faber squatting on a street corner in rags, tootling on her pennywhistle?"

"You shut up, you—"

"Will the crowds hoot and hooray for you then when you are not the brisk young dame that jumps up and down so pretty..."

"Stop it, Amy..."

"Will they say, 'Oh, ain't she the prettiest thing' when... all right, now wait. Stop that. Stop crying. I am sorry I said those—"

"I ain't cryin' you can't m-m-make me cry, you can't, you can't..."

"Please. Come here. There, there, I did not mean it. I know you mean well and have a good and open heart. That's the problem. Please stop crying now, Jacky, please... here, dear, let me hold you. Come, dear child, put your head on my breast. Collect yourself. And then we will go down for dinner, which we will have in the kitchen. Then maybe to the piano? I will start to teach you to play it. There, that is better. Quiet now. Quiet."

That night, in bed, we start off sleeping without touching, each of our backs toward the other, but by morning we are snugged up as usual and I am forgiven. Again.

Chapter 42

We're back in Boston and we could have come back on horseback with Randall as escort but Amy would have none of it, so we came back by that damned rattly coach. But we're back and hardly the worse for wear.

Amy's right, of course. I always think I know what I'm doing and I don't. I always think I'm in control of everything and I ain't in control of nothing. I always think I know everything and it always turns out that I don't know nothin'. I do know, though, that I'll watch that Mr. Randall Trevelyne real close.

I just wish that I'd get a letter from Jaimy. Something. Anything. It's been five months since I sent that letter with Davy and, I know, maybe the wakes of their ships didn't cross, maybe they'll never meet, I don't know.

It's hard, Jaimy, it is. It's hard enough for me to be good when I know you're waitin' for me, but if you ain't...

I attend to my studies. I got to, 'cause I ain't got much freedom around here no more. Since my last outing when I come back with the smashed eye, Peg has told Herr Hoffman I ain't to check out no more horses and Mistress Pimm won't let me spend the night with the Byrnes sisters no more—ladies don't associate with servants, you know. Amy, too, has her eye on me constant. So I must be good. I must content myself with going over to the stables to see dear Gretchen and just ride her around the paddock and walk her and comb her down.

And we have been to see Ezra again, under Amy's watchful eye. I would not be surprised if she has not been given a club by Peg and the Sisterhood and ordered to drop me in my tracks should I show any interest in straying from the straight and narrow. But I am good as any angel, and except for a few growls from Amy when I look longingly toward the Pig, things go smoothly. Ezra has nothing new to report, other than the fact that people are beginning to remark upon the Preacher's growing strangeness.

They do let me out for Rachel's wedding, though, mainly 'cause Peg's goin', too, in all her finery and I get to go under her watchful eye. Peg's kids are all grown and gone, but she considers us all to be her brood, too, so she bawls most uncontrollably when the words are said.

Amy gives Rachel a fine leather-covered family Bible that has a family tree in the front where they will put in all the names of their babies and the babies that the babies have down the years. I, of course, give 'em each a portrait, which is all that I seem able to do of a lasting nature in this world. Annie and Betsey and Abby and Sylvie give two needlework pillow slips that they all worked on and put in their names and wishes, and if you ask me, it is as fine as any of the framed needlework in the school. And Peg, some kitchen tools, and Ephraim gives the bridegroom a fine wood plane he made himself, and Henry, a finely worked bridle.

Across the Alleghenies, imagine that...and she the oldest of us and in some ways the calmest and the wisest, and I can't stand to see her go 'cause I know for certain I'll never see her again and to keep from blubberin' we promise to write and never forget each other and then Rachel and Paul Barkley get on the seat of the loaded wagon, wave, and are gone.

Along with my other studies, I keep working on the miniatures, and I have taken them to a new turn—now I have the sitter turn a little toward me, a three-quarter view, as Mr. Peet would have it. It is harder than the profile view, but it does let the painter fix the eye of the viewer with that of the sitter.

I have had two miniature-portrait commissions that Mr. Peet got for me, and I made a decent penny out of them, too. One was of a prosperous shipowner, and I did him in his office at the end of Hall's Wharf. I think the portrait was a present for his wife. I brought along my long glass and had him cradle it in his arm as I posed him. I gave him a little more hair than he actually has and slimmed him down a touch. He was enchanted with the result and tipped me most handsome.

The other one, curiously, was a portrait of a young bride whose new husband was about to go off to sea, and she brought me into a private room and she locked the door and she took off her cloak and revealed herself in a *very* sheer slip, one so sheer that parts of her upper self were plainly visible through the filmy garment. "Paint me as you see me," she said, sitting down on a stool, "and don't leave anything out." I did it and I made the parts to which she was referring most plump and proud and pink. When she saw the result, she blushed and squeezed my arm and said, "It is just the thing. That will keep him warm and he will look to no other soft breast for comfort."

You'd better not, I thinks, *or this fierce young bride of yours will make short work of you.*

I have shown Maestro Fracelli the Lady Lenore and my intent to try to learn her. He sucks in his breath as he picks her up and cradles her in his arm and puts the bow to her and plays.

"It's like one cannot play a false note on it," he says in wonder, and examines her most closely. "It is Italian, without a doubt," he says, with a hint of national feeling and pride. "And if you should ever want to sell it..."

"Ah, nay, Sir," says I. "I could never sell her, as I am but keeping her for...a sometime friend, who will one day return to claim her."

"Ah," says Maestro Fracelli, handing the Lady to me. "Then hold her thus, and put this under your chin and put your left hand just so, and take the bow..."

And the Lady Lenore and I are off on a long voyage.

The Preacher is losing his congregation. As I look about the church I see the hapless Pimm's girls are really all that's left, and they look at each other and cringe at his rambling, disconnected sermons and keep their gaze down in their laps. His twitchy actions during the service have made even the most hidebound Puritans, them what's used to taking their lumps in church, feel weird and discomfited and they know they have only to go down to the Old South Church to find a preacher that, though fierce, at least ain't crazy. And there they have gone.

I do not meet his eye, because if I do, I think he will know what I have been doing for Janey. I pass the time during the service today wondering how he's dealing with his own board of directors. Those collection plates been looking mighty thin.

I think he sleeps on one of the hard pews, afraid to sleep upstairs, where sometimes he hears the scratching of fingernails or the moaning of a young girl saying, "Please, Sir, don't..." over and over. Sometimes I'm there and sometimes I ain't, but I know he hears her anyway.

One more haunting should do it, I think. I must call the Brothers and Sisters together, one more time, before Amy and I return to Dovecote and the Great Race.

Chapter 43

"You see how he comes around with the dog every hour on the tolling of the Meeting House clock?" I whisper. The bell sounds off in the distance. There is the call of a night watchman down in the town sayin' that all's well. "He is not a smart man, as he never varies in his rounds."

Ephraim nods in the dark, and he and I duck around the side of the school as the man with the dog appears in the graveyard under the pale moonlight. Betsey is there in the shadows, too, and she clutches Ephraim's arm as he comes back to her from our scouting mission.

"So I will distract him when he is at the far end of his round, on the other side of the church?"

"Right. But you must give no sign you know anything about this school or anyone in it, or the Preacher will know that it is not ghosts who are after him, but real people. And that I know he can deal with."

"How long, Jacky?"

"Just five minutes is all it will take."

I have a special treat for Reverend Mather tonight.

———

We are arrayed. I put on my costume with the aid of Annie and Betsey and Sylvie up in my old room into which we have all snuck. Ephraim is given a bottle to portray a wandering drunk. And in my sack, I have my Other Item.

At the appointed hour, Ephraim heads to the east side of the church and I make my preparations by the wall. I can see the man and his dog over there, and then I see the dog raise his head suddenly and pull at the leash. "What is it, boy?" the man asks and follows the dog out of sight. This is my cue to rise up, go to the wall, and kneel down. I'll then crawl to the grave and stand up and wait for the Reverend. If he don't come to the window, then the night's work is lost.

I'm standin' there weaving back and forth, hopin' I don't hear Ephraim's warning whistle, which'll signal that the watchman is comin' back to this side, when Reverend Mather appears in the window and he sees me right off. He starts backward, as usual, but then he comes to the window and opens it and leans out and says in a low voice, "I know what you are and what you want but you won't succeed…you won't…you…"

I think he's just noticed my Other Item. Cradled in my arms I have my baby doll that I used in our act when we sang "Queer Bungo Rye," and I am rocking it back and forth like any young mother, 'cept more slow and sad. And I hum a lullaby, slow and sad. More of a soft keening, as strange and not-of-this-world as I can make it.

At the window he lifts his arms and crosses his fingers in the cross sign in front of his face to ward off evil. *Well, Preacher, that ain't gonna work, 'cause the evil ain't down here. Look within yourself. I hope this will help.*

"No. No," he croaks. "No, I didn't…I didn't…"

I have taken the baby doll from my breast and I slowly extend my arms and hold it up to him. I have blacked out the doll's eyes and blackened its nose and drawn skull teeth across its mouth so it looks just like me.

I hear a low but clear whistle and I pull back the doll to my chest and slowly bend my knees more and more, so it looks like I'm sinking back into the grave, till I'm on my knees and then I bend forward till I'm hid behind the wall and then I quick crawls away. Done!

We meet back in the upper room. We are quiet and I wish Abby could be here, too. I am glad we all come together in good fellowship for I feel an ending coming. A good one or a bad one, I don't know. But an ending, for sure.

PART IV

Chapter 44

We are back at Dovecote, but there is to be no getting in my sailor togs this weekend, oh no, as many of the area's finest people, as well as some that are not so fine, will be coming here for the Great Race tomorrow. Colonel and Lady Trevelyne arrived yesterday and we paid our respects and Mrs. Trevelyne said she was glad to see me and how nice Amy was turning out, I guess you are good for her, Miss. The Colonel nodded and grunted and headed for the stables. When I am in front of him, I have to keep myself from bowing my head and putting my knuckle to my brow, and force myself to curtsy instead, as he is so strongly in command of his family and his holdings that it brings out the lowly ship's boy in me. Would that he was equally in command of himself.

The field for the Sheik to conquer has been narrowed to ten, they being the very finest of all the horses in the North-east. We have been watching them being brought in, just as we watched that day the Sheik was brought in, from the same hill that is again turning green and will soon be once more covered in daisies.

We are mounted, sidesaddle, Amy on her Daisy and me on a little bay mare named Molly. She ain't my dear Gretchen, but she's nice. Millie races around as usual, delighted with our company.

"Here comes another one," I say. It's a big chestnut that is being just as difficult as Sheik can be when he's in a foul mood. I look over at Amy and catch her heaving a great sigh. She, also, is in a foul mood, and no wonder—tomorrow could be the end of her life as she knows it.

I don't want to do it, but I got to ask. "Will you really lose everything if the Sheik loses?"

Amy nods. "Everything."

"How fast would it happen?"

"Oh, it would take a while for the mortgages to be called, for the creditors to pick the place apart." She looks out across the fields of her home. "My tuition at the school is paid until the end of the term, and then I would have to leave. I...I don't even know if I could bring myself to go back with you after all this is over. All of them will know of...the shame. I don't know..."

"Clarissa will still marry Randall?"

"I think so, unfortunately. It's the name Trevelyne she wants, not the money. Her family has lots of money."

"She arrives today?"

"At any time."

"How will she come?"

"In a coach-and-four. That is her usual style."

She is quiet for a while and then says, "If the Sheik loses, and I leave for school on Monday, I will know then that I will never see this place again."

I reach over and put my hand on her arm and say, "He

416

will not lose, Amy, he is too much horse. But if he does, we will go out in the world together, and we will make our way. And we will not make that way by being governesses or by making dull marriages. Do you believe me on that, Sister?"

She puts her hand on mine and manages to smile. "Of course. Are we not the wild and contrary Valentine Sisters?"

"Yes, we are," I say, sitting up in my saddle and cocking my head to one side. "Now, what's that?" I thought I'd heard a far-off trumpet call and a rattle of drums.

"The local regiment of militia is having their Spring Muster today, as part of the festivities. Over in the field across from the paddock. They came in yesterday and are camped in their tents. They march about and shoot off cannons and other foolishness."

As if to echo her statement, a dull thud of a cannon is heard.

"But why did you not tell me?" I shout joyfully. "Let's go!" and I give Molly my heel and we're off.

"Why not, indeed," I hear Amy say, with a certain weariness in her voice.

We get to the parade ground and I size up the battlefield. There are four companies of about one hundred men each and they seem to be drilling by company, as they certainly are not all moving together. In fact, their drill seems pretty sloppy all around, but then, what can be expected. They are only militia, after all, and not regulars. The uniforms of the men are varied at best, ragged at worst, but the officers are well turned out. There is a lot of bellowing of orders and the ranks lurch back and forth like unwilling beasts being prodded with sticks. I see that Randall and his company are the ones nearest to us here by the road. That is good. I look back up the road and note that I can see up it all the way to the two stone pillars at the entrance.

Perfect.

We dismount and go to the edge of a slight rise and watch. I know that Randall spots us right off, 'cause of the way he straightens up and struts all the more. I swear he is flexing the muscles of his tail for my benefit. He has on his blue uniform with the tight white breeches and the shiny black boots and his sword scabbard hangs by his side. He has his sword drawn for the giving out of his orders and has on his hat, which I have not seen before. It is like the hats that the officers on the *Dolphin* wore, 'cept that it's worn with the peaks front and back, rather than sideways. *Contrary Yankees,* I thinks, but it does look quite dashing.

I check the road. Nothing.

Down next to the drilling troops, not far from us, is a tripod of rifles and next to it, a drum, with sticks and straps. Like my old drum from the *Dolphin. Hmmm. Even better.*

Randall gives an order, "To the right flank, march!" and half the unit goes right and half goes left. Randall sneaks a glance up at me to see if I have seen the mess. I put my hands to my mouth to stifle my laughter, and Amy says, "Shall I remind you that it was just such a rabble that defeated…oh, never mind."

Down below, Randall rains a torrent of abuse upon his hapless troops and, kicking and swearing, tries to get them back in order again.

And then I see it. A coach-and-four just passing the pillars and heading down the road toward us, about a half mile away.

"Amy, dear, will you take Millie by the collar so she doesn't follow me. I want to get a closer look at their equipment."

"I do not have to hold her collar. Here, Millie. Sit. Stay. Now what…"

But I am already heading for the drum.

I hang about the tripod of guns, pretending interest in the old flintlocks and keeping an eye on the road and its approaching coach. About a quarter mile now.

I dip down and pick up the drum and slip the harness around my shoulder and take it up a few notches till it sits on my hip just like my old drum on the *Dolphin,* and I take up the sticks and rattles off a drumroll and then settles into a pattern, and then I sings out as loud as I can.

> *"Lord Randall he was tall and slim,*
> *And he had a leg for every limb.*
> *But now he's got no legs at all,*
> *For he ran a race with a cannonball!*
> *With me rue dum dah,*
> *Faddle riddle dah whack!*
> *For the riddle with me rue dum dah!"*

When I come to the whack! I give the drum rim a hard hit with the stick so it sounds like a rifle shot. All the men are facing me and their delight is plain. They are trying to keep from laughing at their gallant commander's discomfort, but some are not succeeding. Randall's back is to me and I can't see his face, but his head seems to sink down behind his high blue collar, and while I cannot see his ears, I got a real suspicion that steam is comin' out of each. I keep the drum rhythm going and go to the second verse,

"Oh, were you deaf or were you blind,
  When you left your two fine legs behind?
  Or was it sailing on the sea,
  That wore your legs right down to the knee?
  With me rue dum dah,
  Faddle riddle dah whack!
  For the riddle with me rue dum dah!"

Still not enough, Randall? All the companies are now watching this play out. Very well, here's another verse,

"Lord Randall he was long and tall,
  Till he lost a race with a cannonball,
  Now he sits with..."

That did it. He jams his sword back into his scabbard and turns to chase me. I squeal and slip off the drum and run back up the rise toward the road and I can hear him poundin' up behind me and I run fast...but not too fast.

Now run, Jacky, that's it, a little bit more now. Let him get right behind you, now get close to the road. Now trip, Jacky, oh poor dear, now trip and fall to the ground, you frail female thing you, and feel the tangle of his legs with yours as he falls on top of you and pins your wrists to the ground. Now look up into his face, Jacky. Why, he don't look half mad at all, does he, Jacky, he looks more, well...lusty like.

He brings his face down to mine and I turn my face to the right and feel the rasp of his jaw on my cheek, and he tries again and I turn my face to the left and again he misses. Then I face forward and he's about to come down for the prize when he hears the rattle of the coach-and-four and he looks up into the wide-open and unbelieving blue eyes of Miss Clarissa Worthington Howe, staring out the window.

The coach rumbles on. Randall thrusts himself to his feet and calls me a name I wouldn't have thought he would have known, him bein' a gent and all.

I get up on one elbow and watch Lord Randall follow the retreating coach to the house. Then I feel Millie's cold nose poke me in my cheek and I hear Amy say, "Take her back to the house."

I do not take my dinner with the Trevelynes this night, as I am banished by Amy to the kitchen. Fine. Just as well. Let the lovers stew.

I have a fine dinner with Mrs. Grubbs and the downstairs staff, and afterward, I walk out into the evening and go to see Pete in his room. There's a line of rooms built into the grandstand for the visiting jockeys and grooms and it sounds like there are parties going on in several of them, but I look at Petey and know for sure he ain't goin' to any of 'em, as he don't look good at all. He tries to put on a brave front, but I place my hand on his forehead and feel that he's burning up with fever.

"Don't worry, Lass, I ain't never missed a race yet."

"Ain't there no one else what can take your place tomorrow? Take the load off you, like, in case you need more time in the kip?"

"Nah. There ain't enough jocks to go around, and the other owners…" He stops to cough, long and deep, and it racks his small frame. "The other owners ain't gonna be

421

lendin' their jocks to the Colonel—there's a lot of money ridin' on this race. Plus the Sheik don't like nobody on 'im but me. No, 'e wouldn't run for 'em."

There's a noise at the door and two jockeys in silks burst in and say, "Come on, Petey, there's a rum bash in...ah, now, he's got a girl. Old Petey! Just like 'im! Bring her along, then. Three doors down!"

Pete waves and says, "Righto!" but he don't move.

I ask him if he wants me to get him anything to eat— chicken soup, perhaps—but he says that he couldn't keep nothin' down. Maybe another blanket, though, and so I find a clean horse blanket on a shelf and throw it over him. He says, "Thanks, you're a good lass," and appears to go to sleep, shivering in spite of the warmth of the night and the blankets that are piled on him.

I go to sit with the Sheik for a while, petting him and talkin' low and soft to him while he whickers in the dark.

I sit and I think for a long while, and then I go back to our room.

After I'm all ready for bed, I open my seabag and take out the asafoetida bag that Mam'selle Claudelle put around my neck that night in Boston, and I lay it out with the things I'll be wearing tomorrow.

Just in case.

Chapter 45

Amy wakes up with a huge, worried, shuddering sigh and gets out of bed. We get up and get ready without speaking much. There is not much to say. We can only hope that Petey is better.

Breakfast is a grim affair. I eat, she don't. I put my hand on hers. "Don't worry, Amy, it'll be all right, either way."

"I know," she says. "I just wish it was over."

Well, it will be over at two o'clock, five hours from now, 'cause that's when the race is to be run.

"Come, let us walk down to the sea. It's a fine day. It will take your mind off things." And we do it, and we sit on rocks by the shore and take off our shoes and stockings and wade in the gentle surf. The sea, as usual, calms me, and it calms Amy, too.

The grandstand is full, there's trumpet blasts and horses are being paraded around and there's excitement and gaiety in the air. There's finely dressed women with parasols and there's fine gents decked out in bright jackets, smoking cheroots and hallooing to one another, some placing bets and others covering them. There's plenty of men who look slightly shady and there's some women that wouldn't look out of place at Mrs. Bodeen's, too. And, oh, look! There's a pair of Royal Navy officers! Next to Amy's mum and dad. They must be guests. A captain, no less, and a lieutenant! I must get next to them later to see if they know anything of Jaimy. Maybe at the ball tonight. And they brought some midshipmen with them. We'll have dance partners tonight, that's for sure.

The Trevelynes and their party are in a boxed-off area, I guess to keep the riffraff away from the quality. Well, it ain't gonna keep this piece of riffraff out. "Come on, Amy, let's join your family." She don't want to, but I prod her and up we go.

The Colonel is in his finest uniform and his wife is a froth of pink silk and Randall looks absolutely smashing in a dove gray velvet jacket and Clarissa, of course, is the very picture of beauty in white with touches of lavender. I am in my school dress, it being the only one I have except for my blue one that I made on the *Dolphin*, and *that* one I'm saving for tonight's dinner and dance. Amy has lent me a fine hat, 'cause us ladies can't be in public without one and I sure can't wear my mobcap or my school bonnet to somethin' like this.

Besides the Royal Navy crew, there's bunches of other swells and nobs about, but nobody introduces me to none of 'em. Guess it's 'cause of the excitement of the moment. That midshipman looks like he'd like to be introduced, though, but of course he can't move from his spot. These boys weren't brought here to have fun—they was brought to serve the Captain and the Lieutenant. The Captain is a loud, garrulous fellow, but he seems a decent sort, for a captain, while the Lieutenant is a tall, thin, dark cove who's got a pair of mustachios that he continually twirls as his eyes go over the nearby girls. I know what's on his mind, and it ain't horse racin'.

Randall is standing at the rail with Clarissa on his arm. She must have forgiven him, or maybe she just considered it his right as a lord of the manor to cover whatever lower-class girls he wanted. Or maybe Randall came up with a real good explanation, which I wouldn't put past him—he's a clever one, he is, as I know right well. Whatever, she sends a glare in my direction, which I return with a smile and slight, ever so slight, curtsy.

I go to the rail myself, but not close to the young lovers, as I don't want to get into a down-on-the-ground-hair-pullin'-face-scratchin' fight with Clarissa just now, what with everything goin' on, and if I know anything about proud Clarissa by now, it's that she wouldn't be afraid to do it anyplace, anytime.

So I look out over the track, and the jockeys are starting to get on their mounts, the little men all in their colorful silks, each one different depending on the farm they're racin' for. I look around for the green-and-white stripes of House Trevelyne, but I don't see none—I don't see Pete, neither.

Uh-oh.

There's the Sheik, dancin' and prancin', but it's a groom what's leadin' him about, not Petey. I look at the Colonel and he's lookin' down at the track, too, and his mouth is set in a grim line around a cigar that is clenched tight in his jaws.

I spy the groom George working his way through the crowd toward us and I know what that means: Petey ain't gonna make it. I hope he ain't dead, 'cause I've grown fond of the little man. George leans in and says something in Colonel Trevelyne's ear and the Colonel nods curtly and bows to his party and leaves the grandstand, but before he does, he motions for Randall to follow him.

I grab Amy's arm and pull her along. "Let's go, Sister. Things are going wrong and we must do what we can."

"But what...?"

"Petey ain't gonna make the race." I turn and look at her, and her face is now empty of all hope. "Please, just go along with whatever I say, no matter what. No matter how crazy. Will you do it?"

She nods and follows me out of the box, her face ashen.

We hit the ground and race toward the jockey rooms and we meet the Colonel and Randall as they are coming out of Petey's room.

I give Amy an elbow and hiss at her, "Ask them what's the matter." as it ain't my place and I don't want to spook 'em.

"Father. What is the matter?" she says.

"Jarvis can't race. He's barely conscious," growls the Colonel. He takes his cigar and throws it to the ground. "Damn it! Damn it all to hell!"

"Can't you forfeit? Call off the bets?" asks Amy without much hope in her voice.

"I can forfeit, but I cannot call off the bets, and what, Daughter, gave you the idea that you can talk to me in this way?" His face is bright red and his tone is dangerous.

"I shall ride him, Father," says Randall, and he begins to unbutton his jacket.

"Aw, you're too damned heavy, boy, you'd surely..."

It is time, Jacky, I says to myself, and I pulls out my asafoetida bag and clutches it in me hand and I steps forward.

"Beggin' your pardon, Colonel Trevelyne, but I have here in my hand an answer to your problem." I ain't used to talking up to large powerful men, so my voice shakes a bit.

"What?" shouts the Colonel, shock and outrage on his face as he stares down at me.

I pushes on. "I have this here powerful voodoo potion that I picked up when I was sailin' on the Caribbean Sea," I says, and waves the bag decorated with its strange symbols in front of him. "It's powerful strong magic, Sir, as it was put together by Mama Boudreau, herself, a most famous hoodoo conjure woman."

"Let me see that," orders the Colonel. He reaches out a meaty paw for my bag, but I shrinks back and holds the bag tighter to my chest.

"Oh no, Sir! Don't mess with the *gris-gris,* Sir, it's very dangerous in unschooled hands. It's very powerful stuff and no tellin' what would happen." I shivers and looks all scared at the very thought.

"Rubbish," says he. "Has this girl ever been to the Caribbean?" he asks Amy. It looks like he is ready to grasp at straws.

"Yes," says Amy, and then, incredibly, she says, "she has often spoken of her knowledge of the mysterious arts of that region."

The Colonel squints at me. "It's powerful enough to cure someone as sick as him?"

"Sir, it was made to raise the dead. It may not cure Mr. Jarvis, but it will get him up."

He hooks a thumb over his shoulder. "All right. Go get him up. And hurry."

Ah. And now for the hook.

"I have terms, Colonel Trevelyne, and you may not like them." I'm puttin' up a brave front, but I'm shakin' inside. To talk to a colonel like this…

"What! What terms, girl?"

"If I rouse up Peter Jarvis enough so he can get on the Sheik and win the race, you must swear, on your honor as an officer and gentleman, to *never* again bet on *anything*. Not a penny, not a pound, not a dollar, not a dime. *Nothing* wagered ever again."

He balls his fist and lifts it high above me. "Why, you insolent piece of baggage…!"

I cringe and hunch my shoulders, and wait for the blow, but the blow does not come.

"Father, please!" say both Amy and Randall together.

I open my eyes. The Colonel is standing there, and he is a bit shrunken, like the air has gone out of him.

I have no mercy. "Do you so swear?"

"Yes," he says, quietly. "I swear."

"All right," I say, all brisk. "Amy and Randall, I'll need your help. Randall, get everybody out of Petey's room." I cross my arms at the wrists over my chest like I'm a voodoo princess and I put my head back and slit my eyes and start into a low chant, *"Hey-ya, hey-ya, hey-ya, hey!"* over and over and follow them in.

We surge into Petey's tiny room and there are people in there standing around him lying there in the bed. Petey's mouth is open and his face is gray and he looks half dead. "Everybody please leave," says Randall, curtly. They look confused. "Out!" he roars this time. "Now!" And out they go, falling over each other in their haste. Randall's blood is up.

As soon as the door is shut, I say, "Randall, put your back to the door and let no one in! Amy, help me!" and I flip my hat to the floor and start to struggle out of my dress. "Randall. Turn around!"

Petey's silks are hanging on the wall with his boots beneath them. Amy has undone the buttons on the back of my dress and I flip it over my head. Off with the shoes and stockings and I pull off my slip and—"Randall, turn around!" *Oh, to hell with it, there's no time!* I put my thumbs in the waistband of my flouncy drawers and pull them down and step out of them. I reach for the silk pants...

"Don't...don't let 'em..."

Petey's talking! His eyes flutter open. I dash to his side. "Don't let 'em what, Petey? Don't let 'em..."

But he passes out again and there's no time to try to bring him back.

I go to the wall and get the silks. I sit on the edge of the bed to pull on the white stockings and then stand and tug on the tight pants and buckle 'em below the knees, then the loose, blousy green-striped top, which'll hide what I got up there. On with the boots—they're a little big, but they'll serve.

There's the call of a trumpet outside. *Hurry!*

I take the white silk scarf I had seen last night when I visited Petey and I wrap it around my lower face. "Tie it in back, Amy! It can't fall off or all is lost!"

"But why...?"

"'Cause the other jocks won't race against a girl, is why! Male bleedin' *pride,* is why! Now, tie it! Tight!"

She does it. I take the green cap and cram it way down on my head and head for the door, Amy, terrified, in my wake.

At the door, a red-faced Randall stands and says, "I…"

"Later, Randall," I say. "Let us out and let *no one* else in. When we come back we'll give three raps and then two. Got that?"

He nods and opens the door and we rush out.

There is a roar from the crowd as I head for the track and the Sheik. I stop halfway there and make a great fakery of doublin' over and coughin' loudly, as if seized by a spasm. I steal a glance up at the Colonel, who is back in his box lookin' at me and standing a little straighter. I give it a few more coughs, as deep and disgustin' as I can make 'em, makes a show of bein' a bit weak and wobbly on me pins, and then I go to the Sheik and put my foot in George's intertwined hands and I'm up in the saddle, and *Oh, he knows me, he does.* The Sheik gives me his big rollin' eye and whickers a greeting as I get my feet in the stirrups and settle in and take the riding crop from George and stick it in my right armpit. I don't want this small whip 'cause I wouldn't want to use it on the Sheik, but I take it anyway 'cause it'll look wrong if I don't. I pat his neck and he dances around a bit—he is ready to go, no mistake.

"Glad you could get up there, Petey," says George. "I had my doubts, for sure." He adjusts the cinch on the saddle. "Now watch out for the big bay horse—that jock Muir from Tenbrooks Farms don't mean us no good. At the start you'll have him on your right, and that bastard Thayer over there on that hammerheaded roan'll be on your left at the start, so you know what that means."

What? What what means? I thought we just started running and the fastest horse wins and that's the Sheik, who'll run away from all the others and we'll win. All of a sudden I'm thinking that there might be more to this and maybe I don't know what I'm doin'. I want to blurt out to George just who I am sitting up here and what the hell is he talkin' about, but the fewer people what know about this the better, or the secret will be out and the race will be forfeit and all will be in vain, so I just give a low grunt and another cough.

"I'd go wide on the first turn if I was you. You'll lose some ground but the horse'll make it up on the straightaways. Good luck to you, Pete. There's a lot ridin' on this."

I nod and grunt and throw in a racking cough and there's the trumpet call for the horses to parade by the grandstand and I take the reins and somehow get him in line and it's all I can do to keep him there. What with all the other stallions and mares around, he's in a fine lather and in no mood to be good. Fine. It's his job to win the race, not to be good.

We come off the line and head for the starting positions. The crowd noise is nothing like anything I've ever heard— there must be a thousand people here, counting the grandstand and those circling the track. Grooms take hold of the bridles and pull the horses to their spots, and it is a very brave groom who puts his hand on the Sheik's bridle. We are third in from the rail, it having all been decided by the drawing of lots, and George was right about the two to either side of me—they look like the meanest of blokes and they're both glaring at me. I can't let 'em look too close, so I coughs and leans forward and hisses in the Sheik's ear, "Scream, Sheik, scream!" and he rears back on his hind legs and does just that, he screams out his defiance to all those who would dare to come here to his own kingdom and challenge him, to shame him, and to take his mares. It is a fine show.

"Mind yer mount, jock!" shouts Muir.

"Sod off," growls I, as deep as I can. "Mind yer own nag!"

A tall man with a red sash across his belly goes to the end of our line and then takes ten paces forward. He has a pistol by his side. All eyes are on him now, so I don't got to worry about Muir or Thayer peerin' at me.

The man holds up his hand and the crowd falls silent. He takes a deep breath and bellows, "Ladies and Gentlemen! The race is to be twelve furlongs, once around the track and up to the finish line in front of the grandstand." I look forward and see the white line drawn with lime on the track! He raises the gun, "Ready." There is a hush. All us jocks point our tails skyward and lean forward.

He fires! The crowd roars as twelve thousand pounds of muscle, hide, and bone surges out of the gates, and the first thing that happens is that Muir brings his horse a sharp left, right into us and forces the Sheik to miss his footing and stumble, and Thayer on the other side does the same thing and the Sheik almost goes to his knees, and Muir and Thayer pull ahead of us. The Sheik screams in anger and I can hear his teeth snapping at the other horses, but I urge him forward—*run now, fight later*—and he gains his footing and his muscles gather under me and he charges down the track after the rest of them. A sob chokes me—I messed up, I messed up bad—we are dead last!

But the Sheik don't sob and cry—all he wants to do is run and beat the others back to wherever the hell they come from and he don't care about nothin' else and he flies down the track with his ears laid back, and by the time we are approaching the first turn, we have passed one, two, now three, four! We are catching up! We are flying!

We lean into the first turn and I see that Muir and Thayer are running first and second, with a big chestnut running third. There's a short straightaway before the next turn and we pass two more horses, leaving only the front three. As we get close to the middle of the turn, Thayer, who's on the inside, lets his mount drift a little to the right, leaving an opening at the rail.

An opening! If we can get through there we'll save distance being on the inside 'cause there's less ground to cover and we'll be in the lead and we won't never let go of it! I urge the Sheik forward toward the opening and he goes for it. Poor trusting horse to have such a poor *stupid* rider. As soon as we get close, Thayer pulls back to the rail and Muir comes alongside to the right, and I realize to my horror that we're trapped! Boxed in!

That's what Petey was tryin' to say—"Don't let 'em box you in," you incredibly stupid girl! And George said, *"Stay outside on the first turn!" Oh, why didn't I, why do I always think I know everything about everything and all I ever really do is make a hash of things!*

As we come out of the turn, Thayer slows his horse, just a little, not so the people in the stands could notice and cry foul, but just a little bit slower so a horse can come up behind us to keep us from escaping that way and the chestnut can come up on the outside to take the lead. It's a setup! A scam. I've been scammed again! Muir and Thayer never had no thought of winnin' the race! All they wanted to do was keep the Colonel's horse from winnin'! *Stupid, stupid, stupid...*

The chestnut is now four lengths ahead, now five, and if he gets too far ahead, there'll be no catchin' him even if I do get out of this. In desperation I veer the Sheik to the right to try and force Muir away enough to break free, but Muir don't move. Instead he brings up his crop and *crack!* he brings it down on my leg, and it's like a hot poker was laid there. The pain shoots up me side and into me head and I lets out a howl of pain and sorrow and desperation right into the Sheik's ear and he hears it and the muscles of his neck swell up and he darts his head forward and bares his teeth and clamps down on the arse of Thayer's horse up there in front of his nose. The roan screams and breaks stride and there's an opening, and this time we make it through. We are free!

But the chestnut is now at least twelve lengths ahead and we're in the backstretch.

"Catch him, Sheik!" I shrieks. "Catch him!" The leader is so far ahead I despair of closing the distance, but I urge the Sheik on anyway, bouncing up and down in the saddle, tears of pain and desolation runnin' out the sides of my eyes—*how could I have been so stupid*—and the Sheik pounds on ever faster and I can feel his hatred for the horse ahead of him and I start to babble, *"Oh come on Sheik come on boy he's gonna beat you he's gonna shame you he's gonna take your mares he's gonna beat you boy,"* and the horse pumps faster and we've gained a length or two but that horse up there ain't no scrub, neither. He's fast and he's strong and he's at the end of the far stretch and he leans into the last turn and clods of dirt are flying up at us from his hooves what are diggin' out to the side as he leans. But we don't care, we just pound on and the white rail posts and the screaming people standing and waving their arms flicker by in the corner of my eye like they ain't even real, just pieces of a crazy dream—*come on boy come on boy*—and we're in the last turn, too, and we go right up to the rail 'cause there ain't nobody to box us in now and we gain another length in the turn, and when we come out of it, we're only four lengths behind!

The roar of the crowd in the grandstand hits us like a wall when we turn onto the homestretch and the race for the line. We're only four lengths behind but that'll be enough to doom us if the chestnut don't weaken, and he ain't showin' no signs of that, no he ain't, so I keep babblin'. *"Beating you Sheik he's beating you,"* and the sun is in our eyes now and *"He's gonna beat you boy he's gonna beat you to the bright shinin' sun he's gonna beat you,"* and I know I ain't makin' no sense but it don't matter. What matters is that the Sheik would rather die than lose and he finds the strength somewhere down in him and now we're up to two lengths and now one. The other jock is flailing away with his whip but it ain't doin' him no good 'cause we're gainin', and now the Sheik's nose is up level with the chestnut's flank and now up to the jockey's knee and now the horse's shoulder and the crowd is howling. There's the white line up ahead and now we're neck and neck and now we push forward by a nose and then by a head and then are goin' away, and then the line flashes by underfoot and…

We win!

I pull the Sheik back and slow him down and turn him so I can get back to the clubhouse, but he don't want to quit just yet, no he don't—he rears up and screams out all the rage and defiance that's in his bloody, glorious heart. No, he ain't done yet at all—he wants to get at the other horse and fight him and beat him into a bloody mess. He squeals in anger as if to say, "I didn't catch him just to let him go. Let me *go!*" and it's all I can do to hold him till George and his grooms come runnin' up to take his reins and calm him down.

Uh-oh.

The grandstand is emptying and people are pouring onto the track. I slide off the dear Sheik's back, give a few coughs, and wipe the tears from my eyes with an end of the scarf and wave off the grinnin' George's "Well done," and head for the clubhouse. I take three steps and then fall down in the dust, and this time I ain't faking. It's the pain in me leg, but I get right up and start a runnin', limpin' lope for Petey's room 'cause I see the Colonel bearing down on us but I can't let him catch me and fold me in his manly embrace, which is what the big, burly, grinnin' fool seems intent on doin'.

There's Amy and she throws her arm around me and helps me the last several yards. She gives the signal rap on the door and we fall into the room. Randall puts his back to the door again and looks at us with a big question in his eyes—and I don't think he really wants to hear the answer 'cause he's lookin' at me with the tears runnin' down through the dust on my face and he fears the worst.

"We won," says Amy, and Randall lets out a huge breath and sinks down a ways on the door. I whip off the scarf and go to the washstand and splash water on my face. *Stop crying,* I tell myself, *don't mess it up now. It's just the excitement. Stop it.* And I do, and I dry my face and straighten up and go to Petey's bedside.

"Pull back his covers," I orders. Amy furrows her brow in question. "Just do it!" I say, and she does it.

Poor Petey's skinny legs lie there helpless, the black hair on them standin' out sharp against the dead white of his skin. I swing the riding crop back over my shoulder and bring it down as hard as I can on Pete's right thigh. Amy gasps at the sound of the whip hitting flesh.

Petey's eyes pop open—I didn't think he'd wake, but he does. I kneel down by him. "Sorry, Petey, but you got that on the near turn. Muir give it to you. You won, Pete, you got that? You won and Muir give you that welt on the near turn."

"That son of a bitch, I'll get him for that," says he, all weak. A small smile comes to his lips. "Nice tattoo, Jack-o."

"You rogue," says I, putting my hand to his forehead. He is covered in sweat now, but his head is cooler. The fever has broken. "Worse luck. You'll prolly get better." His eyes close again.

The pounding on the door is loud and insistent.

"We can't keep them out forever," says Randall, his back to the shaking door. "You'd better hurry and change." His arrogant smile is back.

I cuts him a narrow-eyed glare. *Right, Randall.* I reflects that the I-know-Jacky's-got-a-tattoo-and-I-know-where's-she's-got-it club has just added two new members. *Only one show for you today, Mr. Trevelyne.*

I turn away so that my bare back is all that's for him to look at as I take off the silk top and flip it to Amy. "See if you can slip that over Mr. Jarvis, if you would, Amy."

She goes to do it, and since there's a little more time for a bit more modesty now, I take my dress and pull it on over me and then reach up under and pull off the pants and stockings. *Carefully* pull off the pants—the welt looks all purple and wicked, but there ain't no blood and that's good. I fling the silks to the floor as if Petey had just thrown them there on his way back to bed. I bundle up the rest of my clothes and tuck 'em under my arm. The cap goes on the bedpost and, "Button me up, Amy!"

"All right, done! Let 'em in, Randall!"

Randall steps back from the door and people pour into the little room, showering the half-conscious Pete with praise and congratulations. The Colonel was first in and he rushes over to Petey and shakes his senseless hand, and Amy speaks up with, "He will need salve for his leg, Father," and the Colonel nods and says that all saw the blow and that damned Muir shall never ride a horse at Dovecote again. A groom hustles over with a jar and the covers are pulled back and all around the room there are gasps at the soreness of the slash. Well, maybe I didn't have to hit him *that* hard...

A man who has to be Mr. Thayer bursts in and shouts, "Your horse bit mine! That's a foul!"

"Your nag had his fat, *slow* ass in my horse's face, and that's even more of a foul!" retorts the Colonel, puffing up. "And if you'd like to continue this discussion with pistols on the field of honor, then say one more word, Sir! One more word!" But Mr. Thayer don't say that word but instead turns red and storms out. Needless to say, he and his lady will not be joining us this evening. *And how much sure money did you lose today, Mr. Thayer, hmmm?*

Colonel Trevelyne looks over and sees me standing there. "Get these girls out of here. This is no place for females!"

I put the back of my hand to my forehead and close my

eyes like I'm a poor, weak female about to swoon from tossin' around heavy spells and stuff, and Amy leads me out saying, "The poor thing needs rest," which, of course, I do.

The sheets feel so cool and nice, and I feel I could lie here forever in this delicious doze, their light weight resting smooth and easy on my skin. A great wave of tiredness sweeps over me like it always does after the wildness that comes on in me slowly ebbs away.

"Yeow!" I say, without meaning to. Amy has turned back the sheet and is putting some salve on my welt.

"I am sorry," she says. "I should be saying it serves you right, you could have been killed and all that. But I did not say that before you took the ride, so I have no right to say anything at all. Except thank you."

"Aw, g'wan. All I did was go out and ride a horse."

"That, and extract that promise from Father."

"Do you think he'll be as good as his word?"

"He will. Male honor and all that." Amy looks about her room and I know she is seeing it in a far different light than she did this morning, or anytime in the near past. *Go ahead, Amy. There's no sin in loving your own little room.*

There's a tap on the door and then it opens and Randall walks in.

"Randall! She's not dressed!" says Amy, and she brings the sheet back over my leg. I bend my other leg at the knee to make a tent so that the salve don't stick to it.

"Oh, it's all right," I say, all sleepy and drowsy, running my tongue quickly over my lips and parting them slightly in my best Dying Juliet's last-gasp pose. "The sheets are to my chin, so what's the harm?"

Randall comes over to the bedside but he don't say nothing, he just looks at me. He reaches down and, with one finger, gently pulls a lock of hair from my face. I smile all weak and frail.

"What can we do for you?" he finally asks.

"What?"

"How can we repay you? What will you have?"

I goes to say I don't want nothing, but then I changes my mind and says, "The silks. I want to keep the silks."

I don't know what he says to that, 'cause I slip off to sleep.

Later, when I wake up, the silks have been cleaned and are folded on my seabag, and by them is a pair of supple black riding boots. And they fit, too.

"We shall dance and we shall be gay. That tall midshipman is rather cute, don't you think?" I'm all rested up and ready to go to my first ball. Little Mary Faber, late of London's better gutters, is dressing for a ball with Captains, Colonels, Lieutenants, swells of all kinds, and the finest of Ladies, what a thing.

"Ah yes," smiles Amy, "Miss I-Am-Promised-to-Another Faber." Amy's been smiling a lot since the race and that is good.

I feel a wave of sadness slip over my gaiety, and I am quiet. Yes, and no word from the one I am promised to for over nine months. Not one word. Amy says mail comes to Dovecote on Monday, but I dare not hope.

"I shall be good," I say. *But I shall also be gay.*

We had crimped up our side curls with the curling iron warmed on the cooking fire in the kitchen, being careful to stay out of the way 'cause mighty preparations are being made for tonight's dinner and Mrs. Grubbs ain't puttin' up with no silly girls, not even if one of 'em is the daughter of the house. There's steamin' pots and great joints of meat, but thankfully, no little suckling piggy. Her serving girls are being run ragged and well I know the drill, so we get done and get out. But not before I lifts us a couple hot cherry tarts from a tray. Ain't lost me Cheapside touch.

We then go up and watch the doings in the great hall— men stringing banners and a chamber orchestra setting up their music stands, and that's sure to be a treat, dancing to music provided by someone other than myself. The men have also set up a long table with crystal goblets set out on it and another man brings in a huge punch bowl in the center. The great chandeliers are being lit and the place just glitters with light...and promise.

Entering the dining room we find the table set, with the silver polished and the gold-rimmed plates placed just so, and the wineglasses winking in the light so cheerily. I walk around the table, peering at the name cards.

"Hmmm..." I muses. "I think there's been some mistake. You and I are all the way down at the end. Surely whoever did this didn't know I must sit next to the Royal Navy officers to get the news. So we'll just put this Mrs. Cabot in my place at the end. Who is she, anyway?"

"An old lady, but—"

"Good. She won't notice. And we'll put me next to this Captain Humphries and we'll take this Mr. Adams and put him here..."

"Jacky, you can't put an Adams down at—"

"I just did. And I'll put you in his place next to that Lieutenant—what's his name...oh, Flashby, the one with the mustachios. And Clarissa is there and Randall there, and I believe we've got it right now.

"Our work here is done," I say, all grand. "Let us go dress for the ball, dear Sister."

We are dressed and ready to go. I have on the blue dress that I made myself and I know that Amy does not quite approve of it, being as low cut as it is, but it is all I have. My hair is up and my dress is on. I am powdered, pampered, and perfumed.

There is a tinkling of a bell in the hall. It is time.

"Are you ready, Miss Faber?"

"I am, Miss Trevelyne."

We put on the Look and glide down to the dining room.

We enter the room and introductions are made, bows and curtsies all around, and then we go to our places. The place is a blaze of color, what with the ladies in their finest and the gentlemen in their jackets that go through all the colors from bright blue to deep purple, light mauve to kelly green, but never, oh never, red. None of these Yankees want to risk being taken for a redcoat. I mean, the war is over long since, but some things linger on. The naval officers are, of course, in blue with much gold.

I am handed to my place by Captain Humphries, who's beaming and twinkling away at me, having already consumed a good deal of wine, I'll wager. He pulls out my chair and I sit. Would it pain him to know that he had just performed a courtesy for a ship's boy, I wonder?

I settle in and grin at Amy across the way. She looks absolutely wonderful in her rig, a black silk thing with red ribbon worked into the bodice and puffed sleeves, and I think she knows it. She has the Lieutenant on her right and Randall on her left and Clarissa next to him. Clarissa, of course, looks gorgeous and is laying the charm on all about her. She even smiles upon me, which makes me wonder what she's up to.

The grace is said, the wine is poured, toasts are drunk to the host and to several of the guests, and the soup is served and the conversation begins.

"Isn't it wonderful that Amy could have two of her dear classmates from Mistress Pimm's here?" warbles Mrs. Trevelyne from the head of the table. The three of us allow that it is indeed wonderful.

"How is the old witch?" says a woman with hooded eyes and parted lips a few chairs down.

Ah.

"Mistress is well, Madame," says I, taking a chance. "You would find her skill with the cane is quite undiminished." Laughter all around. *Whew, I'm glad that went over well.*

I take some soup and look across to see that Lieutenant Flashby has taken an avid interest in me...or at least in the rise and fall of my chest. I sneak a quick look down to make sure I ain't dribbled something down there, but no, it looks all right.

Each of the officers has a midshipman standing ramrod straight behind their chairs, to get them anything they might need, but it's mainly for show: *This is what Royal Navy discipline looks like, Yankee rabble.*

"Expecting weevils?" says the Captain, his eyebrow raised in question.

"Excuse me, Sir?" I say, confused. "I don't underst—" Then I realize I've been tappin' my biscuit on the tabletop without thinkin'. *Damn!* "I'm sorry, Sir, it's an old habit."

"That's all right, Missy. Here, a little more wine with you." He gestures and the tall midshipman goes to the sideboard and takes a bottle and fills my glass. Too bad. I had meant to fill my glass with water to dilute the wine, but I didn't get to it in time. Ah, well. Next time. I take a sip.

"So, schoolgirls, eh?" says the Captain, and then he leans in close and whispers, "Thanks for being here. I thought for sure I'd get stuck next to some old biddy and I sure didn't come all this way to talk to ancient dames! Har, har!" He laughs out loud at his wit and I gulp and nod. Under the table he places his hand on my leg and gives it a squeeze. I gulp again. I don't know what to do about it.

The soup bowls are taken away and the main courses brought. The Captain, needing both his hands to dig in to his dinner, frees my leg and I squirm and move a little out of his range. I know the serving girls a little bit now and I wink at them in thanks as I am served. They know me for one of them, and I think they delight in my being here.

Clarissa speaks up. "Perhaps, Classmate, you'll tell us something of your family." She smiles sweetly and brings her glass to her lips.

Uh-oh... I look at Amy but she shakes her head and mouths *Not me,* and then I look at Randall and he just looks back at me as if he's mildly interested in my answer. Clarissa, however, looks me right in the eye, and there is a wicked merriment in her gaze. She knows, and how she knows, I don't know—prolly looking through Amy's scribblings when she wasn't around.

I lift my chin and say, "I have no family. I was orphaned as a young child."

"Oh, what a pity!" says dear Mrs. Trevelyne. "Who took you in?"

"No one took me in," I say. I put my hands in my lap and look down at them. "I was left on my own." I know what's comin'. A pity. This would have been such fun. *Oh, well.*

Amy tries to change the subject. "Captain, could you tell us of the exotic ports you have—" but Clarissa rides right over her.

"But what did you *do,* you poor thing?" she purrs. "Left on your own as you were?"

I stick out my lower lip and say quietly, "My parents died when I was a little girl and I was put out on the curb to live or to die. I fell in with a gang of street children and I ran the slum streets of London with them for several years." I put my napkin on the table and look Clarissa in the eye. "You ask me what I did, Clarissa? I was a beggar and a thief. What kind of beggar was I? I was a naked beggar and a filthy beggar. Any kind of beggar you can imagine and I was it. I begged pennies and I stole bread. I lived under a bridge, but I had good mates in Rooster Charlie's gang, I did, a lot better mates than some I have now."

I take a sip of wine and I will my hand not to shake in rage as I continue. "Actually, if you must know, I was a better thief than a beggar. I stole bread and I pickpocketed fancy handkerchiefs and I stole clothing off of clotheslines and I stole anything that would keep me and my friends alive. In fact, I picked pockets at the very foot of the gallows, the gallows that were sure to be my fate someday."

The whole table is lookin' at me with open mouths, their knives and forks and glasses held motionless in midair. It would be comical if this were a play, which it ain't.

"Then I find it a shame, dear Jacky, that you did not remain in your chosen profession," purrs Clarissa.

I look at her without expression. "It is true, Miss Howe, that my estate was very low. So low, indeed, that it was very like that of the slaves you hold in bondage. Except that I was free."

There are rumblings around the table as some of the guests realize that Clarissa and I could actually go at each other, right here and right now, and they try to soothe ruffled feathers with *there, there,* and *all right, now,* and suchlike.

But Clarissa is not to be soothed.

"Free? Ah, yes. Free," says Clarissa, tilting her head as if what I had said amused her. "Free to beg. Free to steal from honest folk. And free..." Here she pauses and her tongue flicks over her upper lip as if she is about to taste something delicious. "Free to have yourself *tattooed*."

There is a common gasp from the guests at the table.

"Why don't you tell us about your cunning little tattoo, Jacky?" says Clarissa, relentlessly plowing on. "What is it? An anchor? How daring of you, Jacky. I do declare you leave all the rest of us poor girls far behind in the pursuit of new fashion."

The game is up now, for sure, for there are no tattooed ladies in this world, not outside of freak shows. I get to my feet and I turn to my hostess. "Mrs. Trevelyne, you have been nothing but kind to me here at Dovecote and I thank you for it and I beg forgiveness if I have brought dishonor to your table. I am sorry. Sometimes I get above myself. I'll be excused now." She sits there stunned.

I get up to leave the room but a rough hand comes down on my bare shoulder and shoves me back down in my chair. "Oh, nonsense!" says Captain Humphries. "Sit down! That's the best story I've heard all day!"

I take up my napkin again and look over at Mrs. Trevelyne, but she's just all a-goggle with the turn of things and simply takes another dainty sip of her wine.

"So how did you get from there to here? From the rags to the riches? From an urchin in the streets to a neatly turned out young lady in the very bosom of New England society?" the Captain booms out. "We must hear! Leave nothing out!"

Before I say anything I turn to my hostess again, "Please, Mrs. Trevelyne, if anything said here causes you pain, just tap your knife on your glass and I will be out of here in an instant. All right?" She manages to nod. I look at Amy and she is stunned. I look at Randall and he is astounded. I look at Clarissa and she is smirking. I look at Lieutenant Flashby and he has left off looking at my chest and is instead peering at my face, as if trying to figure something out.

"Actually, Captain Humphries, I had a bit of very good luck," I say. "I had the great good fortune to be taken into your own service."

"The Royal Navy?" he says, perplexed. "How? In what capacity?"

"First as ship's boy, then as midshipman, on board the…"

"*It's Bloody Jacky Faber, by God!*" shouts Lieutenant Flashby, bringing the flat of his hand down hard on the table. He points his finger at my nose. "*It's the Jackaroe!*"

"Wot! Can it be? The girl from the *Dolphin*?" says the Captain, all incredulous. "Are you sure?"

"Yes, yes!" says the Lieutenant. "Look! She's still got the mark on her neck where they tried to hang her." That scar has mostly gone away, 'cept when I get excited, like now, and then it flares up all red. I pull my hair around to cover it.

"Is it you?" asks the Captain.

"I don't know...yes, I was on the *Dolphin*, but I had no idea my poor adventures had—"

"Oh, Trevelyne, you dog!" says the Captain to the Colonel, who's sitting there like he's been hit with a bludgeon. "You set this up for us, didn't you! Oh, what a fine thing! It's too perfect!" The Captain's hand has found my leg again, higher up this time, but I am too amazed to move.

"But this can't be..." I stammer.

"Oh yes!" says the Captain, giving my thigh an affectionate squeeze. "It is the talk of London, it is all around the fleet! On all the broadsides! You there, Padget! Sing a few verses of the song! 'Jackaroe'!"

Midshipman Padget, the pretty one, flushes in mortification. He will, of course, obey, as he would obey if his Captain told him to drop his breeches and waddle around the table clucking like a chicken, but he does not have to like it. He fixes his eye on a wall lamp, and dying a thousand deaths, he opens his mouth and gives forth:

> *"She brought herself unto the dock*
> *All dressed in men's array,*
> *And stepped on board a man-of-war*
> *To convey herself away,*
> *Oh, to convey herself away."*

I am completely astounded. The melody sounds like a faster version of my "Ship's Boy's Lament," done in a major key instead of the minor. I think I hear Liam Delaney's hand in this.

> "'Before you come on board, Sir,
> Your name I'd like to know.'
> She smiled all in her countenance,
> 'They call me Jack-a-roe.'"

It warn't like that at all, I'm thinkin'. I have recovered my senses enough to reach down and lift the Captain's hand off my leg. He does not seem to mind. He merely uses the hand to refill my glass. *Sailors,* I swear, *be they Captain or be they seaman, it's all one and the same.* Midshipman Padget launches into what proves to be the last verses.

> "'Your waist is light and slender,
> Your fingers are neat and small,
> Your cheeks too red and rosy,
> To face the cannonball.'
> Oh, to face the cannonball.
>
> 'I know my waist is slender,
> My fingers neat and small,
> But it would not make me tremble
> To see ten thousand fall.'
> Oh, to see ten thousand fall!"

"Poor Captain Locke," I say, after the applause for the mortified midshipman stops. Poor Jaimy, too, what he must think, he being so upright and all. And I can well guess what his mother must think. I take another deep swallow of the wine to calm myself. *Next time I must water it.*

"Poor Captain Locke, nothing! He has drunk for free on that story for months!" chortles the Captain. "He has a grand speech on the matter—I myself heard him deliver it at our club." Captain Humphries puffs up and puts his hand to his chest like a grand orator. "'I will bear the ridicule of any man who has stood on a ship's burning deck with the masts coming down and the air thick with hot cannonballs, a man who has smelled the foul breath of the cannon and seen the scuppers run red with the blood of his friends, yea, a man who has seen all that and yet did not run and hide to save his own life. I will suffer that man's insults and call him brother. But should any man who has not seen those things, one who has sat comfortable at his table with his pipe and his dinner while we were on the cruel sea, should such a man dare make sport of me or the *Dolphin* or any who were on her, then I will gladly meet with him in the morning and cheerfully put a hole in his unworthy chest! I put it to you like this: The girl stood by my side in the heat of battle and she did not run!'" The Captain finishes and lurches to his feet. "A toast! A toast to Bloody Jacky Faber!"

All cheer and rise and I try to sink into my chair. Amy beams at me over her glass. I look over at Randall and see that he is stricken to the core. *Uh-oh.* I see that male pride has been wounded and is in need of repair. I know he is thinking that for all his arrogance and posturing, it is I who have faced combat and come out of it with some honor and he has not yet been tried, and he wonders, in his heart of hearts, just how well he will perform. After the toast Randall sits down heavily and seems to sink within himself. At his side, the good ship Clarissa is in flames, her plan for the sinking of the good ship Jacky having gone awry. She crosses her arms and looks straight forward in a storm of anger.

More wine is poured, the dessert brought, the Captain's hand is back, and the Lieutenant has resumed his leering, but I am soon saved by the announcement that the dance is about to begin and all are invited to the main ballroom. I toss off the rest of the wine and rise up on the Captain's arm and am escorted in to the dance, my head up, eyes hooded, lips together, teeth apart, the finest of the ladies.

Many more people pour in the door to the ballroom and are announced as the band strikes up the first tune. There are people, both young and old, from all over the county, as this is the ball of the year by all accounts. The place fairly glitters with light and color and wild excitement.

First we have a Virginia reel, which is good 'cause it frees me up from the clutches of Captain Humphries, who's a good sort in his way, but I really want to get close to that pretty Midshipman Padget—to ask him if he's heard of Jaimy, of course—so during the reel when there's two rows of dancers and everybody sort of gets to touch hands with everyone else for a moment, I give his hand a squeeze.

On the next dance, a minuet, he comes up to me and, blushing, asks me to dance and I bat my eyelashes and say yes, and then we go to the floor with the other couples and we dance and it is lovely and he is so pretty and nice, but I wish so much that Jaimy was here with me to see all this. He would look so dashing and I would be so proud. After the dance I ask Mr. Padget if he knows of Jaimy, but, alas, he reports that he does not.

My gallant escort takes me to the punch bowl, which has a big chunk of ice floating in it, and he gets me a cup of punch and it's good and I wonder what's in it, but I don't wonder long because I am stolen from the midshipman by Lieutenant Flashby for the next dance, and he is a very good dancer and is very charming and smells of cologne water, but somehow I don't quite trust him. Then there's another dance, a quadrille, and another partner and my head is spinning and I have some more punch and I have a vague notion of Amy coming up to me and warning me about something but I can't remember what it is...

And then there's another dance, and then, wonder of wonders, Clarissa comes to me and says, "Oh, don't mess with that silly punch, dear Jacky. Here, have some of this. We call it a julep, yes, we do. A mint julep, as a matter of actual fact. Oh yes, Jacky, it is just the very best thing. No, no, there's no rum or whiskey in it, just a little of our own fine bourbon...Here, refresh yourself, you must be exhausted, poor thing. You dance so well, I declare you put the rest of us to shame, you really do...you really are the belle of the ball, Jacky...Let me get you another, why, it's no trouble at all, dear Jacky..."

I taste it and it is sweet and smooth and cool and good and it must be all right 'cause it's not harsh at all, not like rum, which burns its way down, and this is just so lovely. Why, it's just like that root beer. "Oh, thank you, Clarissa, I'm so glad we can be frens...er...friends." Only it's soft, so soft. *Another dance?* "Well, Sir, I be delighted. 'Scoose me, Clarissa. Sir, let us whirl onto the floorn..." I mean, floor, I mean...I don't know what I mean. "Whoops, I'm sorry, did I stumble? Isn't this all so lovely isn't this just the best night ever, isn't this just the finest..."

Chapter 46

I wake up looking at the bottom of a chamber pot by which I am kneeling and into which I am throwing up.

"Ooohhh...pleeeeease...God...," I hear myself say.

"God shall not help you," I hear Amy say severely. "You brought this on yourself." I dimly see that she is standing above me as I swim back into full awareness and total misery.

"Please, Lord, take me now. I can't stand this." I cough and spit up some more vile juice. I have never been this sick before, ever, not even when I was seasick. "Please...I want to die now. Please, Lord."

A long string of spittle hangs from my lower lip down into the mess at the bottom of the pot. I wipe it away with the back of my hand and then look up at Amy for sympathy and forgiveness, but I do not get it.

"Who...who undressed me...how did I get back here?" I see that I am clad in my under-linen and stockings.

"I undressed you, Jacky," she says. "But as to how you got here, that story is a little more...vivid, shall we say. Would you like to hear?"

"Noooo...," I say in a very small voice. My back suddenly bucks and a stream of sick comes out of my mouth and into the pot. There is a strong, sour smell in the room.

"Oh, hear it you shall, Jacky," she says, disgusted. "Make no mistake about that. Shall I start with a description of the dance you performed? On the tabletop? It was quite well received by those sailors and other low males in the room."

"Oh no..."

"Oh yes. And the song you sang up there, Jacky? Oh, that was such a hit! Why, it brought the house down! Do you recall? It was the one about bullies rowing other bullies, the one that ends with—"

"Please, no more..."

"Oh, there is more and plenty. It gets better and better. After you came down from your stage... well, actually, you *fell* unconscious from your stage, right into the arms of that loathsome Lieutenant Flashby, who picked you up and strode off out of the ballroom looking for a convenient room to put you in. I suspect you and he would discuss naval tactics or tell sea stories. I'm sure that was his intent. He had gone down the main hall kicking open doors, finding nothing appropriate to his needs until he came to one of the guest rooms and was about to enter, when Randall came storming furiously into the hall, confronting your naval comrade and bidding him put you down.

"'I've got the strumpet and I've got the time, now get out of the way and sod off, Puppy!' roared the bold Lieutenant and our own *beau sabreur* Randall roared back, 'Puppy! I'll give you Puppy, by God!' and swords were drawn and crossed. I'm sorry, Miss, that you weren't awake for that because I know how you love it all so, all that dash and gallantry and derring-do, but you were dumped in a pile on the floor, rather unceremoniously, I thought, for the supposed prize in this encounter. By the by, you might notice a pain in your derriere, as that is the part of you that hit the floor first, with something of a dull thud. The impact did seem to rouse you a bit, because you did manage to get to your hands and knees and try to crawl down the hall for a space, but then you passed out again, with the aforementioned bottom remaining in the air, leaning against the wall. Your arms were splayed out and your face was against the carpet and your mouth was open, and, I believe, drooling slightly. Most elegant. It is an image that will stay with me a long, long time."

"Oh, please…" I don't know what feels worse, the sickness or the knowing of what I had done. I moan again, my head down. More gagging, more spewing.

"Anyway, as I said, the swords were crossed and Randall made an ill-considered lunge at our lustful Lieutenant Flashby, which that experienced officer easily parried. As Randall was unbalanced, his opponent brought up the hilt of his sword and smashed it into Randall's face, bloodying his nose and opening his cheek…"

"Dear God, no…not Randall…not hurt…"

"…and rocking him back against the wall. The bold Lieutenant did then draw back his sword and was about to put it through our Randall and into the wall when our jolly little party was joined by Father and Captain Humphries, who stepped up and ordered his officer to stop since, as he put it, sitting at a man's table and then putting a sword in his son, well, it just isn't done, old boy, not even in America. Then Randall wipes the blood from his mouth and snarls, 'I'll meet you in the morning, you filthy son of a bitch!' and Lieutenant Flashby says, 'Fine, I'll kill you then, Puppy! Name your Second!' Then Father draws his own sword and says, 'You'll not hurt the children of my household, by God, my son will second me and I'll meet you, myself, you British bastard!' Captain Humphries holds up both his hands and says, 'I absolutely forbid it! All we need is an international incident over a dumb girl!'"

Amy sniffs and says, "Actually, Jacky, he did not use 'girl' in referring to you. He used a short, harsh word that I did not know the meaning of, it probably being of low Anglo-Saxon origin, and, I'm sure, quite crude."

"I am so sorry…"

"Sorry? Sorry? Of course you are sorry! You are *always* sorry. Every time one of your cockeyed schemes goes wrong you are *sorry.*"

A spasm racks my body and my mouth opens but nothing but sour spittle comes out.

"Why…why are you…so cruel to me, Amy?" I am crying now, the tears running down my face and dripping into the pot with the other. I start keening in distress, "I thought you was my friend. I said I was sorr*eeeeeee…*" Millie, outside the window, howls at the sound.

"You can stop making that noise. It will not help." She primly folds her hands before her. "Do you know what I think, Miss? I think that when you first came to our school and were treated badly by Clarissa that you vowed that someday and somehow you would bring her down because the good Lord knows that nobody *ever* runs roughshod over Bloody Jacky Faber and gets away with it. Isn't that right? And do you want to know what else I think? I think that you used me to get close to Randall, and you used him to get to Clarissa, and you…"

I stop keening and a coldness comes over me that is stronger than the sickness. "That you should think that, Miss," is all I say and I look up into her face.

"Jacky, no, I'm sorry…" she says, uncertainty now in her eyes. "I didn't mean…"

"That you should think that, Miss," I say again. I begin to get up.

"Please, Jacky, forgive—"

And just at that instant came a pounding on the door and a girl's voice calling, "Miss! Miss! Your mother wants to see you in her chamber right now!"

"Tell her I'll see her in a while!" says Amy, all frantic.

"No, Miss! She wants you right now! She's hoppin' mad, and if you don't come she'll have me beat, she will!"

"All right, all right! Tell her I'll be right there!"

By now I've sat back on my heels and am staring straight forward, saying nothing.

"I must go see what Mother wants, Jacky. Do not leave this room."

"I hear you, Miss," is what I say.

"Please, Jacky, please don't try to leave."

"I hear you, Miss Trevelyne."

"That's not an answer, Jacky, please—"

"Miss, please, now!" the wretched girl pleads and Amy has to follow.

"You sit right there, Jacky. I'll be right back."

When she comes back, she will find me gone.

———

"Millie, you silly dog," I plead, "please go back. You can't go with me. Go back. Shoo, now." But she will have none of it, she just grins her joyous grin and leaps about. Maybe she'll go back when we get farther along.

I plan to walk along the beach till I meet a road and I'll take that road till it meets the Post Road and then I'll head down to New York, as I think that's the best place for me. I sure can't go back to Boston—Clarissa will spread the news of my disgrace at the school and Mistress will surely boot me out, this time for good and ever, and I can't just go down and live at the Pig 'cause the Preacher'd find me there and that'd be the end of me. And I sure can't go back to Dove-cote, what with Amy so mad at me. Her mother was prolly calling her upstairs to tell her to get rid of me quick 'cause I was stinkin' up the place. No, New York's the place for me. Maybe they'll be more forgiving of my ways there. I'll worm my way into another tavern and do the music, and I've got my colors and some disks, so maybe I'll do some portraits of sailors to send to their girls. There's letter writing, too, just like my dad used to do and I...

I stop to be sick again. *Oh, Lord, if you're gonna take me, please take me now...* This is so awful... The drink sure tasted better going down than it does coming up. *Damn that Clarissa!* I had her in flames and now I'm the one that's burnt to the waterline and *Oh, my poor head. You sure showed me, Clarissa, just who was the thoroughbred and who was the mutt.* I sit down on a rock to rest and I put my throbbing head in my hands. I know, I know, Liam, as you've often said, "'Tis the iron fist 'neath the velvet glove," and it is.

Millie comes up and puts her chin on my knee and looks

up at me with her big brown eyes. I put my two hands on the dome of her forehead and I say out loud, "I swear, by the sweet, gentle soul beneath my hands that I will never, *ever,* take a drink of spirits again. Amen."

I've got a little money in my money belt, but I think I'll be sleeping out tonight. It don't look like rain and I'll have to watch what I spend, 'cause now my plan is to make enough to buy passage to England and see what's up with Jaimy. I can't wait no longer, I got to know, so I can get on with things, no matter which way it goes with him. So I'm sorry, Ephraim and Betsey, sorry that I didn't finish up the Preacher, but he's almost done so maybe you can finish the job yourself and, if not, I hope you can put all that behind you and get married and have lots of fat, happy babies. And Sylvie and Henry, be happy in the company of each other. I'm sorry, Amy, that I couldn't stop Randall from marrying Clarissa, I did what I could but it wasn't enough. I never did really learn to fight like a lady, to fight like Clarissa knows how to fight. She showed me that, for sure. I had my foot on the neck of my enemy yesterday but still she wriggled free and beat me down. And, Amy, I'm sorry that I made a mess of things and brought dishonor to your house and family, and I'm sorry, Randall, that you got hurt in protecting me when I was helpless, I really am. And helpless I was—all my cunning and cleverness gone because of my wanton ways. It's funny that you, Randall, the one who mounted the most ardent assault on my poor virtue, should be the one to save it. I thank you for that. Sorry, Gully, that I left the Lady Lenore back at the school. I thought I'd be back, but now I ain't gonna be. Maybe Amy'll save my stuff—though she sure seemed to hate me last time I saw her, so I don't know.

And I'm sorry, Mistress, that I didn't turn out to be a lady. I know you tried.

Dear Millie, why do you leap and bound about so? You've nothing in this world but your hair and hide and bone and your foolish doggie grin and yet you are full of joy and think it just the very best of things to be going down an unknown dusty road with one such as me. Go back now, Millie, you must know I am so *very* hard on my friends.

I open my seabag to pull out my serving-girl gear, as I think I'll cause less comment that way. Bad enough, a girl alone and on the road, let alone one dressed in a blue party dress. As I'm getting it out, I feel a pang as I spy the bright racing silks all folded up there. Was it only yesterday that I had that triumph on the Sheik and was looking forward to my first ball like any silly girl?

I'm starting to feel better. *Maybe I'll live, after all,* I thinks as I finish dressing. The weskit feels good cinched up tight against my ribs, my shiv and my whistle nestled in there all snug where they belong.

Millie, will you not go back? No? Ah well, then, stay and herd your one black lamb, as she certainly needs it. Shall we have a tune, then, to cheer us and speed us on our way? *What?* "The Boys Won't Leave the Girls Alone"? Why, that's one of my favorites, too. A perfect traveling song! What, and you dance, too? You foolish dog, of course you would! All right, here we go…

> "*I'll tell me ma when I get home,*
> *The boys won't leave the girls alone.*
> *Jacky's fair and Millie's pretty*
> *And they've both gone to New York City!*"

Chapter 47

[Delivered to Dovecote on May 21, 1803]

James Emerson Fletcher
On board the Essex
At Sea
April 18, 1804

Miss Jacky Faber, the Best Girl in the World!
Dovecote Farm
Quincy, Massachusetts, USA

Dearest Jacky,

JOY! Pure and absolute joy! The heavens open and pour forth their celestial light, the angelic choruses shout "Hosanna!" and my heart, which was at my feet, leaps to my throat in total joy!

In short, dear one, I got your letter.

Shall I tell you of the way I got it? Yes, I shall, for I have the time, the quill, the ink, and, oh yes! I do have the inclination! Joy!

Anyway, it was an ordinary day—watches, patrols, eat,

sleep, more watches, all unrelieved by any thought that you still cared for me—when word comes that Nelson, the great Nelson, himself, will come over today on the Raleigh to visit the Essex!

Well, having spent your time before the mast (and how you were able to endure it, my poor frail creature, I do not know and scarce can think of it, even now), I know you can well imagine the mighty preparations that were made prior to the arrival of the very Hero of the Battle of the Nile. The ship did shine, I can tell you, with every piece of brass at its highest glint, every flag snapping, every man scrubbed pink and in his finest uniform.

The frigate Raleigh, forty-four guns, came by and heaved to, and the great man descended from it into a boat and came alongside, and in a moment was standing on our deck, followed by Captain Fishburne and the senior officers of the Raleigh. I, of course, was drawn up stiff as a ramrod on the quarterdeck, near the rail. Lord Nelson was bowing and shaking hands with our own Captain and I'm drinking in this historic moment when I hear a pssst! Shocked at this breach of etiquette, I look over the side and there, as a member of the boat crew, is our own Brother Davy! The boat's coxswain was looking at him most severely, a look that grew from severe to incredulous as Davy left his oar and scrambled up the ladder and thrust a letter into my hand and whispered, "She said no other hand but yours," and then retreated back down to the boat. The coxswain reached out and backhanded Davy a terrible blow across the face and then settled back down, but I knew that would not be the end of it—I knew he would be flogged when he returned to his ship.

What could be so important as to risk a flogging, I thought, and then I looked at the packet in my hand and saw that it was from you. I was almost unmanned on the spot, almost sinking to my knees in joy and dread, but I did not. I stood there in a high state of agitation for a good twenty minutes while the captains and Lord Nelson exchanged compliments, and then, when it was time for Captain Fishburne and Lord Nelson to return to the Raleigh, I stepped out and said, "Begging your pardon, Sir, but I must have a word with you," thereby ending my naval career, "but Seaman Jones of your ship has just delivered to me a letter from one I hold most dear and I would prefer that he not be flogged for doing that, Sir. If you would be so good."

Captain Fishburne was transfixed in shock and my own Captain Warren was astounded that one of his junior officers could act in such a manner. I was fully convinced that my naval career was over, but, can you believe it, Nelson himself comes over to see what the matter is and says to me, "Explain yourself."

I am afraid I am going to faint dead away from even being spoken to by such an august person, but I manage to blurt out some gibberish the sense of which could barely be made out, but which was, essentially, "My lord, when Seaman Jones and I were boys together on the Dolphin, he and I and several others on the Dolphin came together and formed a Brotherhood, a club, if you will, such as young boys will do, and we swore great oaths of fraternal loyalty and promised ever to be watchful of each other and Seaman Jones here has brought me a letter from one of the group, one who was especially dear to me and from whom I have not heard since she...er, the person was taken from...and the person made Jones swear to deliver it to no hand but mine, so you see..."

"Ah," says Lord Nelson, and I say no more. "The Dolphin...Yes, I have heard of that incident. And so you are the young rogue who was involved with the girl, then?"

My face betrays my answer before I could say, "Yes, my lord."

He considered this for a while while I died a thousand deaths over my temerity, my probable punishment, but mostly the pain of waiting, waiting to see what you had writ.

Lord Nelson turned to Captain Fishburne and says, "Do you mind terribly if we grant this young man his wish, John? It is entirely your decision, of course."

"The sailor shall not be flogged, my lord," said good Captain Fishburne. What else could he say?

"And Captain Warren," said Nelson, turning to my own Captain, "would you be so good as to assign this young man to my staff when I return to this area?" My captain nods and Lord Nelson continues, "Good. I like to have about me men who are bold in the defense of their friends and are handy with the ladies." He paused. "Then what shall be your punishment, Mr. . . . ah, Mr. Fletcher, for some punishment you must surely get, having broken sacred naval tradition. Hmmm. I suppose it shall be the usual one: Up to the foretop, Mr. Fletcher, and do not come down till the bell rings for the second dog watch."

My heart leaped for joy and I saluted and said, "Thank you, Sir," and I was about to head for the ratlines when he said, "And leave the letter down here, Mr. Fletcher; there will be plenty of time to read it when again you return to the deck."

He could not have devised a more exquisite torture.

The bell had not ceased ringing when my feet hit the deck and I scooped up the letter and raced down to the stateroom I share with Elliot and leaped into my bunk and tore open the packet and the portrait of you fell out into my hand.

Again, I felt on the verge of shedding not very manly tears upon seeing your bright countenance shining out from the tiny disk. That open and trusting face, lips slightly parted as if to speak, and, knowing you, capable of either declaring eternal love or challenging me to a race in the rigging. When I had read the letter and discovered that you had painted the picture, I could not believe it—that you had gained such a skill in such a short time. A short time!—listen to me—it's been an eternity, waiting for word of you!

I devoured your letter as a starving man devours bread. I care not a whit that you have been demoted, as I know that you were brought down by that same excess of high spirits that I find so endearing in you. You are a fine girl and never forget that, whether you are dressed as chambermaid or as lady. Rest assured, too, that whoever in my household has been keeping your letters from me shall be dealt with. I shall write to my mother directing her to look into it immediately.

When I was in the foretop, I watched the boat with Davy in it go back to his ship and I saluted the departing boat and held the salute till all aboard climbed up the Raleigh's ladder. That he would risk a certain flogging to deliver the letter…I cannot even speak of it…We have such good friends in this world, Jacky, and I am glad you have found good friends there, too.

I shall lie here in my bunk and gaze at the picture of you until it is time for me to go up on watch. I cannot tell you how happy you have made me.

Your most humble, obedient, faithful, and overjoyed servant,
Jaimy

PART V

Chapter 48

Colonel John Trevelyne
Dovecote Farm
Quincy, Massachusetts
May 23, 1804

Beadle and Strunk, Private Investigations
30 Devonshire Street
Boston, Massachusetts

My dear Sirs:

I am writing herewith to engage your services in the pursuit and return of a young female, named Jacky Faber, formerly associated with members of my household.

This person was last seen at my house in Quincy three days ago and my daughter believes the girl will try to go to New York. She is penniless, so she will in all probability take some time in gaining her objective. She will probably play music and dance in various roadhouses along the way and you would be well advised to inquire in such places.

You know my name and that I will pay you the going rate for such an undertaking.

Sirs, I relate to you that this is a matter of utmost importance as my daughter will not eat and my son has broken off his engagement to a fine girl and is trying to climb into a bottle. Bring me that wretched girl!

I am your most humble and obedient servant,
Colonel John Trevelyne

Chapter 49

My hands are tied behind me and my ankles are bound. I am facedown on the floor of a coach. I can hear my kidnappers outside, bartering with someone over something. I guess that something would likely be me.

"Well, Sir, as long as we had the girl, we figured that we'd see who'd be payin' the most for her. I mean, Colonel Trevelyne did hire us, but we figured you might pay a bit more, Sir, considering you had hired us to keep an eye on this one before he did, and who did we owe our loyalty to, Sir, I ask you?"

I hear a low rumble of a voice and chills run up me spine.

"Aye, Sir, she's the one. Tattoo on her belly and all. We checked." He gives out a low chuckle, the bastard. "Oh no, Sir, we didn't do *that*. She's in exactly the condition in which we found her. We're not that sort, Sir, we are professionals!"

Professional thugs, I'd call 'em if I could call 'em anything, which I cannot, havin' a gag in me mouth. I've been spending my time chewing on the gag, it bein' a single piece of thin cloth put across my mouth, pullin' my lips back and tied tight in the back of me neck. I figures if I can chew through and free my voice and shout out at the right time, well, I might yet be saved. I can see that darkness is falling outside and that's not good. As if reading my thoughts, a clock chimes out nine o'clock. It's spring and night comes late. That clock. Does it sound familiar?

"Yes, Sir, we caught her on the Post Road heading south. We found her the night before, playing her whistle and singing in a roadside tavern. Pretty good show it was, too. We all enjoyed it hugely. Anyway, we let her spend the night there and then took her when she was out and on the high road the next day. Aye, the Colonel's daughter told us where to look for her."

Amy? Oh no, not you, Amy... You couldn't hate me so much as to betray me, could you?

"Now, as to the matter of money, Sir, it's like this. If it was just the apprehendin' of a wayward child, a helpless girl, like, then the price wouldn't be so much, but this is a different case altogether, yes it is, Sir."

I notice that the wind is really whipping up out there.

He's the leader of this bunch, the one called Strunk, I think. He clears his throat and goes on. "But, Sir, it warn't no helpless child, 'cause after we got in a circle around her there on the road and she saw there was no escape, the slut come at us with this wicked blade, yes, Sir, she did, and she cut poor Dick Beadle sore after he killed her dog. The vicious beast laid about very free with its teeth, it did, and then sunk them in poor Dick's leg, which is when he brained the cur..."

Poor Millie, you was the bravest and best of all of us, you was... Tears roll down over the bridge of my nose and onto the floor of the coach. *You stood your ground, Millie, and you tried to save me. And now you're dead for it. I am sorry, Millie, I am. I am so very hard on my friends.*

"We would, Sir, have dearly wished that either you or the Colonel had warned us that she was armed with the knife and willing to use it. And it's not like we can bring charges against the female, 'cause we wasn't workin' in an official capacity, like, and we still ain't, so we would like compensation for poor Dick's wounds, we would, as we got added medical expenses, like. And his pain and sufferin', too, poor devil, only doin' his job like he was. Oh, like a serpent's tooth, Sir, the fury of a woman."

There is the clink of coins. I have been bought and sold.

"Why, that's very handsome of you, Sir. Very handsome, indeed. I hope you'll keep Beadle and Strunk in mind for any future business of this sort. Where do you want her?"

I can't hear the man's reply, but the man Strunk says, "Help me wrap her in this here rug, Dick, and we'll carry her inside. Here's her bag. Toss it over there." I see Strunk's hateful face for a moment and then the rug floats over me and I feel it tucked around me and then I'm flipped and rolled up in the thing. They ain't too gentle about it, neither. I'm thinkin' they got to sneak me in someplace, someplace where I could be spotted and maybe saved if they didn't cover me up somehow. Then I am lifted and carried inside. I can tell 'cause I hear echoes like it's a big enclosed place.

I'm dropped to a floor and given a kick for good measure.

"That's it, then, Sir. I wish you the joy of her," and there is the sound of the men leaving and the sound of a door closing. And then the sound of a latch being thrown.

Footsteps approach. An edge of the rug is taken and tugged and I am rolled out onto the floor. I see high windows and a high lectern and pews. I roll over and look up into the crazed eyes of Reverend Richard Mather.

"Ah," he says, "the little witch. At last."

"Yes, Grandfather," says the Preacher. "Yes, I have the witch now and…"

He cocks his head as if to listen to a voice. "Yes, Grandfather, it will not be long now."

I tuck me legs under me and struggle to a sittin' position so's I can face him. I shake my head back and forth and try to say, *"No no I ain't no witch please I'm just a stupid girl now let me please go,"* but all that comes out past the gag is a strangled mumble. I'm scared beyond clear reason but I keep on grinding me teeth on the gag.

"Yes, and now we have all the evidence we need to kill the witch with a clear and open Christian heart. No Court in the land could ignore the damning proof—the mark of the Devil, the very pitchfork of the fiend, burned on her belly…"

No no you lunatic it's an anchor, not a pitchfork! It's not—

"See, Grandfather, come look. You will be amazed…" He takes down a lighted lamp and puts it on the pew next to me and then he reaches for me.

I try to wriggle away but he leans down and grabs my arm and brings me to my feet. He pulls down me skirt and drawers, farther than he needs to to see the tattoo.

I squeal in terror. *See? See? It's an anchor! See?*

Suddenly, his head snaps up and the color drains from his face. There is a scratching at the door! A scratching like

I'd scratched as Janey Porter on his roof all those times! *Maybe, oh God, maybe…*

The door is at the side and there is an aisle leading to it. The Preacher throws me back down to the floor and takes me by my feet and drags me a bit up the center aisle so that I can't be seen by anybody when he opens the door, and the scratches come again and he recoils and puts his hand to his throat in horror.

I wriggle like a worm back up the aisle to get my head to where someone could see me if they looked around the Preacher when he opens the door and I get my head there and I've got my eyes glued on the door when he opens it a crack. He looks out, and it is not a horrid specter coming to haul him down to hell but instead a medium-sized black and white dog looking in at me from between the Preacher's legs.

Millie! Oh, Millie, it's you! You didn't die, you wonderful dog you didn't… I try to call to her but I can't. All that comes out is a mumble.

Millie tries to get in to get to me but the Preacher blocks her with his leg and closes the door on her. She yelps and retreats. "Begone, Fiend!" says the Preacher, and he turns his attention to me. And to old dead Grandad. "Her familiar has found her already, Grandfather, and she not here ten minutes. You see what a trial it has been to me. Who knows what other minions she has about her. We must be quick."

Millie's still alive! My mind is churning for a plan. If Amy is next door at the school and she sees Millie, she'll know that I'm nearby 'cause we ran off together, so…How to alert Amy? Maybe if Millie sets up a huge barking, Amy'll hear and come down. The girls'll be in the dorm now, getting ready for bed. I almost choke on my gag, I want to be there with them so bad. *Calm. Calm yourself.* Now, I can't shout to Millie, but I can whine, whine like a hurt dog, I can keen.

Eeeeeeeeeeeeeeeeeeeeeeeeeeeeeeeeeeeeeeeeeeeeeeeeeeeeeeeeeeeeeee...
Millie sets in to barking, loud and sharp.

"It won't do you any good to cry, now," says the Preacher. "No one will hear you."

Someone has already heard me, murderer. I do it again as high-pitched as I can—*Eeeeeeeeeeeeeeeeeeeeee*—and Millie goes into a wolflike howl and she keeps doing it. *Good girl.*

"What's that?" he says all fearful.

It's the Hound of Hell come to take you, Preacher, take you down for the murder of Janey Porter and me! That's what it is! I keep grinding on the gag—about halfway through now.

Millie's unearthly howl suddenly stops, followed by a yelp. A shiver runs through me. Was that a yelp of delight upon seeing Amy come down to her, or a yelp from being kicked by someone to just shut her up? I can't tell. I only know my life depends on which one it was.

The Preacher takes the lamp and hangs it on a hook on the stairway wall. He comes back and pulls me to my feet again and we start toward the stairs up the back of the church. I struggle and twist and he hits me and I fall and pretend that he knocked me out so I can play the dead-weight to the full without bein' hit again. He drags me to the foot of the staircase. Prolly wants me up in his office, where I'll be hidden for the rest of the time I'll be on this earth.

"And when I tell the Court of her openly practicing witchcraft at that horse race, why, they'll applaud my send-ing her back to Hell and wonder why I did not do it sooner," says the Preacher. "Can you believe it, Grandfather? The boldness of the beast, casting spells in front of multitudes, the fiendish boldness! Oh yes, I had my spies there, too, you may rest assured, Sir."

Me bein' all limp is provin' a harder bundle to get up the stairs than he would have thought. In floppin' my legs about I manage to stick my feet between the posts of the railing and hook my toes to stick them there. The Preacher curses and tries to free my entangling feet by tuggin' at me ever the harder, but it don't do him no good, so he throws me down and when he lets me go I try to slither headfirst back down the stairs, but he comes after me, and this time he picks me up with one arm under my knees and the other under my back like you'd carry a child, with my feet toward the wall. He's huffin' and puffin' with his labors and I can feel and smell his breath on my face.

We go past the lit lamp on the wall and I kick out with my feet and I hit the lamp and it comes off its hook and falls to the stairs behind us. The Preacher don't notice 'cause he's wheezin' away with the effort of gettin' me up to his lair and 'cause the lamp hit the carpet on the stairway, which muffled its fall, but I notice 'cause I can see over his shoulder and I see that the lamp has spilled out all its oil onto the stairs and the wick flickers in the middle of the mess like it's gonna go out but it don't, it lights the spilled oil on the wooden floor and it flares up with a *whoosh*, but he don't notice, no he don't notice 'cause he's still mumblin' with his gramps. He just pushes us through the doorway at the top and, with his foot, slams the door shut behind us.

He lurches forth and we go into a room, but it ain't his office like I'm expectin', no, it's a plain room with a single bed with high bedposts and a bedstand with a pitcher and a basin. There's a window, but the curtains are pulled. There is a chest of drawers and one of the drawers is half open and I can see some things inside. Girl things. There is a neatly folded handkerchief on the top.

It is Janey Porter's room. The one she died in. And the one I'm going to die in, too.

He throws me down on the bed.

"You recognize your old chamber, do you?" He leans over my face and peers into my eyes. "Yes, I have quite figured it out, you see. I did not punish you enough last time and so you came back to haunt me. To tempt me again into sin. To make me do it again. I did not kill you enough then. I did not punish you enough then. I shall not make the same mistake this time. Oh no, I shan't."

Great plan, Jacky. Oh, this worked out just fine, Jacky, you fool!

He reaches into one of the deep outside pockets of his coat and pulls out me own shiv. *Oh, to be killed with me own shiv!*

I can smell smoke.

He takes my knife and very carefully cuts the cords from my ankle. I wait a moment and then lash out my foot to kick him and I connect, but not hard enough 'cause he just goes *ooof!* and sits down on me and takes a piece of the cord and ties my right ankle to one bedpost and then pulls me legs apart and ties the other ankle to the other bedpost. He does the same thing with my wrists and I can't do a thing to stop him. He don't notice the smoke curling under the door, but I do.

He puts me shiv on me breastbone and I thinks, *This is it, I'm sorry Lord for everything I done,* and it's at this moment that I finally chew through the gag and the slimy pieces fall to either side of my mouth and I gathers all the fear and terror in me and I opens my mouth and I lets out the longest, most bloodcurdling shriek I got in me, *"God help me I don't want to burn!"*

It ain't God who comes smashin' through the door in a shower of splinters—it is Ephraim Fyffe, but he looks damned good to me! The door falls off its hinges and Ephraim stands there lookin' like the very Avenger of the Lord, with his fists clenched, his shirt torn, and rivulets of blood coursin' down his face.

The Preacher gazes at him as if at Beelzebub himself. Ephraim brings his fist around, and the Preacher's mouth falls in on itself and blood and teeth spatter against the wall as he sinks to his knees and moans.

"Ephraim! Get the knife!"

Ephraim bends down and picks up my shiv and starts cutting me loose. There's loud crackling now and the smoke what's comin' in is thick and black and—*Hurry, Ephraim*—and he's done with my hands and he flips me the blade and I catches it and saws through the ropes on my ankles while he goes after the Preacher, who's staggered to his feet and out into the hall.

I'm on me feet and I stick me shiv back in me vest and grabs Janey's hanky and puts it over my mouth and nose 'cause the smoke is chokin' me and me eyes are runnin' from the sting of it and I gets to the hall and see that the flames are roarin' up the staircase and I follows Ephraim's white shirt in the black smoke and he shouts, "Jacky! In here!" and we fall into a side room where the smoke ain't so bad yet. I see it's the Preacher's office and Ephraim goes to the window what's been busted in and what has jagged glass pointin' in all around the inside edges, which is how he got all cut and bloody, coming through that window. He kicks at the glass from the bottom edge and looks out.

"Look out, she's comin'!" The flames are at the door behind us and the floor is hot.

"I can—," I shouts over the roar.

"No time!" says he. "Keep your arms to your sides till you're clear of the window!" and he lifts me up, one hand on the scruff of my neck and the other in the clothing bunched up around my crotch, and holding me level-like, he pitches me out the window like a sack of grain, clear of the cruel glass.

I hit the blessed cool air and expects to kiss the hard ground but instead land on something soft that gives beneath me and I look up and see all around me people holdin' the edges of the blanket they held there to break my fall. There's Henry and Annie and Dolley and Betsey and Sylvie and sturdy Peg on a corner, and there's men and women I don't know but can only gawk at in wonder, and there's more people pouring up the hill with buckets and axes, and there's water wagons and men in helmets, and the people holding the blanket let it down to the ground and I roll off it and I find, wonder of wonders, that I have rolled up next to my seabag. It's here by the door where my kidnappers had thrown it.

They pull the blanket up taut again for Ephraim, who's now standing in the window. The flames are right behind him now. All the windows below have melted out and thick tongues of fire lick out at the wooden sides of the church. It is going up fast.

"Jump, Ephraim," cries Betsey, tears pourin' down her cheeks. "Oh, please! Jump!"

He does. He lands feet first on the stretched blanket and it serves to break his fall enough so he is not hurt. He still hits the ground hard, though, the upper windows bein' real high and him bein' real big. As soon as he's upright, Betsey's arms are around him and cryin' about the bloody cuts on his face and arms.

"Nay, it's nothin', Betsey, they ain't deep. See, they're stoppin' already."

"Reverend Mather," sobs Betsey, still clinging to him, "did you…?"

Ephraim shakes his head. "Kill him? Nay. He ran up to the steeple. Let his God kill him."

And then it's Millie's lovin' tongue I feel on my face and I starts into blubberin' from all the shock and terror and the chokin' smoke and I don't make much sense just, *"Millie you sweet sweet dog you saved my life you did you did you did."* And then my friends are pullin' me to my feet and kissing my cheeks and pullin' me away from the heat of the doomed church and the sparks that are dartin' about everywhere like fireflies in the wild wind that's swirlin' about. I see Sylvie's sleeve next to my face and there's little burn holes in it from the embers floatin' down and about. *Poor Sylvie, your shirt,* I think crazily, as if that was important now in all this. My mind is churnin' around and I got the mad urge to run—*run!*—'cause I'm the one what started this fire and everybody's gonna be mad at me and oh, God, there's Wiggins and I know he's lookin' to arrest someone for all this and I know who it's gonna be and I pick up my seabag and start weavin' away.

There's the rest of the upstairs girls in their white nightgowns blowin' about them in the crazy wind, wringin' their hands and wailin', and there's Amy runnin' toward me and Millie loping out to meet her...

Then all eyes go to the church steeple, 'cause it's now completely engulfed in flame and from inside it comes this high awful shriek, a long scream of a soul in terrible pain and in utter desolation. Then there's this rending sound of something giving way and the great bell comes loose from its belfry and falls seemingly slowly through the burning timbers to the ground, and when it hits the cobblestones, there's this deep, sad *bonggggg*. I wouldn't have thought that something that heavy could bounce, but it does and it turns over slowly in the air and comes down again and *bonggg* still softer and then one more faint *bongg* and then it rolls over and comes to rest.

Finally, Janey, the bell has tolled for thee.

But the screaming continues. It can't still be him...No, no, it's not. It's horribly not. The roof of the stable has caught fire from the sparks and the horses trapped inside are screaming in terror.

Amy is runnin' to me but I yell at her, "Amy! The horses! Let the horses out!" and I point at the stable, its roof ablaze. She stops and turns, confused, and then runs for the stable, followed closely by Henry and Herr Hoffman.

"Look!" shouts one of the girls. "The school!"

The school, too, is on fire. The embers blew into the bushes around the foundation and they flared up and the first floor is already in flames. "Is everybody out?" I shout and Peg says, "All mine are!" and the upstairs girls look at each other and can find no one missing. There's more men streamin' up the hill with buckets and axes to help…there's John Thomas in that bunch filling buckets at the pump and passin' 'em along a line to throw the water on the base of the fire but it ain't gonna do 'em no good, it's too far gone, it's—

"Oh, my God!" says someone, pointing up. "It's Mistress!"

I look up and sure enough, there she is, standin' at an upper window, lit from the light from the burning church. She is in her nightgown and her long gray hair is loose and flying out wildly from her head. The big entrance doors are a sheet of flame. There's no way out that way and if the first floor is gone, then she can't come down through the kitchen. She's trapped.

"What's she doing?" asks a girl on the edge of hysterics.

"Jesus," says I, "she's takin' her precious needlework off the walls, that's what she's doin." *Damn!*

I start runnin' to the side of the school and I bellows out the sailors' call for help "John Thomas! To me! To me!" He jerks up his head and hands his bucket to another man and follows me.

"Get a ladder! There, on that shed!" I order as we round the corner. "Put it up there by those rungs!" He does it and I'm up to my old window in an instant. I throw it open. *Thank God they didn't lock it when I was gone.* "Follow me up! I may need you to carry her!" and with that I'm through the window and in my old room.

Good. No smoke yet. I race across and open the door and head down the stairs to the hall. I can smell smoke now. I can see tendrils of it comin' up between the cracks in the shrinkin' floorboards.

There she is, calmly taking down the framed examples of fine embroideries, samplers, and needlework from the hallway wall and tucking them under her arm.

"Mistress! Come on! You've got to leave!"

She calmly turns and faces me. "Why?" she asks. "The British are coming?"

"Only one, Mistress," I say.

She looks me in the eye. "You. Of course. You."

"Even so, Mistress," I reply. "And now we must go. The school is on fire."

"You were the worst of my girls, you know…"

"I know, Mistress, and I'm sorry, but we've—"

"And here you are at the end of things. How appropriate. How utterly appropriate."

The smoke is getting serious now and I can see the flames below through the cracks. The floor is hot, the varnish on it curling in the heat.

"Where are my girls?"

"They are safe, Mistress. Now you must go join them."

"No, I can't leave my school."

"You must take care of your girls, Mistress. They are outside and they need you. There will be another school. You must go, now." *John Thomas, where the hell are you?*

"Now, look at this one," she says, conversationally. "This was done by one of the Cabot girls. Now, *that* was a girl! And that one was done by a Lowell and…"

And, finally, I hear John Thomas's boots on the stairs.

"Take her!" I shout, and he scoops her up and heads back up the stairs. The framed things fall from her hands and crash to the floor, their glass shattering. I pick up the Cabot one and follow them up. The far end of the hallway floor gives way as I make it back into my room.

John Thomas and his load, which is protesting vigorously, are disappearing out the window when I spot the Lady Lenore hanging on the wall where I left her weeks ago. I put the strap over my shoulder and bid farewell to my sea chest and I, too, go out the window.

When I hit the ground, I sling on my seabag and go around to the back of the school. The girls are enfolding Mistress into their midst, their hands fluttering about her like little white birds. The stable doors are open and horses stream out, screaming, their eyes wild and rolling with fear, and in the middle of them is Amy.

And there's Wiggins with his rod, again, and the vile Dobbs is with him and he's pointin' at me and Wiggins is comin' at me and I got to go.

My mind is reeling and bent on escape and I see dear Gretchen and I call to her and when she goes by me I grab her mane and swing up onto her back and away we pound, away, away from Boston burning behind me, 'cause sure as hell they're gonna blame this on me, and it warn't all my fault.

Epilogue

Jacky Faber
New Bedford, Massachusetts
June 20, 1804

Miss Amy Trevelyne
Dovecote Farm
Quincy, Massachusetts

Dear Amy,

I hope you read this letter and do not just throw it away, seeing it's from me who you were so mad at last time we spoke because I brought shame and disgrace to your family by my actions. I guess all that lady stuff just ain't going to stick to me.

Anyway, Great Good News! I've been taken aboard a whaler! Can you believe my good luck? It seems that these Quaker whalers ain't shy at all about sailing with women, as all they care about is the profit to be made. The Increase, they call it.

When I rambled into New Bedford town I, of course, went straight to the docks and there in front of the ship was a table set up and the Captain and his First and Second Mate were signing up crew members for a voyage to the North Sea grounds and I marches up bold as brass and says that I am the notorious Jacky Faber what can climb the rigging in a living gale to trim a luffing sail, and after they're done laughing, the sods, they take me on for a quarter share. Not as a sailor, of course—I'm to be Companion to the Captain's wife, who is big with child, and to help her when her time comes. Also to tutor her young son, who is also coming along. After the child is born, she and her brood will get off in England to be with relatives and I'll be put off then, too, and I can go see what's going to happen with Jaimy. Either way, I got to know.

The Captain's wife is a real sweet lady and I know we'll get along fine. The Captain's a bit of a queer duck, what with him stumping about on his peg leg, shouting orders like he's the very Angel of the Lord, and glaring out from beneath his shaggy brows, but the crew says he knows his business, one leg or not, and so I am easy in my mind.

We're leaving real soon, so I got to hurry and get this off in the post. Say good-bye to the Sisterhood for me, and tell them they'll always be held close in my heart for as long as I live. And dear Peg, of course. Tell her she was like a mum to me and I'll never forget her for the love and care she gave to an outcast stranger. The boys, too. I never got to say thanks to all for my daring rescue. Say farewell to Randall for me, too, and give him my thanks for saving my rather shaky virtue. Tell him to mind his studies at that college and to leave the girls alone. And a big hug for the blessed Millie. Tell them all not to worry about me. It's funny, but lately I've been getting the feeling that I'll be a lot safer at sea.

I left the sweet Gretchen at a farm near the shore. I saw two children playing with a ball and I stopped and they petted her and she seemed to like them and their father came up and there

*were cries of "Father! Father! Can we keep her, please? Please!"—
and I told the father how I came by her and didn't want to just
sell her to anyone who might abuse her and he seemed kind and
agreeable, so I gave him a paper showing where she came from
and all, and he gave me a ride back into town in return. I believe she is well placed, Amy. Tell Mistress she can take the cost
of her off the money still in my name with the school.*

*And as for you, sweet Amy, I pray that someday you will
find it in your heart to forgive me and once again call me Sister, that dearest of names.*

*The Captain calls and we must obey. The gangway is pulled,
the sails are loosed, and the lines are cast off.*

Pray for me, Sister, for I go to the home of the whale.

*Your friend,
Jacky*

Don't miss the latest Bloody Jack adventure!

Under the Jolly Roger

Being an Account of the Further Nautical Adventures of Jacky Faber

The feisty Jacky Faber sets sail once again.

A pirate at heart, Jacky Faber returns to the sea in a truly swashbuckling tale filled with good humor, wit, and courage.

After leaving the Lawson Peabody School for Young Girls in Boston—under dire circumstances, of course—she boards a whaling ship bound for London, where she hopes to find her beloved Jaimy. But things don't go as planned, and soon Jacky is off on a wild misadventure at sea. She thwarts the lecherous advances of a crazy captain, rallies the sailors to her side, and ultimately gains command of a ship in His Majesty's Royal Navy. But for Jacky, the excitement doesn't end there....

Turn the page to see Jacky leading her crew into battle!

We come down on the unsuspecting smuggler like the pack of hungry dogs we are.

He is running up there ahead of us, and I take the glass and run up to the foretop and train it on him. Sure enough, the other Captain has his glass trained on us and, from what I can see, is looking mighty worried. *Why is this English ship bearing down on me?* he's probably thinking. *Have not the bribes been paid?*

Oh yes, Frenchy, you have paid. But not quite enough. Not yet, anyway.

"Mr. Harkness!" I shout down. "Give him one across his bow."

Crracckk!

The bow chaser barks out its nine-pound ball. It hits a few yards off to the left of the ship. *Good shooting. We don't want to hurt the prize,* which looks to be a nice little two-masted schooner, maybe ninety feet long. Good and beamy and sure to hold a fat cargo. Little Mary, Cheapside Mary, that greedy little thief who still lives within me and is never very far from the surface, is in full control of me now, and my heart beats in a state of high excitement as we bear down. *Better than rollin' drunks, eh, Mary?* I think.

"Another on his side, Mr. Harkness!"

Crraacckk!

The ball hits about ten yards to the right of the schooner, but she shows no signs of heaving to. *Give up nicely now, Frenchy. This is strictly business, nothing personal. Don't want anyone to get hurt.*

I swing back down to the quarterdeck. Drake has already been told to issue cutlasses and they gleam in the hands of my sailors.

"We'll come along his port side and take him there," I say to Jared.

Booommmm...

There's a blast from the other ship, a high whistle and a neat round hole appears in the mainsail right above our heads. *He's firing on us, the sod! The cheek of the man!*

"Close now!" I shout to Jared. "Man the Boarding Party on the starboard side!" The drummer boy starts his drum roll and I pull my sword.

We're comin' up fast on the prize, only about fifty feet away...now twenty...ten...we are on her!

"Starboard gun crews, hold your positions!" yells Robin, lifting his own cutlass. "Grappling hooks, away!" He gets up on the rail.

The hooks are thrown and the ships are pulled together.

I lift my voice in the chant, "Were-wolves! Were-wolves! Were-wolves!"

And the chant is taken up by the entire crew, until the very sky seems to shake with it.

With Robin in the lead, the Werewolves surge over the rail, waving their cutlasses and yelling like very devils from Hell. Jared and I swing aboard and we find the crew of the smuggler cowering against the starboard rail. Their Captain stands up before them and unbuckles his sword.

"*Capitaine?*" he asks of Robin. The French Captain is plainly outraged by the turn of events, but I guess he intends to do things in the right way with the giving up of his sword and all. Robin shakes his head and directs the Werewolves to disarm the smuggler crew and herd them back onto the *Wolverine,* where they will be confined below.

"*Capitaine?*" he says again, holding his sword out to Jared.

Jared grins his mocking grin and bows low, sweeping his arm toward me. "No, Sir. *This* is the *Cappy-tan*. May I present our own Captain Puss-in-Boots?"

The Frenchman's mouth drops open. "*Une femme! Une jeune fille!*" he says and pulls his sword and I drop down in the ready position, but he pulls the sword to use on himself, not me. Jared comes up next to him and knocks the sword out of his hand.

"You'll get over it, Froggie, count on it," says Jared. "After all, we did."